GOD OF DUNG

By A.A. Jordan

First American Edition August 2015

Manufactured in the United States of America

Text set in Cambria

ISBN-13: 978-0996803410

ISBN-10: 0996803416

Religion (n). From the Latin *religare,* "to bind."

Chapter 1

Clarence never completed a curse. This was inspired by the acronym SOB. Whoever invented that was a genius. As far as he was concerned, profanity was for the profane, so he took it upon himself to preserve the lost and sacred art of subtlety by turning expletives into crossword puzzles: you only get a few letters; the rest you can fill in for yourself. Besides, a cursing old man was a cliché, and he had no intentions of dying a cliché.

He did intend to die at a retirement home though. The brochure for the Golden Age Retirement Home promised bliss amidst beautiful surroundings, but all he saw on his way there was a ghost town so void of life that it could have passed for a graveyard. The only sign of life was a stray pile of crap, which his foot narrowly avoided.

"SOB!"

The evasive maneuver took its toll on his old bones, which had long ago retired their rapid reflexes. He heard a few cracks and pulls, like an old machine that had just been kicked on, and had to throw out his arms to keep from toppling over. He teetered this way and that before finally settling himself into a balance. That was a close one.

To make sure he really did avoid the crap, he had to go through the tough part: bending over *and* lifting his left foot, both at the same time. Once again, the old machine of his body grinded and groaned as he slumped forward to tip his foot and tap it with his walking stick. So far, so good: nothing fell from the heel. Next, he tried scraping the sole of his shoe with the end of his cane. You never could be too sure. Crap had a way of stubbornly clinging to most any surface, especially footwear. But it looked like he was in the clear.

"The last thing I need is to check into a retirement home smelling like dog S. People will think I crapped on myself already," Clarence muttered as if anyone were around to listen. "Folks need to learn to clean up their S."

"Whoa, wait a second. Don't move, sweetie."

A voice as rough and raspy as sandpaper had just called him "sweetie." He turned around and saw a woman as large as a burlap bag full of butter, gripping a briar pipe in the corner of her mouth, wobbling in his direction. *Who the H. is that?*

"Matylda," she introduced herself, reading the question in Clarence's eyes. "Don't move, sweetie," she ordered again, pointing at his feet. "What kind of dung is that?"

"What the H. difference does it make?"

"It makes a lot of difference," she insisted, annoyed by having to explain the obvious.

He laughed once, thinking her response to be a joke, but as he watched the woman studiously hovering over the dung, he realized she was serious. Despite her rotund figure, bending down to get a good look at the poo was a comparatively simple matter for her—so much so that she was able to casually fondle her briar pipe at the same time.

She examined the crap long enough for Clarence to realize that this was no idle curiosity. This was her hobby. She leaned in a little closer and her arm reached out as if threatening to touch it. Thick, butter-like fat squeezed from her sides, which made Clarence flinch. Had she stayed in that position much longer, the blubber might've splattered like batter on his feet, but just as quickly as the fat inflated from her squat, it deflated as she effortlessly straightened herself and took another blow of her pipe. An obscenely fat woman with an obscene habit and an obscene obsession with filth—a cliché of a woman if Clarence had ever seen one. He threw up his hands dismissively.

"Bah." She did the same, practically stealing the words from his mouth. This made Clarence freeze with contempt.

"Did you just flip me off?"

"So you *can* see!" she snapped.

"Of course I can see."

"Well, you sure as shinola didn't see the big pile of crap you almost marched over, and you already admitted you don't even know what kind it is."

"You crazy broad, who else craps in the middle of the side walk? It's dog crap!"

"Well, you should have opened your mouth and said that the first time before I came all the way over here, bending over in front of you like some kind of stripper. But it's a good thing you didn't open your mouth

6

because you're wrong! I don't know where you went to school, if at all, because you have your letters all backwards. It's not dog crap. It's God crap. This crap came from a *God!*"

"Jesus!"

"Good guess, but no," she answered. "I don't think he would do that, at least, not out in the open like this. Wait! What do you know about Jesus? You wouldn't happen to be one of those old people who hang around on street corners trying to convert others, would you?"

"Say what?!?"

"A Bible? Do you have a Bible on you? If you do, jump to the back and see if there's anything in there about Jesus having kept a pet dog. Also, see if he blessed the dog."

"I think he might have owned a mule," Clarence clarified, scarcely able to believe that he was entertaining this woman's madness.

"He diiiid." Her eyes ignited. "Wait. No, he didn't! He owned a donkey. But I see where you're going with this: you're thinking this came from Jesus' Ass. Highly unlikely, but there's only one way to know for sure..."

She dug into a witches' waist-satchel and pulled out the infamous *graffito blasfemo*, so named because it depicts a crucified man, presumably Jesus, with a donkey's head. The original carving was discovered in Rome near the Palatine Hill, but Matylda had somehow scored a bootleg reproduction. Early Christians and even Jews reputedly used the donkey as a totem for their deity, which could only mean that the so-called *graffito blasfemo* was not blasphemy at all, but rather onolatry—donkey worship. Matylda, however, was simply using her blasphemous bootleg print as a kind of dung detector. Clarence watched as she hovered and rotated it over the small stool.

"Woman, you flipped your wig."

"Shhhh! I'm testing to see if this is donkey dung."

"With *that?*"

She scoffed at his ignorance and pointed to the inscription written just below the drawing: *Αλεξαμενος σεβετε θεον.* "Tell me what this says, right here."

"I can't read that!" Clarence protested.

"Well, I can, so shut up and listen. It says: '*Alexamenos worships his God.*'"

"Who the H. is Alexamenos?"

"Just call him Alex. He carved this image on a wall in Rome two thousand years ago." She looked both ways and whispered: "I stole it from a museum two days ago."

"Is it an original?"

"Of course it's an original."

"Then why is there a price tag on the back of it?"

"What are you talking about?" She checked the back and blinked several times when she saw he was right. She brooded as a scientist would over a failed experiment, shook her head and left.

Just like that, the conversation was over. Clarence looked at her with befuddlement. Only now did he notice her folk get-up: a grey and gold tunic with an earthy-green apron tied about her waist, a dozen chattering necklaces draped from her neck with a spiraled silk scarf and, the oddest accessory of them all, pink bunny flip-flops that actually flipped and flopped as she waddled off. He didn't expect to see bunny flip-flops on a woman like her, but he decided that the rest of her—from the ankles up—was a walking cliché. He closed the matter by flipping her off.

"Same to you!" she called out, having somehow detected the gesture even with her back turned to him.

She returned to a run-down, rustic shop just across the street—a building only slightly wider than its door. It looked as if someone had crammed a storefront into a narrow alley. Just above the door was a small, dusty window that framed a wooden idol of Triglav—a frightening figure with three heads fixed to a pole and eyes that appeared to be alive.

She closed her door shut, not with a slam, but with enough force that it caused a bell hanging from the sill to let off a soft chime. It was a delicate clamor, like the crisp chirping of a bird, but it stopped suddenly, as if swallowed by the quiet, predatory silence of a desolate street. Clarence looked around again for life, but there was none. No traffic,

8

no pedestrian clutter, not even the dog who left poo on the sidewalk.

"Crazy old hag," he muttered to himself. Just as he turned to leave, he looked down one more time at the small, smelly mountain near his feet. Maybe this dog crap really was God crap. After all, it was strangely spherical. *What kind of dog craps in spheres?* he wondered. He leaned over and poked the turd with his walking stick, which did not escape the attention of the curious eyes of Triglav. Satisfied, the eyes closed shut, as if going to sleep, and pulled away before Clarence could notice their piercing stare.

By now his attention switched from the turd to the tavern he just now noticed in front of him. It had to be the most depressing bar he had ever set eyes on. There were no neon signs advertising cheap beer or even a store sign. Still, suddenly he felt an urgent thirst for a Budweiser and decided that the open door was all the sign he needed to welcome himself inside. Right away, he felt like he had walked into a medieval dungeon smelling of old stones and moldy wood. But what grabbed his nose was the unmistakable pungent smell of...

"A dog!" he exclaimed.

A full-bodied Finnish Lapphund with a healthy white coat and a white muzzle rested lazily, spread out in a corner. Her ears twitched from Clarence's voice.

"I knew it was just dog crap. I don't know what that broad was talking about."

As Clarence drilled home his point by tapping his cane into the floor, the Lapphund sat with her tongue sagging from her mouth and her eyes wandering around the room with a far-away look that told Clarence this mutt wasn't paying him the least bit of attention. Her ears only came alive at the sound of a toilet flush. An old door opened and out came a small boy with a head so disproportionately large that his scrawny legs, buried inside brown jeans, trembled like crutches as they strained to carry the dead weight. Covering his small torso was a blue apron with Egyptian patterns and a hawk's head as the tavern's logo. He walked past Clarence with as much disinterest as the dog had shown him and a strange gait that took him behind the bar, where he disappeared. What he was doing behind there, Clarence could not imagine, but it sounded like the kid was stacking phone books. That must have been it because a minute later the top of the boy's large head peeked over the edge of the bar.

"Is this your dog?" Clarence asked, but the boy didn't answer. "I asked you a question, son. Is this your dog?" Still no answer. "Scared to fess up, are ya? I'll take it you know that there's an ordinance against leaving dog crap for people to step in, especially old—"

Before Clarence could get into a rant, an old man, bulbous and dressed in dyed gray burlap, walked in. Despite his grungy appearance, his manners proved to be much better than the boy's. He greeted Clarence with a nod before taking a stool near him. He must have been a regular because the boy immediately set up a glass of ale the size of a small barrel in front of him. The old man didn't wait to dive in. He made three audible gulps before resurfacing for air and showing that his thick, white beard had soaked up the beer like a sponge. His lips and tongue came out from hiding to lap at the dripping excess. The rest was wiped away with a single swipe of his sleeve. A second swipe cleared away an unrelated mess lingering under his blocky, Swiss-cheese–textured nose. With the urgent matters of beer and hygiene finally resolved, he turned his attention to Clarence, motioning for him to join in the drinking.

"Does this kid talk?" Clarence asked, ignoring the invitation.

"You don't have to call him 'kid.' Just call him 'Barkeep,' like I do," the old man answered in a Finnish accent, although to Clarence's untrained ears he sounded Irish. "And yes, sometimes he talks, but not often. The last time I heard him open his mouth and say a word was exactly two years ago."

"Two years!" Clarence looked at the roof of the Barkeep's head. "What's wrong with him?"

"Nothing's wrong with him. He just prefers silence. If you're going to stand there and tell me there's something wrong with a child who prefers silence, then I'm going to sit here and tell you that something is wrong with *you*!"

"No, I get that, but this kid is taking the Fifth Amendment a bit far, wouldn't you say?"

"What are you talking about?"

"I'm talking about the mess out there on the sidewalk." Clarence thumbed towards the door and then pointed an incriminating finger at the dog. "And I'm talking about that crap hamster over there in the corner, trying to look all innocent."

"How do you know the dog did it?"

"I don't! That's what I was trying to find out. I asked the boy, but he refuses to answer."

"He's not 'refusing' to answer. He's just waiting for the right time to answer."

"The right time?" Clarence's voice went up an octave. "How about after I ask the question? That seems about right to me."

"For some questions, maybe, but not for every question. Sometimes we ask the right question at the wrong time, and we're not ready for the answer. The trick is to ask questions only when we know we are truly ready to hear the answer. I'll give you a demonstration." The old man grabbed his mug, dipped his head backwards and poured what was left of his beer directly into his beard. Presumably, some of it actually made it into his mouth. He assertively pushed the empty mug towards the kid. "Barkeep! *Yksi tuoppi kiitos?*"

Clarence assumed that meant something to the effect of *another pint, please.* The Barkeep nodded and complied by placing a second beer on the counter.

"See?" the old man quipped. "I was ready for that one. But now watch this." He propped himself up slightly from his stool to talk to the roof of the kid's head. "Barkeep! One more thing if you don't mind: I think my wife might be having a wee bit of fun on the side when I'm not around. Do you think she's being unfaithful?" He waited for an answer, but none came. "See?" He turned back to Clarence. "It's not the right time for that kind of question."

"Right." Clarence rubbed his forehead, fighting back a mocking laughter. "All I wanted to know was if his dog soiled the sidewalk. What kind of question is that?"

"The kind that is none of your business would be my guess."

"It's my business if I almost slipped on it!"

"But you didn't. And what's your deal anyway? What kind of man comes into the best and only tavern in town bellyaching about a turd when his belly should be aching for a *beer*? Why worry about a stray stool you nearly stepped on when there's a perfectly good stool right here for you to sit on?"

It was an odd invitation that came with the old man slapping the seat with his hand. Clarence looked around and begrudgingly obliged.

"We've exchanged three hundred sixty-five words so far—not counting the ones I just said—three hundred and sixty-five! And not one of them was a name."

"You counted?"

"Of course I counted. Now we're at three-hundred ninety-eight words and still no closer to exchanging names."

"And no closer to understanding why you're keeping a word count," Clarence mumbled.

"Why am I counting? Look, do you want to exchange numbers or exchange names? Because I don't think I'm comfortable with giving you my number just yet. But you're welcome to my name—it is Väinämöinen."

"Vy—" Clarence was screwing up the name already.

"Väinämöinen."

"Vy-na-m—"Clarence took a breath and tried again. "Vyna-monen."

"Väinämöinen."

"The way you say it sounds like you're singing."

"I wasn't, but good guess, stranger, I *am* a singer."

"What do you sing?"

"Wait! First tell me your name."

"Clarence."

"I sing songs, Clarence. Now ask me what I drink."

"What do you drink?"

"I drink beer, Clarence. Now, I can tell from the stool you nearly stepped in that you are more of a complainer than a singer, but I can also tell from the stool you're sitting on that you're a drinker, much like myself. What I have not been able to put my finger on is what it is you're planning on drinking and how much of it you intend to drink."

"What do they serve here?"

"They serve beer. Would you like a beer, Clarence?" To help Clarence make up his mind, Väinämöinen sunk his mouth and beard into his barrel and finished the last drop of ale, which he announced by smacking his lips and slamming the bar with his glass.

"We're back to counting now, Clarence: Shall I order one beer for just myself, or two beers to celebrate two new friends? Now, before you question why I'm calling us 'new friends'—or as we twist it in my tongue, *uusi ystävä,* which is a bit formal, but at least it's respectful—let the record show that while yes, we are two *old* men, we're *new* friends nonetheless. How many beers, *ystäväni?*"

"Two," Clarence answered, assuming that ystäväni meant 'friend.'

"I love the number two. It's the antidote to loneliness. The Germans have a word for it: *Zweisamkeit.* It's like saying *twoliness.* To my knowledge, they don't have a word for *threeliness* because three is a bit of a crowd and nothing good ever comes of crowds, let me tell ya. Reminds me of the old Finnish folktale of Tobias, who was out searching on his hands and knees below a streetlight when a friend walked up to him and asked, 'What are you doing, Tobias?' and Tobias said to him, 'I'm looking for a lost key.' So the friend got down on his hands and knees to help Tobias look for his key. Then another friend came by and joined the search. And then another. And then the neighbors. Before you knew it the whole town was out on their hands and knees searching for the key. This went on all night until finally someone asked, 'Tobias, where exactly did you lose the key?' and Tobias answered, 'I lost it in the house.' 'In the house! Then why are you looking for it out here?' they asked and Tobias answered, 'Because there's more light out here under the streetlight.' Tobias wasn't the brightest of fellows. That's why he stayed near the street light. But where was I going with this?"

"Crowds," Clarence answered flatly.

"Right. *Joukossa tyhmyys tiivistyy. Stupidity comes in crowds,* ystäväni. Yes, it does. Then again, sometimes even the number two can be a bit of a problem, like in the old Finnish folktale of a priest who was known for his wisdom. He was also known for being a bit cranky. People kept bothering him with questions about love and life, so the priest decided to start charging for his wisdom—100 markkas per question.

Tobias became his first customer and paid him 200 markkas for two questions. After he paid the priest, he asked him, 'isn't 100 markkas per question a bit expensive?' 'Absolutely,' the priest answered, 'and what is your second question?'

"So you see, crowds can get a bit crowded, and two can be a bit of a trickster too, but not when it comes to drinking. All you need is two good drinkers to cure the lonesome feeling of drinking alone. Do you know what I'm trying to say to you?"

Absolutely not was the blank and bewildered answer in Clarence's eyes, and he had no idea how to respond to these two fruitless folktales. Thankfully, the Barkeep made the save by planting two small barrels of beer on the bar. The joyous sight of beer had wiped the slate clean, and Clarence watched as Väinämöinen plunged his mouth into a head of foam, swallowed a quarter's worth, sleeved his mouth and moved on to a new question.

"So what brings you to the best and only tavern in town, Clarence?" He paused and thought about this. "Ah, never mind. I suppose that one answers itself."

"I'm on my way to a retirement home."

"Oh? Do you have a God there that you're going to worship?"

"A G— A what?"

"Oh, stop your stuttering. I said a *God*! Are you going to see your God? Why else would you be going to the retirement home?"

"To check myself in."

Now it was Väinämöinen's turn to look at Clarence incredulously. He leaned his head to the side, re-appraising Clarence from head to toe. His lips moved and muttered while his eyes made incremental skips, cueing Clarence that he was, quite literally, being *measured*. But Clarence's old man's hunch made it a difficult task to do accurately. Unsatisfied with the results, Väinämöinen examined Clarence's attire. Generally speaking, Gods have a regal glow, but Clarence had more of an old and dull matte finish, which was strange considering that he wore a green shirt—a color that usually signified new life and fertility. Then again, he also had a limp, grey phallic symbol hanging around his neck, suggesting impotence. Perhaps he was a God in his winter season, but if that were the case, why wear green? Even the most dismal Gods would decorate themselves in a lively lapis lazuli, a radiant red or even a badass black with hints of grey. Or, if they were going for the purity palette—pretentious as it may be—they robed themselves in all white. Clarence didn't look like a God at all, quite the opposite: he just looked mundane and, even worse, *real*. There was no imagination to his appearance. Just to be sure, Väinämöinen recalculated the poor and obviously confused man one last time and shook his head at the results.

"Perhaps," he began, trying to put it politely, "you should retire in your own home."

"I can't. Rent's too high. And I have a neighbor who has no control of her two-year-old son. All he does is run around their apartment screaming 'MINE!' MINE!' MINE!' I'm looking for peace and quiet and"—Clarence paused—"well, *twoliness*."

"Ah, be careful, ystäväni," Väinämöinen cautioned. "Like I said, the number two can be a bit tricky. They have two major problems at the retirement home: one, it's overcrowded; two, they always think there's room for one more; three—"

"Three?" Clarence frowned. "You just said there were only two problems."

"I know, but there's a strange math going on over there. If you haven't been in the habit of counting before, I suggest you start now if you're going to live there. So that you don't get more than twoliness."

"Wait a second, how do you know which retirement home I'm talking about?"

"A better question is: How will *you* know which retirement home *I'm* talking about?"

"Aaargh!" Clarence grumbled to himself. To put an end to the riddles, he searched his pocket until he found the retirement home brochure he brought with him. He tried showing it to Väinämöinen, but the old man refused to even look at it.

"I know what a retirement home looks like. You're sitting here worried about fancy pictures when what you need to be worried about is *counting*. Any man who doesn't know how to count in this world is lost!" Väinämöinen finished those words by throwing his head back and finishing his beer. He slammed the mug down on the bar and looked at Clarence. "I'm ready for my third beer. What about you? Are you ready for your fourth?"

"You mean... My second? And *your* fourth?"

"Aaah!" Väinämöinen pointed and growled approvingly at Clarence. "Well done! Well done! I was testing you. Barkeep! Give me my fourth ale, and since I don't like drinking ahead of my friends, bring Clarence three more."

"Three more?" Clarence protested.

"There's an old saying, ystäväni." Väinämöinen smiled as the Barkeep lined up four beers on the counter. "It's easier to keep up than it is to catch up."

True words. No matter how quickly Clarence guzzled his ale, his "new" drinking buddy remained two or even three beers ahead of him. They soaked their brains in beer for hours, and while the Sun was making its swift descent on the horizon, the two men were crash-landing into the bar, knocking over glasses and plates of food. The Barkeep seemed unbothered by their rowdiness. He just kept lining up the pints and keeping up the tab.

"How many beers has this been?" Clarence shouted as if Väinämöinen were sitting all the way across the room.

"I— I don't know," Väinämöinen shouted back. "I lost count a while ago."

"Aha! See that? See that?" Clarence pointed at Väinämöinen and then held up two fingers. "This from the man who lectured me *two* hours ago about counting?"

"I can count."

"Not while you're drunk, apparently."

"I can count!" Väinämöinen raised his voice.

"Whoa! Easy there. I was jok—"

"I can count!!!" He slammed his palm on the counter.

"What the H. is wrong with you? Getting all worked up over counting.

Of course, you can count. Everybody can count. And even if you can't, the last thing I want to do is get into a bar fight over some D. numbers." Clarence tried to place an assuaging arm around Väinämöinen, but he shoved it away.

"You fool! You know the problem with your kind?"

"My kind? Exactly what *kind* is that?"

"The kind that takes numbers for granted, just like you take names for granted. What kind of name is *Clarence*?" He practically spat the name out. "I wasn't going to say anything before—didn't want to hurt your feelings—but the moment you told me your name, the very sound of it seared my ears, like nails on a chalkboard. You just took random letters, threw them in the air and whatever order they landed in, that was your name."

"This from a guy whose name is *Vanamorninn*?"

"Väinämöinen. There's a perfect order to that name. Just because you say the name imperfectly, that doesn't make it imperfect. And while I'm at it, the same goes for the world around you. Can you imagine what our world would look like if it were just thrown together with random numbers?"

"It *was* thrown together! It's called the Big Bang!"

"Perfect. Let's go blow up a garbage can and see if all the pieces fall together into a royal wagon. Might as well. That's how you came up with a name like Clarence. There's no order to that name. The rhythm of the seasons, the patterns of the animals—there's an order to all of it. Reminds me of the old Finnish folktale of Tobias' dog, who took up the work of a cobbler and promised a wolf a pair of shoes. The only problem was that dogs don't make shoes and wolves don't wear them! The contract was broken even before it was made, and it resulted in a turf war between the wolves and the dogs, but the dogs outnumbered the wolves and drove them out of the parish. As a reward, the dogs were given an official government license that guaranteed that they be fed no matter where they went. Well, all was fine until the dogs decided to go for a swim on the beach and placed the license under the tail of one of their companions. I know you know where this is going, but I'm going to say it anyway. They dove in the water and the license got lost in the stream, but they didn't know it. So when they got back on the beach, they started sniffing each other under the tail to see who had the document. But it was gone, and no one has found it since. And still to this day, the dogs are looking for this license. And that's why when two dogs meet each other, the first thing they do is sniff each other under the tail. *That*"—Väinämöinen gaveled the bar with his glass—"is what I'm trying to tell you."

Once again, Clarence was dumbfounded and speechless, which Väinämöinen took as proof that his point had been sufficiently made.

"Put flour in your mouth, haven't I?" Väinämöinen said and nodded his head with cocky certainty. "In my tongue, we call that *Laitoin jauhot suuhun.*"

"Put flour in my— What? What the H. does that even mean, and what was the point of that story?"

"You're hopeless." Väinämöinen sighed and shook his head. "Fine, let me *count* this out for you: *One*, dogs don't make shoes. *Two*, wolves don't wear them. *Three*, governments don't give licenses to dogs anymore and that's because—*four*—they give them to the owners, whose job it is to feed the dogs. That's called order, ystäväni. Not random order— intelligent order. Unintelligent order is for *your* kind!"

"Oh, now I get it. Intelligent order. Like intelligent design." Clarence nodded his head with revelation. "I was wondering why you kept your face buried in that Johnny Christmas beard, looking like you fell from the ceiling of the Sistine Chapel. You're a religious nut, aren't you? Let me ask you a question. Ever pay attention to your hygiene? When was the last time you washed that beard? Cleanliness is part of order too, in case you were wondering. And since we're on the topic of dog licenses, it's illegal to leave dog crap on the sidewalk. Did you even notice the dog crap on the sidewalk before I mentioned it to you?"

"It's not dog crap."

The argument came to a grinding halt as they both wondered who had just spoken. They stared at each other blinking before turning their heads in tandem at the large head sticking up from behind the bar.

"Sweet words from the grapevine, the boy just said something!" Väinämöinen said in a hushed tone.

"It came from a Dung Beetle," the Barkeep added.

"Finally." Väinämöinen finished his beer and got up to leave.

"Where are you going?" Clarence asked, wanting to finish their argument.

"Are you or have you ever been married, ystäväni?"

Clarence, slightly taken aback by the question, didn't answer.

"Right." Väinämöinen nodded. "Not the right time to answer that one. Okay, fair enough. Well, let me tell you before you even ask: I *am* married. To a woman with an obsession for dung. That's what marriage is, ystäväni. You marry into each other's strange obsessions. That's how you know when two people are crazy in love. The number two is tricky, is what I'm trying to tell you, and I'll tell you something else: there are only two words that are sure to ruin a man's self-esteem—'*I do.*' Don't worry. This isn't a pity party, and even if it were, the party was over years ago. I blame no one but myself for being tricked by twoliness and standing next to that woman and saying 'I do,' and after *I did*, I've been putting up with her crap and collecting it for her ever since. I wish someone would tell me why I go home to that harebrained harlot every night."

"Because she is loyal," the Barkeep inserted just as Väinämöinen was leaving. This stopped him in his tracks and made him spin around.

"Ah, bless you, boy, bless you." Väinämöinen's eyes lit up. Somewhere beneath his beard he was smiling. He turned to Clarence. "See? The right time. The boy just saved my marriage."

"The gypsy looking woman is your wife?"

"My *loyal* wife! And I have to get home to her. She will want to hear this news." With those words and without leaving a dime on the counter, Väinämöinen hurried out of the bar, leaving Clarence alone with the kid and his dog.

"He forgot to pay," Clarence said, blinking. He turned to the Barkeep. "We're not on the same tab, just so you know. How much is my tab, by the way?" The Barkeep didn't answer. "Not the right time for this type of question? Gotcha." Clarence chuckled and stumbled as he backed away. "I'll come back in, say, two years and see if you have an answer then."

He slipped from the bar and out into the twilight and saw that the small spherical stool was gone. Väinämöinen, the old crazy coot, had taken it.

The air had cooled considerably, but somehow, even though the surface of his skin felt the brisk breeze, the cold didn't whisk through his body or into his bones as it normally did. In fact, he felt a little on the warm side. *Must be the beer,* he thought and began to walk, but even with his cane, he found himself stumbling into a street pole. *Definitely the beer.* He took a minute to steady himself before looking up at the sign, which bore the word *Religare.* Not *Religare Street* or *Religare Avenue.* Just *Religare.*

As far as street signs go, this one was a bit ambiguous, but it was best to assume that whoever put it there knew what they were doing, and so Clarence assumed he was on Religare Road, Street or Avenue. He looked westward, where the Sun was setting behind a grand gilded cube-shaped building which glowed a crimson hue.

The retirement home!

The words leapt in his mind. Forgetting his age, he almost leapt from his feet. But it only took two or three steps before he nearly collapsed into another stumble. He steadied himself again, but for some reason the world was still moving. Still spinning to some new rhythm. Dancing around him. He nodded his head, as if to a silent beat. He knew why the world was spinning.

Mother Earth, that harlot, went and got herself drunk!

Chapter 2

♪ I said that I've got a new kind of pain
I've got headache in my heart, heartache in my head ♪

Great Googly Moogly, what the H. is that? Clarence wondered as an electric boogie travelled through the walls and hummed in his ears.

♪ I've got headache in my heart, heartache in my head ♪

His eyes fluttered open as the funk hit him: the '70s were back! He placed his hand on his forehead and felt a throbbing heartbeat inside his skull, as if his brain and his heart had swapped places and the old pump was trying to beat itself out of his head. The smallest movement only made it worse. Slowly and carefully, he levered himself upward and swiveled to the edge of his bed, where he slumped over and, as old men are wont to do, tried awakening his legs with a massage, but the tune coming through the walls and the throb in his head were too distracting.

He lay flat again to level off the cranial earthquake and slowly relocated his hand from his brow to his breast. With the palm of his hand, he listened for signs of life in the cavity of his chest. Really, he was just checking to see how his brain was making out in there. He felt no heartbeat, but this didn't alarm him. The brain is nothing like the heart. The heart is an extrovert: alive and always on the go. The brain, on the other hand, is the very symbol of the introvert: reposed on the outside, but inside hides a nightmare of more clutter and restless activity than most hearts can handle. There are also memories locked away in there. With his hand still on his chest, Clarence thought back to when he was a lifetime younger and survived his first hangover. Like losing one's virginity, you can only have your first hangover once, but there's nothing to say that the experience can't be relived.

He was at a wedding. The DJ was spinning Funkadelic's "Some More." Clarence was underage, loosely dancing and recklessly drinking champagne with no thought given to how the tide of inebriation would slam down on him and wash him up later on the shores of someone's lawn. He did not wake up on a friend's couch or even at home to await the reprimand of a parent. He woke up alone to the smell and feel of vomit and grassy overgrowth. There were no witnesses to his revival, no prankish laughter of drinking buddies who would later share stories of the night before. There was only Mother Nature's voice, which, though serene and pleasant, was nevertheless indifferent. The birds couldn't have cared less about his partying like a champion, and their morning hootin' sure as H. wasn't to applaud his hangover.

Clarence recalled nothing particularly ceremonious or climatic about that morning. It happened and that was it. Now it was happening again, as if his younger days were a foreshadowing of a life to come in his senior years. He had no friends or family to help him through this hangover.

He lifted his hand from his chest and the memory blinked out, as if turned off by a remote. The hammering in his head and the song's wet-electric guitar riff was finally receding, but now a new and different thumping took their place. The pounding was coming from outside his apartment door. He looked in that direction and saw the doorknob vibrating. It was every old person's worst nightmare: loud rap music. Hangovers weren't big fans of it either.

"Man alive," he grumbled to himself, as he pushed up from the bed and plodded to the door to thrust it open. "Holy sh—" he nearly broke his no-cursing policy at what he saw. Not a rap band, but a parade. An indoor parade. In the hallway. Just outside his door.

Thanks to Väinämöinen, Clarence found himself in the habit of counting, even when it seemed a trivial detail. His finger bobbed up and down as he numbered no more or less than twenty-four men, all wearing large masks of animals: a Lamb, a Bull, a Crab, a Lion, an Eagle, a Scorpion, a Rabbit, a Monkey, a Rat, a Tiger, a Dragon, a Snake, a Horse, a Rooster, a Dog, a Cat, a Hyena, a Pig, a Squirrel, an Elephant, a Jackal, a Zebra, a Gazelle and a Beetle. Eight were in front, leading the group while shaking a strange metal instrument that made the sound of soft rattling cymbals. Eight were in the rear, holding drums almost the size of their bodies and striking them with amazing synchronicity. In the center were another eight, carrying on their shoulders long horizontal beams supporting a platform mounted with the emblem of the Sun.

Man alive! Clarence thought, *I'm still dreaming.* Or maybe he was still drunk. Old people get drunk faster than young people, and thanks to a doddering metabolism, booze works its mojo on their minds markedly longer. In other words, contrary to popular belief, even the most juiced-up juvenile is nowhere near as much fun as a soaked senior, hence this old folks freak festival. All of these fools were drunk. *Unless*—Clarence hesitated as a third possibility entered his brain—*I'm dead.*

He placed his fingers on the inside of his wrist to feel for a pulse. He felt a tick, like the struggling hand on a grandfather clock. *Meh.* Clarence shrugged his shoulders. If he were dead, there was nothing he could do about that anymore. Now it was only a question of whether he was in heaven or in hell.

His answer lay just outside the window, where he saw in the distance the drab grayness of the ghost town he had left behind the night before. In the foreground was a vast and verdurous field that wasn't entirely unfamiliar. He looked to his left and saw his jacket slumped over the back of a chair. Peeking from the edge of a pocket was the retirement home brochure.

Now it was coming back to him. He grabbed the brochure, held it out at arm's length and adjusted his peepers. He compared the brochure's photo with the landscape just outside the window. They were a match.

Just then, the twenty-four–fogey procession slowly marched into his peripheral and halted in the window frame. The thumping and thudding, at last, came to a stop. For a few long minutes they stood noiselessly, as if waiting for something. Still observing from his window view, Clarence could not help but to wait with them, wondering with terrified fascination what had made twenty-four crazy codgers throw on togas and stand in the cold at the crack of dawn.

He didn't have to wait long. The Sun came up with a flash of light, ambitiously cutting through the air and gradating across the animal masks of the twenty-four old men, causing them to glow. Slowly, they swayed their bodies and chanted a strange mantra.

Stunned, Clarence fixed his attention back to the brochure. Surely, this thing said nothing about early morning fetish festivals. He opened it up and saw the picture of a concierge. Thankfully, he was not wearing an animal head. But he wasn't exactly a PR poster child either. Clarence studied the congenial photo of an African man who seemed to have misplaced himself in a polyester business suit. In fact, it looked as if he had been shoved into it by Photoshop. Whoever this huckster was, Clarence needed to speak with him. *Now.*

*

Clarence opened the lobby door and walked into a wall of P-Funk. At maximum volume, a new song was jamming. This time, it was "Mothership Connection (Star Child)" by Parliament.

♪ Well, all right, starchild
Citizens of the universe, recording angels
We have returned to claim the pyramids...♪

The lobby rattled like a disco. It even flickered like one. Every square inch of the four walls was lined by an unusual number of large lit ivory pillar candles—three hundred sixty-one in total. Smoke burned and rolled in calligraphic patterns before dissolving into a thick marijuana-like haze.

Clarence fanned the air to break a hole through the smoldering wall of smoke and identified the Concierge, though he was nothing like the man in the brochure. For one thing, he was high—literally, high, as in levitating. He bobbed his head to the music while his body buoyed in the air. Clarence checked his pulse one more time and refocused his pupils to confirm that yes, this man really was floating.

What he saw seemed to be less an act of will and more an act of physics, as if no matter how hard the Concierge might have tried, the poor guy would never be able to get his feet to touch the ground. Consequently, he had no use for shoes, so he reclined in the air barefooted.

Clarence also noticed that the pseudo-salesman style of his brochure photo was scrapped and swapped with a vibrant orange patterned dashiki and narrow sunglasses. This too-cool counter jockey was pretty good at multi-tasking too. He could read a book, listen to P-Funk and plough through a box of Rice Krispies—using chopsticks, no less—like nobody's business.

But he wasn't particularly good at paying attention to his guests. Two customers were waiting impatiently at the front desk for his attention. Clarence was one of them. The other was a short dark misshapen man whose ogre appearance was belied by a self-assured, aristocratic attitude. Fed up, the ogre reached over the desk and turned off the music. This got the Concierge's attention.

"What's up, brotha? What can I do for you?"

"Yes, hello, brother," the ogre answered in a proper British accent. "We apologize for interrupting your voracious quest for knowledge. In fact, it pleases Us to see people of your generation still reading, and, We will add, you handle those chopsticks effortlessly, as if they were your own fingers. But We do have a few questions for you, if you don't mind. First, what is the maximum occupancy for this building?"

"Are you a fire inspector?"

"Well, occupationally, no, We are not fire inspectors. But We are generally worried about fire and brimstone hazards, yes." The ogre nodded and looked around at the overabundance of candles.

"Aww man, that reminds me of The Bootleggers' song 'Fire and Brimstone,'" the Concierge cut in with bass and funk in his voice. He closed his eyes and nodded as he heard blue-grass music in his head. He sang the lyrics.

> ♪ *I felt the rumbling beneath my feet*
> *And the whole world was shaking free*
> *And the sun was standing still*
> *It was dark, but I could see.*
>
> *I saw fire, fire and brimstone coming down on my head*
> *I saw fire, fire and brimstone coming down, down on me.* ♪

Clarence blinked while taking all of this in. He wondered about the odds of witnessing a British ogre gentleman who referred to himself in the plural hold a conversation with a P-Funk, blue-grass, country-rock concierge who dined on breakfast cereal with chopsticks.

"You don't need to worry about fire and brimstones, my brotha—or the candles," the Concierge replied, finally opening his eyes and popping some Rice Krispies into his mouth. "We have regular fire evacuation drills."

"Yes, of course. But we weren't thinking of evacuations. More of an *eviction*."

"Is someone being too noisy?"

"No, no, no, that's not the problem here."

"Are you complaining about the morning procession?"

"No, that doesn't bother Us either."

"Well, it sure as H. bothers me!" Clarence interjected from behind. From over the roof of his sunglasses, the Concierge eyeballed him. Even the British gentleman was obliged to turn to get a look at the source of the rude interruption. It also gave Clarence a chance to get a good look at *him*, which immediately made him wince. He had a meaty slanted forehead awning over a pair of bright bulbous eyes that seemed to lack eyelids. His hairline receded in not one but two places, forming a "W" across the roof of his head. Clarence could tell that he invested most of his time taming his vanishing hair because the rest of his face, which was half-shaven and scruffy, suffered from neglect. Finally, his hunchback posture, which somehow mingled with a dignified poise, lent him the look of a troll, but one with impeccably good manners.

"I beg your pardon!" the ogre-like gentleman said sternly. "You'll get your chance to complain soon enough. Not that it will matter anyhow because when We are done here, you too will be promptly evicted."

"Me?" Clarence exclaimed.

"Him?" the Concierge added.

"Yes, him"—the ogre drilled his finger into the counter—"and everyone else in this bloody building! Except for you, of course." He nodded to the Concierge. "A well-read and cultured concierge is always good to have around. But your memory skills might need some refining. You neglected to answer my question about the maximum occupancy of this building."

"Thirty-three million," the Concierge answered flatly.

"Well, please let Us know how we can assist you in whittling that dreadful number down to *one*."

The Concierge didn't reply. He just looked at him dubiously while leaning on one elbow and continuing to feed himself from his cereal box. Clarence, meanwhile, couldn't believe his ears. In fact, he was beginning to think that he was not drunk, dreaming or dead at all. *No,* he decided. *The problem isn't me. It's them! This troll and this concierge are both crazy. Somehow, I ended up in a madhouse. I have to go back to town and find the real retirement home.* He turned and made his way for the front door. His old bones still had enough strength to slam the door so hard that it came off its hinges.

"Good to see that some are willing to cooperate," the gentlemen troll said, watching Clarence exit. "One is a good enough start. Now let's get rid of the rest of them!"

*

26

"Well, look who's come back with his tail between his legs, looking for forgiveness," Väinämöinen announced with a celebratory drink, emptying a half pint of beer into his beard. After he had his fill, he shared some with the Lapphund.

"Forgiveness? Try directions," Clarence corrected.

"Ah, no hard feelings. At least none that can't be washed away with a warm pint."

"Beer? At this hour?" Clarence said dubiously. "The Sun just came up, you know."

"Kyllä! I know. That's why I'm drinking."

"In the morning?"

"Kyllä! That's usually when the Sun comes up."

"Don't you think that's a bit early?"

"Maybe. But if I waited too long, it wouldn't be morning anymore, now would it?"

"What about the afternoon? Or the evening?"

"Oh, I'll be having a pint at those hours too," Väinämöinen said, finishing the last half of his beer and signaling the Barkeep for another.

"Okay, okay. As long as you are aware you have a drinking problem."

"Here, we don't call it a drinking 'problem.' It's a drinking *ritual*. A problem is when you don't know when to do what you're doing or why you're even doing it, so you end up doing it all the time for no other reason than that you can. That's a problem. A ritual means you do it every time at the right time, and what better time to have a drink than during a celebration. By the way, it's good to have a good friend join me for this important observance, ystäväni." Väinämöinen leaned to whisper in Clarence's ear while thumbing towards the kid behind the bar. "I like the Barkeep here, but he's not the most festive fella in the world."

"Celebration? What are we celebrating?"

"Well, to be honest, a friend's return to the bar is a good enough reason to drink, but the real reason for our celebration is the return of the Sun. It just came up this morning, if you hadn't noticed."

Clarence blinked a few times before walloping him over the head with his eyes, but Väinämöinen was impervious to the silent smack-down.

"Comes up every morning, actually," Väinämöinen added solemnly. "Poor *läjä*. That kind of due diligence warrants a 24-ounce salute." He karated his forehead, military-style, then took a drink.

"So you celebrate the Sun? Why?"

Väinämöinen slammed down his mug. This time, it was his turn to look at Clarence as if he were the village idiot.

"*Olla pihalla kuin lumiukko!*"

"English, man."

"What difference would that make? You're *like a snowman in the yard*, in any language. Why am I celebrating the Sun? What planet are you from, ystäväni? Wait! Let me answer that for you: the one with third row seats to an actual star! Put a person within a few cubits of a movie star and he doesn't just lose his mind but abandons his brain entirely. But put him 327,360,000,000 cubits in front of a *real* star and *meh*"—Väinämöinen shrugged, mimicking a vapid attitude—"*I've seen a million of those. What's the big deal? It's only a sun.* No, it isn't 'only a sun.' It's *the* Sun—capital S—and it's the only Sun we have. It's our own personal star! It's *your* star. You remind me of the old Finnish folktale of Tobias' pig and the squirrel."

"Oh gawd, here we go with Tobias again."

"We're not going anywhere. We're going to sit right here until the end of the tale." Väinämöinen shoved a finger into Clarence's shoulder. "This is a tale of knowing your place in the world. The squirrel didn't know his because he had the nerve to call the pig a fool for not being able to see the sunrise despite being a fathom taller than the rodent. Quite naturally, the pig was put off by the squirrel's insult. So the two made a bet on who would see the sunrise first. The problem was the Sun never came up that next morning."

"It didn't?"

"Not for the squirrel. The pig ate him," Väinämöinen chuckled. "But then again, the Sun didn't come up for the pig either because Tobias ate him. So the lesson of this legend is: Don't ever take for granted that you'll see your next sunrise. Celebrate the Sun you have while you still have it. Now have a beer and drink to it. "Barkeep! *Yksi tuoppi kiitos.*"

Clarence took a big sigh, rolled his eyes and conceded. The Barkeep set down a beer in front of him and stood there as if waiting for something.

"Oh, right! Last night's tab." Clarence searched his pockets for his wallet but realized it was still in his jacket at the retirement home. "Can you add this to yesterday's tab and I'll square up with you later?"

The Barkeep, of course, didn't answer.

"C'mon. This is an ordinary question I'm asking."

"We're not waiting for you to pay your tab, ystäväni." Väinämöinen laughed. "We're waiting for you to give a proper thanks to the Sun so that we can start drinking."

"Give thanks?" Clarence asked and Väinämöinen nodded. Clarence cleared his throat, raised his beer at eye level and began making a toast. "Okay, well, thank you for the warmth"—his voice broke with joking embarrassment—"and, um, thank you for the light and for never sending me a light or heat bill. 'Cause I can't afford it."

Väinämöinen released a hearty and approving laugh and pounded Clarence's back with an open hand, encouraging him to drink up.

"Okay, so now that we have that out of the way, tell me about where you're going."

"I'm still trying to find that retirement home."

"You mean you didn't find it last night?"

"I'm not sure where I slept last night. I was little drunk when I left here."

"A little?" Väinämöinen chuckled incredulously.

"Whatever. The point is that when I woke up this morning, I saw a bunch of men in animal masks having some kind of cel—" Clarence paused as a realization hit him. "Wait a minute. They were having a celebration of the Sun, I think."

29

"Men in animal masks? Do you know how many?"

"I counted twenty-four."

Väinämöinen's eyes lit up. He was probably smiling too, but it was hard for Clarence to tell from behind his beard.

"Aaah. *Hyvin tehty. Well done.* So you're finally keeping tally. Good. If you're sure there were twenty-four, then I can tell you exactly who they were."

"Who?"

"The Gods of the Decans. Some people call them *the Watchers*."

"Watchers of what?"

"Watchers of the Sun and the stars. Mostly, they just watch the hours. They keep track of time, ystäväni."

"Why?"

"Because it's useful to know what time it is, that's why. Just like it's useful to know the direction you're going. That reminds me. I have useful news for you. I know the way to the retirement home."

"You do?"

"Kyllä. Just go exactly the same way you did last night. You found it."

"Like H. I did."

"If there are twenty-four Watchers living there, then you found it, ystäväni."

"Yeah, but I overheard the Concierge. He said there were a lot more than twenty-four living there."

"I warned you!" Väinämöinen wagged his finger. "Don't say I didn't warn you because I did. I told you they had a weird math going on there."

"Yeah, but he said there were thirty-three million people there."

"Not people, ystäväni, *Gods*." Väinämöinen looked squarely at him. Clarence reciprocated, but for a different reason. He appraised the wild look in Väinämöinen's eyes and decided that yes, he was crazy.

In fact, it would seem that everyone in this town had lost their mind. Väinämöinen misunderstood Clarence's silence, figuring that he had finally gotten through to him. This encouraged him to continue his disclosure.

"To be honest, ystäväni, I thought it was a bit odd when you told me you were planning to check yourself in there since you don't look like a God. No offence, but you lack the order of a God. The Gods are all about order, ystäväni, and there are three things you can always count on them ordering: time, space and pizza."

"What?"

"You heard me. But before the Gods ordered pizza, they ordered time and space, and they did this with number. That's why counting is important. It's a good thing that you're finally learning how to count. Maybe that's why you were brought into this town. Maybe the Gods finally came to their senses and want you to replace the Concierge. He's a total hack if you ask me. Not a true number's man like myself. He got the position because he *claims* to know the ancient myths, and I'll admit he knows a few, but he doesn't know the myths and the folktales as well as I do. He certainly doesn't know the tall tales of Tobias, of which I'm an expert. And you have to be an expert of *all* the myths if you're going to keep count. Reminds me of the old tale of Tobias and his—"

"Keep count of what?" Clarence interrupted

"The Gods. Don't believe that Concierge when he tells you there are thirty-three million of them. That's the *maximum* occupancy, but they've exceeded that number a long time ago. I don't know where they're cramming all those Gods anymore. I'll grant you, a God is really just a symbol and you can fit any number of symbols into even the smallest space, even on the tip of a needle. That reminds me of—and don't interrupt me this time, ystäväni. It's kind of rude, you know—it reminds me of an old riddle:

I once knew a one-eyed ugly old lady,

And, my God, she only had one tooth!

Made of bone, wood or even metal

And had a bite as sharp as truth.

When she went for a stroll,

She'd slither like a snake,

31

And her tail was just as long.

Until she slithered so far

That by the time she got home,

She discovered her tail was gone!"

Väinämöinen stopped there with a con-man's smile, certain that Clarence was too much of "a snowman in the yard" to solve the riddle.

"A needle," Clarence said flatly.

"Wh— Did you hear that one already? Who told you?"

"You did! You said 'tip of a needle' and that it reminded you of the rid—"

"Kyllä! That was my point. Almost lost it there. It's true, ystäväni, you can fit any number of symbols on the head of a needle, but not so many in the head of a man. The mind can only handle so many, and when you pack too many symbols into the same space, it starts to get a little crowded, like the old Finnish folktale of Tobias and the lost key—"

"Yeah, yeah, yeah." Clarence waved his hand impatiently. "The whole town was searching with him under the streetlight where he didn't even lose it."

"You've heard that one before?"

"Yeah. Anyway, too many symbols are too much for the mind."

"Kyllä! That's when the mind stops paying attention and the symbols begin to lose their meaning. If you let that condition stay for too long, you come to the conclusion that there is no meaning. And a life without mind or meaning is unmindful and meaningless." Väinämöinen paused to let this sink in and took another drink. Then he continued: "I'm not a pig or a squirrel, ystäväni, so I don't make bets about the sunrise, but I am willing to bet someone wants you to take the Concierge's job. While I wouldn't mind seeing that hack on the streets, I'd hate it more to see you behind that desk. It's not an easy job, ystäväni. I used to work it myself and was darn good at it too, until some crippled kook checked in and started insisting to me that he was the one God—the *only* one. He kept saying it so much, he made me lose my count. Now before you doubt my math like you did before, let me just say that if you tried counting when someone kept throwing numbers into your ear, you'd fumble your arithmetic too. That's exactly what that ogre did to me, and that's how I got fired. Been unemployed ever since."

"You mean the guy who looks like a troll?"

"So you met him already." Väinämöinen shook his head. "I don't envy you. He's still on that one-man mission, isn't he? Wait until you meet the rest of him."

"What are you talking about?"

"He's a three-for-one special is what I'm talking about. Three personalities! All wrapped up with a bow in one crazy head. I said it before and I'll say it again: Nothing good ever comes of crowds."

"Who is he?"

"His name is Balaam. Don't get me wrong. He's a nice guy, polite and courteous. At least, that's how he comes across at first. But the problem is that he used to be an avatar, and once you become human, even for just a short time, it's hard to rub that crap off. Reminds me of the old Finnish folktale of the old man who spent morning, noon and night at a tavern. He'd go home to his wife and she'd ask him where he'd been, so he'd tell her that he was out admiring the roses and sniffing the sunshine. But every time she kissed him, she'd smell the ale on his breath and the odor of the tavern in his beard. 'The next time you come home, you better smell like a job application!' she'd scream at him right before throwing him out of his own home. Alas, he had no choice but to go back to the tavern and start the cycle all over again."

"That's an old Finnish folktale?" Clarence asked, incredulously.

"Kyllä," Väinämöinen said with a nod and took a drink. "Old as me. Maybe even older. Anyway, what was my point in telling you that?"

"Balaam became hu—"

"Oh, oh, that's right. The human experience is a lot like the smell of humans. Once it gets on you, it's there to stay, like an odor that gets into your beard. It doesn't help that humans usually kill avatars, and from what I heard, Balaam got it pretty bad—the kind of stuff that can mess up your mind, if you know what I mean." Väinämöinen circled a finger near his temple. "The poor guy is shell-shocked. But worse than that—in my humble opinion—is that the moment you become human, you start thinking like them. The problem with people is that they see what they want to see, regardless of what's looking right back at them."

"Symbols," Clarence said, rewinding a bit.

"What about them?"

"You said the Gods are just symbols. But symbols aren't real. They're products of the imagination."

"There are many things that are products of your imagination, ystäväni. Geometry is the product of your imagination, as are numbers. But it is these products of the imagination that produce the products of *your* real world."

"Is there a chance that everything that is happening to me is just a symbol too? Maybe this is all in my head."

"Well, it's all in *someone's* head, that's for sure! The head is the home of the Gods, and there are a lot of heads out there in the real world. Although lately the Gods have had fewer and fewer heads to make a home in. That seems to be the problem. Whosever head we're in, they seem to have a job for you. I suggest you do it, so that you can get back into your own head."

"A job? I'm not looking for a job. I'm looking to retire!"

"What are you telling me for?" Väinämöinen wiped away beer from his mouth. "I'm not the one offering you a job. I'm still trying to find one for myself. If you're really desperate for work, I have a house that needs cleaning, but I can't pay you anything. The only job I can think of around here is as the Concierge, and whether you like it or not, that means you need to walk back to the retirement home and give him his walking papers. This may come as a shock to him, so after you break the news, tell him there's a nice warm stool waiting for him at the pub," Väinämöinen finished with a devilish chuckle. "Tell him that Väinämöinen will be waiting for him."

*

The Concierge was just about done fixing the broken door when Clarence returned. Though Clarence expected a swift and much deserved chastening, the Concierge appeared to be a mostly unflappable personality. He stood up, smiled and sang a sweet sample from Lionel Richie.

34

♪ *Hello. Is it me you're looking for?* ♪

"Uh... Yes. You're the concierge, right?" Clarence stammered and the Concierge nodded. "What is your job description? I mean, what is it that you do?"

"I do check-ins, brotha."

Clarence waited for him to say more, but he didn't. Clearly, the Concierge was deliberately withholding information, no doubt because he knew this day was coming and he wasn't going to give up his job without a fight.

"So that's all you do every day? Check-ins?"

"Oh, that's right," the Concierge added. "And I fix the door."

"Guilty as charged," Clarence conceded by holding up his hands. "Sorry about that. Okay, so you fix doors and check people in? Do you ever check people *out*?"

"What do you mean?"

"I mean when people check into a hotel, they don't stay forever, right? Eventually they leave."

"This isn't a hotel. It's a retirement home."

"Good point. But if all you do is check people in, then shouldn't you have a computer or something to help you keep count?"

"Don't need one." The Concierge tapped his temple, then sang a sample from Nelly.

> ♪ *'Cause it's all in my head*
> *I think about it over and over again*
> *I replay it over and over again*
> *And I can't take it yeah I can't shake it* ♪

Clarence looked at him and blinked. It felt as if he were talking to a jukebox.

"Sooooo... You're saying you don't have a computer?"

"Nope."

"Not even a pocket calculator?"

The Concierge shook his head.

"But what if you need to do some math?" Clarence knew that his questions sounded like they had an agenda attached to them, but the Concierge, still unfazed, smiled and pointed to his head, as if to say, *it's all worked out in here.*

"Bull S." Clarence objected. "I'm old but I ain't senile. Nobody does math in their head. What's two hundred eighty-four plus two hundred twenty?"

"Five hundred four," the Concierge answered effortlessly. Clarence's eyes roamed the roof of his head as he crunched the numbers to see if this was correct: *four plus zero, drop the four; eight plus two, drop the zero and carry the one...*

"Okay," he moved on, "what's the square root of twenty-five?"

"Five."

"Too easy. Square root of... sixteen hundred?"

"Forty."

"Still too easy," Clarence said while reaching into the front pocket of his shirt to pull out an outdated pocket calculator. He tapped out an equation, which he covered with his hand. "What's the square root of... two?"

"One—"

"Aha!" Clarence pointed at him, jumping the gun.

"Point four one four two one three five six two three seven three zero nine five zero four eight eight zero one six—"

"Okay, okay, stop showing off," Clarence conceded by putting his calculator away.

"Look, brotha, why are you interviewing me for a job I already have?"

"Actually, a friend told me *I'm* supposed to have the interview"— Clarence swallowed—"for your job."

"Friend, huh? You mean Väinämöinen?" The Concierge smiled, shook his head and didn't wait for Clarence to answer. "Man, that fool is just mad because I replaced him. You probably noticed that his train of thought has a few train wrecks from time to time."

"Yeah. I noticed."

"Väinämöinen's problem is that he thinks only the old myths are worth remembering. That's how he lost this job. He refuses to accept that human beings never stopped singing about the Gods, even to this day. And as the old saying goes, *singing is believing*."

"You mean seeing is believing."

"No," the Concierge countered, "believing is seeing. People see what they believe. Reality is the opium of the masses, man. But the ears..." He tapped his and hummed a hymn. "Oh, listening is love, my brotha. Boombayala!

"Boombaya— What?"

"Boombayala. It means 'listen.' Like 'The Message' by Dr. Dre and Mary J.

♪ *Listen listen listen... whoahh... Listen* ♪

"Listen to the lyrics, my brotha. Listen, there are three recurring things you hear in myths and music, man: Love, the World and God. Why is that? I'll tell you. Because nothing disappoints a man more than a broken heart, a broken world and a broken God. Broken hearts and broken worlds are the main reason for man's break-up with the Gods. Jerry Harrison called us 'Casual Gods.' He named a whole album—and a band—after us! Classic stuff, man. Also, one of my favorites: 'Jesus of Suburbia' by Green Day. Peep this:

♪ *I'm the son of rage and love, the Jesus of Suburbia*
From the bible of none of the above ♪

"BOOMBAYALA! That's some deep bleep right there, my brotha. But I'm not finished. Arcade Fire's album 'Neon Bible.' The whole album recorded in a church. First words:

♪ *A vial of hope and a vial of pain*
In the light they both looked the same ♪

"That's what I'm talkin' 'bout, right there. Broken Gods, man. But then you get the flip side from cats like X-Clan. What did they say in that song 'Funkin Lesson'?

> ♪ Born in a cosmos, with no time and space to exist
> Vibe in the midst of the chaos
> Mortals label me as illogical, mythological ♪

"Okay, you got that, right? That was from their first album—first song too! Now, fast forward to album two, second song—'A.D.A.M.' This joint was about the first man, and what do they say? Boombayala. Pay attention.

> ♪ I'm not measured by tradition, or any type of religion
> Not even cosmic dimensions ♪

"But wait a second! You just told me you were *'born in a cosmos.'* What's up with that? I'll tell you what's up. It's like the Joni Mitchell 'Woodstock' song.

> ♪ I came upon a child of God
> He was walking along the road
> And I asked him, where are you going
> And this he told me…
> We are stardust, We are golden
> And we've got to get ourselves
> Back to the garden. ♪

"Not my words—hers! Not the Word of God. Not even the word of man. This is the word of *Woman*. That's what *she* said, and what I'm saying to you is this…" He took a deep breath before continuing. "*They* know. You hear me? *They* know. They know that they come from the stars. *'Born in a cosmos'*… *'We are stardust'*… They know. Like a kid who discovers his absentee father, human beings are trying to figure out their relationship to the stars—the *Casual Gods.*

"So they make songs about us, man. 'Space Truckin' with Deep Purple. Pink Floyd and 'Astronomy Domine.' And who could forget Bob Marley's joint:

> ♪ The stars up above, that play with Laughing Sam's dice…
> The Zodiac rise, that dreams that come through the skies. ♪

"Songs are sermons, man, even when they try not to be. And that's some deep bleep, for real!"

The Concierge's train of thought came to a grinding halt, and Clarence was more than happy to get off.

"I'm too old for this." Clarence lowered his head.

"I'm glad you figured that out for yourself, bruh. I didn't want to be the one to say it. Some people can get a little sensitive about their age. Besides, only a God is fit for this job."

"Just to be clear... You are a God, right?" Clarence asked.

"God of Music." The Concierge proudly pounded his chest.

"So what am I supposed to do? Why am I here?"

"Hey man, you're here. You don't seem like you're in a hurry to start working again, so in the meantime hang loose and enjoy your golden years." Those words, of course, warranted a song-quote. This time it was David Bowie's 'Golden Years.'

> ♪ Golden years, gold, whop, whop, whop
> Golden years, gold, whop, whop, whop
> Don't let me hear you say life's taking you nowhere ♪

Suddenly, the Concierge reverted back to the person in the brochure, sounding like a salesman closing the sale. He swayed his arm, as if presenting a brand new car.

"You didn't even have to die to make it to heaven. Here, you'll always see the Sun rise and set without obstruction. We have pearly white clouds that will never rain on your parade, procession or party—and we have all three of these festivals, not all day, but every day. It's a beautiful place. Hang out, have some fun and get some rest—in that order. Judging from your condition last night when you stumbled in here, I'll safely assume you already know about the pub up the street. Have a drink. And then have another. You'll have plenty of time to work, right after you spend the rest of your life playing," he finished with a smile.

"This is impossible." Clarence sighed again.

"Quite the opposite, my brotha. Don't believe me? Put a gliiiide in your striiiide"—he thumbed towards a door just past his shoulder—"and you'll see that here, at the Golden Age Retirement Home, anything is possible."

Clarence felt as if it were a dare. Or maybe it felt like making a deal with the devil. Or even worse, like making a deal with a game-show host: Do you quit while you're ahead or take what's behind door number three? Like all foolish contestants, Clarence picked door number three.

*

"THIS CONTEST IS SCHEDULED FOR ONE FALL. TO MY LEFT, FROM NIGERIA, KNOWN FROM WEST AFRICA TO LATIN AMERICA AS THE GOD OF THUNDER AND HAILED AS THE KING OF THE OYO EMPIRE... SHANGOOOO!"

The winged Goddess of victory, Nike, stood front and center of a wrestling ring as she heralded the massive bodied Shango. The energy of her voice brought hundreds of African Gods to their feet as they howled and hooted ear splitting battle cries. Shango stuck out his barrel chest and broad shoulders, confidently showcasing his formidable frame. Nike gave him a short minute to receive his audience before turning to the regal Olympian in the opposite corner.

"AND HIS OPPONENT, HAILING FROM MOUNT OLYMPUS, ALSO KNOWN ALL OVER THE WORLD AS THE GOD OF THUNDER, THE REIGNING HEAVYWEIGHT CHAMPION OF THE WORLD AND SELF-PROCLAIMED KING OF THE GODS... ZEUS!"

The room erupted again as Zeus slow strutted around the room, bobbing his head as he spiked both hands in the air. Cocky as hell, he flexed into a crowd-pleasing exhibition of his zero-fat figure by shedding every layer of clothing until he was butt ass naked. This went back to the original Greek custom, where Olympic athletes competed in the nude. Shango stoically looked on, his steely visage showing no affect to Zeus' nude showboating.

Clarence opened the door to a hallway electrified with lightning as the two deities wasted no time charging into each other with thunderous force. The walls trembled from the tension of two thunder Gods in a locked-arm tug of war that ended with a bone-cracking body slam.

Clarence couldn't believe his eyes. The retirement home exploded with carnival colored confetti as scores of African Gods cheered for Shango when he gripped Zeus into a neck-breaking headlock. But Zeus broke the hold with a spine-splitting back body-drop that made all the Gods of Olympus roar.

Stray limbs seemed to whip through the air every which way as jeering Gods recklessly punched the air, nearly elbowing Clarence off his feet. This was no place for an old man and right away he wanted out. Muscling his way through was like trying to push through a concert crowd, but after much jouncing and jostling, he finally saw the light at the end of the tunnel.

A very long tunnel.

The hallway appeared to stretch on for miles and was dissected by several intersections, each with its own mob of pedestrian traffic passing to and fro. Clarence's eyes expanded all over again and his mouth fell agape with disbelief. If he hadn't known better, he would have sworn he walked into a busy New York City intersection.

Before Clarence could get a second look, a chariot zipped past, nearly sideswiping him. He lost his balance and could feel that he was toppling over, but some portly fellow with the head of an elephant caught him, making the save.

"Easy kiddo. Gotta watch it out here," the elephant man said with a friendly wink. He helped Clarence find his balance and then went on his way, leaving him with a hard pat on the back that sent him tumbling to the ground.

Clarence used his third leg—his walking stick—to get back on his feet. Just as he did, he found himself standing face to face with an exotically handsome man with blue skin and long hair spiraling into the shape of a tower. He was showered in wild colors of gold that beamed as if they had their own source of light. But none of this was brighter than the man's glaring white smile, which made Clarence shield his eyes. As he looked down, he noticed that the man had four arms.

"Holy Sh—"

"Shiva!" the man announced himself with a rich Indian accent and his hands perched on his waist, as if he were a superhero. He extended one of his arms for a handshake. Instinctively, Clarence obliged and became the victim of the firmest, fiercest non-arthritic handshake he had ever experienced. They sized each other up, Clarence taking inventory of Shiva's arms while Shiva smiled, making an appraisal of Clarence's stick. Without warning, Shiva burst into laughter.

"Hey, Ganesh!" he called out to the elephant man. "This guy has three legs!" With three of his arms he grabbed the stick from Clarence and held it like a piece of antique furniture. "Beautiful! Gorgeous! But why only three legs, why not four?"

"I have two legs"—Clarence snatched back his property—"and you should only have two arms."

"Aaah, you're right," Shiva agreed, snatching back Clarence's stick. "This isn't a leg. So what is it then? Oooh. It's a staff... of poooower!" Shiva's words echoed.

"No! It's a walking stick." Clarence snatched his cane again.

"So then it *is* a leg. That's what I said the first time. Odd numbers are hard to walk around with. You should consider adding a fourth limb."

"I'm doing fine with three. If I need a fourth one, I'll borrow one of yours. You have plenty to spare."

Clarence shouldered past him, dismayed by the rudeness of anyone, even a God, who snatches property away from an old man.

"Wait, three-legged prophet!" Shiva called. "You must tell me your name?"

"What did you call me?"

"Three-legged prophet. But I wanted to know your name."

Prophet! The word leaped and somersaulted in Clarence's head. *Maybe this is my job. No,* Clarence decided, *there's no way I'm qualified for that position. I have no work experience!* Then again, he wasn't qualified to be a concierge either, and he still wasn't convinced that this wasn't the position he was summoned to do. But as he looked around at the crowded chaos surrounding him, he was sure that even if it were, he wanted no part of it.

Clarence walked away from Shiva, having forgotten to give him his name. All of the commotion had made him weary and he decided that it was time for a rest. It was difficult to navigate the turbulent hallways, let alone find his room. Every door was identical and he had long forgotten his room number. This was going to be a trial and error process with plenty of errors, but so be it. He needed to get back to his room.

The first room was a clear miss. He opened the door to find a Goddess, beautiful and busty, wrapped in a white towel after a hot shower. Clarence blushed and found himself frozen with embarrassment. The room was misty from shower fog, which helped conceal her half-nakedness, but that didn't stop her from fast-forwarding with blurring speed to the mouth of the door and slamming it shut in Clarence's face. He recoiled from the force, knowing that he deserved that.

He thought twice about opening the next door, but it had been carelessly left open, practically inviting Clarence to take a peek.

Inside, he found an ancient Persian man with a long curly beard rolled into a cylinder. Whoever he was, he was berating some Japanese guy with porcelain skin and a white walrus mustache that flowed down his face like silk strings. Clarence watched as both men bickered back and forth without pause.

"All I'm saying is that you didn't ask permission to use my name on your cars!" the Persian fogey protested, slamming down his fist on a table.

"They are not *my* cars. How many times do I have to keep telling you that?!? If they were, my name would be on them. Besides, no self-respecting Japanese God would call a Japanese car *Mazda*," he spit out the two sour syllables as if they swathed his tongue with a bitter flavor. "Yuk! I'm not even sure why anyone would want to drive a car named *Mazda*."

"Because nobody in their right mind will drive a car named Kamikaze, that's why! And good luck getting insurance with a name like that."

"That, Mazda-san, is not my name."

"No one would drive a car named *Omiokane* either!"

"Please, Mazda-san, say my name with royalty," Omiokane demanded.

"Not until you pay your royalties"—Mazda leaned forward and raised a single eyebrow—"or shall I take this matter up with my legal department?"

"Ha!" Omiokane threw back his head. "And you mock me, Mazda-san! The Great God of Truth is threatening to go running to his lawyer."

"Make no mistake, you will be running to yours after you hear from mine!"

The old quarrelling fools were so busy bickering like kids over lost marbles that they didn't even notice Clarence slowly hobbling past them, headed for their window. Realizing that he might be knocking on doors all day and night before he found his room, Clarence decided it was time to get away from the hustle and bustle of the retirement home. The window of these two squabbling seniors looked like the perfect emergency exit.

Clarence propped the window open and a strong wind current swept through the room, practically blowing Omiokane's kimono off his body. This made Mazda fall over into laughter. Omiokane turned in the direction of the window where he heard Clarence lifting one arthritic leg on the windowsill, straddling it like a horse and releasing a distressing groan for reasons that most men would understand. He took a deep breath and resigned himself to a broken hip as he allowed his body to drop.

Omiokane and Mazda both gasped as Clarence suddenly vanished from the window.

Chapter 3

His ears interpreted it as the sound of a crushed bag of chips. *Man alive*, he yelped in his mind, *that was my bones!* But the sound of his body crunching didn't bother him nearly as much as the smell. He lay prostrate for several seconds, while his nose twitched every which way, sniffing out the source of a sour stench. At first he thought it might have been coming from himself, but Clarence knew his own smells. Ripe as they were, this stink was even riper—it was ancient.

He turned his head to the subtle sound of grass being disturbed by tiny footsteps and spotted the culprit—a little bastard pushing along a ball of crap twice its size. It looked just like the little ball of shit he saw on the sidewalk.

"You," Clarence whispered at the Dung Beetle, but his nose wiggled again, overruling his decision. The funk wasn't coming from the ball of dung, but from what was just beyond it: a pair of funky feet in sandals.

The decomposing smell of a pair of destroyed feet can easily rival the predictably pungent output of bowels, and these craggy, callused feet were beyond toxic. Clarence blocked his nose and looked up to see the already familiar sight of an ogre in a long white tunic and wine-colored scarf wrapped crosswise over his shoulder and across his chest.

"Balaam," he whispered.

Without invitation, the ogre plopped down next to him with a glass of wine in hand, sipping from it like a true connoisseur.

"Good on ya, mate. Better to go arse over elbow out the window then spend another second with that bloody botch of Beelzebubs. Turned this temple into a two-bit tin house is what they did."

"So what? You want to throw everybody out—including me?"

"Actually, it would appear that you threw yourself out."

"Good point." Clarence hoisted himself on his butt and leaned against the back of the wall. "Give me some of that wine, will you?"

"Barmy! And share germs? Not a chance, ol' chap. Whores and lepers We can handle, but catching cooties from a commoner is where We draw the line. Did you bring your own glass?"

"No, and I didn't bring a British accent either. Who are you, man?"

"Who do you think *We* are?"

"I think you are crazy."

"BLASPHEMY!" Balaam shouted in a booming bass voice.

"Blasphemy is the King of the Jews using the Queen's English," Clarence snapped. "That's blasphemy."

"Oh, hush, you sour ol' scrote. Don't you watch movies? We've always had a British accent, even two thousand years ago. Now, did you bring a glass of water or no?"

"Water? For what?"

"So that We can turn it into wine, obviously."

"You're driving me crazy with this 'we' business! Why do you keep saying *we*?"

"Because We are three."

"But there's only one of you!"

"Brilliant observation. We are also one."

"Jesus." Clarence shook his head.

"Yes, my son?"

"I thought your name was *Balaam*."

"Indubitably. I was also known by that name at one time."

"How come I never heard it before?"

"Presumably for the same reason We've never heard of yours before." Balaam threw up his nose. "Pray tell, how did you come by the name *Clarence*?"

"My mother gave it to me!"

"Perhaps you should have given it back and demanded a new one." Balaam shook his glass, oxygenating his wine before tossing his head back and finishing it in one gulp. "Oh dear, it appears We're out of wine, my son, leaving Us with only two choices: either We find some water or"—he pointed down the long stretch of lawn in a direction all too familiar to Clarence—"we continue our libations at the tavern."

*

"Ah!" Väinämöinen cheered at the sight of Clarence walking in. He took a drink of his beer and shared some with the Lapphund, who lapped from the mug eagerly. "You're becoming a regular already. This pleases me." His salute stopped as he saw Balaam walking in behind Clarence. "Oh, just tickle my testicles with a hammer. Why'd you bring *him* here?"

"Because We're thirsty," Balaam retorted. "And so is Clarence."

"Well, don't bother sitting down. One beer is all you get and then it's back to the nuthouse with ya."

"Beer? Bollocks to that. My taste buds would never forgive me. This tongue tinkers exclusively in a closed palette of vintage reds."

"We're doomed. All of us." Väinämöinen shook his head.

"What are you talking about?" Clarence asked.

"I'm talking about the old Finnish folktale of Tobias and the three trolls."

"Oh, not him again."

"That's what I said when *he* walked in." Väinämöinen flung his finger at Balaam. "Three trolls just like him showed up at Tobias' church and did communion. They did okay with the bread but immediately got drunk on the red wine and went crazy. Turned Tobias' church upside down and to this day, you'll never see a troll step foot in a church, not even the British ones. Trolls don't do well with wine, ystäväni."

"Oh, rubbish. One glass of water, please."

The Barkeep set down a beer mug filled with water, which Balaam immediately inspected for blemishes. Sure enough, he found plenty. He grabbed a handful of napkins, rubbed down the entire outer surface and gave the rim a good once-over. He raised the glass to the air and examined it against the light, little knowing —or, perhaps, little caring— that Clarence and Väinämöinen were examining him and frowning at his fussiness. Satisfied, Balaam stuck his finger into the water to check the temperature, then swirled it around. Just like that, it became wine.

"Oh, look at the fancy troll and his wine. Would you like me to *cut some cheese* to go with your wine, sir?" Väinämöinen tilted and raised his butt cheek to let one rip.

"Very cosmopolitan," Balaam replied, sipping from his wine. "Is it not enough that I'm drinking it from a beer mug? But if it makes you feel more at home, I'll belch periodically. Now tell me, how is that darling but demented wife of yours?"

"Demented? At least she's not walking around thinking she's three people."

"FOOL!" Balaam bellowed. "YOU DARE INSULT MY SON!"

The tavern shook from this outburst while storm clouds gathered just outside the window. Heaving like a dragon and trembling with rage, Balaam aimed a bent finger at Väinämöinen, as if on the verge of passing judgment. Suddenly, as if a switch had been hit, the trembling stopped and the clouds abated. Balaam sat down and regained composure.

"Calm down, Father. He knoweth not what he sayeth," Balaam soothed himself.

"See what I mean about wine and trolls?" Väinämöinen whispered to Clarence. "Crazy as a carnival is what I'm trying to tell you. Speaking of which, Balaam, we're all still waiting to see this one-man parade you keep yappin' about. What's taking so long?" Väinämöinen sniggered.

"We're still downsizing the band, thank you. But if you want to be a good Christian, you can start clearing out all the clutter from that abysmal shack of yours and make room for a few million homeless derelicts that We'll be sending your way."

"Don't count on it." Väinämöinen laughed and gripped Clarence's shoulder. "That's *his* job!

"Hold on, now. I never said I got the job."

"You mean that cuss of a concierge didn't want to give up his position?"

"Apparently not." Balaam sipped more wine. "But if it's employment you're after, We have a job for you. You can help Us downsize—"

"Oh *Gods*, here he goes again." Väinämöinen palmed his face. "Listen, ystäväni. I have another idea."

"Oh *God*, here he goes again." Balaam slouched and twirled his finger in his wine.

"Just hear me out." Väinämöinen patted the air. "There's an old God who may know why you're here. He lives in the forest, not even a Reindeer's piss past the temple. He calls himself Ptah—a name that is short, sweet and to the point. But unlike his name, Ptah is only short and to the point—he's not sweet. Don't expect good manners from this God because he has none to spare. Not anymore at least. He won't even live in the retirement home with the rest of the Gods."

"Sounds like a wise old fellow," Balaam inserted.

"Wise and old, yes." Väinämöinen nodded but then lowered his head ominously. "But it is wisdom and age that made him so ornery. If ignorance is bliss, as they say, then what does that say about wisdom? Approach Ptah the same way you would approach an angry dog. Don't reach out to pat him on his head, that's a no-no."

"Don't pet an old man on the head." Clarence firmed his lower lip and nodded. "Sounds like sage advice."

"Not an old man—and old *God*. You can pet an old man on the head as much as you want. But Gods don't go for small talk or small pleasantries. And don't try winning him over with a cute voice either. Now, assuming old age hasn't slowed your legs as much as your head, you'd be wise to leave now if you want to talk to him. Here"—Väinämöinen waved in for his beer—"I'll finish that for you."

"What about my tab?"

Clarence and Väinämöinen turned to look at the Barkeep, who stood silently. Väinämöinen looked at Clarence and shrugged his shoulders.

"Guess you still have to wait for the answer on that one. Say, you don't mind if we keep your tab running while you're gone, do you?"

"What?"

"Okay, okay. Doesn't hurt to ask."

Clarence rolled his eyes while he turned to leave, but his pupils stopped on a sign hanging just above the doorway. Someone had written the word "STENTIALISM" on a blank sheet of used copier paper, still smudged with toner, and buttressed it next to the exit sign just above the door, which now read: EXIT-STENTIALISM.

Clarence laughed mildly through his nose at the prank. This hadn't been there before, he was sure. He wondered who was behind the joke. *Väinämöinen, maybe?* He turned to confirm this and found the demented deity in the middle of a counting competition with Balaam, who already had him screwing up his numbers. Enraged, Väinämöinen shoved aside every empty mug with his arm and dove from his chair to choke that obstructive British accent out of the ogre. *Nope, it wasn't him*, Clarence concluded. It couldn't have been Balaam either, and he doubted the Barkeep had enough phone books to stack to reach this high.

Exitstentialism and its cognate *enterstentialism* are not words anyone will find in the dictionary, but should. They refer to the human condition of exiting one room and entering another without any idea why, the reason for having made the effort in the first place having been inexplicably forgotten. Such incidences increase with age. Domestic animals are suspected to suffer from this as well. Dog owners, for instance, have observed how a dog will pick up and leave one room and then stand pointlessly in the other, as if the reason for making the move had been forgotten. Exitstentialism can also refer to life choices, particularly when a person goes from one life phase to another and suddenly discovers that they have no clue where the hell their life is going. *Wherever you are, there you are.*

Oh well, Clarence shrugged, putting the matter of the authorship of the sign behind him and turning to pass through the door of "exitstentialism." He pushed the door open and felt the air changing. His skin felt the shift more than his mind, so that as he disappeared through the door, he mindlessly stepped into a distant memory of a long, open and empty corridor of another lifetime.

He was standing alone in a gallery made of long concrete walls mounted with trophy cabinets, embroidered banners, faculty photos and other paraphernalia of school patriotism. But the place had been deserted. The hallway should have been teeming with hyper, hormonal teenagers, but they had all long since graduated, grown up, lived their lives and died.

Clarence remembered having stood here once before, at the ripening age of sixteen, when his younger upstart self was on the cusp of discovering his career passion. Showing an early interest for invention and a fertile imagination, he created an artistic method he proudly called *starchitecture*—another word never to be found in a dictionary. He took star-watching hobby books and made black and white photocopies of the constellations. He set the copier for invert so it would churn out white pages full of black dots. That's where the fun began. He'd re-connect the stars into new constellations that took the form of organic buildings. The results were a fusion of Frank Ghery and Louis Khan—sprawling, erratic forms and wayward lines that congealed into artifices from an ancient future. But at that time, Clarence knew nothing of either Ghery or Khan, nor did he know that *starchitect* was already a term reserved for celebrity architects. But that didn't matter because he wasn't even trying to do architecture; these were just crazy renderings from his budding imagination. At the very least, it was bait for reeling in his classmates, who would stand over his shoulder and watch him connect the dots, wondering what cool shape would emerge next.

Clarence snapped out of that old memory when he realized that there was something in the palm of his hand. He looked down, saw a hallway pass and the rest of the story came back to him. Starchitecture was how he garnered his share of attention in school, but sometimes it was the wrong attention. After one too many incidences of getting busted for being a master starchitect while in class, he was slapped with a hallway pass with explicit instructions to go see the guidance counselor.

Oh yeah, I remember that guy, Clarence sneered. It wasn't a fond memory. This was the guy who told Clarence that we live in a, quote, *rabid economy*, unquote. He also said that there weren't any more welfare checks for artists. He called art impractical. But the world, he said, would always need architects. *That* was a practical profession. With those words Clarence's imperial imagination was dethroned.

He had always promised himself that if he ever saw *that guy* again, he'd punch him. Of course, by now *that guy* was long gone and dead, presumably just like most everyone else in this school, but if the hallway pass in his hand was hinting at something, then maybe *that guy* was still alive and well in Clarence's memory. People spend their entire lives being beat up by their own memories. Now it was time for a little payback.

Clarence crumpled the hallway pass into the ball of his fist as he stormed to the guidance counselor's office. He did his best to kick the door open, but with his old legs, the best he could manage was a pathetic knock with his foot. While he was winding up for a second kick, a familiar voice asked him to come in.

It was *that guy*, the guidance counselor. His dirty-blonde chevron mustache arched into a smile. He was exactly as Clarence remembered: an innocuously looking vanilla man with a mullet. He hadn't aged a day, nor had his awful '80s fashion.

You! Clarence's eyes darted.

"Mr. Moody," he announced with a smile while waving for Clarence to come in and sit down. "Have a seat. Tell me, how have you been?"

"Crappy."

"Crappy? C'mon, Clarence." The counselor was still smiling. "A cranky old man who says he's feeling crappy is a cliché, and you know it. You hate clichés. Why don't we try this again. How have you been?"

"Crappy."

"I see." The counselor's smile collapsed. "Okay, what's wrong?"

"You gave me bad advice."

"Yeah, well, the odds of giving good advice are—"

"Shut up! You told me to consider architecture as a career. "

"The operative word there was *consider.* You could have considered something else, you know. There are many practical profess—"

"Aaargh, there's that word! You killed me with practicality, you punk! I ended up being a lousy, run-of-the-mill architect. I became a 'practical' project manager working on cheap skyscrapers and strip malls! I should sue you for malpractice."

"Ha! Good luck with that. I'm dead! But feel free to sue 'my estate.'" He chuckled. "I'm sure whatever I left behind is sitting somewhere on a dusty old shelf at your local Goodwill selling for thirty-five cents, including the mediocre paintings I used to do. Those are probably going for a dollar. So you're upset with me because you became a mediocre architect? So what? Join the club. We're all a bunch of lukewarm professionals. I was paid thirty grand a year to give bad advice to bad kids who barely cared about the bad education they were getting, let alone the bad education they were going to pay good money for to get in college. Now that I'm dead, I finally realize they were right. Why get excited and motivated over nothing?"

"Did you just say that an education is *nothing*?" Clarence intoned.

"No, you're saying it and I'm *agreeing* with you. You were a good kid, Clarence, and you worked hard, harder than most of those bastards, anyway. Probably worked hard in college, too. You did everything you were supposed to do, including listening to me, and look at you: you still ended up being a schmuck—just like me. The difference between you and me is that you still think you're pissed about having been a failure. But I know that you're not pissed; you're just disappointed, and that's even worse. Because unlike being pissed, when you're disappointed there isn't much you can do about it. When you're pissed, you can take it out on somebody, like me, for instance. You came in here wanting to punch me. Yes, I know this. But who are you going to punch when you're disappointed? Maybe you want to take it out on yourself, but if you do that, you're a fool. Are you a mediocre architect? Sure. But that doesn't make you a fool, Clarence."

Clarence sighed as his rage left him. What he had just heard had to be the most well-rationalized ramble since... well, since the last time *that guy* talked him into thinking practically. Now he was doing it again and it was working. A shame, too. Clarence really had planned on punching him.

"So what do I do now?" Clarence asked.

"Are you actually asking me for my advice?"

"No, definitely not," Clarence answered and the guidance counselor smiled approvingly. Clarence didn't smile at all. He just turned around to leave.

"Actually, wait a second," the counselor called after Clarence. "I don't usually give unsolicited advice but on second thought... Maybe you *should* punch me. In fact, I'll make a deal with you. To cure our disappointment, instead of beating up on ourselves, let's beat up on each other, kind of like a Dead Man's Fight Club, like the students used to do. Whaddya say? Want to smack me in the teeth with that cane?"

Clarence shook his head and resumed making his way to the exit.

"Where are you going?"

"To see another guidance counselor." Clarence grabbed the door handle. "I have to get a second opinion."

He passed through the door, and Mr. Mediocre Architect, as he secretly called himself, re-entered the world of mediocre Gods. *They must be mediocre*, he mused to himself. *They are all retired. Couldn't have been that good at what they did.*

Clarence stood at the mouth of a long cobbled pathway leading to the Golden Age Retirement Home. At this distance, he had a full panoramic view of the building, an opportunity he had before, but hadn't taken. He had purposely avoided looking at the building, which was uncharacteristic of him. Usually, he couldn't stop himself from studying every standing structure he passed by. In fact, he had developed a somewhat annoying habit of critiquing and grading them, often accusing them of being glorified boxes that amounted to nothing more than prisons for the middle class. Yet, his own career was a long stretch of building the same glorified boxes he had come to criticize.

That's what made the Golden Age Retirement Home so peculiar. It was, quite literally and brazenly, a glorified box. Its builder abandoned the battle against the cube, opting instead to magnify it, to enlarge it to a monumental scale and to open it up to the sky by wrapping it in reflective windows. The result, in a word, was *heavenly*. At dawn, the cube glowed golden hues with the Sun; at noon, it turned blue and marble; at dusk, it blazed a fiery crimson until cooling into the serene and soft lunar lights of a starry heaven. By camouflaging itself with Mother Nature and the Cosmos, it became not just a home but also a symbol of the Gods, who assumed plant and planet, stone and stars as their bodies.

More importantly, and contrary to everything Clarence believed about architecture, the grand cube did not distract from what was outside its walls but pointed to it, bidding the viewer to look up and around and remember the beauty of the world: the crisp air and white mountain-like clouds marching across the horizon, moved by winds that whisper to the ear that the Earth is very much alive.

B minus, Clarence graded it, being either too jealous or too jaded to appreciate such sappy romanticism. Any hack can plaster walls with reflective windows. This wasn't a sign of genius; it was a sign of giving up and resorting to the architectural equivalent of a Photoshop filter.

Clarence rolled his eyes and allowed them to wander away from the cube and across the vast plain until they landed at a grayish-white obelisk in the distance. It seemed to be a sort of landmark, or perhaps its overtly phallic form signified fertility—or a *forest*! Yes, Clarence could see the grove just behind it and remembered that this was his destination.

He took off in the direction of the obelisk. When he reached it, he realized it was not an obelisk at all, or, at least, it wasn't as plain as the ones he had studied in the past. This one was totem-like, marked on all four sides with figures and faces. Its peak terminated with four heads, crowned with a phallic looking hat and aligned with the cardinal directions. Perfectly vertical, it commanded Clarence's respect as he stood in its long shadow.

He retreated from the weight of the massive monolith to a nearby solitary bench, where he noticed a structure that looked like a small doghouse. He eyed it dubiously, remembering that there was supposed to be a strict prohibition of pets at the retirement home. But then again, the home itself turned out to be one big safari.

Clarence circled around, examining the exterior of the doghouse before kneeling down, as low as his bones would allow, for a peek inside. He pulled open the door, allowing sunlight to dissipate the thick darkness. He thought maybe he'd find a sleeping dog, but instead there was a small stone idol of a plus-size woman with enormous breasts. Two offering bowls made of bronze rested in front of the stone figure, but they were empty. Clarence stepped away and looked at the doghouse again, realizing now that it was a *God*-house, a temple. The stout statue was a Goddess, apparently one with a large appetite—she had two offering bowls.

He graded the tiny temple a *C minus*, mostly for its shabby, unkempt condition, both inside and out. Frank Lloyd Wright was known for being impossibly meticulous with his buildings, obsessing over even the trivial placement of a pencil holder. Clarence, despite having never elevated to such greatness, had similar obsessions. He felt that the plight of the starving artist was embarrassment enough to Western civilization. To have *starving art* on top of that was beyond embarrassing; it was plain offensive.

He looked at the hungry idol, crawled inside and helped himself to her dry and dusty bowls. He backed out into the sunlight and peered back at the retirement home. He considered going back there to clean and fill the bowls, but as he looked back at the grove, he decided there must be a water source closer by.

"Maybe I can also find some food in there too," he muttered to himself.

He stacked the bowls and, with the help of his cane, made his way inside the forest. There was a surreal shift in the air. The wind had moved freely along the campus grounds, but in here the trees obstructed its swift transit. The stillness of the air was filled by the voice of branches stretching out like long arms and rubbing elbows, as if the trees were enjoying a conversation by soughing constantly. It was a pleasing sound for Clarence, one that reminded him of a running river.

The trail took him deep into the forest and up a steep mound. As he ascended, the air was changing again. It was becoming moist. Sure enough, the mound leveled off, with the trail ending near a moving stream that crept from behind a small thicket.

Clarence seated himself on an unusual rock that seemed to have been purposely shaped and polished into a perfect cube. He placed the offering bowls at his feet, where they clinked the rocks, triggering a domino of sounds. Animals suddenly came to life, scrambling and scurrying off, leaving only the sound of slow, careful steps crunching the leaves—the signature of a predator patrolling its prey. Not that Clarence's ears could notice such subtlety.

The tip-toeing continued for a while until the predator tripped and toppled. Clarence spun around and sprung to his feet. He could see only a single set of eyes that had been watching him. They advanced forward revealing a hazy, hunched silhouette walking upright, bow legged, like an animal that had learned to walk.

"Thief!" the shadowy silhouette claimed with a thick, heavy African accent.

Clarence flinched and the pursuant pulled back, scrambling his arms in defensive retreat. Having scored himself a little time, Clarence frantically foraged every pocket on his body looking for a weapon until he realized he already had one in his hand—his walking stick. Not exactly the choice weapon for combat, but it was all he had. His assailant responded in kind. As if a switch had been hit, a set of arms sprung from behind his back clenching a hammer, a ruler, a compass and a T-square.

Clarence swallowed hard. The stakes had been raised. He blinked and readied himself. As he looked at his opponent's weapons, he felt a chill run down his spine. He was too old to fight an armed man, let alone a six-armed one. The thought of retreat entered his mind, but just as soon as it did, and as if his opponent had heard his thoughts, a set of legs sprung from his waist. Clarence swallowed again and waited for the predator-man to lunge from out of the shadows and attack.

But the odds evened themselves when the would-be attacker took a single step forward that ended with a pitiful moan. He watched the man drop his drafting tools and retrieve a bottle of rubbing cream from behind his back to soothe the ache in his knees. Clarence knew both the cream's scent and the painful yelp all too well. *Arthritis!*

No longer afraid, Clarence hobbled forward, pronged the man with his cane, then reached his hand inside the protective thickets and pulled out an old man with a skull cap peeled over his bald head. Clarence stared at his dark, bark-colored skin, realizing this man wasn't just old—he was ancient!

"You scared the bejeezus out of me, man! How old are you?" Clarence probed bewilderedly.

"Do not ask elders of their age, boy," the man answered.

"Boy!" Clarence objected. "Do you see how old I am?"

"What I see is that you are too young to inquire after my age and too old to be stealing from a shrine. Where are your manners, boy?"

Clarence didn't answer. His mind had detoured from the question and back to the extra limbs that were hanging by hinges from the old man's back. They were fakes.

"Not nice to stare at an elder's handicap, boy," the old man reproved firmly.

"You have artificial arms and legs?"

"Eight of them! Compared to your one." He swatted away Clarence's walking stick.

"This helps me walk better."

"And these help me *fight* better."

"Fight? With the tools of a carpenter?"

"Carpenter? I'm an Architect, boy!"

"You're an architect?"

"Architect!" the old man corrected.

"That's what I said!"

"With a capital A!" he demanded.

"How can you tell the difference?"

"I can tell the difference because there *is* a difference. Open your ears, boy! And open your eyes while you're at it. I am *the* Architect."

Clarence had to think about this for a moment, but then the light bulb went off.

"Oooh. You built—"

"The Golden Age Temple, yes! And the shrine you pilfered."

"No, no, no." Clarence stepped forward in apology. "You have me figured out wrong. I'm an architect too!"

"Then where are your tools, boy?"

"I'm retired."

"Retired?" the old man repeated indignantly. "Then you are *not* an Architect."

"No, I *am* an architect. I'm just a *retired* architect."

"Architects do not retire—they build. They have tools, not idle time on their hands. They build temples and shrines, not steal from them."

"I wasn't stealing from the shrine. I was going to fill these offering bowls."

"Oooh, so now you are telling me you are a Priest. Ten seconds ago you were an Architect. Okay, tell me, *Priest*, with what were you going to fill the bowls?"

"Water."

"Two bowls of water? I guess that is one way to cure a bashful bladder. Okay, *Priest*, here's a tip for you: Only one bowl is for water. The second bowl is for *what*?"

"Piss?" Clarence responded with slight agitation in his voice.

"Oooh, so now you're a Comedian. Hopefully a retired one."

With those words, the old man threw out an arm to swat Clarence. The force, however, was a bit much for even his craftsmanship, and his artificial arms unscrewed themselves and fell to the floor in shambles. As he struggled to catch the falling parts, his prosthetic legs gave out too, followed by his real ones. He tumbled to the ground. As if this happened to him all the time, he promptly began rubbing his knees with more arthritis cream, moaning hopelessly.

"No offense," Clarence said, sympathetically. "But it looks like you're a retired architect, too. What's your name?"

"Ptah," he answered proudly.

"Ah, so it's you." Clarence's eyes lit up. "Vynamonen—"

"Väinämöinen," Ptah corrected.

"Yeah, he sent me to talk to you."

"To talk, perhaps. Surely, not to steal."

"I wasn't ste—"

"What is your name?" Ptah cut him off.

"Clarence."

"That is not your name. What's your *real* name?"

"I don't know what you mean."

"Pffft." Ptah rolled his eyes. "And you call yourself an Architect?"

"Yes, I do call myself an architect. Forty years I've been building—under the *real* name of Clarence."

"Your real name isn't Clarence."

"Fine. My full name is Clarence Moody. Satisfied?"

"Satisfied? The question is, are *you* satisfied with that atrocity of a name? Your kind is either all form and no function, or all function and no form, especially when it comes to architecture and words. You use words for show only. A name for you is a suit: You try them on until you find one that fits. Pffft. Verily, I say, boy: If your name is true, then it is true for you."

"Well, verily, I say back to you that I verily have no clue what the H. you're talking about. But if you're looking for a yes-man, then yes, my kind knows nothing about true names. We use a first and last name, occasionally throwing something in the middle, but true names, whatever the H. that means, never enter the equation."

"Never enter the equa—" Ptah blinked, dumbfounded. "Tell me, boy, what kind of Architect are you?"

"I already told you—the retired kind."

"Thank Heavens!" Ptah sighed with relief. "The last thing the world needs is more empty buildings made with empty equations."

"The buildings are empty so that people can walk into them."

"And when people walk out of them, then what?"

This brought Clarence to a standstill. It seemed like such an odd question, but somehow he understood it. Buildings were built to be populated. If for some reason they became ghost towns, like abandoned strip malls, then they were eventually torn down. The modern world would have only a few ruins to survive it.

"Foolish boy," Ptah scoffed. "A building should never be empty. A building should be *alive*. And all living things have names. But you're building dead buildings. Your world is full of them."

"Guess you've never been to Las Vegas. Los Angeles. New York," Clarence retorted.

"Bright lights and flashing signs are not signs of life, they are signs of life *support*. A city that never sleeps is too afraid to close its eyes. It is afraid of what might happen if it does. It is scared of darkness—of dying. So you chase away the night with light and noise. But real Architecture embraces silence, do you hear me, boy, SILENCE!"

"Yeah, I can hear you." Clarence cleared the ringing in his ears with a finger. "Let me ask you something: When was the last time you've been to the retirement home that *you* built?"

"You call it a retirement home. I call it a temple."

"I call it a carnival, actually!"

"Do not change the topic." Ptah grunted as he bent over to retrieve his T-Square. "We are talking about true names and Architecture."

"We don't *name* buildings, okay? We give names to people, pets and sometimes boats, but that's about it."

"Of course you do not *name* a building, boy. The name is already there *if* you build it properly. Each stone in a building has its own name. See that stone you were sitting on without my permission? I built it and yes, it has a name—a *true* name."

Clarence rotated to see the perfect cube behind him. It was just the diversion Ptah needed. He pounced on Clarence, knocking him to the ground where they struggled, grunting and groaning in the process. Frustrated by his feisty opponent, Ptah widened his eye sockets and flashed a blinding light into Clarence's eyes. This bought him enough time to raise his T-Square like a sword, readying to bring it down on the roof of Clarence's skull.

"You lied!" Clarence muttered. "You're no Architect. You're a *murderer!*"

"For the punishment of theft!"

"Without a trial?" Clarence rebutted. "Your T-Square isn't square at all, is it?"

This brought Ptah to a pause. Clarence had made a point much sharper than any blade a man might wield. Ptah's hands and arms trembled while his eyes fumbled around inside his head, searching for a counter-point or even just a snappy come-back. He had always been wise and witty with words, but on this day, his old mind had gone as dull as his judgment. He lowered his arms and, with a deep grumble, reluctantly relented and stepped away.

"A wise thief, I see. We will see how your wisdom holds up against the Judges."

"Judges? How many judges are we talking about here?"

"Forty-two."

"Good Lord, how many trials is this going to take?"

"Only one. But you'll stand before forty-two adjudicators, and they are all very wise and very old and, unlike you, *not* retired. And, unlike me, they are not forgiving when it comes to justice. Don't expect to con your way out of this like you did today." Ptah dusted himself off and began walking back towards the bushes.

"Wait!" Clarence called after him. "Vynamonen sent me here to get advice from you!"

"Väinämöinen," Ptah corrected. "And the only advice I have for you is that you find yourself a suitable lawyer."

"How many lawyers? Forty-two?"

"No, boy. Just one." He continued walking away.

"Wait!" Clarence called after him again. "Where am I supposed to find a lawyer?"

"There are plenty to choose from in there." Ptah pointed down the path leading back to the retirement home.

"You mean the freak fogies back there?" Clarence exclaimed. "That's a retirement home! What good is a retired lawyer?"

"Funny," Ptah sniggered. "I have the same question about retired Architects."

Clarence winced at Ptah's whip-like wit, but held his tongue from lashing back. Wars of wit were just like Western gunfights: There's no honor in shooting a man in the back, not even with words, and Ptah was already walking away. Indeed, without so much as a glance backward, he vanished inside a cluster of bushes.

Chapter 4

♪ *Counting the days (yeah)*
Until some freedom can scream my name
Counting the days (yeah)
Until the Gods break these chains ♪

With Collective Soul cranking in the foreground, the Concierge danced in the air, lighting all three hundred sixty-one candles lining the perimeter of the walls—all except for one. The last and lonesome candle was placed in the center of the room with nineteen ominous idols forming a circle around it.

The Greeks referred to the number one as *Monad*, meaning "alone." It is the exact opposite of *Zweisamkeit*. To be number one is to be the only one—a status aspired for by type-A competitive personalities. But it can also be lonely at the top, and so, as a condition, "alone-ness" is avoided by almost everyone, except for the most sincere of introverts. Consequently, it is the natural impulse of the number one to seek out company, and this it does by begetting numbers. How this happened is anyone's guess. Maybe it was an elegant genesis, like cellular division, where one divided itself into two and kept dividing until becoming a cancerous overgrowth of numeric possibilities. Or, perhaps, the Monad spontaneously combusted, like a big bang, and crapped out an infinite number of chaotic possibilities. Or, maybe this never happened at all, except in the human mind. The Universe had its own big bang of matter, while the Mind had a big bang of numbers. The two are, despite incredible odds, compatible. *Zweisamkeit.*

The three hundred sixty candles were a tribute to the Monad's name, but also to the Egyptian calendar year, which lopped off five "epagomenal" days. Lighting each of these candles and periodically replacing them was a tedious job, but it was, quite literally, a job suited for a concierge. After all, the word *concierge* means "count of candles" (from the French *comte des cierges*) and refers to a servant whose task it was to maintain the lighting of the medieval palace. They also assumed the role of security guards and kept count of prisoners. Modern hotels have since changed their job description to simply guest services, which means when a customer is angry, it is the concierge's job to stay cool.

So it was that when the lobby door burst open and came off of its hinges, *again*, and Clarence, completely irate, stood in the doorway with the light of three hundred sixty-one small flames flickering across his visage while he violently breathed and wielded his cane with ill intention in his eyes and fire fuming from the wax in his ears, the Concierge, true to his job description, stayed cool.

"What can I do for you, brotha?"

Clarence stormed over to the front desk and turned off the music, then stormed back to face the Concierge.

"I need to talk to a lawyer," he said through his teeth. The word *lawyer* made the Concierge blink.

"Aaah..." Clarence shook his finger. "Typical. Typical. Soon as you mention the L-word to people, it's like you dumped a big bucket of cold coffee all over them. Suddenly everybody wakes up. Good morning, sunshine. Did you have a nice nap? Are we ready to talk about the chaos going on in this miserable excuse of a retirement home? Or should we have that conversation with a lawyer? Yes, let's talk with a lawyer about how you're either unfit, uninterested or just plain unqualified to do your job!"

The Concierge, of course, broke out into a song.

> ♪ Bring your lawyer
> And I'll bring mine.
> Get together, and we could have a bad time ♪

The needle skipped when Clarence swung his walking stick for the Concierge's head.

"Whoa, what's wrong with you, brotha?"

"Sing another song," Clarence growled. "Do it, GD-it. Sing another song."

"That was George Harrison, man. 'Sue Me, Sue You Blues.'"

"I don't give a fartin' F. who it was. I'm trying to discuss legal matters with you."

"You're going to sue me to get my job?"

"To H. with your stupid job! I'm not talking about that. I'm talking about the old man in the forest who completely fell off his rocker. I'm talking attempted murder."

"Here? Who?"

64

"*He* is probably going to tell you that I tried to steal from the shrine, but I'm telling you right here, right now, that this is a bold-faced lie. I thought the GD shrine was a doghouse, which should tell you a whole lot about its disgraceful condition. I was trying to do a good deed by attempting to fill her dishes with food and fresh water. And for that I was tackled to the ground by the old man and almost bludgeoned with a T-Square!"

"Oh, you mean Ptah." The Concierge nodded.

"Yes! Him! The Architect."

"*Former* Architect."

"What?" Clarence blinked.

"He's retired. That's the reason the shrine—and this home—are in such bad shape."

"But he told me—"

"That he's *still* an Architect?" the Concierge finished his sentence. "That's his pride talking, but trust me, his bones will tell you a different story."

"Maybe. But he still had strength enough to almost split my head open with a T-Square, and I'm the one he wants to put on trial!"

"Listen, dude. Your first problem is that you entered a sacred temple without authorization."

"Somebody had too. Did you see the condition it's in?"

"Yeah, yeah, I know. But you wouldn't invite yourself into the CEO's office, no matter what condition it was in, now would you?"

"CEO?" Clarence frowned. "Who is that woman in there?"

"That's Big Momma. They don't get much bigger than her."

"Well, I can tell you right now Big Momma is missing her meals."

"Yeah, that's true. But I don't mean big like that. I mean big as in the Big Man on campus, except this isn't the Big Man; it's Big Momma, and this ain't just her campus—it's her world, you see where I'm goin' with this? You don't go into her sacred sanctuary without authorization, or at least, without knocking first. That's your first problem." He paused for a brief moment. "Your second problem is that this is your second time pulling that stunt. I got a complaint from Veritas that you walked into her room without knocking."

"Veritas? Who the H. is Veritas?"

"The woman you walked in on without knocking."

"Not on purpose. I was trying to find my room."

"Doesn't matter. The name *Veritas* means 'truth,' which means it's your word against the truth. So who do you think the Judges will be more likely to believe?"

"This is madness."

"Did you happen to read the sign that was on her door?"

"No. I didn't even see it."

"Do you know what it said?"

"I just told you that I didn't see it!" Clarence shouted, but he noticed the Concierge staring at him with a coy grin, waiting for Clarence to at least take a guess. "I don't know what it said... *Please knock*, maybe?"

"No. It reads: *I am all that has been and shall be... And no mortal has lifted my veil.* Do you know what that means?"

"She doesn't do nude scenes?"

"Exactly. The truth doesn't like people looking at her, especially not crusty old men. And I know this is the twenty-first century and things are more liberal, but she doesn't like women checking her out either. You busted in and saw her half naked. That's more than what most people get to see." The Concierge leaned forward, checked to his left and right and smiled ribaldly. "How much did you see, man? Is she hot?"

"Listen," Clarence shoved the question aside. "I will put on a blindfold and go back and apologize to her, okay? I was just trying to find my room."

"I know. But it really is a good idea to knock first. That's neither here nor there, though. The problem is that when this goes to trial, Veritas is going to testify against you, which is going to make Ptah's case even stronger. If I were you, I'd start making friends, and that ain't gonna be easy because rumors spread at the speed of sound around here. Busting in on two women is not the kind of rumor you want running ahead of you. I'm not sure how many of those Gods are going to want to be seen talking to you, let alone be your lawyer. If I were you, I'd start praying that out of thirty-three million Gods, at least one of them is willing to take your case."

"Praying? To who?"

"To who- or *whatever* you believe in." The Concierge shrugged. "The point is, it's time you start making friends in high places. Go door-to-door and do a bit of a meet-and-greet. Who knows, maybe someone will answer. But this time, homie..." He leaned forward and looked over the rim of his shades to emphasize his last point, which came as an Oscar Brown, Jr. song.

♪ *Knock and then enter,*
You'll be more than welcome here!

Opportunity, just knock,
Opportunity, please knock! ♪

*

Clarence expected the hallway door to explode open with all of the frenetic big-city energy from before, but instead he was swallowed by an ancient silence, empty and hollow, like stepping inside an old, abandoned warehouse. When it was crammed with Gods, the building felt irredeemably small, but this new and sudden vacancy revealed how open and massive the temple truly was. The walls were made of granite, something he didn't see much of, especially in commercial buildings. And yet the interior style felt like ancient industrialism, a factory for the Gods.

He didn't realize he had set off into a soft stroll until he felt his shoe make an irregular step and crunch down on something metal. He looked down and saw a tiny pin trapped between the floor and his foot. He didn't like clichés, but this one seemed so unlikely that it was worth the effort of bending over so that he could pick it up, hold it over the floor and drop it. He actually heard it hit the floor. The tiny sound it made reverberated.

The pin bounced a few times before it settled into its new spot and, with a little stretch of a superstitious imagination, pointed at a door. With so many rows of doors to choose from, this seemed a good way to make up his mind on where to start. This time, Clarence made sure to check for any cryptic *please knock before entering* signs. There weren't any, but there was an odd room number. Instead of being a whole number, it was a fraction: 5/8.

Clarence was slightly bemused by this but shrugged it off. He balled his hand into a fist, but before he could get off a knock, the temple began to rattle and roll into an interminable convulsion.

"Earthquake," Clarence said, but as soon as he did, the convulsions stopped.

A strange light pierced and permeated the door and began to swirl into a vortex, lifting him off the ground. Frantic, he threw his arms wildly around in search of an anchor, but all he could find was that miserable pin floating in mid-space. For whatever reason, he reached out to grab it, but before he could, the whirlwind sucked him into its spiraling eye. Just like that, as if the vortex had satiated its appetite for human meat, it returned to its ruse as a door. The air and gravity returned to normal.

The pin dropped.

*

Clarence was strangely content inside the bowels of whatever had just eaten him. Perhaps he was just relieved that it didn't have teeth. To be swallowed is traumatizing enough, but to be chewed by a vortex is just plain overkill. Happy to be in one piece, he sat back and waited for digestion to ensue. He had never been inside a gastrointestinal tract before, and this one wasn't all that bad. The smell was okay and instead of bowel darkness, there seemed to be nothing but light—a scarlet light that was warm and comforting, like sitting next to a fire when the air is brisk.

The light began to flicker and threatened to go out. Clarence panicked as the light retreated, but it didn't vanish. It receded into a single source, contracting into a form that was now approaching him. Instinctively, he shielded his eyes.

"I didn't see you," he lied.

"It's okay," she replied softly. "I am fully clothed in light. You may look at me."

Clarence opened his eyes and then opened them wider, so as to pack his pupils with every pound of the plus-sized pin-up girl floating before him. Full-figured and well-rounded, she wore her extra weight as comfortably as a skintight bathing suit, flaunting every curve. In fact, 'girl' wasn't exactly the word for this big-boned buxom. The only *girlish* thing about her was an obvious hobby for boy toys. Though Clarence was a senior, he was still just a pup in the pupils of this hungry cougar.

With one hand on her hip, just as she would have done in her modeling days, she passed the other hand through her maroon muffin hair and curled a few gray strands, proudly showcasing her age and celebrity. Clarence was enraptured.

"Oh. My. God," he whispered. She could hear the desire in his voice and smiled approvingly.

"Not quite," she whispered back.

Hypnotized, Clarence reached out his hand for her, but the cougar threw out her paw and swatted him.

"Wait!" she demanded, then looked over her shoulder and shouted: "Make up!"

A team of winged, tired-looking angels appeared from nowhere to powder her face and reset the two buns that flanked the side of her hair. One angel held up a small mirror for her approval. She nodded and flapped her fingers to dismiss them.

"Now, where were we?" she asked.

Right away, Clarence saw that there were two sides to this sexy lady. She was all work *and* play, and right now, she was ready to play.

"Who in the H. are you?" he asked.

"Lucifer."

Whoa! Clarence felt himself go limp, but Lucifer was still ready to play, still smiling and still seductively swaying her head and hips left and right as she extended both arms, inviting an embrace. Clarence flinched.

"Oh, come on!" Lucifer flapped her arms against her sides. "Do you know how long it's been since I've had guests?"

"Really? I thought this place would have been packed."

"You've been watching too many movies. My name just means 'bearer of light.' You may know me as the Morning and Evening Star. Like the Decans, I rise in the East with the Sun as the most bright and beautiful star."

She paused waiting for the light bulb to go off over Clarence's head, but he looked more like a deer in headlights.

"I'm the planet Venus, idiot," she relented, dropping her arms to her sides again. "Yeah, I know. I've put on a few pounds, but in my thinner days I was a scarlet starlet. All who laid eyes on me marveled at my splendor. At least, they used to before they made me into (A) the demon of darkness and (B) a *man*! That one really gets under my skin. Do you know how hard it is to meet a man when everyone assumes you are one?"

"Times have changed. I probably know a few men who pitch for that team."

"Are they from Mars?" she asked, but then immediately waved it away. "Oh, never mind. What's the use? Just forget *Lucifer*. From here on just call me Luci, okay?"

"Got it."

"And what shall I call you?" she asked flirtatiously.

"Clarence."

"So what brings you here, Clarence?"

"A vortex."

"You mean you were sucked in?"

"Yup."

"Did you knock?"

"Hey, I was about to, but that door is broken," Clarence said defensively.

"If you don't want people coming in unannounced, then you need to fix it."

"Fix it? I made it that way." Luci folded her arms. "Somebody told me that if I wanted to find a man, I needed to be more aggressive. Apparently, men are intimidated by big-boned bikini women named Lucifer."

"We are," Clarence admitted. "But vortexes are a little scary too."

"Fine. I'll turn it off. The door is *that* way." She pointed and turned to leave.

"Wait!" Clarence raised his hand. "Uh... Are you a lawyer?"

"A lawyer? Trust me, no judge would ever let me step foot in their courtroom. With these curves I can convince any jury of anything."

"Would those curves convince forty-two Judges of a man's innocence?"

"Probably. But that's not the kind of work I do. I use these persuasive pounds for the field of advertising."

"I'm sorry?"

"I'm a model." She proudly posed to prove the point, then went off into a rapid-fire recital of her résumé. "Actually, I'm more of a Renaissance Woman. I like to think of myself as a muse with my hands wrapped around a lot of minds and a lot of men. Most importantly, I am an inspiration to women—big women. Thin models have their purpose; they're good for an appetizer, but only a full-figured woman can fill the eyes and appetite of a *real* man. Would you like a small, medium or large, sir? Or shall I super-size you? Nothing wrong with leftovers, you know."

She licked her lips and for a second there, it seemed the cougar was ready to pounce, but after a single blink she was back in business mode.

"That reminds me. I'm thinking of starting a restaurant franchise that caters to the pleasantly plump mature women with a cougar's appetite. What do you think of this slogan: *The good thing about fat is that when it's hot... it sizzles.*™ " She paused to let that sink in. "How does that make you feel, Clarence?"

"A little hot." He tugged at his collar. "Where's the AC? Do you have central air?"

She blew down his neck, which sent a shudder down his spine.

"Better?" She smiled devilishly and he nodded. "Good. I've trademarked that slogan, but you have my permission to use it. I've chosen you, Clarence. I've summoned you for a purpose."

"Actually, I've already been sum—"

"I want you to help me inspire the world. I've written a book. A Bible, if you will." She pulled out an advance copy from her bra, flipped a few pages and began to read with a little Maya Angelou sass and spice in her voice.

"Big Girl, Big Girl, look around you,
Marvel at the world and see that Mother Earth
Does not strut in straight lines, but with curves.
From the flower's petal to the butterfly's wings,
It is the curve that gives them their form,
Their elegance and their swing.
Even the anorexic caterpillar
Seeks out its curves in the cocoon
So that it may someday spread its wings and bloom.
Big Girl, Big Girl, full-figured and fertile,
Flap those curves! Get your big ass over that hurdle.
Get off the ground. There's no mountain too high.
Come on, you can do it. Flap hard... and fly."

She closed the book and wiped a dry tear from her eye. "I want you to take this message to big women everywhere, Clarence. Will you help me?"

"You want an old man to tell large girls to show off their curves? They might think that's a little icky."

"No, Clarence. I've already cornered the plus-size market. I want to expand this message to the *mature* market. I want old people to feel sexy again. Listen"—she turned to another page in her Bible—"this is a gospel hymn that I wrote.

"Old Girl, Old Girl!

Yeah, you still got those wrinkles,

But you still got that tingle,

Still got the fever for the flavor of a Pringle,

Life's too short to die single,

There's still time to shag,

Dust off that swag

And let those rude boobs sag."

"Okay, okay, I get the point," Clarence said.

"I still have to get permission to use that line about Pringles. But otherwise, what do you think? Will you help me spread my light into the darkness?"

"I don't know. It's an ugly world out there."

"Then let's make it beautiful. Everyone deserves to feel beautiful. Don't you agree?"

He did. But he wasn't sure about how he felt about making a deal with the devil. He tossed it around in his head for a short while before deciding.

"What the H." he said, sticking out his hand. "Why not? After I clear my name, I'll do whatever I can to help you."

Elated, Luci grabbed his hand, shook it once and pulled him into a loving embrace. Clarence was more than happy to be swallowed by her cleavage. The deal was done and Clarence grinned eagerly at her, as if to ask *so what next?* But it was too late. She was already back in business mode.

"You've made the right choice, Clarence. I'll have my lawyers contact you about the details. Do you know your way out?"

Before Clarence could answer, she let loose all of her contracted light. It expanded with such blinding force that he was blown backwards. He shielded himself with his arms, but the light had long since hit him. In fact, when he finally dared to peek over the edge of his forearm, he saw that he was already back in the hallway.

"You crazy, psycho B—"

Before he could break his no-cursing rule, the vortex reopened and shot out his cane. It grazed past his shoulder, nearly spearing him in the face. This time he knew better to keep his mouth shut.

*

The next room was numbered 108. Clarence stood in front of it, let out a sigh and knocked. He looked down at the door's four doorknobs, which turned in tandem. The door opened and right away he recognized the burly, blue man with four arms.

"Shiva!" he announced himself in his characteristic thick Indian accent. "Namaste," he greeted while clasping all four hands together and bowing. He then reached out his four smothering arms to embrace Clarence into a chiropractic man-hug. Clarence heard a loud crunch and, much to his surprise, actually felt... better.

"Your spine has just spoken a great truth, and that is that love may break hearts, but never bones!" Shiva pointed at Clarence. "You ran off without telling me your name. Ah, don't worry about it. I know your name now, Mister Clarence."

"How do you know my name?"

"You're famous now, Mister Clarence. I've heard four rumors about you already."

"What rumors?"

"I hear you are to be our new concierge. And that you sneaked a peek at the naked truth, or at least half of it. That you ran off with Madam Big Momma's offerings—never a good idea, by the way—and that you went on a date with Madam Lucifer. I suppose we should also include your name as rumor number five. I didn't want to believe it. Is that really true? Please tell me it isn't. They told me your name is 'Mister Clarence.'"

"They? Who exactly are *they*?"

"*They* are everywhere. *They* hear everything. *They*... *We*... are the Gods."

"Did *they* also tell you I need a lawyer?"

"Oooh, so there are *six* rumors. Interesting number. Please, come inside."

With four arms, Shiva obliged Clarence into his apartment to meet his roommates, who were consumed by a chess match. If Clarence's bones hadn't been so old, he would have leapt right out of his shoes at the sight of them. They were even more wildly exotic than Shiva, starting with Brahma who not only had four arms but also four heads, each with its own thick ivory beard. Brahma scratched and twirled all four beards with all four hands while studying the next move on the chessboard. Sitting opposite of him was Vishnu—another four-armed God—who used one of his arms to ambivalently wave at Clarence as Shiva made the introductions.

"Brahma and Vishnu, I would like you to meet Mister Clarence—" Shiva interrupted himself to quickly whisper to Clarence: "I'm sorry, did you confirm that your name is Clarence?"

"Yes."

"That is your name, for sure?"

"Yes."

"This is not a joke? You must tell me now if it is."

"No, it's not a joke. My name is definitely Clarence."

"This is definitely Mister Clarence!" Shiva looked up and announced again. "Mister Clarence is our new concierge."

"Uh, no, that rumor isn't true. I'm not a concierge. I'm an architect. Retired."

"Mister Clarence is our new retired Architect! Mister Clarence, I cordially invite you to meet Lord Brahma and Lord Vishnu."

Several hands waved at Clarence, who waved back with only one. This somehow felt inadequate so he decided to wave with both, which gave Shiva a chance to notice his cane.

"Oh! Where are my manners? Would you like me to take that staff of power off your hands?"

"It's just a walking stick," Clarence answered.

"Ah, but you're not walking," Shiva countered while taking the stick from

Clarence. "You're standing, and it appears you do not need three legs to do that."

"Actually"—Clarence tried grabbing his cane back—"I was planning to *walk* up the hallway to find a lawyer, so I'm going to need that."

"So you said. But I can't let you leave without hearing more about this sixth rumor."

"It's not a rumor. I really do need to talk to a lawyer."

"But you *are* talking to a lawyer."

"You're a lawyer?"

"Absolutely."

"Okay." Clarence nodded. "Good. Well, you need to know that the rumor of me stealing Big Momma's offerings is not true."

"What about the other rumor? Are you dating Madam Lucifer?"

"No. And who the H. cares? We're supposed to be talking about my case."

"What case? You just said you most certainly did not steal Big Momma's offerings. Case closed, no?"

"Well no, it's not that simple. I took her bowls. I'm admitting that, okay? I'm putting that on the table, right now. I took her bowls, but only so that I could wash them and fill them with offerings. I went into the woods to find food and water but was attacked by a maniac who thought I was trying to steal them."

"Oooh, I see. This is juicy," Shiva said, eating this all up. "It is also very complicated. You definitely need to talk to a lawyer, Mister Clarence."

"You just told me you were a lawyer!"

"I am, but not that kind of lawyer. Neither is Brahma or Vishnu. We practice law, but not that kind of law—more like the laws of the Universe. What you need is a criminal attorney. Probably a very wise one too."

"What kind of attorney are you?"

"Lord Brahma is a creative attorney, Lord Vishnu is a preservation attorney and I am a destruction attorney."

"What the H. is a *destruction attorney*?" Clarence intoned incredulously. "You mean like, destruction of property?"

"Close. More like destruction of the Universe."

Clarence blinked, then asked with disbelief: "This is your day job?"

"Day job? Oh no. I am not flipping burgers, Mister Clarence. A day job takes only a few hours to finish many repetitions of the same task. We are talking a career here, where it takes days, weeks, or months to do only one task. In my case, as well as with Brahma and Vishnu, it takes us many years to do what we do for a living."

"How many years?"

"Billions!" Shiva threw out his arms, and then saw the look of awe on Clarence's face. "Yes, Mister Clarence, *billions.* I'm an obsessive-compulsive perfectionist. I like to take my time when I work. I refuse to settle for mediocrity. Only with humans is world destruction an event. But with me, it is a process. I allow all my subjects to mature and peak with age before escorting them into the great mystery of renewal. Humans, as usual, prefer to cut to the chase. You drop a quick bomb and—poof—everything's gone. You have more of an appetite for destruction than an appreciation for it."

"I think we just want to get it over with. There's not much to appreciate about dying."

"Mister Clarence, every time the seasons slowly shift, the scent of spring fades and the leaves radiantly change their hue before withering and falling away, those are my laws at work. I light up the darkness of the void with exploding stars, and I do it so that new worlds may emerge again. But that part is delegated to Lord Brahma."

"Exploding stars, huh? What about exploding appendices? Is that your work, too?" Clarence shot back. "Watching leaves wither and die is one thing; watching someone you love fade away is another. Having to watch yourself kick the bucket isn't exactly a picnic, either. You don't even watch it—you *feel* it. Birthdays begin feeling like they come twice a year. While your body is slowing down, time speeds up just to get you off its conveyor belt. The world pushes you into the slow lane so that it can zip past you because while they're on their way to live young, you're on your way to a retirement home—to be around other withering leaves. And you do this not because there is strength in numbers, but because there's comfort in them. Trust me, the last thing anyone wants to be is the last dead leaf falling from the tree."

The room went silent as Clarence's words reverberated noiselessly in Shiva's head. He stared at Clarence with eyes noticeably dilated. Even Brahma and Vishnu had finally snapped out of their chessboard trance, mesmerized by Clarence's poetry.

"Magnificent. A Masterpiece," Shiva said, clasping all four of his hands together. "Slander barks and sarcasm bites, but sincerity bores through the cynical flesh to tap the heart and bring it to beat again. I am impaled by your poetry. You, Mister Clarence, are my finest work."

"What?"

"World destruction is not a waste, Mister Clarence—it is a craft. Yes, Mister Clarence, a craft. You see, Mister Clarence, I am an artist."

"Destruction as... *art*?"

"Most certainly, Mister Clarence. If there can be an Art of War, why not an Art of Destruction?"

"Five seconds ago you were a lawyer. Now you're an artist."

"I multi-task." Shiva smiled, flashing his four hands.

"Artists *create*," Clarence argued.

"Some do. But I am an artist who *destroys*."

"An artist who destroys," Clarence skeptically nodded. "It all sounds so postmodern. But you do realize that postmodernism is dead."

"Not dead, Mister Clarence, *destroyed*," Shiva bolstered, beating a fist against his chest as if claiming sole credit for its destruction. Clarence sighed, realizing this could and would go on forever.

"Can I have my leg back, please?"

"You mean your staff of power? Absolutely." Shiva handed it back to him. "But remember... Before it became a staff of power, it was a limb from a tree whose leaves had to first wither and die. There is great potential in destruction, Mister Clarence. And there is even greater potential in renewal."

*

The next door didn't even have a room number; it had a store signage reading *Café des Aveugles*. Clarence didn't know what to make of it, but he knocked anyway, resigning himself to whatever was on the other side. The door opened almost instantly, revealing a shadowy, dusk room inside.

From out of this darkness, and apparently from out of the eighteenth century, emerged the Victorian version of a video vixen—a dangerous looking woman with a butt that boomed into a bell-shaped silk dress, courtesy of the original booty implant—the bustle.

"Clarence, *bienvenue*," she said in a sultry French voice. She practically sprayed him with pheromones as she extended her hand. "I am... *Raison*."

She took his hand to escort him into a pitch-black darkness, then closed the door. After a short second, she struck a match and lit up a cigarette, which made her face glow. A soft light came on, revealing that she had stripped down to a bodice, briefs and nothing more. She held out her hand, but Clarence hesitated.

"My hands are clean, *mon chéri*," she promised, as if her hands were really the issue.

With a titillating smile, she strutted forward, circled around him and swathed her arms across his chest until her palm came to a rest against his heartbeat.

"Your heart is strong," she whispered.

"No, it's not," he replied, feeling weak.

"Then you must sit down."

"I have three legs. I can stand."

"I insist, mon chéri."

She guided Clarence to the edge of her bed, pulled back and circled her arm for him to take in every element of the Café des Aveugles. Instead of sensual trappings, the room was trimmed with images of revolution. A mural of a woman with her blouse falling from her shoulders and carrying the French flag while leading a score of men into battle occupied an entire wall. This suddenly gave Clarence an idea of where he was and who was standing before him.

Raison was, quite literally, a Goddess born from a revolution brewed in the underground cafés at the Palais-Royal in eighteenth-century Paris. Within these subterranean chambers, Newtonian machines mingled with Epicurean delectations. Drinks, drugs and derrières were all part of the basement-level debauchery enjoyed by the mostly male clientele, but no dirty indulgence was more perverse or pervasive than the pressing issue of politics. Whereas patrons today sit together at café tables and trifle on with small talk, these perverted patriots formed tribunals that sentenced the Catholic Church to be overthrown in an unprecedented revolution. After the guillotine dropped, the blood was mopped and the smoke cleared, there emerged a theatrical cult of Reason, where Nature itself was the Supreme Being. God as most knew him was duly deposed and replaced by a whore, randomly conscripted off the streets and elevated as the living emblem of the cult's Goddess—Raison, or Reason.

Clarence returned his eyes to her and saw that she had never taken her eyes off him. He also saw that just over her shoulder was a long row of cavalry swords, a long-barrel blunderbuss rifle, Nock guns and a few muskets. Even more intimidating was a red oak guillotine sitting ominously in front of the French flag.

"What the H. is that?" Clarence whimpered.

"That," Raison began as she sat next to Clarence and crossed one supple leg over the other, "is *justice*."

From out of nowhere, she pulled out a four-barrel flintlock pistol and waved it in front of Clarence's face.

"You've come to the right place, *monsieur. Je vais vous aider.* I have heard about your problem, and I'm going to help you *claim* your justice." It was the way she intoned the word 'claim' that made Clarence swallow hard. He turned his head at a random noise behind him, but Raison, with two fingers under his chin, pulled his attention back to her. "Do not worry. You can speak freely. We are alone, mon chéri."

"Alone? Where is your roommate?"

She answered by cocking her pistol and pulling the trigger. Thankfully, it only snapped. The gun was empty.

"You can kill Gods?"

"*Oui.* I can. And only I," she answered, gently pressing her lips against Clarence's ear.

"Who did you kill?"

"Yahweh *and* Allah. They wouldn't stop bickering, so I killed them both. And so, mon chéri, I am the only one who can help you with your problem."

"There's been a mistake. I'm looking for a lawyer, not an outlaw."

"And I am looking for a new roommate."

"Raison, I'm twice your age."

"*Au contraire,* mon chéri, I am twice *your*s," she corrected.

Clarence's eyes rolled to the roof of his head as he did the math. While he counted with his fingers, he noticed the mural again in his peripheral. He saw the title at the bottom: "Liberty Leading the People" by Eugène Delacroix.

"That's *you* in the painting, isn't it?" Clarence asked.

"Oui. I am the Goddess of Liberty, Truth and Reason," she proudly intoned in her French accent as she raised her pistol at shoulder level. "I brought man from the cemetery of superstition and into the light of enlightenment, from the ruins of religion to the true sanctuary of science. When I came to be, the Gods ceased to be."

"This place is full of Gods!" Clarence exclaimed. "Millions of them."

"Then *we* will need reinforcements."

"We?"

"Oui."

Raison stood up and sashayed to the blunderbuss hanging from her wall.

She turned and looked back at Clarence. Her eyes twinkled with dare and passion as she slowly grabbed the rifle and in a single motion recklessly tossed it to Clarence, who caught it, looked at it and cringed.

"No, thank you," he said, tossing it back.

"You plan to fight them with that wooden leg?" She pointed at his walking stick. "You think you can kick them to death?"

"It's a staff of power!" he rebutted.

"There are no such things, Clarence." Raison rushed over to him. With an aggressive yet seductive push, she lunged him backwards onto her bed and allowed her busty body to collapse on his.

"My bones," Clarence groaned.

"*Mon chéri*, you must listen to reason. The Gods are not real. They are figments of the imagination, which is why we must be rid of them. We must kill them all."

"You want to kill imagination?"

"Oui."

"But I need it."

"For what, mon chéri?"

"To create."

"Create what?"

"Art and buildings."

"You are retired, no?"

"Yes. But I still need my imagination."

"You need reason!" she snapped.

"I need both."

"You need me, and me alone."

"I need a lawyer." Clarence shoved Raison aside. "And a restraining order."

He grabbed his cane and made a slow, hobbled escape. Raison rushed to cut him off at the door, but he made the interception with his staff of power, blocking her and brushing her off to the side. He dived through the door and pulled it shut, but could already feel Raison trying to reopen it. This turned into a tug of war, which lasted for a long minute before finally the commotion settled.

He kept his grip on the doorknob, half expecting the door to yank open and for him to be sucked back inside. Instead, a pulverizing force carried by a loud blast exploded past his ear, leaving a gaping hole in the door. Clarence peeped through it to find Raison, armed with her four-barrel flintlock pistol, poised to pop a second hole through the door—or through him.

He fell to the ground, barely escaping a second and third shot. A fourth shot nearly took the door of its hinges. He watched her as she threw down the gun and reached for the blunderbuss. His eyes leaped from his skull and his bones crackled as he rolled over and retreated to the next apartment. From the ground, he banged on the base of the door for dear life. Thankfully, it opened. Clarence looked up to see a group of Jehovah's witnesses. They looked down at him and without so much as a second thought slammed the door shut in his face, yelling: "We're not interested!" Then he noticed a copy of **The Watchtower** being slid underneath the door.

Clarence rolled his eyes and rolled to the next door. Before he could even get off a first knock, Raison's door exploded into splinters and dust. A thick cloud smoldered through the hallway, smothering Clarence's vision. He rubbed his eyes and saw the misty silhouetted figure of Raison marching towards him with her rifle clenched in both hands. She emerged from the fog with a last pounding step. *This is it*, he thought, *my goose is cooked*. He clenched his eyes and waited, but reopened them again when, after a painfully long minute, nothing happened. To his bewilderment, he saw Raison reloading the blunderbuss, a ritual that required so many tedious steps that she was obliged to mumble the loading instructions.

"*Une*, for safety purposes, set the hammer on 'half-cock.'

"*Deux*, grab a charge from the ammo pouch.

"*Trois*, tear the top of the charge with your teeth while pressing down a ball of lead into your mouth with your tongue.

"*Quatre*, pour the powder down the barrel.

"*Cinq*, spit the ball of lead from your mouth into your palm and stuff it down the barrel followed by the package wadding.

"*Six*, stamp it all down with a ramrod.

"*Sept*, add gunpowder to the flash pan and, last but not least...

"*Huit*, cock the musket and..."

She looked up, lifted the musket to aim it and stared over the long barrel. Clarence swallowed hard.

"Hold still, mon chéri," she insisted with a terrifying detachment in her voice. "I am not trying to kill you, just the foolish ideas you have in your head."

This meant a bullet straight to the cranium.

Shoving aside the knock-first etiquette, Clarence grabbed the knob to the nearest door to force his way inside. Raison fired her shot, and the rifle kicked back and puffed gunpowder. She lowered the musket and waved away the lingering smoke.

Clarence was gone.

He toppled forward into an apartment full of old books. His first, hopeful impression was that this was the room of a lawyer, or even a librarian, but he was wrong on both accounts. It belonged to a Cheetah, whose head turned sharply at his sudden arrival. Her eyes glowed like embers as she prowled in his direction, but as she came upon him, she swiveled in a half-circle and angled her back towards him.

"Do me a favor, handsome," she began in a thick voice. "Scratch my back, please."

Clarence had no idea why, but he reached up and obliged. He felt a soothing vibration as she purred. She basked in the massage for several minutes until, finally, she swiveled around to face Clarence. Her fangs showed as she spoke.

"Would you mind doing the same for my roommate?" she asked.

Still on his back, Clarence felt the room shaking from the approach of the roommate, who stopped at the roof of his head and hovered over him. He looked up into the face of a Hippopotamus, whose wide-open mouth was spiked with enormous, pillar-like teeth. Presumably, she was smiling.

"So you need a lawyer, I hear," the Hippo said.

His frail fingers gripped into his chest as his heart skipped a few ticks.

"No," Clarence mumbled in a dizzy. "I need a hospital."

*

It was Clarence's sense of hearing that brought his consciousness back. He listened for repetitive electric beeps, clinical evidence of life still ticking, but he didn't hear them. What his ears did hear was the pulse of life from his own heart, which was beating at a normal rate again. He moved a little and felt his bones respond with a sharp but fleeting ache. Never had he been so thankful to feel the arthritis in his limbs. This meant he was still alive.

He opened his eyes and found himself surrounded by herbs and plants of all types. A wandering wave of incense filled the air. It was peaceful. Relaxing. *I can retire here*, he thought to himself. But as he made small movements to ensconce himself in this luxury, the feeling of being watched interrupted his thoughts.

His eyes slowly pivoted towards the familiar face of an old Japanese God with a roundish head and a walrus mustache raining down from underneath his nose and chin. There was a silent sadness and a grayish-blue emptiness in his eyes. He was blind. He hovered over Clarence as his ivory skin cracked into a wizened and wily smile.

"My name is Omiokane. I will be your lawyer."

Chapter 5

Omiokane, reposed as he was on the outside, was a bit of a closet diva on the inside. In the old days he was seen as a wizened God committed to ritual and right methods, but these days his insistence that things be done this way or that resulted in rumors that the old God suffered from OCD. There may have been some truth to that, but the retirement home really had strayed from the proper order of a true temple, leaving him no choice but to escape from the chaos to a private open-air shrine atop a humble hill. A wise man he was, but not a handyman, so setting up his sanctuary was limited to hanging animal-shaped wind chimes from tree branches and erecting a crudely constructed vermillion gateway called a Torii. The result was miserable, but a Japanese philosophy known as *wabi-sabi* not only excused such imperfections—it embraced them.

The wind blew and the chimes kissed, singing in the process.

Omiokane could hear Clarence at the base of the hill, using his third leg to leverage his weight as he trudged up the incline. He could also hear Clarence cursing in acronyms, demanding to know why this, of all places, would be the place to discuss legal matters. To Omiokane, the answer was obvious. It was picked for its privacy, its serenity and its vista. It was a small hill, yes, but it still provided enough elevation for a fruitful view of how the flatlands buttressed against the blue sky. Omiokane, of course, saw nothing but blackness, but the breeze that wafted over him gave description enough of what his eyes could no longer see.

Finally, he heard Clarence's feet crunch the grass at the peak of the hill. He arrived grumbling and glowering at Omiokane, who waited to hear if Clarence had brought his prize. His answer came from a gust of wind carrying a hoppy scent to his nose.

"You brought it." Omiokane inhaled deeply. "My offering."

"You send an old man on three legs to a tavern, across a yard as long as a football field and then up a D. hill? You're no God of Wisdom," Clarence hissed. "You're a God of Torture."

"And you are a whining prophet," Omiokane countered and patted a small altar in front of him. "Place it here," he instructed.

Clarence obliged and watched as Omiokane searched the air with his

86

hands until they found the handle of a large glass barrel of beer. The old God smiled approvingly and sunk his lips into the froth. He was far more disciplined than Väinämöinen when imbibing his booze, even to the extent of being elegant. With ritual-like movements, he tipped and poured the beverage into his mouth at measured intervals, as if it were tea. He indulged a soft and audible exhale to express his satisfaction. Finally, he placed the mug down in front of the mat and stared through the darkness at Clarence, ready to begin. Clarence, still wheezing from the walk, made himself comfortable and waited to see if this blind old God of Wisdom would live up to his reputation.

"There is a great wisdom—"

Clarence cracked into a rude laughter. Omiokane, though blind as a bat, stared at him with steely contempt.

"I apologize," Clarence said, still sniggering. "It's just... Your voice reminds me of those old Japanese wise men I used to see in the movies. I'm sorry. I interrupted you. Continue. You were saying something about wisdom."

"Do you drive, Clarence-san?"

"Nope. Too old."

"I am too old as well. And too blind. And yet I am still accused of being a car thief."

"By your roommate."

"*Hai*," Omiokane nodded. "Ahura Mazda. He is the Persian God of Wisdom and Light. He is also the namesake of the famous Mazda automobile line, which is owned by a Japanese car company. Ahura Mazda is upset with me because the Japanese borrowed his name without permission. He tortures my ears everyday with his protests on this matter."

"The Japanese couldn't name their cars after one of their own Gods?"

"That is exactly what Ahura Mazda said and is still saying and will continue saying to anyone who will listen. But the Japanese didn't just borrow his name for a car; they borrowed *cars* and the technology for making them. Cars were foreign to Japan and did not find their way to her shores until the Meiji era. Among the many alien things that were imported was the word for 'nature.' Prior to this, the Japanese did not separate Nature from the Gods; they were indistinguishable. This concept of separation was borrowed, and so the Japanese had to invent a word to accommodate this new idea: *shizen*. Before this, the Japanese word for encountering the Gods was the same as for encountering Nature: *Kami*. It is a word that refers to anything that inspires a sense of awe.

"These days people are no longer in awe of Nature. Sometimes I wonder if it would have been better if the Japanese had not followed the Western world into the ways of industry. Though you know that Nature is alive, the eye of industry sees her as if she were dead. Rock, trees and water are the remnants of her carcass, and industry is a business of gravediggers. This is the real root of Ptah's anger. He is not angry that you have stolen from Big Momma. One cannot steal from the Gods, just as one cannot steal from Nature. But one can be disrespectful to Nature, just as one can be disrespectful to one's own nature."

"Hey"—Clarence shrugged—"what goes around comes around. I think the reason we have become indifferent to Nature is because she has always been indifferent to us. In fact, it has been our industriousness that has kept Nature from killing us."

"Hai, Nature kills, but human beings murder. You stay Nature's hand, only to die at your own."

"So you're saying it's better to die at Nature's hand?"

"Clarence-san, you must understand that Nature kills with one hand, but she feeds with the other. Your fear of one hand has compelled you to sever both. That is all that I am saying. People spend too much time conquering their Gods and not enough time conquering their demons. Your fears, your arrogance, your recklessness and the strongest demon of all, your illusions—these have made you enemies of Nature and of each other. You must show Ptah that you have respect for Mother Nature and for your own nature. If you do this, you will solve your real problem."

"*Real problem?* What real problem?"

"Initiation."

Clarence fell silent. It was one of those moments when a word is used outside of its own comfort zone, suffers an identity crisis and loses its meaning.

"I— I don't follow you," he said while watching Omiokane take another drink.

"I want you to rebuild the temple," Omiokane answered, setting down his glass.

"You mean the retirement home? Why?"

"Because the Gods have deviated from their Nature, and we need a new temple to restore order. And because I would like to have my own room. I can no longer listen to Ahura Mazda accuse me of stealing his name. It is driving me crazy."

"You? What about me? I was accused of stealing from the CEO. You're asking me to rebuild the entire temple? What about my acquittal?"

"I will ensure your acquittal. In exchange, you will rebuild the temple so that all of the Gods can have their own sanctuary. Especially me."

"Okay, stop right there. Enlarging a temple requires planning, resources, contractors—none of which I have here. I'm not sure you understand how architecture works."

"On the contrary, it is you who does not understand. There are secrets to the true science of architecture, secrets that you will only learn if you are initiated."

"Initiated? By *who*?"

"By Ptah."

"The guy—the *God*—who tried to kill me? Are you kidding?"

"No, I am not kidding. And he will try to kill you again, just to be clear."

"Just to be clear?" Clarence repeated. "Okay, duly noted. He's going to try to kill me again... Anything else?"

"Hai," Omiokane nodded. "I admit that this is a tricky situation. It is even trickier when we consider that if you are found guilty at your trial for the charges of stealing from Big Momma, you will be sentenced to death."

This time, Clarence was at a loss for words. He tried mustering up a mocking laughter, but failed at even that. All he could do was shake his head.

"Death has somehow cornered you," Omiokane continued. "But it is precisely the moment when an animal is backed into a corner by a stronger opponent that it will make its attack. Therefore, it is best to go headfirst into battle. If you delay, death will find you unprepared, but if you move expediently, perhaps it will be the other way around—you will find death when it least expects you."

It was the way Omiokane said that last part that made Clarence realize that this God of Wisdom had a dark side. He angled his head forward, squinted his vacant eyes and broke into the hardened smile of a War General.

"You mean a sneak attack?" Clarence blurted.

"He won't even see it coming."

"You want *me* to launch a sneak attack on Ptah and convince him to 'initiate' me? Yeah, that'll win him over."

"Winning him over will come later. First, you must *win*."

"He's a lot stronger than me. Trust me, I already know. The man has six arms and four legs. I only have three! Plus, he has this thing where he flashes light from his eyes. What will I have?"

"You will have the element of surprise. You must see yourself as a samurai, and *that*"—Omiokane pointed to his walking stick—"is your *katana*."

"My *what*?"

"Your weapon, Clarence-san."

Clarence rolled his eyes. Thirty minutes ago his walking stick was a staff of power; now it was a samurai sword. He tried to imagine himself, a senior citizen, unsheathing his stick from the ground, slicing it through the air and cutting down Ptah in a single blow. Ptah's body would linger in suspended animation before realizing it had just been struck and, after a few seconds of shock, collapse to the ground. Victorious and, no doubt, with his back to a Full Moon, Clarence would hover over him, look down at his fallen opponent and...

"And then what?" he asked.

"And then you will offer him flowers, handpicked from Mother

Earth's bosom. *That* is how you will win him over," Omiokane nodded conclusively and reached forward to finish his beer.

"I can't believe it." Clarence shook his head. "This is what qualifies as wisdom these days."

"Oh no, Clarence-san, not wisdom—*war.* This is a battle strategy. Wisdom will come when it is time for your trial."

"You said you would ensure my acquittal!"

"Hai."

"With *wisdom*?"

"Hai."

"Wisdom? Not... *evidence*?"

"I was not aware that innocence required evidence."

"Everything requires evidence."

"Even wisdom?"

"No, wisdom is sort of... It's like a... Well, to use an analogy you might understand, wisdom is like an antique car, like a Mazda or something. You admire it when you see it, but nobody drives it anymore."

"I see." Omiokane stroked his long walrus mustache twice. "Then we must correct that. If it is evidence of your innocence that you seek, then I suggest we produce an eye-witness to the event."

"An eye-witness, sure." Clarence sarcastically bobbled his head at the obvious. "Yeah, that would be a good place to start."

"Hai. So who else saw what happened?"

"That's the problem. There was no one else there."

"Are you sure? Maybe there were some frightened animals nearby. Animals can be very observant, you know. Perhaps they saw everything but are too afraid to come forward."

"Frightened animals." Clarence blinked incredulously. "You mean like... the Easter Bunny?"

A gust of wind chimed in with a familiar song that stopped Clarence mid-sentence. He looked over Omiokane's shoulder and saw dozens of wind chimes all in the shape of animals, including one that took the form of a running rabbit. His eyes lit up with revelation as he remembered the animal-headed fogies at the retirement home.

"Vynamonen."

"Who?"

"Vynamonen," Clarence repeated, still butchering his name. "C'mon, the guy who looks like Santa Claus. He was the concierge before the other guy."

"Oooh, him." Omiokane frowned. "I don't know. Are you sure you want *him* as a witness? This Easter Bunny sounds like a better lead."

"No, I don't want Vynamonen as a witness. He wasn't there," Clarence answered, "but I think he knows who was."

*

There is a famous oil painting of an after-hours diner with its lights still on, illuminating an otherwise dark and desolate downtown alley. The diner's long window offers a fluorescent snapshot of nightlife on a weekday. Seated at the bar and under bright theatrical stage lighting are a barkeep and only three patrons: a couple and one guy, with his back turned, sitting alone. The artist, Edward Hopper, generously called them "Nighthawks," as if it were James Dean, Marlon and Marilyn lounging at the bar. But Gottfried Helnwein, who did his own adaptation of the painting, saw that these so-called nighthawks were not desperados, just desperate. He renamed the painting "Boulevard of Broken Dreams."

Väinämöinen, Balaam, the Lapphund and even the Barkeep looked a lot like Hopper's heroes, who wandered in from the boulevard as day orphans, adopted by the night. Three Gods and one dog with nowhere else to go but where they were. Even the Gods have broken dreams. Jealous Gods dream of monogamy and monotheism, but as made clear by Balaam, who was slumped over on his stool and wasted to the world, the hearts of men wander from one God to the next.

Väinämöinen also had his share of broken dreams, albeit only one. He used to be a famous folk singer for the Gods, but not anymore.

The Lapphund, who propped herself on a stool next to Balaam with her mouth hanging open while gazing off into nowhere, was the only one who seemed content with the company she kept.

Soft sunlight crept into the tavern to break up the gloomy emptiness inside. But the light didn't travel much further than the window. It hung around like a misty haze, leaving the dark and dingy bowels of the pub untouched. The Barkeep made rounds collecting empty glasses—the aftermath of a war between wine and ale and two Gods who had settled their disputes by drinking each other under the table. Väinämöinen, the clear victor of the competition, relaxed at the end of the bar, nursing a victory beer as casually as if it were water. He reminisced about the old days when the Gods gathered around to hear him sing. What time took away, imagination gave back. Instantly, the bar became a stadium filled with fans. Väinämöinen made his hand into a visor as he looked around surveying the crowd and then waved to them.

"Thank you, thank you. You're too kind. Thank you."

He patted the air, trying to calm the ovation. A hush washed over the stadium and the old singer God began his hymn—an ode to the Gods of Time.

♪ *What is time? Is it two hands on a clock*

With a watch on their wrists?

No, no, no. Time is a bitch,

But at least not a four-legged snitch,

She'll never open her mouth to spill secrets,

But she'll open her jaws to spill blood

Because Time is all the time speechless,

But still all the time hungry for a stud.

She preys upon youth, she'll devour your prime.

Better run for your life if someone asks you for Time.

Do you have the time? No! Time only has you.

Wrapped in her jaws, gripped by her claws.

Can you tell me the Time? Kyllä! Now that I can do.

Time is the Sun, Time is the Moon. Time is the Planets.

Time is a Zoo.

A Zoo? You heard me right—Time is a Zoo!

93

Lions, Bulls, Two Fish and a Ram,

Time is a quickie, be careful she even has Crabs.

You're better off with the Virgin, ask her out on a date.

You two love birds can go splurging on a milkshake or Milky Way.

But don't be so certain, I just remembered to say

That first the cruel Virgin must give you the Time of day. ♪

A door opened and closed shut, like a swift rejection, but Väinämöinen, so enraptured by his own melody, took it as a sound effect to his song and continued singing.

♪ *Oh well, don't sweat it. Here's a tip from the God of masturbation,*

All you need is time and a wee bit of imagination,

And the Virgin will be there—and all the other constellations!

Because the real beauty of time is that it's all in your mind.

Don't listen to Einstein, just take heed to this rhyme.

You won't survive Time!

Run for your life because you won't survive Time ♪

Väinämöinen stopped and came alive as he heard applause—real applause—coming from behind him. He spun around and saw Clarence proudly putting his hands together.

"Just in time for the victory party," Väinämöinen slurred and pointed to the bombed-out Balaam. "As you can see, ystäväni, I've conquered the British."

"Vynamonen," Clarence cut him off. "The men that I saw with the animal heads—there was twenty-four of them—who were they again?"

"Gods of the Decans."

"You called them the Watchers."

"Kyllä." Väinämöinen nodded. "They watch the hours. The Decans are Time Gods. Time is Nature's eyes and her memory. They are the most ancient Gods of all."

"But why are they animals?"

"Because they are the Zodiac, ystäväni—*the Circle of Animals*. The

Decans are the constellations, the first measurers of Time."

"Perfect. So, theoretically, if someone wanted to know what time it was, they could just check with them, right?"

"Kyllä."

"And if a certain incident happened, it's possible that they saw it, right?"

"Where are you going with this, ystäväni?"

"I need to talk to the Decans. Is that possible?"

"Sure. But first you will need to fast for a month, at least."

"A month! Why would I have to fast for a month?"

"So they have no interest in eating you."

"Eat me? Why would they want to eat me?"

"Because they're *animals*, ystäväni. Weren't you listening to the song? Every animal knows a good meal when he sees one. That's why you fast—so they don't see you as a good meal."

"Has that worked before?"

"It worked for Tobias."

"Oh God, not him again."

"This one is from the old Finnish folktale of Tobias and the seven-headed Dragon. Now, the first thing you need to know is that Tobias was as poor as pigs and whistles. The poor guy was so poor that it was hard to imagine him being any poorer, and yet every year, he became poorer still. He lived on rocks and cheese is what I'm trying to tell ya. But Heaven works in mysterious ways because a diet of rocks and cheese is what saved his life when he came across a fire-breathing and starving Dragon. One hungry dragon is bad enough, but this dragon had seven heads, and each head was hungrier than the last. Tobias would have easily ripped into seven portions of soft, succulent meat, but the poor guy was nothing but skin and bones like I told you. So the Dragon passed.

"They decided to go in search of food together, but, like I told you before, twoliness is good over two glasses of ale but not one portion of food. The two of them came across one tree—the World Tree—and in its branches was a buffet of beasts: every creature that ever creped and crawled in the past, present and even the future.

"Now, the Dragon had no problem flapping its wings and reaching the creatures at the top of the tree, but Tobias had neither the wings, strength or courage to climb the World Tree, so he cried and whined for his share of the kitty—a common problem with humans.

"The Dragon grew tired of his whining and pulled down the top of the tree so that Tobias could eat. But there's an old saying about humans: *Give a man a fish and he'll eat for a day; give him a buffet and he'll eat everything.* Tobias had lived on rocks and cheese all his life, so when he finally had some real meat, he couldn't control himself. He dove into the tree and stuffed himself like a pig in a sty, and the fatter he became, the more delicious he looked to the Dragon. Dragons have an old saying too, you know: *Every delicious dinner deserves a dessert!* Besides, the Dragon hadn't known Tobias that long, so it wouldn't be that rude if he ate him. But the Dragon hadn't reasoned the whole matter through because opening his mouth to eat the poor guy meant he had to first let go of the tree, and well... That is how Tobias learned to fly."

Väinämöinen wrapped up the tale by bowing his arms across his chest and nodding. Only an idiot would miss the moral of this one. Clarence, being the idiot that he was, just looked at Väinämöinen, bewildered and blinking.

"My point is..." Väinämöinen huffed with frustration. "Approach a dragon after having fattened yourself with a meal and you'll soon become one. The same is true with the Decans. Better to approach them when you're skin and bones and already on the brink of death. If they see that, they may not bother with you."

"I walked right by them at the retirement home," Clarence rebutted. "They didn't bother me then."

"You walked by the *Gods* of the Decans. The Watchers."

"Right."

"No, ystäväni." Väinämöinen shook his head. "The Gods of the Decans watch the stars to track the time. The Decans *are* Time. They are the stars that men used to know the hours of the night. The Decans are dangerous animals. There is nothing with a more voracious appetite than Time, ystäväni. Do not approach the Gods of Time unless you are willing to approach the hour of your own death." Väinämöinen drilled in the warning with a piercing stare.

"Come with me," Clarence pleaded.

"Not a chance."

"Come on!"

"*Oma apu paras apu!*" Väinämöinen declined in his own language.

"Translation, please."

"*If you want something done right, do it yourself.* Besides, you don't even have anything to defend yourself with."

"I have my walking stick."

"Have you ever used it for running?"

"Jesus!" Clarence shook his head and Balaam raised his to look around, certain that he heard someone call for him. "Fine. I'll go on my own."

"Wait, ystäväni." Väinämöinen grabbed Clarence by the shoulder. "This is a suicide mission. You must know this."

"I don't have a choice."

"You could *not go.*"

"Didn't you hear what happened? The God you sent me to consult with accused me of theft. I need a witness to prove my innocence. And the only witness at the time *was* Time."

"Ystäväni"—Väinämöinen leaned towards Clarence—"that ache you always feel in your bones is Time slowly chewing on your limbs. There is another saying in my land: *Ei elämästä selviä hengissä. You won't survive life.* Time preys upon us all."

"Then I guess it doesn't matter if I die now or later."

After this clever counter, Väinämöinen bobbed his head and conceded: "You are right. Because you insist, I will take you to one of the Decans."

Clarence looked at him as if to ask, *you will?* Only a fool would be this eager to meet one of the Decans, but Clarence had already proven himself an idiot unable to connect the dots on a simple precautionary parable. Now he was proving himself a fool as well.

"Kyllä." Väinämöinen shook his head. "Come with me."

He said this as if they were going on a faraway journey, but they walked only a few feet to the other end of the bar, where the Finnish Lapphund kept Balaam company. She still had the same far-away look in her eyes, but her ears showed otherwise by turning in the direction of Clarence's voice.

"This *dog* is one of the Decans?"

"Kyllä."

"She doesn't seem that fierce to me."

"That's what spending all your time at a tavern will do to you, ystäväni. But in her salad days, she was nothing short or shy of a savage beast. Definitely not someone you'd just walk up to and ask to be your witness at a trial. But she's perfectly tame now and prime for talking. So go ahead and ask her if she saw anything." He encouraged Clarence with a nod and a smile. Clarence frowned skeptically.

"Has this ever been done before?"

Actually, it had.

In 2008, a Labrador went down in history as the world's first animal to appear as a witness in a French murder trial. A woman found hanging from a ceiling was ruled an apparent suicide by the police, but others were not so sure. A murder suspect was identified and taken into a preliminary trial, where the deceased owner's Labrador was escorted to a witness box to see how the dog would respond to the alleged perpetrator. According to reports, the dog reacted by barking ferociously. In honor of this service, the Labrador was given the nickname *Scooby*.

Clarence looked at the Lapphund who looked off into nowhere. Desperation has a way of trumping all logic and skepticism. With no other recourse, Clarence fought back a sinking feeling of embarrassment and mumbled his question.

"Did you see me steal from Big Momma's temple?"

The Lapphund looked at him only briefly before her eyes retreated back into oblivion. Still, this didn't stop Clarence from waiting another half-minute for his answer. It took that long before he dropped his head in embarrassed defeat. Väinämöinen consoled him with a hand on his shoulder.

"Don't take it personally, ystäväni. The Decans have a no-snitch policy, and maybe it's a good thing they do. Stealing from Big Momma is a big deal. What were you thinking?"

"I didn't steal. That's why I need a Decan. To prove my innocence."

Clarence dismissed this whole desperate experiment with a wave of his hand and walked off.

"Where are you going, ystäväni?"

"To find a witness. One that will talk. Or, at least, bark."

"But I haven't told you where to find the other Decans."

"Yeah, but you told me who will." Clarence stopped in the doorway and looked back at Väinämöinen. "It was in your song—the God of masturbation."

With mild embarrassment, Clarence blushed and left.

*

Back at the retirement home, Clarence lay in bed. There was no drumming, or thumping or any electric music sizzling through the walls. He was surrounded by silence, the kind of silence perfect for privacy. That isn't to say it had been this way all day. No doubt, in his absence, the Gods were jamming in the hallways, but as soon as they got word that the Peeping-Tom pervert was on his way back, they scattered like roaches to their rooms, leaving the lewd leper to work out his loneliness with the only deity that would have anything to do with him—the God of masturbation.

Prostrate, beneath his blanket, Clarence replayed Väinämöinen's song in his head.

♪ Here's a tip from the God of masturbation,
All you need is time and a wee bit of imagination,
And the Virgin will be there—and all the other constellations!
Because the real beauty of time is that it's all in your mind...♪

It was the first time Clarence didn't want to blow his brains out from having a song stuck in his head. In fact, that was the point. In the ancient past, when writing was still considered taboo, songs and stories were designed precisely for this purpose. They were made to cling tightly to the imagination, searing into the mind's eye of the listener a map of the stars. Moses and the twelve tribes of Israel, Jesus and his twelve apostles, Hercules and his twelve labors—the twelve beasts he battled—were, in fact, the twelve signs of the Zodiac.

Every child stargazes at one time or another, but star-watching was a true science, supposedly started by the Babylonians. Not enough credit is given to the Egyptians, though, who invented the system of twenty-four hours that we still use today. This they did by devising their own Zodiac, a useful method for knowing exactly what stars you are looking at. These stars were subsequently segmented into twelve intervals, so as to measure the twelve hours of the night.

Clarence left his bed, looked out the window and for the first time since he was a little boy, he tried to count the stars. There were too many of them. He tried to make out their animal forms but couldn't. It wasn't like seeing forms and faces in the clouds, where all one had to do was look for a few seconds and a shape emerged. With the stars it wasn't so easy. Connecting these dots, he realized, must have taken a vivid imagination, and according to Väinämöinen's song, that was exactly what Clarence needed to see the Decans.

He pulled his window open, hoisted himself to the ledge and sky dived a few feet to the ground. He heard a loud thud as he hit the dirt. It was a hard fall and Clarence's limbs, in complete protest, refused to move. That was fine. Here, in the chill of the night, prostrate on his back, was exactly where he needed to be. Like a boy making angels in the snow, he spread out his legs and arms, and did nothing more eventful than stare into the stars—actual stars, not facsimiles of them. With his mind, he connected them into lines, and the lines connected into shapes until, at last, a form emerged. *Starchitecture.* He created a house of the Zodiac, out of which emerged an animal.

A Lion. Leo. Whoa!

Another animal emerged, but it was only a Lamb. Aeries. *Jesus*, he exhaled, *that was close*. But just as soon as he had relaxed, another animal leapt from the sky, this time a Bull. Taurus.

One after another, more animals emerged, slowly stepping from a seething celestial miasma, like primitive life moving from water to land. They were evolving, advancing in Clarence's direction.

He grabbed his walking stick, spiked it into the ground and groaned as he tried to scramble to his feet. He withdrew the stick from the dirt like a warrior, wielding it like a sword. His legs trembled the entire time, threatening to buckle and cast him right back down to the ground.

He watched as the straight line of animals splintered off into two directions, slowly encompassing him. He pivoted around, surveying the surrounding animal army and taking inventory: a Lamb, a Bull, a Crab, a Lion, an Eagle, a Scorpion, a Rabbit, a Monkey, a Rat, a Tiger, a Dragon, a Snake, a Horse, a Rooster, a Dog, a Cat, a Hyena, a Pig, an Elephant, an Owl, a Jackal, a Zebra, a Gazelle and, finally, a Beetle. But no Virgins.

Their formation complete, they stood side-by-side, sealing off any opening for his escape, a realization that nearly caused him to panic. But then he remembered Väinämöinen saying that these were Decans— Time Gods—and their circle formation had created a cage, yes, but also a clock.

He cleared his throat to speak but was lock-jawed from fear. He could see in their eyes the same objective scrutiny that most animals afford to the scent of a stranger: *Is this a potential kill, a potential killer or a fleeting curiosity?* After only a minute or two of deliberation, they decided it was the last of these three. Like a jury adjourned by a gavel, they broke apart and dispersed, moving at the slow pace of a herd of cows, showing not even the slightest interest in looking back. Time's interest in killing us is cruel, but her disinterest is even crueler.

Clarence watched, despondently, as they drifted away. His power of speech was returning and he wanted to call out to stop them, but it was too late. They were gone.

He was ready to abort his mission when he saw a new animal drifting towards him. This one came from a separate herd than the others. It emerged from the North and was much larger than the other animals. The celestial contours of its body were much broader and, whatever it was, it exuded greater power.

A gust of wind rushed ahead of the beast, sweeping Clarence off his feet. He tightened his grip on his stick and tried re-anchoring himself by stabbing it deeper into the Earth, but after multiple jabs he realized there was no ground. He looked down and discovered that the Earth had retreated from his feet. He was hovering within a void of darkness. He would have panicked, but he felt a warm, wet breath swath across his neck. His reflexes made his eyes shoot upward to discover that he was looking directly into the ferocious red eyes of a Great Bear. The enormous animal continued respiring into Clarence's face, each breath having the force of a solar wind. His eyes glowed radiantly, fiercely. As much as Clarence wanted to look away, he couldn't help but to stare deeper into them, wondering what was behind them. He was in a trance.

A sudden movement broke the spell. It was a low frequency that made Clarence's body shake from the inside. He could feel his bones almost ready to crack and splinter from the force. He thought it was an earthquake, but beneath his feet was only space. No, the vibration was from the creature's voice.

"Who are you, little man, who are you? Tell me now, who are you? Speak well and speak true, or be consumed by the emptiness of hollow words."

"My name is Clarence," he answered, his voice shaking as much as his bones. "I am a human being—a man who has lost his way and wandered into a world of the Gods."

"Humans belong to the Earth. How come you to the stars?"

"I was accused of a crime I did not commit. I am looking for a witness."

"Of what crime were you accused? Speak well, speak true, human."

"Of stealing Big Momma's offerings."

"BIG MOMMA?!?"

The Bear roared. That was all he needed to hear. In a single suction, he swallowed Clarence up and paused to lick his lips. *Delicious*, he thought to himself. He hadn't enjoyed the taste of human flesh in quite some time. But he wasn't able to savor the rare delicacy for long. He felt a clamorous tumor in his throat and began to choke until he was forced to spit Clarence back out.

"What the H! Is there any justice in this world?!?" Clarence coughed and gasped. "I just told you that I didn't do it, and the first thing you do is eat me! You didn't even give me a chance to tell you that the offering bowls were already empty. How can I steal something that isn't there."

"I know that you are innocent of this crime, little man. I know, too, that you were attacked by your accuser."

"If you know all this, then why the H. did you try to eat me?"

"Hold your tongue! I was not trying to eat you. But I am binding you to your duties to Big Momma."

"My duties? What duties?"

"The humans have created a new God who is starving the Earth by devouring her offerings. It will be your duty to expand the temple. Then you will return to your world. And you will bring this new God back to the temple... for an *early* retirement."

"So now I have two jobs? What about my acquittal? I need a witness."

"You shall have it."

The Bear leaned forward and, for a second time, gobbled Clarence with a gulping chomp, this time making sure the old man went all the way down. He licked his lips, delighting again at the rare taste of human flesh, one that appeared to have a faint flavoring of ale. He savored this for as long as he could before he stuck his paw into his mouth, inducing himself to gag. This turned into three dramatic convulsions and ended with a violent heave. Clarence shot from his mouth again. This time he didn't come back empty handed. In his palm, he held a ball of unhewn iron.

"You have in your hand, little man, the Heart of the Pole Star. Present it to the forty-two Judges. This will prove your innocence.

"But know this: Once you are proven innocent, your attacker is proven guilty of his attempt to kill an innocent man—a crime punishable... by death."

"No, no, no. He can't die. He has to initiate me so that I can expand the temple. Wait! Where are you going?"

The Great Bear ended the conversation, rather abruptly, by marching off. Clarence watched as he nested himself back into the Northern sky, merging with the stars.

"Did you hear me?" Clarence shouted. "He can't die. I need him to ini—"

He stopped mid sentence from the feeling of dream-falling, or, at least, that is how the sensation felt as he dramatically descended back into his rational mind. He looked down and saw the ground rapidly rushing to his feet. This time he didn't hear a loud thud, but felt it as he remembered dropping out of the window and smacking the ground. Everything should have gone black, but it didn't. Instead, Clarence opened his eyes and saw light.

The morning Sun was rising.

Chapter 6

The three hundred sixty-one candles in the lobby had the same mesmerizing effect as a massive neon store-sign buzzing and coruscating with electric life. Pulling the plug, then, was the same as a great wind sweeping through the lobby and blowing out all the candles at once. Just like that, the fire of life blinked out and was gone, leaving some to wonder where it went, if anywhere at all.

That's what Clarence asked himself when he entered the lobby and saw that someone had put out the small fires and removed every candle, rendering the room and the walls as bare and lifeless as a naked corpse. For Clarence, it was like being back at his office, where he spent countless hours inside the grey bowels of a compact, constipated cubicle. He even heard the sound of an outdated dot-matrix printer, screeching like a newborn baby while violently inhaling reams of perforated pages, then shitting them out on the floor. He followed the nerve-racking noise to its source and saw something he thought he'd never see in the world of the Gods—*a computer*. The Concierge had dismissed them before, but now here it was on his desk, quietly humming to itself, or perhaps to the newborn, which was still joined to its mother by an umbilical cord.

Meanwhile, the Concierge was AWOL. Just as Clarence wondered about his whereabouts, the hallway door burst open and out came a portly woman who looked like a cross between a '60s bank teller and an austere government agent. Clarence watched her sit down at the computer to crunch numbers, type up terms, print out the results and store each page to the top of a ream of papers stacked nearly as high as her beehive hairdo.

"What the H. is going on here?" he protested.

"Can I help you?" the woman asked, looking over her retro cat glasses.

"Yes. You can tell me what the H. is going on here."

"An audit."

"An audit of what?"

"The Gods."

"The Gods? Where's the Concierge?" Clarence demanded.

"He's no longer employed at this establishment," she answered flatly, removing a newly printed page at its crease and adjusting the position of her glasses as she reviewed it.

"No long— Who are you? What's your name?"

"Name?" She looked at him as if he were some naive pollyanna. "Governments don't identify people with names. We use statistics, polls and numbers with hyphens."

"Fine. What's your number?" Clarence conceded.

"Double-O-Seven"—she paused—"Dash Two."

"Double O Seven... Dash Two."

"Correct. And you are?"

"Clarence. I'm the new Ar—"

"Just a moment, Clarence," 007-2 excused herself and went back the way she came. The hallway door closed and the lobby went silent. Minutes later, the door exploded open and she re-emerged, holding Balaam by the collar as he kicked and flailed his limbs in protest.

"What in Our good name are you doing, you beastly boiler of a woman?"

"Downsizing."

"Downsizing? Us?!?"

"This retirement home has violated several building codes, not the least of which is exceeding the allowed maximum capacity, which constitutes a fire hazard."

"We've been saying this for years! Why are you evicting Us?!?"

"Because drunkenness is a violation of Article V, Section XIII, Line XXXIII," she recited robotically.

"We are not *drunk*!"

"You *were* drunk when you arrived here last night, trashing the lobby!"

"We flipped over *one* table!"

"That was the merchant's table."

"*Merchants*? Is that what you're calling thieves these days?"

"It was *you* who ran off with *their* money."

"Yes, well..." Balaam huffed. "Still, you can hardly call that trashing the lobby."

"You ran naked through the hallway in the middle of the night, banging on the doors of all the tenants, demanding that they get out immediately. That's called disorderly conduct and disruption of peace, violation of Article VII—"

"Oh, muzzle the ol' moose. We get it."

"Good! Would you like me to keep going with your other violations?"

"That won't at all be necessary. And We'll thank you to remove your hands from Our person." Balaam yanked free from her clutches, and dusted himself off. "We have no desire to stay in such an abominable abode, anyway. You'll be hearing from Our lawyer."

"That reminds me," 007-2 excused herself again and marched back into the hallway, reemerging a minute later with Omiokane, whom she hauled along by the collar of his kimono.

"What did he do?" Clarence exclaimed.

"Consuming an alcoholic beverage on campus grounds," she stated and released Omiokane with a slight toss, causing him to stumble forward.

Just like that, as if the whole thing had never happened, she went back to her station to resume her tasks, never once bothering to look up and give the two dejected deities so much as a second glance. This pissed Balaam off something fierce and, without warning, he erupted: "INSOLENCE! YOU DARE DE—"

"Can it," she cut him off and pressed the PRINT button, allowing the robotic scream of the printer to have the last word.

Balaam slowly lowered his fist in defeat. Omiokane, blind as he was, could feel the gesture and turned his grey eyes towards him.

"So, Balaam-san, I hear you are looking for a lawyer."

"So, I hear you're looking for a new job." Väinämöinen sniggered at the Concierge, who hovered in the tavern doorway—another walk-in from the *Boulevard of Broken Dreams*.

Sun Tzu, the esteemed Chinese military general and philosopher, once wrote: *"If you wait long enough by the river, you will see the body of your enemy floating by."* At long last, that prophecy was fulfilled. Väinämöinen had waited a long while, and here, finally, was his enemy floating by to take his place at the bar.

"You've come to the right place," Väinämöinen continued. "This pub is like a shelter for the homeless—*and the jobless*. Feel free to have a beer or two, we won't judge. You can keep a tab running until you can get back on your *feet*."

He flared up into knee-slapping laughter. The Concierge was genuinely confused until he saw Väinämöinen point at his bare feet floating inches from the ground.

"Sorry, but you *walked* into that one," Väinämöinen roared and grabbed his sides as he nearly tipped over from his stool. All the while, the Concierge just looked at him. The Barkeep sympathetically placed a gratuity beer in front of the poor guy, which he duly imbibed while watching the fat old Finnish fool finish his laughing fit.

"Oh, don't look at me like that." Väinämöinen wiped a tear from his eye. "We both knew this day would come eventually. It happens to the best of us. See the Barkeep here? He was the original concierge until *I* replaced him. And I know he didn't like it one bit because the little brat started a tavern and waited years for me to be fired. He knew that I would come wallowing in here to drown myself in a pit of self-pity. And now it's your turn. Your ship has finally sunk."

The Concierge said nothing. He quietly and coolly sipped from his beer, wondering why a self-described drowning man would take such delight at watching a ship sink. But such is the nature of envy: self-satisfaction quickly turns into self-sabotage.

"Yeah, I know. I'm supposed to be better than this," Väinämöinen continued. "But I'm not. I've waited too long to start taking the high road now. I have every intention of being low and petty, so you best prepare yourself now while you still can. Are you ready?"

"Ready?" the Concierge frowned. "For what?"

"For me to shamelessly gloat over your ill fortune. I'm not going to hold back either."

"Fine. But before you do, just remember that song from the musical Avenue Q.

♪ *That's schadenfreude! People taking pleasure in your pain* ♪

"Kyllä, but like we say in my tongue, *mikään ei kuivu kyyneltä nopeammin. There's nothing that dries faster than a tear.*"

Väinämöinen gave a cocky *hmpf* and rolled up his sleeves as he prepared to engage in, quite literally, a *proverbial* battle. This would be like two squabbling sophisticates sparring with Shakespearean sonnets, but with one difference: this was the old school versus the new. The Concierge went first and fired off by singing some Jimmy Cliff reggae.

♪ *Foolish pride won't bring you happiness
Foolish pride will bring you emptiness* ♪

Väinämöinen spat to the side and fired back:

"But pride is also a pack of lions. And no man has ever been brave enough to tell a lion to swallow his pride."

That was a Väinämöinen original. Technically, that was against the rules. But it didn't matter. The Concierge didn't know any better. In fact, he blinked absently while his eyes wandered around in his skull, lost in this ball of tangled wisdom. Väinämöinen took this as the first sign of a sure victory. With a wily smirk smeared across his face, he bobbed his eyebrows and waited for the counter-attack. The Concierge obliged. He cracked his neck and knuckles, threw back his head and sang.

♪ *When the ego is hungry, it feeds on the flesh of its master* ♪

"Kyllä. Unless the ego is vegetarian. Then it is a healthy ego."

Another Väinämöinen original. The Concierge looked at the Barkeep and raised his hand for a bourbon drink. He slammed it down with no chaser and, with the glass still in hand, sang a little Brandy.

♪ *It's a shame you have to learn the hard way* ♪

109

"Meh." Väinämöinen shrugged. "As the saying goes, *'by the time the game is learned, all the players have left.'*"

"But as Ice-T said," the Concierge shot back:

> ♪ *Don't hate the player, hate the game* ♪

"Ah, but a wise man once said: *'A little hate goes a long way,'* " Väinämöinen retorted.

The Concierge accepted this with a skeptic's smirk. *A little hate goes a long way, huh? Which 'wise man' said that?* No matter. He already had his rebuttal.

> ♪ *Still drunk on that hater flavor haterade*
> *It's home-made but it still won't getcha paid*
> *'Cause ya still drunk on that hater flavor haterade* ♪

"Hey, *'don't knock it until you try it,'* " Väinämöinen rapidly retorted.

"But," the Concierge quipped with a finger in the air, "as Jhené Aiko said:

> ♪ *An eye for an eye leaves everyone blind* ♪

"Kyllä, but as they say, *'Justice is blind,'* and now we know why."

"Okay," the Concierge said with a nod and shot back:

> ♪ *Blind Justice has a sword, so don't lose your head*

He took a single finger and sliced it along his neck as he repeated the last words of the song.

> *Don't... lose... your... head* ♪

Väinämöinen got the message and mulled it over for only a few seconds before he jabbed a heavy finger right back into the Concierge's chest.

"To quote a great American President, *'I do not negotiate with terrorists.'* "

Technically, this qualified. But it was still pretty witless, even by Väinämöinen's standards. The Concierge shook his head out of pity, and scarcely sung his counter-quote.

"Listen to Green Day, bro.

"Besides, you're Finnish, man."

He waited for Väinämöinen to say something stupid. It was a lot like waiting for a slow computer to come out of sleep mode. His eyes were open, sure, but not exactly online. At long last, it would seem that the old fool was at a loss for words.

"BOOMBAY—"

"Aha!" Väinämöinen raised a last minute finger, halting the victory chant. *"Tyhmäkin käy viisaasta, jos suunsa kiinni pitää."* He paused to let this incubate before translating. *"Even an idiot seems wise if he keeps his mouth shut."*

"Oh, alright, you win! Go ahead and gloat. Knock yourself out."

"Kyllä!" Väinämöinen threw up both arms as if he had just kicked a field goal.

Gloating is nothing more than assaulting another person with a smugly gaze, which is all Väinämöinen really wanted. He leaned forward on his stool and planted one balled fist on his waist while an evil grin peeked through his thick beard. Like a staring competition he had already won, he glared and gloated, even to the point of glowing. The Concierge pushed up his slender shades with a single finger so as to protect his eyes from the radiation. Fortunately, it didn't last for very long. The fire of *schadenfreude* flashed and burned itself out pretty quickly, as it usually does. Steam rolled off Väinämöinen's brow as he relaxed into a self-satisfying victory.

"Ah, that felt good." He exhaled, and stretched out his arms and then motioned to the Barkeep for two pints of ale. "Well, I don't hold grudges, so from here on we're friends. From one friend to another, let me give you a bit of advice: *Myöhäistä itkeä kun on kakat housuissa. There's no use crying when the crap is already in your pants.* You did the best you could in this fast moving economy, but the world is like a moving train: it doesn't slow down for anyone, not even the Gods. The only question is: What are you going to do about it? As far as I can tell, there are only three options. You can whine about it like a big baby or you can get back on that horse, grab your guns and chase down that train like one of those train robbers—breaking the law and maybe even getting yourself killed in the process. That leaves option three, which is to do the right thing and give up. Wherever that train is going isn't any of your business anymore. The only business for a couple of jobless Joes like us is right here. Bring all your loneliness and broken dreams to this bar and bury them in the bottle."

He put a period on his point by pressing his lips against the glass to take a drink.

"Hold on, homie," the Concierge stopped him. He cracked a cool smile at Väinämöinen, raised his glass and quoted Billy Joel's 'Piano Man.'

> ♪ *Yes, we're sharing a drink they call loneliness*
> *But it's better than drinking alone* ♪

Väinämöinen nodded and raised his glass. "To twoliness."

"To twoliness." The Concierge nodded back. The two Gods clinked their glasses and ratified their new alliance with a drink.

At that moment, the tavern door opened and in walked Clarence, Omiokane and Balaam.

"Look alive, Barkeep," Väinämöinen announced. "You are about to report record profits."

The Lapphund was just as excited by their return. She leapt up from her cozy corner and rushed to adopt Omiokane into the family by feverishly licking his hands and nestling her head between his knees. Only Balaam didn't share in the homecoming. He threw his fists to his waist and glowered at the sight of the Concierge, who shrugged it off and raised his glass to greet him.

"What's up, brotha?"

"What's up, brother, indeed!" he said raising his British lilt an octave. "We must say that We—and presumably everyone else in this bar— are entirely disappointed in you, Mr. Concierge, sir. We will grant you that you showed initial promise with your avid cultural inclinations, but your work performance leaves a great deal to be desired. On top of doing a completely inadequate and unacceptable job and getting yourself rightfully fired in the process, we find you here, of all places, drowning your ambitions in booze instead of going back to—"

"Oh, shut up before you drive him and the rest of us crazy," Väinämöinen cut him off and motioned for the Barkeep to bring a round of drinks.

"The man just lost his job; the least you could do is let him keep his mind."

"A likely response from someone who also had great difficulty at keeping that position for very long." Balaam rolled his eyes indignantly. "How hard can it be to keep count of a horde of trifling demons?"

"Oh, I can keep count alright. Right now I'm counting four Gods and one human. One of you is lost, three are homeless and only one of us has a couch for the rest of you to crash on. So I suggest you keep that in mind the next time you decide to start running your mouth."

"How many couches do you have?" the Concierge asked.

"One, and since you just lost your job, it's only right that you have the arm of the couch to cry on. All I ask is that you keep it down while the rest of us try to sleep."

"Sleep where?" Balaam asked.

"On the floor, of course. Don't worry, parts of it are clean."

"I beg your pardon! You're putting Us on the *floor*?" Balaam pointed to himself. "No, no, no... This is unacceptable. We must do something about this."

"Something is being done about it," Clarence butted in. He looked around at all the faces staring at him before he finished. "I'm going to rebuild your temple."

"Splendid!" Balaam shouted. "And what will you do with the rest of these heathens?"

"He means *our* temple—all of us—you troll," Väinämöinen chided, and then leaned over to Clarence. "I'm not trying to rush you, ystäväni, but how long before you wrap this up? I trust my wife hanging around all these old farts, but I'm not so sure about this one." He thumbed over at the Concierge. "She has a thing for dark chocolate. I don't mind giving him my couch for a few nights, but it won't be long before he's giving *me* the couch, if you know what I mean."

"Well, it's going to take some time," Clarence admitted. "First, I have to go through some kind of initiation."

"Well, what are ya waiting for? Go and get initiated. *Nasta lautaan. Do it now.* Chop, chop!"

113

"You think I'm in a hurry to do this? First of all, I don't even know what the H. getting *initiated* means."

"Oh, that. Well, if I'm not mistaken, ystäväni, I think what they do is blindfold you and slit your throat. Well, most of them, anyway. But that's only if you chicken out at the last minute. Tobias' initiation was another matter altogether." Before Clarence could object to yet another Tobias tale, Väinämöinen was already knee deep into it. "Oh, that was a dreadful initiation, nearly killed the guy. They sent him wandering the lands aimlessly, giving him neither a question to answer nor an answer to question. Poor Tobias had to figure out on his own that this was his first test, to measure his endurance. He went back and knocked on the temple door and demanded entry, but they refused to let him inside. This was the second test: perseverance. Tobias waited outside their door for forty days and nights with only rocks and cheese to eat. By the time they answered the door, the poor guy was nothing but skin and bones. But even still they didn't let him in. They sent him back on the journey. This time they told him what he was looking for—*Lohikäärme*."

"Loh— What?"

"Lohikäärme—a 'salmon-snake.' Also known as a dragon. Only this Dragon had seven heads, not one. A scary enough prospect by any estimation, but it gets worse, ystäväni. Once Tobias found Lohikäärme, he was ordered to steal its heart. Now, I know what you're thinking. Why not steal the heart of a lamb or even a lion and pretend it came from Lohikäärme. Ah, but the legend says Lohikäärme's heart is as cold as ice and as hard as iron."

"Wait a minute, wait a minute," Clarence cut him off. "An *iron* heart?"

"Kyllä."

"Like this one?" Clarence fished out of his pocket the iron ball given to him by the celestial Bear and all eyes widened, transfixed by the very sight of it. The Gods huddled around, leaning in for a closer inspection. Clarence looked at their enraptured expression. "What the H. is this?"

The answer came from everyone, in a whisper.

"The Pole Star."

Otherwise known as the North Star and currently located in the Bear constellation. The Pole Star was a big deal in ancient times, almost as big of a deal as the Sun and the Moon, maybe even bigger, depending on who was doing the talking. For instance, after King Solomon built his temple, the God of the Hebrews spoke to him saying, *"I have consecrated this temple, which you have built, by putting my Name there forever. My eyes and my heart will always be there."* In this case, His "eyes" alluded to the Sun and the Moon. His "heart" was none other than the Pole Star.

So it was that with stars in his eyes, Väinämöinen pointed at the iron ball and finally blinked as he spoke.

"And you got that from—" Väinämöinen didn't dare to say it, but he didn't have to. Clarence read his mind and nodded. "Holy Dung, he's alive. Tobias is alive!"

"Tobias?" Clarence exclaimed. "No, I didn't get— What the H. are you talking about? Jesus, I don't even know who Tobias is. I got this from a Bear."

"Did the Bear happen to say if his name was Tobias?"

"You know what? Don't say that name anymore. I'm done with Tobias, okay? All I know is that I met a great big friggin' bear and he swallowed me!"

"Nah, bruh," the Concierge cut in. "If *that* is the Heart of the Pole Star, then it wasn't a Great Bear that swallowed you; it was *Ursa Minor.*"

"Ursa Minor?" Clarence intoned.

"Yeah, like the song." The Concierge threw back his head and hymned a Baptist spiritual.

♪ *When the old chariot comes*
I'm going to leave you
I'm bound for the promised land ♪

"Ursa Minor sang that?" Clarence asked with his face wrenched.

"No, man. Harriet Tubman sang it. To let the slaves know when it was time to break camp. The song is about the North Star—the Pole Star—which is part of Ursa Minor. Damn, dog, you don't even know your own history. That's sad, brotha. Real sad."

"We beg your pardon," Balaam interjected, "but *Ursa Minor* simply means *Little Bear*, which is no more helpful then saying *little*

115

human. What this good man is looking for is a proper name of the aforementioned Ursa, which so happens to be Charles."

"CHARLES?" they all said together.

"Indubitably. Charles Wain, to be precise."

From the Old English *carles wæn,* which meant "the Peasant's Wagon," a reference to the apparent wagon shape of the Big and Little Dipper. Harriet Tubman saw the wagon as a chariot.

"Okay, so why did Charles give this to me?" Clarence asked. "And why did he tell me it was his heart?"

"I just told you, man. The Pole Star is the North Star," the Concierge explained. "It's the only star in our sky that stays fixed, like the center— or heart—of a wagon's wheel. But some call it the Eye of the Sky—an eye that stays awake for thousands of years, overlooking the Earth. It sees and watches everything."

"Very good!" Omiokane exclaimed. Until now he had been completely silent, but this part of the conversation woke him right up. Everyone turned to look, patiently waiting as the sightless sage sat at his stool with his back perfectly vertical while sipping on a glass of beer. Clarence, most of all, waited for this so-called God of Wisdom to say more. After a few soft smacks of his lips, Omiokane finally continued: "Yes, this is very good." He raised his finger to the Barkeep. "Another one, please."

"What the H!" Clarence rolled his eyes. "He's not even listening to us."

"Kyllä, but he still has a point, ystäväni. This *is* very good. When you left here, you said you needed a witness, and now it seems you have it. What more do you want?"

"Well, I'd like to *not* have to be initiated into something I've already been doing for decades. But if I *must* be initiated, it'd be nice to not have to do it with the God who tried to kill me."

"There's no use crying when the crap is already in your pants, ystäväni."

"He dropped that same line on me too," the Concierge whispered to Clarence with a slight nudge.

"Dying is no excuse to not get on with life," Väinämöinen continued. "Last time I saw you, you were off to face the Decans, the most fierce animals of all. As it turns out, you stood up to a Great Bear—"

"Little Bear," the Concierge corrected.

"Charles," Balaam re-corrected.

"You stood up to Little Charles and made it out in one piece. It took courage to walk out that door, so explain to me how you came walking back in as a coward?"

"Let me see, hmmm... I think the part where I was swallowed." Clarence nodded. "Yeah, that was when I became a coward."

"Kyllä. But there's an old Welsh saying: *'You need not speed, you cannot stay, a down-hill wagon on its way.'* "

"What the H. does that even mean?"

"It means if you're already on your way downhill, might as well make it to the bottom so that you can at least look up."

"He's right," the Concierge agreed with a single nod and a shrug.

"My good man, if We may add to this motivational speech," Balaam tactfully inserted. "It is written in Psalms twenty-three, verse four: *'Yea, though I walk through the valley of the shadow of death, I will fear no evil: for thou art with me; thy rod and thy staff they comfort me.'* "

"So you're coming with me?"

"Oh, Heaven's no, I've passed through that dreadful forest once before and found nothing but a horde of mosquitoes looking to make communion on my body and blood. But you still have thy rod and thy staff to comfort you. That should be quite sufficient."

"It's a cane."

"No," Omiokane cut in and set down his beer. "It is your katana. But your opponent believes it is only a cane, which means that you still have the element of surprise to your advantage. As your legal counsel, I ardently suggest that you go now and confront the master. It is time *you* finish what *he* started."

Clarence looked around at the group until his eyes landed on Väinämöinen, who approved with a solemn nod.

"There's another Welsh proverb that you ought to keep in mind, ystäväni: 'No hand that is slow will be true in its blow.' In other words"—he put a firm grip on Clarence's shoulder—"go get 'em."

*

The system of initiation has ancient origins and continues to this day, particularly among secret societies that conscript only those candidates that can be trusted with trade secrets deemed unfit for the laity. To impress the urgency of the responsibilities that new candidates will take on as members of this society, they undergo a rigorous rite of passage. What exactly these initiations entail remains a mystery to outsiders, and understandably so, for candidates who betrayed the confidence invested in them by divulging the group's secrets were, summarily, put to death. Needless to say, Clarence's trepidation about his own initiation was definitely warranted.

He had no problem retracing his steps. All he had to do was look just beyond the vast estate of the retirement home, where he could see the tall totem obelisk still standing with its head and eyes overlooking the grove. He made his way in that direction until he was back at Big Momma's shrine. It still looked more like a doghouse as far as he was concerned. The door was securely shut, and this time he knew better than to go poking his head inside. Instead he reached into his pocket, pulled out the Heart of the Pole Star and decided it would make for a suitable second weapon to be used with his katana. He even ran a sparring scenario through his head.

Ptah would try to activate his combat cyborg limbs with some sort of apparatus operated by a switch. Normally it only takes a second or two to hit said switch, but Ptah had arthritis, so Clarence figured it would take him twice that time. That's when Clarence would strike. He'd hurl the iron ball for Ptah's head, causing him to duck and lose his balance and giving Clarence even more time to swing his katana in a shoveling motion, catching Ptah in the chin, hopefully with only one blow. After that, he'd offer him flowers.

Clarence firmed his grip on the iron ball and rehearsed this scenario several times over in his head as he continued along the path leading into the forest.

Though it would have made for great cinematic moodiness, he set aside the idea of waiting until nightfall and went about the business of entering the grove with the relative comfort of daylight. Fate, however, was not to be outdone, and any security offered by the Sun had been obscured by a grey overcast. The first time he took this route, it was tranquil, enchanting even. This time around, the forest looked forbidding, and the way inside was now overgrown with thick, tangled weeds that clung to his ankles. The forest stirred from animals scurrying in every direction, but they weren't retreating. They were gathering like an army ready to pounce. Even after their swift and sudden movements finally settled, the soughing of the trees persisted, giving off an ominous moan that sounded like a warning to turn back. Clarence couldn't have agreed more.

"Screw this S." he muttered to himself. He took the advice of the trees and made an abrupt U-turn. But he didn't get far. The sight of Big Momma's shrine stopped him in his tracks. He stared at it in disbelief. The door, which had been closed only minutes ago, was now open.

The trees soughed again, now urging him to run. Once again, he was in total agreement and hobbled hastily to get away, but it was more than his bones could take. He lost the grip on his katana, dropped it and crumpled to the ground. As he struggled to get back to his feet, he heard a stirring from inside Big Momma's shrine. The trees rattled even more feverishly, now pleading: *run, run, run!*

"I'm trying!" he shouted, which seemed foolish. The trees weren't listening. But someone else was.

"Who in the world are you talking to?"

The voice rolled with a familiar African accent and came from the shrine. Clarence looked up and saw Ptah, having as much difficulty getting *out* as Clarence had getting *up*. It was now a competition between two old fools, and they both stopped short of cursing from the embarrassment of their predicament. This was not how Clarence imagined their epic battle would kick off.

Ptah won the race, but it took several minutes before the old, arthritic deity muscled his way out of the shrine. When he finally did, he used both hands to brush off his dusty robe *and* his damaged ego. He looked up and saw Clarence still struggling. He proudly made his way towards him. Clarence swallowed hard, realizing that his battle plan was already foiled. He looked in the direction of his stray katana, but it was too late for that now. Ptah was already hovering over him, holding out his chest like a boxer who had knocked out his opponent. For a brief moment, the clouds parted and the Sun showed through. Ptah stole the opportunity to purposely position himself against the rays, adding regal flair to his victory stance.

From Clarence's point of view, the Sun was just a nosy spectator, peeking over Ptah's shoulder to see what was going to happen next. Ptah made his move. Clarence flinched and closed his eyes. In a split second, he imagined the sharp and sudden pinch of a T-square slicing through him. Or perhaps it would be the dull thud of losing consciousness. But neither scenario happened. Clarence opened his eyes again and saw an extended shadowy arm offering to help him to his feet.

"Follow me, boy," Ptah commanded.

"Follow you where?"

"To your initiation."

With no other words exchanged, Ptah was already off, leading the way and leaving Clarence with no chance to ask any more questions, which was wise on his part because Clarence had many. For instance, how did Ptah know that he was here to be initiated?

As Clarence watched him march ahead, he heard the trees still soughing, although now it seemed more like they were laughing. *Run, run, run,* they mocked him, rustling their leaves hysterically. Clarence replied by wagging his walking stick as if it were a middle finger, a gesture that Ptah somehow noticed.

"What are you doing?" he asked defensively. Clarence quickly lowered his cane and conjured up a lie.

"I was... pointing."

"Pointing at what?"

"At the totem back there, with the four faces. What is it?"

"Światowid," Ptah answered, but having no interest in elaborating, he abruptly changed the topic. "Your initiation will take three days."

"Three days?" Clarence exclaimed.

"Yes! And let me tell you now that this isn't elementary school, so you won't be running to the restroom every ten minutes. In fact, you won't be given a restroom break at all. If Nature is calling, now would be the time to answer because once we start the initiation, there will be no interruptions."

"Do I get to eat?"

"No!"

"Drink?"

"Haven't you done enough drinking at the tavern?" Ptah scolded. "You can quench your thirst at the river, but don't overdo it. Like I said, I won't tolerate a wandering bladder or wandering bowels for that matter."

"I'm old and constipated."

"Good. Then we should get through this without any problems. Oh, except for one thing." Ptah raised a finger. "Your katana. You won't need it."

"What?"

Ptah spun around and with surprising swiftness snatched Clarence's cane from his hand. He masterfully spun it around in a full circle so that one end of the stick struck squarely into the center of Clarence's forehead. His eyes crossed into the bridge of his nose and rolled backwards, trying to locate the source of a sharp and sudden pain. The blow was hard enough that it should have split open his skull. He could feel himself falling, like waking up suddenly from a dream—or drifting into one. The blinding light of the Sun began to recede and sent Clarence off into the peace of darkness.

*

Day 1: Clarence's Initiation

Death is silence. Sweet silence. Noise dissipates. Sound recedes into tranquility. Peace embraces the twilight of consciousness as the lights go out, bringing about a darkness that is necessary for sleep. Nothingness.

Like sleep, consciousness is absent at first. No one remembers the time when consciousness first awakened, but when it did it was thoughtless. There was only a primal self-awareness triggered by the instinct for survival.

To eat. To live.

Clarence was alive again, but in another body, one that moved instinctively and indiscriminately through a liquid darkness. Had light found its way down here, in this vast ocean, he would have seen an explosion of primordial colors, all collaged together into Nature's tapestry, but it was just as well that such primitive splendor remained hidden from his eye, for he would have been indifferent to it all. The world was vibration to him and nothing more. The slightest movement rippled through the waters and struck his nerves, triggering a reaction so instinctive that he wasn't sure if it was his decision at all to dart off in the direction of the disturbance. Just as soon as he did, he could feel the source of the movement retreating from him. He was after it, hunting it, abruptly cutting right and left as the prey changed its course, sending a barrage of confusing vibrations, effectively ending the desperate chase with escape.

He aborted his pursuit. He could still feel the vibrations, but they were becoming more distant as the prey continued its swift retreat. Soon he could feel nothing at all. The surrounding darkness was as still and empty as his self-awareness. The feeling of hunger lingered and may have heightened his sensitivity to another disturbance. But this one moved differently, creeping with incredible stealth. The pervasive sensation of hunger turned into the uneasy feeling of being hunted. Fear caused him to move and the waters rippled, sending out vibrations that confirmed his location. The predator struck and found him. Clamped down on him. The pressure was deep and the pain piercing. He struggled against it, but it all ended abruptly with a sharp snap of teeth ripping him in two.

The vibrations stopped and the darkness claimed him once again. Life was over. The paradox of life is that it lives on death.

*

He emerged from a state of absence to a state of existence. He was alive again, though he had no memory of having ever been alive before. This was the first time, after the last first time and however many first times before that. The only connecting thread from one life to the next was the primal hunger and primitive fear—the act of eating and being eaten, a ritual repeated a million times over in many forms and a multitude of bodies. Everything was food and everything needed food. He belonged to a living organism that sustained itself through a ritual self-sacrifice, perpetually eating, reproducing and eating again. Killing without opinion, and being killed without opinion—all to satiate the hunger, and to satisfy the will to live. It was all so binary, this algorithm of survival. But its output was a worthy one: immortality of the species.

He was captured again. Relentless jaws squeezing life away from him, suffocating him. The darkness of consumption and loss of consciousness had returned, sending him back into the void.

*

Awareness re-awakened.

He opened his eyes as a new form. There was always a new form. In one life, he had many legs and in another he had four. Sometimes he had no legs at all. As his forms changed, the world changed. He swam through it, slithered through it, crawled through it, climbed through it and ran through it. Each time he was always in search of food and always searched for as food. Each search always ended the same: silence and rest from the struggle.

And then an awakening.

*

His eyes opened.

He looked up at the sky and watched the silver orb that moved across it, changing its location every night and dwindling in size in the process, as if the sky itself were eating it until it vanished. It remained absent, belonging to a void, then appeared again, as if slowly crawling from the womb of the sky that had eaten it. The silver orb was reborn, and, of course, re-eaten and then reborn again.

*

His eyes opened. This time his mind opened with them.

He watched the silver orb moving across the sky again, but this time he *counted* it. He counted its days and phases, marked them as notches and grouped them according to their patterns. Every day, every week and every month was counted, the Moon's many lives and forms tabulated until, at last, there was no more time for reckoning, for he had reached the end of his days. He died with the Moon that day, slipping into the void on the night it was devoured by the sky. This time, when he died, his bones weren't his only remains. He left behind a Baboon's fibula inscribed with a tally of notches—the advent of numbers.

He reopened his eyes for the first time, *again*. This time, he looked East as he watched the dawn and the Sun rising overhead. His black skin soaked in every ray as the radiant orb lifted itself above the horizon. This light of life was even more blinding than the darkness of death, and its powerful glow stretched across sky and land until it reached the reflective limestone surface of a massive pyramid.

This was only one of many pyramids. Indeed, as the Sun travelled the sky, it looked down on a vast papyrus-colored landscape sprawling with vibrant stone temples.

Looking up at the sky was the man of numbers. The builder. The architect.

*

Day 2: Ptah's Initiation

Clarence awakened and instinctively palmed his head. It ached even more than his bones. Memory had been knocked out of him, and as his eyes panned around the room, he realized he hadn't the faintest idea where he was. It appeared as if he were inside a planetarium. The walls were decorated with dots and lines, which his eyes studied long enough to realize that they were constellations. For a moment, he thought that he was back in high school and that he was peering up at another masterpiece of starchitecture. But this fantasy was chased off by a nearby sound.

He turned to find Ptah hard at work, building what appeared to be a new set of prosthetic limbs. Now it was all coming back to him: Ptah had tried to kill him—*again*. Clarence had no intentions of giving him another chance at murder. He looked around the room for his katana and was surprised to find it waiting for him right at the tips of his fingers.

Ptah labored away on his new limbs, lost in that etheric state that the Japanese famously called *mushin no shin*, which means *the mind without mind*. It describes the state of absence that the master warrior feels during combat. There is no time for thought, only action. Artists also experience this when they have mastered their tools to such a degree that the hands override the mind and go about the task of creation without interference from the discursive brain. So the sudden whack he felt on the back of his head from Clarence's cane came as a rude awakening. Ptah slumped forward from the blow. Before he could turn around he felt the cane clenched just under his chin, squeezing into his neck.

"What in the world are you doing, boy?" Ptah wheezed, but Clarence refused to answer. This was the surprise strategy that Omiokane had advised; only there would be no flower offerings at the end of this battle, if battle were even the word. Two old fools wrestling on the floor had all the stale nostalgia of schoolyard brawls from Clarence's time. That was back when two apish boys settled their juvenile competitive claims by bloodying each other's nose and then became best friends the next week. Of course, it was hard to see how a friendship could possibly follow this Grade A ass whoopin'. Clarence hissed in Ptah's ears as he choked a croak from the old God until finally the struggle ended and Ptah's arms and legs went as limp as his prosthetic limbs.

Clarence didn't relent right away, certain that Ptah was playing possum. But after a few prods for good measure he decided Ptah's inert body was genuine. He pushed the old deity to the side and spent the next fifteen minutes convincing his old bones to get back on their feet.

*

This time it was Ptah's turn to wake up on the floor. When he opened his eyes, he saw Clarence reclining in a chair, waiting for him. Ptah thought to stand and retaliate, but a throbbing head thwarted any intentions of combat.

"That's called arthritis of the *brain*." Clarence laughed. "Doesn't feel so good, does it?"

"What in the world do you think you're doing?" Ptah snapped.

"No idea. But I can tell you what I just did: I just kicked your A." Clarence huffed.

"You struck me from behind."

"A strategy I learned from you."

"So what now, boy?"

"For starts, you're going to stop calling me *boy*."

125

"You'd prefer that I call you by that dreadfully empty name of yours?"

"Yeah, yeah, yeah. Empty names and empty buildings. I heard it all before from you. You know, while you were lying there, knocked the F. out, I was sitting here wondering what do with you. But I think you just gave me the idea I was looking for. I'm going to teach you how to be an architect."

"What?"

"You heard me. Time for *your* initiation... *son*," Clarence cynically intoned. "I'm going to tell you how to build empty buildings. You build buildings for Gods. I build buildings for brands, you know, with the little TM and R symbols floating over their letters like little halos. Oh, you'd be surprised at how much the Gods and Corporations have in common. Gods are personified. Corporations have personhood. Legal, constitutionally protected personhood. You say that when a temple is empty the Gods are still there. Well, guess what? When a building is empty of people, the Corporation is still there. You say our buildings lack a true name. And I say that your temple lacks a brand. See how that works? Now, pay attention, son; I'm going to tell you how the real Gods were made."

 Clarence pulled the chair closer and rocked like a grandfather telling a bedtime story to a grandchild.

"In the beginning there was nothing, only formless emptiness. There was only God, whom architects know as... The Client. The Client is all-powerful, and though certainly not always wise, he is always wealthy. And the Client hovered over the void and said, 'let there be light.' And there was no light. You see, there were no electricians to provide lighting because there was no building. So the Client decided to create a building by hiring an architect. The architect sat down and drafted up the best possible building so that form and function, light and shade, shape and line would converge into life and culture. But the almighty Client shook his head and said, 'no, that won't do.' He told the architect to *remove this, change that, put this over here and wouldn't it be nice if we could cut down costs by not using this?* And the architect said, 'No.' For the sake of civility and culture, creativity must not be compromised. He folded his arms across his chest to stand his ground against the Client. And so the client fired him. Just like that. And after the architect was fired for being too passionate about art, the Client came to me. He asked me if I would cut corners, save costs, increase value and be practical and reasonable. And I said... *'Yes.'* So, you see, in the beginning there were no grand, gilded temples. In the beginning there was only a lovely little box with windows. Finally, the Client said 'let there be light' and the electrician came along and turned on the lights."

"So your Gods™ live in 'little boxes with windows?'" Ptah snarked.

"I guess I said that wrong," Clarence corrected. "Our Gods™ live in big boxes with windows. I live in a little box with windows."

"Serves you right for building boxes."

"This from a guy who built a dog house for Big Momma?"

"Call it what you want, but the point is that I built exactly what I intended. You, on the other hand, must postpone your intent before you can build. I see now why you do not capitalize the A in Architect. It is a passive role, without intent or will."

"Listen—" Clarence tried to object.

"No, no, no. I've heard enough. I get it. You served the will of the Gods™ of the real world. And now you're retired." Ptah grunted as he lifted himself from the floor. "Except... you now have one more building to build."

"How do you know that?"

"Never mind how I know. What you should know is that the Gods of *this* world will not tolerate your casual mediocrity. The Gods™ of your world may have killed your career, but did they also kill your creativity? If so, then you truly are a retired architect. But if ideas still have life in your mind, then I believe you may yet have one last work left in you."

"You don't get it." Clarence rolled his eyes and stood up to leave.

"And that is why I call you boy, boy." Ptah hissed. "You have the body of an old man, but inside you are still a boy; storming off like a child, throwing tantrums like a child and refusing to listen like a child. Is that what you do every time you hear something that disagrees with you?"

"I'm leaving because you don't get it. Buildings are expensive. Where am I going to get the materials and money to do another building?"

"Do you really believe that in this world matter and money mean anything? These things are all in your head."

"My head? I thought this was all in someone else's head."

"Not someone else's," Ptah corrected. "*Everyone else's.*"

Ptah saw Clarence blinking from confusion. He removed his skullcap and pointed to his head.

"Everything you see and all the Gods of this world belong to the collective imagination of every human being. There are *billions* of people in the world, and all these people have their own ideas, their own beliefs and their own Gods. Or, in some cases—*thank God*—they have no Gods. In other words, you and I and everything you see in this world belong to the tangible thoughts of billions of people. We belong to the world of the Mind, Clarence. The most powerful element of human beings is their Mind, and the Gods belong to that power. We are the power of thought, and the real temple of these thoughts is the Mind."

"So... To expand the temple, I have to expand the consciousness of people?"

"No, no, no. People have to do that for themselves. That will take too long, and you and I do not have that kind of time. What I am saying is that you must expand the temple of *your* Mind if you are to expand the temple of the Gods. I will help you do the first task."

"Wait. How did you know that I was brought here to expand the temple?"

"I read your mind." Ptah winked, and Clarence couldn't tell if he were joking or not. "But now I have a question for you: Are you *still* a retired architect?"

Somewhere beneath the surface of Ptah's scholarly stare was a smug smile as he waited for the answer. Clarence shook his head knowingly and conceded.

"No."

"Good. Now I can reveal to you how the Gods were made."

"How the Gods were made?" Clarence intoned incredulously.

"Yes. The Gods did not make the Universe; the Universe made the Gods," Ptah paused to polish his shaven head with his hand and continued in a textured voice. "Thirty-five thousand years ago in the Lebombo

Mountains one of your distant ancestors made the greatest discovery of all—a discovery that would unlock the powers of the Mind and reveal the Gods of the Universe. This discovery was numbers. Your ancestor took a baboon's fibula, and with it he began to count. It doesn't look like much, just a bunch of notches, but from these simple numbers emerged the key to the Universe."

"Why a baboon's fibula?" Clarence asked.

"Because the Baboon is a curious animal, maybe even the most curious of all animals—after humans, of course. Your ancestors were curious about the stars and their movements. They were curious about the Sun. But it was the Moon that sparked their curiosity by teaching them the science of counting through her phases. It was like a hint on how to understand the world around them. It was a hint on how to understand the Gods. Your ancestors made the Baboon a symbol of the Moon and the stars, and they personified this symbol with the name *Djhuti*.

"You see, Clarence," Ptah continued, "the Universe yields to numbers, and numbers yield to the Universe of the Mind. The gift of Mind is what made human beings—an especially slow and weak animal—the most powerful of Nature's many creatures. With the Mind, you are able to see the true spirit of the Universe through the power of numbers. With this power, you are able to shape your reality and to create your world. Tell me, Clarence, when you were a young man, did you know that you would be an architect?"

"Sort of. I was doing buildings as drawings. So I guess I thought I was going to be a painter or something."

"What changed your mind?"

"It's not a practical profession."

"So *then* you chose to be an architect?"

"No. I thought I'd be a about a dozen other things before I fell back on the advice of my guidance counselor and chose architecture."

"Exactly," Ptah smiled. "All those possibilities. You could have become any one of them. That is how it is for numbers. The number 1 is the beginning of all possibilities. The only difference is that instead of becoming only one thing, 1 becomes all things. It became 2 and 3 and 4. It became lines, triangles and squares. It became cubes and spheres. It became space and time. These are all the embodiment of numbers. The Universe is arranged by the perfect power of number. A human being who can think like the Universe can think like a God and create like one."

"But also destroy like one," Clarence countered.

"This is because humans have forgotten that numbers are a philosophy, not a utility. Knowledge without philosophy is just a buffet of information to be consumed without discipline. There are some with high IQs but low character, who treat knowledge as a trophy, and there are others who treat it as a toy. But knowledge is the life of the Mind, Clarence. For your initiation to be successful, you must forget everything that you have been taught about architecture and numbers. You must stop thinking of them as utilities and begin thinking of them as ubiquitous. Numbers are everywhere. You will find them if you look and listen for them."

"Look and *listen* for numbers?" Clarence blinked several times at the crazy coot. "Are you sure it wasn't you who was hit over the head?"

"There is only one way to know for sure."

Ptah reached into his robe and pulled out a ball of unhewn iron, which Clarence immediately recognized. Instinctively, his hand clenched at his pockets, and as he suspected, the Heart of the Pole Star was gone. His eyes, hot with fire, shot upward at Ptah, ready to demand back his property. But the order was already obliged. Within the hair of a second, the ball of iron became a blur before Clarence's eyes. He heard a cracking thud and the lights went out a second time. His body went limp and toppled backwards, returning to the darkness.

Ptah shook his head as he stood up and hovered over Clarence, who was as inert as the ball of iron next to his head.

"Hopefully, that will knock some sense into you," Ptah said as he reached down and reclaimed the ball of iron. "We will conclude your initiation tomorrow."

*

Day 3: Clarence's Re-Initiation

Clarence re-awakened. This time he had no trouble remembering where he was. With clouded eyes, he looked to his right and saw the shaky silhouette of Ptah, leaning back in a chair. He was preoccupied with some task, but Clarence's blurred vision made it hard to tell exactly what. He appeared to be repairing his mechanical arms. Clarence shifted his body for a better view. The floor creaked, alerting Ptah that his initiate was finally awake.

"What did you dream about, Clarence?"

Clarence didn't answer right away. His eyes became distant and pensive as he retreated into his memory to grab the dream-images. At first they were hazy, but the deeper he probed into his mind, the more the images came into focus. Without realizing he began to describe them.

"A tree," he said in a voice as dim and hazy as his vision. "Hundreds of objects hang from the branches. I see myself as a—" He stopped at the next word.

"As what?" Ptah asked.

"A boy. I'm counting millions of pebbles spread out around the base of the tree."

"Did you know that your word 'calculus' means *pebbles*?"

Clarence shook his head no. It seemed like such a stupid question.

"Are you telling me that I was doing calculus in my dream?"

"I am fairly certain *you* just told me that. Now, tell me what do you think your dream was telling you, Clarence?"

"To rebuild the temple with calculus."

"Close. But try again."

"To rebuild it with pebbles."

"Aargh." Ptah stood up with frustration and looked at Clarence with disgust. He reached into his white robe, pulled out the ball of iron and taunted Clarence with it. "How about I knock some sense into you one more time?"

"You are a *maniac*. No, you're a *Klepto*maniac! You stole that from me."

"It is only a ball of iron, Clarence. Can dead matter really be that important to you?"

131

"Yes!"

"And why is that? Is it because you treasure the numbers hidden within it?"

"There are no numbers hidden in it. It's just an iron ball."

"Are you telling me there are no numbers in weight?" Ptah tossed the ball in the air and caught it.

"Just because numbers measure weight doesn't mean that they *are* weight," Clarence argued.

"Very good. Then perhaps you can tell me what numbers *are*?"

"Nothing. They don't exist. They're just ideas. Inventions of the mind."

"And in all your long years, have you not heard the expression *mind over matter*?"

"Heard it and ignored it."

"Perhaps you prefer the expression *matter over mind*?" Ptah laughed rather cynically and suspended the ball of iron over Clarence's head, threatening to let go.

"No, no, no. Okay, okay. Mind over matter. I prefer mind over matter," Clarence conceded in a panic. "Just tell me how to do it."

"I have been trying to tell you. You do it with numbers."

"You want me to move this ball of matter with my mind?" Clarence asked, shielding his face with his arms.

"No. I want you to move it with numbers."

"Right now?"

"No," Ptah laughed. "You will do this when it is time for you to rebuild the temple."

"I can't do that."

"You can, if you try to understand what I have told you."

"No, I mean... I can't. Not without the ball of iron. You have to give it back to me."

Ptah hesitated and looked curiously at the iron ball, then at Clarence.

"This is the Heart of the Pole Star. How did you get this?" he asked, but Clarence stayed silent. "Unless you understand what this really is, it will not help you build the temple."

"It's not for building the temple," Clarence grumbled.

"Then tell me: What do you think it is for?"

It's to prove that you accused me of theft and tried to kill an innocent man! It's to condemn you to death! Of course, there was no way in hell Clarence could confess any of this, and that was what was really killing him. Keeping this secret from the same person who had just shared his knowledge felt like the worst kind of treachery.

"You are stalling, Clarence. How will this iron ball help you?" His voice sounded as if he were growing impatient, but as Clarence looked into his eyes, he suspected that Ptah already knew the answer.

"It's evidence," Clarence vaguely muttered.

"Evidence... of what?"

Clarence hesitated again, but a guilty conscience forced him to spit it out.

"Of my innocence... and your guilt."

Clarence braced himself as he searched Ptah's face, trying to read his reaction, but there was none. Not right away, at least. After a long minute, Ptah held up the ball of iron to his ear and... *smiled.*

"I tried to tell you before but you wouldn't listen," Clarence hastened to add.

"Shhhh, I am listening now. Oh my God, you are right! But you have to know that if you want the Heart of the Pole Star to vouch for you at your trial, you have to learn quickly how to wake it up from its sleep."

"What the H. does that mean?"

"It means exactly what I said. Talk to it and wake it up, Clarence."

"How come when I ask a question, you just can't give a straight answer?"

"Did you not just do the same thing when I asked you about this ball of iron?" Ptah stepped closer to Clarence and dropped the iron ball in his hand, returning it to him. "Why not just give me a straight answer? I think it is because you were afraid that either I would not be ready to hear the answer or that I would not accept it. This is my fear with you as well. That if I tell you the real mystery of numbers, you will refuse it. Therefore, is it not better if I leave you to discover it for yourself?"

"Okay, fine. But do you have to keep hitting me over the head?"

"Yes."

Clarence saw it coming and though he didn't know why, he didn't try to avoid it. Ptah's extra limbs sprung out from behind his back. In one hand was the infamous T-square, which he swung with the mechanical swiftness of a guillotine. It found its mark in the center of Clarence's head. This time, Clarence didn't retreat from the darkness; rather, he stayed his ground and surrendered to it. After three days of dying, he finally understood the real meaning of initiation: It comes from the Greek word τελευτᾶν, meaning *to die* and then to open the eyes again, reawakened.

Chapter 7

Human beings don't believe in intelligent design, but they do believe in *good* design. And if human beings designed the Gods, the Gods are good designs, hence the expression: *God is good.*

This spurious syllogism was how the Gods came to have an intelligent discussion about what exactly *they* believed in, albeit that's putting the case rather mildly. Truth is, the Gods debated this subject fiercely, and there were a few brawls and skirmishes before they finally agreed on the doctrine of *Great Design*. This was inspired in no small part by a rumor that outside the Universe of the Mind was another Universe, where all the symbols and ideas of the Mind were real. In fact, some Gods referred to this beyond as "The Real World," while other Gods simply referred to it as "The Other Side." A rumor had circulated that in the beginning, this Real World was engineered by a Grand Designer, who later took up gardening as a hobby. This Grand Gardener designed, curated and planted an award-winning botanical paradise, popularly known as Eden. Though Eden was easy on the eyes, it did not impress the other Gods as much as the invention of Adam and Eve, both of whom the Gods saw as textbook examples of cutting-edge craftsmanship. Their argument was this:

At some point, perhaps while they were frolicking in a forest, Adam and Eve felt a strange sensation in their lower abdomens and realized that something was amiss. However, because this was their first time experiencing this curious sensation, they had no way of knowing what their bodies were demanding of them. It's hard to imagine the Grand Gardener explaining bowel movements to his new human inventions, so he did what all great designers do: he automated this process. The act of shitting, so crucial to the survival of creatures, happens whether they will it or not. This, the Gods agreed, was Great Design.

Human beings were fruitful and multiplied, exponentially increasing the volume of crap they produced. The Grand Gardener, being also an astute business manager, called a creative team meeting. The task of designing efficient ways of expelling excrement was delegated to the Gods, who inspired the invention of the toilet bowl. Humans like to believe that it was their own ingenuity that solved this problem.

However, when the Gods designed the toilet bowl, they didn't automate it, which means the user had to know how to use it. Here is where the toilet bowl excels. Without doubt or exception, the toilet is the most user-friendly invention introduced to man. There's something about the design of toilets that you just can't get wrong. Even doors don't have it that good, as evident by how often they confuse their users. For instance, Burger King franchises once decaled their doors with signs reading: *You can have it your way and pull, but this door is known to be pretty stubborn.*

With toilets there are no "FLUSH" signs or even red arrows pointing to the flush handle. The user intuitively knows what to do and how to do it. This is truly Great Design.

So it was that Väinämöinen, Concierge of the Gods, nominated the toilet bowl as not only the token of their belief, but also its altar. The decree was signed and ratified and has been the religion of the Gods ever since. But like all religions, over the many years attendance declined, and service to this altar slowed down, mostly due to aging and constipation. But Väinämöinen was a diehard and remained steadfast, duly delivering passionate prayers and sermons every Sunday. His most popular hymn was this:

"O' Lord of the Loo, mighty Restroom Redeemer

Blessed of the Bowels, O' great Colon Cleaner

I beseech thee: grant me these three bountiful boons

A good dump and a fresh rump without which we be doomed

But the third of your most beneficent gifts

Is that all men must squateth when he taketh a shit

Every man, woman and child learns to wipeth his own ass

And all men are embarrassed by the first sign of gas,

It begins with a tremor and a belch in the stomach

Lo, it is a prophecy that an earthquake is coming!

"Excuse me," we say before we blast open the door

And then pray to our Lord that we don't shit on the floor

The bomb drops and it's over, save the lingering fumes

The aftermath from the blast in a public washroom

Awkward? Kyllä, and not a single man is excused

But that, dear disciples, is why this be Good News

All mortals are equal in the eyes of this Lord

Who cares little of rank, class, title or score

From Pope's to Prime Ministers, even President Obama
So, too, the great Lama has lived out this drama
Their shit stinketh too, like the rest of us bums
So let us all salute the savior of man the great God of the Dung!"

"TO THE GOD OF DUNG!" they all cheered. Even the Lapphund howled, which made Väinämöinen explode into laughter and motion the Barkeep for another round.

Balaam was the sole exception. Unable to sit by and listen to such sacrilege, he dismounted his stool to storm out of the tavern. At that precise moment, Clarence came bursting through the door, and with speed his bones hadn't known since his youth, he zipped past his friends and disappeared behind the restroom door.

The Gods duly lowered their heads as a show of respect and privacy for the momentous occasion of acquiring a new convert. A long silence followed, maybe a little too long. But finally, as Väinämöinen prophesied in his sermon, a grunting was heard. A plop and a splash followed and then, finally, *the flush.*

The group erupted into a joyous ovation and stood up as Clarence opened the door and emerged a new man. He raised his walking stick signifying a sure victory, to which the small assembly drummed the bar with their mugs.

"Speech! Speech! Speech!" they shouted in unison. Even the reserved Omiokane had broken character as he joined the rowdy college in clamoring for Clarence to follow up Väinämöinen's impassioned poetry. Clarence patted the air with his hands as a call for silence. As the room lowered to a murmur, he cleared his throat and began.

"I don't buy that ol' antique axiom that all old men are wise," he began. "So I don't have any wise aphorisms to share. Life can't be summed up in a few clever words, no more than it can be lived in a few years, no matter how cleverly we live them."

"Shoot! That sounds like a pretty good aphorism to me," the Concierge interrupted as he pulled out a pen and began writing it down on a bar napkin.

"Shhhh!" Väinämöinen shushed him. "Keep going, you're doing fine, ystäväni!"

"All my adult life, I've been an architect. But it is only now that I have a chance to do true architecture. Of course, I never expected my client to be a great Little Bear. But you know what? I've never been as scared of any client as I am of this one, so you can be sure that I plan to do my best work for him—and for all of you."

The speech, short as it was, ended and was extolled with unanimous applause. Before Clarence knew it, he was hoisted up and wrapped up in a four-arm embrace. As he squirmed for air, he looked down and saw Shiva, sanguine as ever, smiling up at him. After a second loving squeeze, he set Clarence back on his feet and handed him over to Väinämöinen, who presented him with a fresh glass of beer, which Clarence consumed eagerly. He wiped his mouth and raised his mug to make a toast.

"It's been a long time since I've felt this inspired," he cheered. "A toast to Charles—the great Little Bear."

"It's not the Bear that did that to you—it's the *BEER!*" Väinämöinen roared and slapped Clarence on the back, causing him to spill his ale on Balaam's tunic.

"So now that you've poured out your heart all over Us," Balaam said while irritably examining his tunic, "may We ask when you plan to get to work on this little Magnum Opus of yours."

"Not so fast," Omiokane cut in. "First, tell us... Did you complete the initiation?"

"Yes," Clarence answered.

"And so you know *how* to build our temple, Clarence-san?"

Clarence paused and looked around at the group. He answered with a sigh.

"No... Not yet."

"Not yet?" Balaam exclaimed. "So then what was the point of the initiation if that freak in the forest didn't tell you how to build the bloody temple?"

"Ptah adheres to the old ways of initiation, which as far as I know is the only way," Omiokane answered for Clarence.

"And which bloody way is that?"

"The way of Nature. She does not reveal her secrets easily. They must be discovered by one's own efforts, either by studying Nature's symbols or by studying man's, which are copies of hers. Clarence-san will have to think hard about the symbols that were shown to him in his initiation if he is to discover how to build the temple."

"How bloody long will that take?"

"That depends on the intelligence and intuition of our new architect," Omiokane said, then appended after a short pause: "Usually it takes about forty years."

"FORTY YEARS!" everyone exclaimed in unison.

"No, no, no. This is unacceptable." Balaam shook his head. "Look at how old he is. He'll be dead by then."

"Kyllä. For once I agree with the troll," Väinämöinen added. "There should be a faster way. I can't have this many men hanging around my wife for forty years. If I'm not dead by then, for sure I'll be divorced. Someone must know who can just tell this man what he needs to know."

"There is someone who knows," Omiokane answered. "But from what I have observed, I don't think he intends to talk."

Clarence looked at Omiokane, and then at the rest of the group. They all recoiled reflexively. They could feel the silent interrogation underway as Clarence scanned their faces to suss out the tight-lipped traitor among them: Balaam, Väinämöinen, the Concierge, Shiva, the Barkeep... His eyes locked in on the roof of the boy's head, and suddenly it was plain as day.

"You," he whispered.

"He won't answer you," Omiokane said.

"Yeah, I've noticed. I've been up this road before with the little runt. Who is he?"

"Harpocrates, the God of all Mysteries and Secrets and, therefore, the God of Silence. He will not waste words answering questions prematurely or ones that the inquirer can answer on his own."

"He told you this?"

"Of course not."

"Then how do you know?"

"Because Lao Tzu says in **Tao Te Ching** that *'those who know don't say, and those who say don't know.'*"

"So you're telling me that all the answers I needed from the very beginning have been sitting right here behind the bar?" Clarence sighed irritably.

"Kyllä," Väinämöinen agreed and raised his mug. "All of life's answers are in the bottle, ystäväni. That's what my mother told me, wise as she was: 'But be careful,' she warned, 'the more you indulge the answers, the more the answers become a problem.' Perhaps I should have listened to her," he finished while guzzling his beer.

"Oh for Heaven's sake, enough of this waffling and whining." Balaam threw up his hands. "He just told you that it doesn't bloody well matter because whatever it is the boy knows, he's not going to tell us."

"Is there some other God who would? What about the guy you just mentioned?" Clarence turned to Omiokane. "Lau... whatshisname."

"Lao Tzu."

"Maybe we can talk to him. Is he here?"

"Of course he is here. But you can't talk to him."

"Why not?"

"Because he is dead." Omiokane poured a small libation for the dead Lao as a show of respect, but some of it splashed on Balaam.

"Bloody hell!" he protested.

"But just because you cannot talk to him, doesn't mean that he cannot talk to you," Omiokane added, taking another drink.

"Please tell Us that you're not referring to divination," Balaam intoned. "A demon divining a *dead human being* is the very definition of backwards."

"That is exactly what I am talking about," Omiokane answered. "And if someone is willing to be my eyes, I can direct you to where this needs to happen."

"*Hurraa!* Then we're off to the *Other Side* to talk with the dead. Not many Gods get to go there, but if I know anything at all about necromancy"— Väinämöinen stopped to summon the Barkeep for another beer—"it has to be done in an altered state."

*

Clarence, the Concierge, Väinämöinen, Omiokane, Shiva and Balaam marched like a small cavalry up a cobbled street with the Lapphund gleefully trotting at the tail end. The sky was pristine blue, crisp and cloudless. The air, fresh and breezy, was practically sweeping them along, as if it meant to hasten their merry parade. Each person carried two mugs topped with foam and full of beer. Balaam was the only exception, sipping carefully on a glass of wine. Shiva boasted four mugs, one for each hand, which he waved to and fro without spilling a single drop. Never particularly partial to ale, Shiva surrendered his share to Väinämöinen, who had already guzzled his last glass and reached back to claim his third helping from one of Shiva's hands.

"Ystäväni"—he gulped and swabbed foam from his muzzle—"now that we're on the first leg of our little road trip, maybe you can tell us about your initiation."

"Yes, Mister Clarence," Shiva blurted with excitement. "I must hear about this epic battle with Ptah!"

"And please," Balaam curtly added, "try not to belabor trifling details or bore Us with amateur adjectives of glistening sweat and the glare of your opponent's blade and the like. A short and sweet summary will suffice. In fact, just tell Us: Who won the battle, you or the heathen?"

"There was no battle," Clarence answered briefly.

"Delightful story! Quick and to the point, as is always preferred. Most importantly, you turned the other cheek. Well done, ol' chap, well done indeed."

"No battle?" Väinämöinen objected. "Then what were you doing for three days?"

"Getting initiated. There just wasn't a battle before it."

"So the flowers worked!" Omiokane raised an approving finger.

"No, there weren't any flowers either. Somehow he knew I was there to be initiated."

"Well, like the troll said, no sense fussing over petty details," Väinämöinen hastened. "Just tell us how the initiation went."

"I don't think I'm supposed to tell you that."

"Kyllä. I get it. Because if you tell us, then you'd have to kill us!"

"No, then Ptah would have to kill *me*, although... He tried to kill me three times already and I'm still here. To be honest, I'm not even sure I understand how that works anymore. When someone dies in this world, what happens to them?"

"Death here is a mystery, ystäväni. No one knows what it's like where the Gods go when they die. What we do know is who comes to take them."

"Who?"

"Ankou," Väinämöinen said in a mysterious tone. "He is the Shadow of Life, following its every step until the light fades. When it does, that's when Ankou pulls you into the twilight. He is known as the God of Death and the Death of the Gods, although neither of those job titles really matter anymore."

"What do you mean? The God of Death *died*?"

"No, we just don't get a lot of Gods kickin' the bucket these days, so we hardly ever see Ankou around. The poor guy is unemployed, like me and the Concierge. I'd invite him to the tavern, but I'm not sure how I would feel about having a beer with the fellow. Might drink myself to death or something."

"So, if he's unemployed, what's he doing?"

"Last I heard Ankou went from being the Grim Reaper to a Grim Repo."

"You mean... a *Repo-Man*?"

"Kyllä. Part-time, anyways. He picks up shifts here and there. He's a good bounty hunter, from what I hear. When you see a guy like him coming to collect, you don't put up much of a fight, if you know what I'm sayin'."

"So Gods don't kick the bucket too often—but some have?"

"Kyllä."

"And Ankou takes them?"

"He doesn't just take them, ystäväni. He swallows them into the darkness. They pass from memory into the deep underworld of the subconscious, where they are all but forgotten, which, for a God, is just the same as being dead."

"Ah, but nobody is ever truly forgotten," Omiokane cut-in. "No matter how distant it may be, a memory is never completely lost—not even in the underworld."

"But what if someone is *condemned* to death? Are they still taken to the subconscious?"

"You are referring to Ptah?" Omiokane asked.

"Yes," Clarence answered solemnly. "If I'm innocent, he's guilty and will be condemned to death. That's what the great Little Bear told me."

"Charles!" Balaam snapped. "He has a bloody name, for My sake."

"If Charles-san has told you that, then it is so, Clarence-san."

This wasn't what Clarence wanted to hear. His mood shifted, and so did the sky. The Sun shut its eye behind a cluster of clouds that convened into a grey overcast. Without its warm rays, the air became steely and brisk. But it wasn't Clarence's change of heart that warped the weather; rather, they had walked into new territory even more dire than where they came from.

If the City of the Gods was deserted, the ghost town they had now entered was completely desolate. A scourge had swept through this town, killing everything in it and leaving only a long line of empty buildings decaying in plain sight like unburied corpses. If there was any life left in these architectural carcasses, it was that of ghosts, paralyzed and lingering around their vacant bodies with nowhere to go. Clarence noticed a slanted street sign with its letters peeling and faded. It was similar to the one he saw near the temple, with no designation of street or avenue, just a random word.

Gnosis

"What kind of street sign is that?" Clarence pointed.

"Not a street sign—a *word* sign, ystäväni. The Mind is a world of ideas and one way ideas are transferred from one Mind to another is through words. There's a conversation going on somewhere on the Other Side and that word sign means we have just entered someone else's head. We'll have to be careful. There aren't many minds left where the Gods are welcome. We may not be wanted here."

"Shoot, I don't think I even *want* to be wanted here," the Concierge hastily added, looking around as if a sudden terror might lunge out at them at any moment.

Clarence looked around with him and agreed. This was like a walk through a dark alley. Shiva saw the unease in Clarence's eyes and wrapped him into a protective, almost paternal embrace.

"Be of good cheer, Mister Clarence," he advised with his always-affable accent. "Look around you. We are walking through a masterpiece. Form follows function, followed by fatigue and festering. This is the art of destruction in all its monochromatic beauty. As we walk through this grand desolation, we are life juxtaposed against the canvas of death; we are light to this shade. To quote the great Picasso, *'Every act of creation is first an act of destruction.'* Even computers have a delete key," Shiva proudly quipped.

"Wait a second, how would you know that?" Clarence looked at him.

"Because you're talking to the bloke who broke the new concierge's computer," Balaam butted in. "Or did you not notice he was evicted like the rest of us?"

"I didn't *break* it, Mister Balaam. I *destroyed* it." Shiva proudly threw out his chest. "And thereby, I *created* a masterpiece."

"Quit bragging already." Väinämöinen huffed, "Nothing's more embarrassing than an artist still carrying on about his old work. If you want to really impress me get to work on destroying these brain cells."

That meant *give me another beer.* Väinämöinen stuck out his hand and Shiva obliged. Clarence noticed that Shiva was the only God not joining in the drinking.

"You don't drink, Shiva?"

"Certainly not, Mister Clarence. That would be a disaster."

"Would?" Väinämöinen interjected. "It *was* a disaster. Nearly destroyed everything."

"What did you do?" Clarence looked at Shiva.

"No, not Shiva, ystäväni. I'm talking about Sekhmet and the slaughter of the human race!

"This terrible tragedy took place in ancient Egypt, long before there was a retirement home for the Gods. In fact, no one thought that one would ever be needed. The Gods were all good-looking in those days, all except for the Sun, who was old enough to have been the great-great-grandfather of all the Gods—and maybe even older still. In fact, he was so old that he began to be a wee bit late in bringing in the year. Nothing big at first, only a quarter of a day, but after a few years, his tardiness tallied into days and eventually into weeks. Schedules became a scrambled mess. But what really roasted everyone's rumps were the long, hot summer days. Seemed like the Sun was crawling through the days with a cane, and people who worked the day shift were up early every morning and didn't get to go home until late. The people prayed to the Gods about the problem, but the Gods replied, *'Oh you ungrateful lot of babies! Be thankful that you have a Sun circuiting around your pitiful lives at all. Can't you see that the man is tired? You try spending your entire life running in circles and see if you aren't crawling by the end of the day, crying like a bunch of broken babies.'*

"Wise words from the Gods, but what they didn't realize is that the scrambled schedules meant that all the sacred rites and rituals were completely out of whack. People began making offerings to the Gods on the wrong days. Finally, the Gods decided to do something. They counted their coins and pitched in to buy the Sun a grand golden chariot and four stellar steeds to pull him around the Earth. The idea was as genius as it was generous, but sadly the Sun was too senile to know how to ride the thing. He hobbled into the seat, grabbed the reins and the horses zipped him around so quickly that now human beings had the exact opposite problem. Whereas before the day shifts were too long, now they were too short. The workdays were even shorter and people weren't making the money they had become accustomed to.

"The whole thing was now becoming a great big joke, and people went from revering the Sun to ridiculing him, saying that he was too old and senile for the job. Laughing at the elderly is bad enough, but some folks became downright angry and decided it was time to put a stop to the Sun. They called a secret meeting with the Earth and said, *'Listen, we have an idea: You're still relatively young and good-looking, so why don't you switch places with the Sun and give this tired, old man a break? We know it's a tough job, but if things keep going the way they are, there's going to be nothing but chaos for all of us.'*

"Now the Earth was a spoiled princess. She had grown accustomed to being the center of everyone's attention, and as far as she was concerned, the labor pains of bringing in new life every year was work enough, but even she had to admit that the Sun had become something of a slacker—a problem which had to be fixed. But she also knew that the Sun was headstrong and would insist that he was the only one fit to do his job. The only way to get around the Sun's stubborn ego was to trick him.

"The Earth devised an earth-shattering scheme. She seduced the Sun with two words and four syllables that everyone, especially the Sun, loves to hear: *Happy Birthday*! For all anyone knew, maybe it really was his birthday, or maybe it would have been his birthday if the days and years had been as they were supposed to be. Either way, the old senile Sun believed her and put on his best suit for a birthday bash that the Earth put on in his honor. She lured him into the center of a room and presented him with his gift—a rocking chair. The Sun was a bit confused by this, but he wasn't at all suspicious. He thought that new shoes and a cane would have made for a much more practical present, but in those days it was bad manners to complain about a gift, so he graciously accepted and sat down in the chair to take a load off. That was the moment she had waited for. Before he knew it, the Earth was tying his legs and arms with chains too strong for even him to break. Her plan had worked and she began dancing around the Sun, never once taking her hands off the chain. The people celebrated this momentous day with a New Year festival. They created new calendars and began re-scheduling all of their daily plans and activities.

"For a while everyone was happy, except the Sun's favorite daughter, Sekhmet—a fierce and hungry lioness, who, for obvious reasons, hadn't been invited to the party. Hurt by the rejection and the abuse to her father, she went off on her own to drown her sorrows in a local tavern. As you probably guessed, the anger and the ale went straight to her head, and she went on a genocidal killing spree, the worst the world had ever seen. The Earth nearly drowned in the blood.

"The whole time the Sun was still chained to the chair, and he could hear the screams of human beings and felt sorry for them. He came to his senses and realized that maybe the people had been right all along. He was old and tired and the rocking chair was actually quite comfortable. He could get used to it. A good thing it was that he came to his senses because the humans pleaded for him to do something about his daughter before she killed them all. *'Look,'* the Sun said, *'undo my chains and let me keep the rocking chair, and I'll try to reason with her, but I can't guarantee that she'll listen to me. She's always been a bit rebellious, this daughter of mine.'* Human beings petitioned the Earth to undo the chains, but she couldn't hear their prayers over the screams and cries of the people. Their only recourse was to go back to the Gods for help, which meant confessing what they had done.

"The Gods responded with a great big roar of laughter, saying, *'The Sun may be old and senile, but you humans are just plain stupid.'* Harsh words, for sure, but it served them right, and they repented for having made fun of the elderly. Satisfied with their contrition the Gods came up with a solution. *'We can't undo the Earth's chains. If we do, you'll go spinning out of control and lose the heat of the Sun. However, we can reverse it, so that it is the Sun who holds the chains on the Earth.'* The humans agreed to this plan, but the Earth didn't like it one bit. She was big and beautiful, but a little too busty for the chains, which were even tighter than a corset. To add insult to her injury, she was still drowning in the blood of the humans. The humans went back to the Gods and pleaded on her behalf, to which the Gods replied, *'A fitting consequence for her conspiracy against the Sun, but very well. Though we will not free her from the bonds she created, we will restore her happy place in the center.'*

"The Gods created a companion for the Earth—the Moon, which revolved around her beauty. It was a win-win for everyone. Though the Earth enjoyed being the center of affection once more, she still grieved from the oppression of her bonds. But the Gods in all their numeric wisdom knew that this problem would correct itself. The Moon tugs on the Earth's chains giving her a brief reprieve of comfort.

"The Sun, at last, was in a more comfortable position to have a long talk with his daughter, Sekhmet. He convinced her to sober up and go home to her husband, who, we can be sure, had more than a few harsh words for his homicidal wife. But at least the great slaughter of mankind had finally come to an end.

"The Sun happily retired from his former occupation, but it occurred to him that the day would eventually come when the rest of the Gods would become as old as he, and that's how he got the idea of starting up a retirement home for the Gods.

"Ever since that day no one has mocked the Sun—quite the opposite. We salute him at every sunrise as if he were still making his daily errand, even though we know that it is really the Earth spinning and screaming and making her annual dance around him, just as the Moon dances around her. Meanwhile, the Sun smiles as he rocks brightly and blissfully in his brand new rocking chair. The End!"

"That is *not* what happened!" Omiokane objected. "Sekhmet was perfectly sober during her rampage. It was the Sun who purposely got her drunk as a way to make her stop."

"You weren't there to see it, old man."

"Neither were you, *older* man."

"Yeah, but at least I could have seen it if I was. I'm tellin' ya, she was a drunken assassin with no respect for life or limb until the tide of intoxication receded from the dry lands of a sensible mind."

"Poetically put"—Omiokane raised a single finger—"but, nevertheless, your accounting of this tale is in error, and I'd like to see you prove otherwise."

"You'd like to see anything at all, you blind fool!"

"Fine. I would like to *hear* you prove it, and it appears you will get your chance, for we have arrived at our destination. Behold"—Omiokane motioned with his hand—"I give you all… *the Library.*"

A quiet awe washed over the group, or, at least, that was Omiokane's impression of everyone's sudden silence. In reality, disappointment dribbled down from every face as they stared absently at this "big" reveal: a small and squalid shed leaning in one direction, threatening

148

to collapse off its foundation. An overgrowth of weeds sealed off the entrance even to squatters and vagrants. It may have been a public library in its heyday, but now it was nothing but a public restroom, particularly for the Lapphund, who sniffed around, chose some random spot and squatted with her back slanted to make a ripe offering to the God of Dung.

"Just what the place needs—more fertilizer." The Concierge shook his head.

"What's going on?" Omiokane asked. "There should be a House of Knowledge here. Is it here or no?"

"Kyllä." Väinämöinen placed a consoling hand on Omiokane's shoulder. "But it looks more like a House of the Dead, and I'm fairly sure the tenants were all evicted."

"No," Clarence said, "the dead are still here."

"Where?"

"Behind us."

They all turned to the opposite side of the street, and once again their faces collapsed into disappointment. This time the library was there. In fact, the small plaque that read *"Library"* said so, but it wasn't the most inspiring sight for a House of Knowledge. In fact, it was as bland as an abandoned suburban home.

"Maybe we should try another branch," Shiva suggested.

"No time for that now," Omiokane replied and motioned for someone to put out their arm and escort him inside.

They opened the door and walked into a wall of mildew. Each person reflexively shielded their nose as they stepped slowly through a musty antique room. It looked as all libraries did before the computer age: a stale space sprawling with vintage card catalog cabinets and matching shelves loaded with old books, brittled by time. Väinämöinen was right: This was the house of the dead, but the rows of dusty shelves were still very much alive, quietly breathing the living words of the past.

With their noses still guarded, the group looked over the titles. Väinämöinen grabbed the first book he saw, a cover consisting of large type only, which he read aloud.

"The Science of Economics." He opened to a random page and balked at what he saw. "This is a strange way of counting, ystäväni. What kind of numbers are these?"

"The kind that runs the world," Clarence grunted, and then turned his attention to a tightly wedged book at the top of his shelf, which he fished out with his cane. He called out to Omiokane as he sifted through the pages. "I found that book you mentioned—the *Tao Te Ching*. But I don't see anything about architecture in it."

Omiokane replied with a murmur as he wandered around through the darkness of his own eyes. He extended his hands and felt his way through the small maze of shelves until they reached a beam of misty sunlight. He paused as his old, furrowed skin soaked in the warmth, then followed the ray to its source—a window. His hand touched the glass and after a few taps to the right, he located the wall.

Clarence searched through all the shelves looking for Omiokane until finally he found the blind God walking through intervals of light and shadows as he used the wall and the windows to guide his footing. Eventually he stopped when his hands found what they were looking for—a stairwell.

"Are you sure this library has what we need?" Clarence asked.

"I am very sure, Clarence-san. The Library itself *is* a temple. And like all temples, the real treasures are kept away from the eyes of the vulgar. I believe what we need is down here." He pointed down the stairwell.

"What's down there?"

"The closed stacks." He grabbed the rail and made careful steps down.

"It's too dark down there. Can you see anything?" Clarence shouted down the stairs but retracted after hearing the blind God grumble at such a stupid question.

"Just bring the dog," Omiokane yelled, then followed up with a sharp whistle.

Four feet trotted hastily across the room and Clarence saw the Lapphund zip from between a row of shelves and down the stairwell, answering the call. Seconds later all the darkness flashed away, consumed by a blinding glow.

150

"Behold!" Omiokane declared, fond of grandiose announcements. "I give you Sirius—the Dog Star *and* our brightest star of the night."

"But it is still daytime," Clarence said, shielding his eyes from Sirius' blinding glare.

"Not for much longer, so I suggest you get down here and get started."

*

Descending into the darkness of the closed stacks felt like slipping into the subconscious, which may have well been the case. After all, they were not really in a library. This was just someone's memory of that old warehouse of words, where the homeless slept, students crammed and authors stowed away. And these were not real books, but the memory of them. Libraries had vanished and bookstores had closed, but words were still extant in the real world. The Internet was a landfill of wasted words. But the permanency of printed pages was another matter entirely. Like all endangered animals, tactile text was romanticized only after it became evident that it was under the threat of extinction. Suddenly, people relished the feel of a book, even savoring the smell as if it were something the author intended. To touch an old book and open it after having only just found it was the charm of every library.

Omiokane sat down with a dusty grandfather of a book, whose spine was bent and cracked from age. Like an old man who greets a friend from long ago, he sat down and took his time turning the pages. He scanned its surface with his hand, reading not the words but the embossed images. His fingers felt out the ridges of a pole and a cross beam until he had the picture in his head: a scale with a heart in one pan, counter balanced by a feather in the other. This was the scene of a tribunal, a test of a man's heart. Would it be free of the burdens of life or weighed down by them? The answer would come from the Judges, who were illustrated and embossed at the top of the page. Forty-two of them.

How strange, the very sight of the Gods scanning through pages written by men, some of whom would claim that their words were ghostwritten by the Gods. Balaam was reading the "Word of God," though the look on his face suggested he was having difficulty making heads or tails of it. Väinämöinen, who sat apart from the group, looked just as confused with the economics book he was still wrestling with. Shiva had found a book on Western art and was engrossed by the Sistine Chapel, specifically the **Creation of Adam**, where a long-bearded God was stuffed in a skull-shaped shawl. The Concierge, always a connoisseur of culture, wasn't even reading but listening to music from an old Walkman while floating around the room.

Meanwhile, Clarence was looking at the stars. He scanned through a book of constellations, remembering how this had once been his boyhood ritual. With his frail finger, he traced out new paths that linked one star to the next until a new organic constellation emerged. This was more of that B.S. starchitecture. He grew impatient with himself and forcibly closed the book, but his eyes stopped and locked on the back-cover image of a woman—*a nude woman*. But the illustration was strikingly asexual in its rendering. Its style was unmistakably Renaissance and its tone somewhere between mystical and medical. The unclad woman stood against a backdrop of stars, holding the Earth in her right hand. Surrounding her archetypal body was the Zodiac. Below her, in small print, was a caption:

> *I am all that has been and shall be…*
> *And no mortal has lifted my veil*

"Hai!" A rare and unusual outburst from Omiokane snapped Clarence from his trance. He turned his head and saw the old God drilling his finger into a book.

"I told you!" Omiokane said. "It was the Sun who got Sekhmet drunk to stop the killing." Sure enough, the embossed illustration showed the Lion-Goddess drunk and spread out in a purring slumber.

"Wait a minute, you old con." Väinämöinen looked at him incredulously. "The Egyptians didn't have Braille."

"No, but they did have relief carvings, which this book has reproduced flawlessly."

"What kind of book is that?"

"A law book," Omiokane answered, "for dummies."

Clarence looked up and his face dropped.

"A law book *for dummies*?" he repeated and looked around to see if the others had heard this. "My lawyer is reading a law book for dummies. Did anyone else hear this?"

Omiokane cracked into a soft chuckle.

"Oh, I wish I could have seen your face just now, Clarence-san. I am only kidding. This is not a book for dummies; it's a book for the dead—*The Egyptian Book of the Dead*, to be exact. Although, in a way I suppose it is a book for dummies since I have never attended an Egyptian trial before, and from what I can see..." Omiokane paused to re-examine the reproductions with his fingers. "It seems you will stand before the Scale of Truth with your heart being weighed against a single feather."

"My heart?"

"A metaphor," Omiokane assured him. "This ritual is called the Weighing of Words, so you will have to speak from your heart, and the weight of your words must not be heavier than the feather. If they are, you will be found guilty and annihilated."

Clarence swallowed.

"*But*... If your heart is lighter than the feather, then you are innocent and will be absolved of all charges. The prosecution, however, will be promptly terminated."

Clarence palmed his face. "Jesus!"

His choice of words apparently triggered an outburst from Balaam, who slammed his book shut and went on a tirade.

"Who in Our good name was the so-called editor of this monstrosity? King James?!? Who on Earth is this King James and why didn't he at least hire a court janitor to clean up this rubbish? Oh well, it figures. The levels of illiteracy in those days were absolutely abominable. It was impossible to find a decent biographer, and if you did, he confused his artistic license with a license to kill the truth. Add to the equation the protection these hacks got from the writers' guilds—writers' *mafia* would be more accurate—and these so-called wordsmiths were virtually untouchable. Which is fine by Us. Why on Earth anyone would want to touch this trifling tripe is worthy of a good mystery novel. Good riddance."

He bunged the book over his shoulder, barely missing the Concierge who was completely oblivious of the near hit. He was too engrossed in the library's catalog of old music, much of it hip-hop from the tape cassette era, and all of it familiar favorites for him: L.L. Cool J posing in his cool Kangol hat for the album "Bigger and Deffer," Brand Nubian and their debut album "One for All," X-Clan and their seminal sophomore classic "Xodus," every album by the immortal KRS-ONE and, of course, "The Low End Theory" by Tribe Called Quest. His eyes really lit up when he found music by Earth, Wind and Fire. He checked over both shoulders, saw that no one was watching and smuggled them all into his dashiki. In the process a stray fell from the bin, but the Concierge caught it before it hit the ground. He looked at the cover: a woman riding the back of a dragon, howling at the Moon—New Age music!

This was unchartered territory, even for the Concierge. He looked at the cover's title:

Building the Temple Within

New Age sap seeped from the author's name—*Wind Whisperer*. But the booklet inside told a different story:

"Hotep! He' ha! Nawo! Boi kom! Καλή ,ήμερα σου! As-salamu alaykum! Shalamu! Shalom! Greetings and blessings to you in whichever language you use, for we are all one spirit and flesh before the All Seeing Eye of the Celestial River, who goeth by many names but flows through our lives as one nectar. I drinketh from this nectar and my cup runneth over. I am intoxicated to bring my musical debut to you. Like a message in a bottle I believe the Celestial River has carried this message to you, my beloved. Hallelujah! Say it again, with me, please: Hallelujah!

"You hold in your hands 'Building the Temple Within,' which features a body of chants and healing vibrations that will help bring you into the Indigo Light of the Aquarian Age. Listen to the soft whispers and wind chimes and feel the light of love within. Our vibrational journey will begin with a story—my story—of how I came to this world with the mission of bringing this music. As a being of light, I am known as Wind Whisperer. *In the flesh I am called Toby, but my mentor knew me by another name..."*

The last part got the Concierge's attention. He looked up and over at Väinämöinen who was still struggling with adding up the math in the economics book. He tapped Väinämöinen on his shoulder, which made him flail his arms around in a fluster and spin around to find the Concierge holding the cassette booklet in his hand and pointing to the author's mysterious name. Väinämöinen's eyes shot open.

"Holy Dung, he's alive!"

"Not he," the Concierge corrected. *"She."*

154

Väinämöinen looked confused. He turned to the cover and blinked at the image of a woman on the back of a Dragon.

"What's going on?" Clarence asked.

The Concierge answered by hooking the Walkman to a pair of speakers. He hit play and waved for everyone to gather around, including Clarence. They all listened in rapt attention as a woman's voice spoke softly through the speakers, telling the tall tale of Toby.

Otherwise known as... *Tobias.*

Chapter 8

Aiieeooooooooooooooo. Sh-sh-sh-sh. Aiieeooooooooooooooo. Sh-sh-sh-sh.

Aiieeooooooooooooooo. Sh-sh-sh-sh. Aiieeooooooooooooooo. Sh-sh-sh-sh.

Greetings and blessings, my beloved spirits. What you just heard was the wolf's cry, followed by the Sistrum. The first set of vibrations you experienced was made with my voice, and the second set was made with a musical instrument that originated with the Ancient Egyptians. By the combination of these simple sounds alone you should have felt an Indigo Light swelling within you, crystallizing in your pineal gland and emerging as a fragrant rainbow from your crown chakra. This is the power of the Indigo vibration. To be perfectly honest, I am not supposed to tell you this. In fact, I am not even supposed to know what I am about to tell you.

The mysteries of the light belong to an ancient tradition of secrecy, but sadly, in this age of darkness, these secrets have been all but completely lost, and so I was dispatched from the vibrational plane of the Indigo Light to re-learn these secrets and to share them with you—even if it were at the expense of my human life.

Coming into this human life was not easy.

When I first incarnated in this world, I was confused. Confused by the attitudes, the politics, the rules and laws, and the materialism. You see, I was not raised as most are. When born, I was abandoned by my parents to the woods, and like the twins Romulus and Remus, I was suckled by a wolf who adopted me as one of her own. Under the stewardship of my Wolf-Mother, I learned to communicate, as all animals do, by telepathy—this would be a useful skill in channeling my spirit guide. My Wolf-Mother also taught me the wolf's cry, the same one you heard at the beginning of this cassette. I remained with my Wolf-Mother for the formative years of my life. I ran with her through the forest, surviving the many adventures of the wild. I also enjoyed frolicking in lakes and ponds, playing in the light of the Sun and also, of course, baying at the Moon. I was living in Eden, a true paradise. That is, until man arrived.

I remember that day. The air was different. The trees were nervous. Their leaves rustled with anxiety, warning the animals of the forest of what was to come. Even the Full Moon portended the coming disaster. It came as a loud crackle, thick like thunder. The animals retreated to their holes and the birds took to the winds and scattered. I was frightened and looked to my Wolf-Mother for comfort, but she didn't respond. That's when I saw her blood for the first time. She was dying. Shot by a gunman. I tried to save her, but the wounds inflicted by men are fatal. Bleeding and coughing, and with only minutes of life remaining, she decided it was time I knew my true name: W—

"Wait, wait, wait, stop it right there," Clarence ordered. "Are you all listening to this S? We're wasting time. This woman is crazy!"

"Shhhh!"

"Hush it!"

"Stop interrupting, man!"

"You're ruining the story for the rest of us!"

"Mister Clarence, you are being very rude."

"Rewind it, please." Omiokane blew his nose. "To where she tries to save her Wolf-Mother."

I tried to save her, but the wounds inflicted by men are fatal. Bleeding and coughing, and with only minutes of life remaining, she decided it was time I knew my true name: *Wind Whisperer*.

Using telepathy, she shared with me my true history.

Before I came into the world of flesh, I was a light spirit named Wind Whisperer. And my teacher was an ancient light known by all as Thundera. She was and is a kind and patient mentor, who devoted many light years teaching me the skill of breathing, a skill I would later need to live in the world of men. She also taught me how to read their vibrations and how to calm their energies using crystals. These teachings were to prepare me for the time when my spirit light would be embodied by fledgling flesh. I would be reborn among the children of the Earth. This return was all part of my special mission.

Thundera said to me, "You will go to the children of the Earth, you will help usher in the Aquarian Age of the Indigo children. But first you must be initiated in the Secret Temple of the Goddess.

157

Learn their secrets and share them with the world, even if it costs you your earthly life. For the secrets of the temple are guarded under pain of death."

Thundera saw the worry in my eyes, but she had no choice but to continue with my briefing.

"When you are eighteen human years, search out and find the Secret Temple and convince the keeper of the house to accept you as his protégé. Tell him that you are an Indigo child. He will refuse you, but do not give up. You will have the help of a spirit guide, and she will show you the way inside the temple. You will have ten years to absorb their secrets into your memory. Commit nothing to paper, lest you lose the trust of the housekeeper. Remember everything. When you leave the Secret Temple, only then can you transcribe what you have learned. Take it to those who will listen. This will not be an easy mission, but if you complete it faithfully, you will return no longer as a student of our world, but as a teacher."

I, of course, wept. I did not want to come to Earth. I told Thundera that I was not ready, but she smiled softly and told me, "Think of yourself as a treasure hunter searching for a lost gem. Imagine the excitement when you finally find it and the joy you will bring when you share this treasure with the world." "I can't do this alone," I pleaded. "You will not be alone," she said back to me. "I will return to the world in animal form. I will find you and nurse you as my own." Thundera saw how these words soothed me and with only a single nod she told me that the time had come. And came it did.

I was born. From my true form of subtle light I became human. As promised, Thundera found me. She had taken the form of a She-Wolf, and now she lay in my arms, dying at the hands of a He-Human. Her telepathy was fading, leaving her no choice but to speak to me with the wolf-tongue. She whispered in my ear: "Arooo-a-ooo-aooo-aoooo."

Because I know most readers have not the ears for this language, I will translate her poignant words: "My murder is your first lesson in the ways of the world. Humans are cruel beings. Use the vibrations of the Wind and Whispers to convert their cruelty into kindness."

Her eyes blinked, her head had gone limp and just like that, the candle flame flickered out. Thundera was gone.

The hunter emerged from behind the bushes, gripping his thunder-weapon. I could see the dark vibrations of cruelty all around him. I was angry and wanted to slay this foe, but I heard the words of Thundera repeat in my memory: Arooo-a-ooo-aooo-aoooo. Yes, Mother. I will heed your words. I will convert his cruelty into kindness.

I stood up, threw out my arms and threw back my head.

"Aiieeoooooooooooooooo!" I shouted the wolf's cry and shook my knees into a dance—a purification ritual. But the hearts of men are dark, and I could feel his vibrations resisting my chant. I sang louder and danced harder. The trees began to shake. They were no longer nervous. They were helping me, using their energy to purify him. It was working. The hunter dropped his weapon, fell to his knees and wept.

"Wooga. Woo-Wooga," I said to him.

I did not yet know English. But the hunter saw the meaning in my eyes. He nodded his head knowingly and apologized for his crime. He saw that I was still but a child, as vulnerable to the world as my Wolf-Mother was to his weapon. He knew the only way to repay his crime was to adopt me as his child. At that very moment, a soft moonlight parted through the sky and from it boomed the voice of Thundera.

"This is my daughter, in whom I am well pleased."

From that day on, I was given the Earth-name Toby.

My new Earth-Father taught me the tongue-speak of men. As I matured, he also taught me the sinister ways of the world: greed, theft and war. Only when he saw that I was ready did he send me out into this so-called civilization to fulfill my mission. As a parting gift, he gave to me a wolf-cap, taken from the skull of my Wolf-Mother, so that she would always be with me. Overwhelmed by gratitude, I hugged my adopted Earth-Father and went out into the world to fulfill my mission and meet my destiny.

Just as a soldier must have his uniform, a priestess must have her gown—and her weapons. Of course, the "weapons" of the

Indigo Priestess are never for inflicting violence but vibrations. I travelled to and fro, here and there, hither and yonder, collecting crystals of all kinds: amethyst, which is purple in color; blue and rose crystals and citrine quartz. The further I travelled, the more my inventory grew, but one special crystal was still missing, one that would allow me to do astral projection.

"Oooh crystals!" Shiva said. "What will she do with those?"

"Absolutely nothing," Clarence grumped.

"Shhhh!" Omiokane hissed. "She's going somewhere. Listen."

I made it to Herkimer, New York, a small village with brick buildings buttressed one against the other and a population of just over seven thousand. The people of this small settlement knew each other. I was the only stranger among them, and I noticed them noticing me as I walked along their main street. I could hear their murmurs. "Look at this New Age nutcase," they whispered. There I was waltzing around in long hair and a lavender tie-dye dress with lapis lazuli looped around my neck and a small satchel of crystals tied around my waist. I could understand their apprehension. The plain-clothed folk of Herkimer were not accustomed to seeing an Indigo Child moving among them in the flesh. Having been well-instructed by my Earth-Father on the ways of men, I said nothing and kept moving up an isolated road with only the occasional vehicle passing by me. As the drivers passed, they would look at me and shake their heads. My journey, I soon learned, was to be a lonely one.

Finally, I had come upon a small gray abode with a stone entrance in the center. It had the appearance of a flattened temple. But the sign told me it was *Crystals Restaurant*.

A kindly woman with a temple apron tied about her waist welcomed me at the door. I responded in kind with my own greeting.

"Hotep! He' ha! Nawo! Boi kom! Καλή 'ήμερα σου! As-salamu alaykum! Shalamu! Shalom! Greetings and blessings to you in whichever language you use, for we are all one spirit and flesh before the All Seeing Eye of the Celestial River, who goeth by many names but flows through our lives as one nectar. My name is Wind Whisperer, but you may call me by my Earth-name Toby. I have travelled far in search of the Herkimer diamond crystals. Will you take me to where I may find this precious rock or, pray, direct me there?"

She looked at me as if I were crazy. She raised her arm and pointed.

"Across the street, sweetheart," she said. "Would you like something to eat?"

I nodded, took a seat and requested a salad.

While I nourished myself, I saw an old man watching me. His gaze was different than that of the other village folk. He seemed not so much perplexed by my appearance, but suspicious of it. His vibrations felt forbidding, so I finished my salad and left.

Across the way, I ventured through an open field, past a steady row of wood cabins until I came upon a rock landscape. It was the Herkimer Diamond Mines. Excited and relieved, I threw back my head and swung open my arms, allowing the sprawling energy of the rocks to swallow me.

"Aiieeooooooooooooooo!" I gave out the wolf's cry. People looked at me, but I didn't care. I removed a rock hammer from my satchel and went to work.

*

Situated near the Herkimer Diamond Mines is a star temple. It is humble and unassuming to the eye, appearing as a mere lodge to the uninitiated. But to the trained eye it is a true temple for watching the stars and has a small sphere with a great eye for gazing up at the Celestial River.

Of course, with the Herkimer diamond crystal I needed no such contraption. I bow-tied the crystal about my head like a headband, and, as Thundera instructed me, I crossed my legs and nested myself beneath the Celestial River, allowing its energy-nectar to course through me.

Aiieeooooooooooo. Sh-sh-sh-sh. Aiieeooooooooooo. Sh-sh-sh-sh.

Aiieeooooooooooo. Sh-sh-sh-sh. Aiieeooooooooooo. Sh-sh-sh-sh.

I shook the Sistrum with one hand and fondled the Herkimer diamond crystal with the other. The ground receded and the stars approached me, appearing in the form of happy animals: a Lamb, a Bull, a Crab, a Lion, an Eagle, a Scorpion, a Rabbit, a Monkey, a Rat, a Tiger, a Snake, a Horse, a Rooster, a Dog, a Cat, a Hyena, a Pig, a Squirrel, an Elephant, a Jackal, a Zebra, a Gazelle and a Beetle. They danced a friendly circle around me while whistling and singing sweet psalms. It reminded me of the animated movies my Earth-Father used to show me. These starry-eyed celestial creatures were kind and eager to share their many myths. The Pig and the Squirrel were the first to share their story about a bet they made over the sunrise. The bet did not end well for either of them. Gambling is risky, appears to have been the moral. Then came the Dog who told me about how he lost an all-you-can-eat city license during a careless swim at the beach. Always cover your ass was the conclusion of his wise counsel. For hours I listened until the last of their stories had been exhausted. I thanked them and promised to share their wisdom with the world, as per my mission. That's when a seven-headed beast emerged. I asked him his name and he answered: Lohikäärme, the Salmon-Snake. Otherwise known as a Dragon.

"F-f-f-feeeed me," one of his heads demanded. He had a terrible stutter and a bad case of Tourette's, which included erratic head ticking and erotic lip licking.

"Feed you what, brother Dragon?" I asked. He smiled and licked his lips again.

"S-s-s-salad."

"Of course." I nodded.

I took the seven-headed Dragon back to Crystals Restaurant, where he dined on a garden salad. He was vegan. His table manners were impeccable. He looked into my eyes and pledged to me his undying love.

"S-s-s-stay with me," he pleaded with one of his ticking heads.

"I cannot. Not until I finish my mission. I am searching for the—"

"S-s-s-secret Temple."

"The Secret Temple!" I exclaimed with excitement. "You've heard of it? Where can I find it?"

The Dragon answered with gagging convulsions and, after several heaves, spat out an iron ball on the table. It glistened with saliva, like a crystal.

"What is this, brother Dragon?" I asked.

"M-m-m-my heart," he answered and then ticked his head.

"That's so sweet," I said, clasping my hands at my cheek. "But what about the Secret Temple?"

"Y-y-y-yes, I will take you there."

"Thank you. Perhaps you want to take back your heart until I return."

"K-k-k-keep it."

"What shall I do with it?"

"Y-y-y-you will know," he answered, licking his lips. "When the time is right... you will know."

"Of course. Speaking of time. Shall we go now?"

He nodded and we gathered our belongings and made off for the Secret Temple, though it didn't turn out to be the secret I thought it would be. It was a two-story greenish-gray flat-roof home "hiding" in plain sight, with a silver maple tree as its only cover. I began to doubt if he had taken me to the right place, but when I turned to confirm with the Dragon, he was already gone.

Temples are large and grand, but this one was small and unremarkable. The door was made of glass, allowing me to see that no one was inside. The room was completely dark. I pulled on the door but it was locked, so I knocked. After a short wait, an old man appeared. It was the same old man from the restaurant. He must have had an unusually voracious appetite because when he answered the door, he was still eating. His speech was like a dog's bark, and bits of bread and meat shot from his mouth as he told me, rather tersely, that they were closed.

"A true temple is never closed, and the light of knowledge never sleeps," I said back to him. But he just smacked his lips and looked at me.

163

This was a test. I needed only tell him my true identity.

"I am the child of the Indigo Light," I declared.

"What the hell is that supposed to mean?" he barked.

He was agitated. I reached into my satchel, grabbed the amethyst crystal and flagged it around to calm his vibrations. I puckered my lips and blew a soft wind into his face. This helps to soften their energy, like blowing on a hot cup of ginger tea to cool it off. I blew again and he blinked from too much air.

"What the hell are you doing?"

"Calming your energy," I told him.

He moved to close the door on me, but the gust of wind from my lips and my arm stopped him. I don't often use these powers, but I was determined to get inside.

"Have you lost your mind?" he asked me. I had been asked this question before.

"The crystal tied around my head ensures the safety and stability of my brain," I assured him. "And in case you were wondering, the lapis lazuli necklaces help retain my vibration at its optimum equilibrium. There. I have told you more than I tell most people. By declassifying my identity, I may have put us both in danger. Now, please, by the will of the ascended angels, I demand entry."

"I just told you we're closed."

"Impossible. I am here to discover the lost treasure. I am a treasure hunter."

"What on Earth are you blathering about? Does it look like there's a lost treasure in here?"

"Let me take a look inside and I'll tell you."

"We're closed! Unless you're personnel, I can't let you past this door."

"Too late," I said and pointed at my foot lodged between the door.

"Move it or lose it," he ordered.

"Lose it," I elected and dared him to make good on the threat. He slammed the door on my foot.

"Aiieeooooooooooooooo."

That was not an Indigo chant, but a cry of agony. I raised both hands in the air and blew frantically to lower the vibration of the pain, but the aching spell cast on my foot was too strong. His voice, from behind the door, was even stronger.

"Crazy woman, you have enough treasure dangling from your neck and strapped around your skull already, although if you ask me all of it is worthless. But if it's more sticks and stones you're after, go to the Sangertown Square. There may be a shop for New Age nutcases. Happy shopping."

"Shopping? Do I look like I need make-up?" I snapped at him.

"Yes! I'm sure a shopkeeper will be more than happy to sell you some. Don't give up."

Don't give up?

Thundera had used these same words. What did he mean by that? He sounded sarcastic when he said it, but I believed that to have been part of his ruse. Suddenly it hit me, and I felt foolish for not having thought of this from the beginning. The Secret Temple was a Secret *Society*—for *men only*. Sadly, sexism had long since been a convention for these fraternities, but whatever, I was not going to give up. I closed my eyes and channeled my spirit guide.

Channeling a guide is like walking up to a one-way window used in interrogations and knocking. You can't see them, but they can see you. But some say it's like walking up to a *mirror* and knocking, because the true spirit guide is *you*—your higher self. Whatever the metaphor, I knocked and my guide answered in a uncharacteristically deep baritone. She told me she had seen it all and that she agreed with the temple guard. Agreed with him? "Yes," she said. "Don't give up." "But what should I do?" "Do exactly as he said. Go shopping."

I hated shopping. Whenever it was time to dress me in the cloth of the common ruck, my Earth-Father would drag me to an oversized hut called a mall. I hated it then and I hate it now. Just imagine a young woman dressed more like she belonged in the woods or even a psychic fair, marching among a carnival of kids dressed like branded corporate citizens. These logo-lovers never notice each other, but they always notice me. No amount of meditation or energy cleansing could prepare me for the tangled web of reckless and restless vibrations of a mall.

It was a six-hour journey to Sangertown Square. The old man of the temple must have known this. He was testing my fortitude. And since my mission was more important than my objections, I accepted the challenge and deigned a visit to the village mall. Of course, the moment I entered, I attracted attention. My spirit guide had warned me not to wear the wolf-hat. It has cute grey ears at the top, but the brim sticks out as a muzzle with fangs—a warning to these brand-zombies not to cross me. But they missed the message. They always miss the message, especially if it isn't pounded in their heads every five minutes. Okay, okay. My spirit guide is in my ear right now reminding me that underneath their onion-layered cosmetics is a soul trying to find the switch to turn on its own light. I am a light worker, she just reminded me. Exactly. Time to turn on some light. I threw back my head and let out a great howl.

"Aiieeoooooooooooooooo."

Everyone stopped and looked at me. I could hear the murmuring and snickering from a few people. I raised my arms and swayed them. I began circling around, shaking crystal energy at them. But their vibrations were as thick as a stonewall, a sign of their mental density. My guide warned me that this would not work. "If you can't beat them, join them," she said. She was right.

I removed my wolf-hat and tossed it. Then came my necklaces and, sadly, my head crystal. All of it came off, even my clothes. They all gasped as I began to strip down to only my panties. Then I stood there, arms flat at my side, as one of them.

"Brothers and sisters," I began lovingly, "I bring blessings and good tidings from the Other Side. We are a species of light, but here, in this form, we are but mere flesh, just as you see me now. My guide has told me, 'when in Rome, do as the Romans,' and this sad civilization is most certainly Rome."

166

"If it's true that all roads lead to Rome, then it's also true that they lead out of it," Balaam interjected. "Our advice for this gormless gally is to drop everything, including her knickers, and run. Don't bother looking back."

"Shhhh!"

"Don't shush Us. Clarence was right. She's clearly off her trolley, but at least not as much as the Romans—the most abominable people We've ever encountered. And unnecessarily violent, We might add."

"Balaam-san, please go upstairs if you cannot keep quiet. Rewind it again, please."

"My guide has told me, 'when in Rome, do as the Romans,' and this sad civilization is most certainly Rome. Taking her wise counsel, henceforth I will walk among you as one of you. We are, after all, brothers and sisters of the light. Please, will one of you direct me to a shopkeeper who will sell me branded apparel and expensive footwear?"

Sangertown security would later escort me out of the square with all my belongings rudely shoved into my arms. They were, however, kind enough to direct me to a Goodwill store—another six-hour walk.

The good folk of the Goodwill were more accepting and helpful than the lost souls of the local mall. I told an assistant shopkeeper that I wanted to "fit in" and look more "worldly." She nodded and took me around the store, which turned out to be a warehouse of treasures, including several shelves of old books. Next to those, I noticed a few paintings selling for only a dollar each. The shopkeeper told me that they were the work of a retired guidance counselor who used to work at a high school in the area. She then directed me to the other end of the room where racks of clothing hung on display. The clothing, she advised, was a bit "dated," but still more with the times than the wolf hat and witches robe I was wearing. During my guided tour, I noticed a dusty shelf with old music from the '70s, '80s and '90s. I was taken by the cover art, particularly the fashions. Many of the musicians' hair was as long as my own, or it was big and spiked like a porcupine. I asked the shopkeeper if these musicians were animal whisperers. She never answered my question. Instead, she laughed and proceeded to introduce me to a music form called hip-hop. These musicians were all heavily branded in their fashions. One

musician caught my attention. He was wearing expensive footwear, leather jeans and jacket, but more importantly, on his head was an animal totem—a kangaroo cap called a Kangol. To prove that he was the priest of an animal cult, he was accompanied by a panther with a sacred gold necklace wrapped around her neck.

"That is what I want," I said, putting my wolf hat away. I looked at the collection of music and realized it might be of some use. "And I'll take all of this music too."

Two weeks later, I returned to the temple. This time I arrived at sunrise. The door was locked, but I could see the old guard inside. He was still smacking his lips and spitting bits of food. I suppose in two weeks time, I couldn't expect for the old man to have changed his coarse appearance—even if I had.

He sized me up in my baggy denims, my leather jacket, African medallion necklace, Addidas sneakers, sun-spectacles and, of course, the Kangol. Though every inch of me was covered in branded fashion, the look on his face suggested that he wasn't buying it. I swallowed hard as he examined me closely. I couldn't tell what he was thinking. In the end he appeared to be more concerned about the time than about me; after making a passing glance at his watch, he simply walked away.

Perhaps he expected me to leave. If so, he was to be gravely disappointed because I pulled out my newly purchased Walkman, turned on my newly acquired "Walking With a Panther" music and stayed put. This race would not be given to the swift, nor to the strong, but to the one who endures to the end. I waited.

An hour later he returned, looked at his watch and left again.

Another hour passed and he was back. He looked at me, then at his watch. He walked away again, but this time the temple lights turned on. He returned to unlock the door. He opened it only slightly and asked for my name.

I answered in a baritone borrowed from my spirit guide and this time, I gave him a male name: "Tobias."

Suddenly, I remembered the advice of my Dragon brother. I dug into my baggy pants pocket and pulled out the iron crystal.

"And I have this."

I presented him with the Dragon's heart, but he ignored it. He seemed more interested in my face, inspecting it, perhaps for its gender. After a long minute he gave a reluctant nod and stepped aside, allowing me inside. I had to hide my limp as I walked past him. It would take more than two weeks for the injury to my foot to fully heal, but it didn't matter. My excitement was a natural anesthetic for the pain. Besides, I was no longer walking; I was floating. The lost treasure was here, all around me. As always the mystery was obvious once discovered. The treasure was books.

The Secret Temple was a library.

The last library I remembered was from a previous lifetime in Alexandria, Egypt, when I was incarnate on Earth as Theophilus. It was in this confused form that I ordered the closing and destruction of the Alexandrian Temples. The Serapeum was burned to the ground, and with it all public knowledge. This was done to depose paganism and pave the way for Christianity. When I stood in this discreet and humble library, I knew why I had been conscripted for this mission—to balance the karma of my past deeds. Apparently, I alone was dispatched for this sacred duty. I know this because the entire time I stayed within these hallowed halls, not a single soul entered. There was only me. And the guard, of course.

After an entire day of reading, his only words to me were that the library was closing. He advised me to come back the next day two hours later than I had today. That was the library's opening hours. In my faux-baritone voice, I thanked him and departed.

As instructed, I returned the next day two hours after sunrise.

Once again, I was the only visitor. There were no other movements to compete with the sound of my footsteps. The walls were listening to my steps, following them. In some strange way they were guiding them, leading me through a maze of bookshelves to a stairwell, leading downstairs to a goldmine of books. I grabbed the first book I could find and opened to a page with a most peculiar phrase:

"I am all that has been and shall be...
And no mortal has lifted my veil."

My eyes lit up at these words, which belonged to an ancient Goddess. I turned the page for more and found an entry on an ancient cult known as the Gnostics. The founder of one of the cult's sects, Marcus, was blessed with a vision of a Goddess, whom he referred to as Tetrad, a word that, curiously enough, means "Four", but figuratively it also means "Truth." According to Marcus, this Goddess of Truth appeared to him unclothed, revealing to his humble eyes every naked limb of her body. Even more perplexing, sacred letters were written on each limb. I wondered if these were the letters of the Indigo chant.

"Aiieeooooo—" I couldn't help myself. I started the great cry, but quickly stopped when I realized I had blown my own cover. Footsteps were approaching. I quickly closed the book shut and saw that on the back cover was the very image of the Four-Goddess, Tetrad, except her limbs were not inscribed with the sacred letters, but with the signs of the stars—the Zodiac.

The footsteps stopped at the top of the stairwell.

"This is the closed stacks department," the guard called down to me. The tone in his voice suggested that I was not supposed to be here. I must have stumbled upon the temple's secrets. I tucked the book inside my shirt and went back up the stairwell, pretending to be empty-handed. But he was on to me. He grabbed my arm and forced me to show him what I had stolen.

A History of Numbers

He looked at me, then at the book and then back at me. I was sure he would expel me from the temple, but he did not. He nodded his head and motioned for me to take a seat at a table in the open stacks. I obeyed.

This time, I opened the book to the first page. Here I found an ancient painting of Fu Xi and Nu Wa, two sibling heroes from Chinese mythology, whose upper bodies were human and lower bodies dragon-like. In the hand of Fu Xi was a compass, and in the hands of Nu Wa a T-Square and plumb line. With these instruments, the chaos of the world was meted. Opposite of this image was a similar illustration, from the thirteenth century, which showed the Christian God holding a compass to *"inscribe a circle upon the face of the deep."*

The next two pages spread out into an ancient temple carving of the Goddess Seshat, "Counter of the Stars." She was a strange looking Goddess with a bizarre seven-petal plant growing out of her head and a Cheetah's robe wrapped around her elegant body. She was engaged in an even stranger ritual that involved taking one end of a measuring cord and offering the other end to an Egyptian Pharaoh. Together they geometrized—they measured the Earth and created the temples of Egypt.

I turned the page from here and learned that mathematics and geometry came from Egypt and Mesopotamia, and that the Gods of Egypt and Babylon had all been linked to numbers. Men who had mastered the science of number were deemed kindred to the Gods. But as the world entered a new era, such men were regarded as demons, or even rebels. Such was the case of a man wanted by the Romans for the crime of sedition. A "hue and cry" notice calling for this man's arrest read:

WANTED FOR SEDITION AGAINST THE STATE
A dark-skinned man, mature of age, three cubits high, hunchbacked, long nose and connate eyebrows, scanty hair and under-developed beard. They who see him might be affrighted by his appearance. Goes by the name BALAAM THE LAME.

Also known as JESUS.

"What did We tell you?" Balaam blurted again. "Absolutely abominable those barmy barbaric Romans were. They were mean and violent with no hope for salvation. And for the record, it took a bloody resurrection to get out of that country alive."

"Quiet!"

But not just him. There were other men who became Gods by virtue of number. I read about them all, committing their names to memory. It took a month to read the entire book, but when I finished, I went to the guard and told him that it was time.

"Time for what?" he asked, looking genuinely confused.

"It is time that I spoke with Seshat," I said.

"Who the hell is Seshat?"

I opened the book and showed him the picture. Specifically, I pointed to a small cluster of hieroglyphs inscribed above her head.

"Lady of the Books," I translated.

"You mean... a librarian?" he re-translated.

"I mean *the* Librarian," I re-re-translated.

"You're talking to him," he claimed.

"Seshat is a woman."

"And I'm a man."

"I thought you were a guard. Why are you pretending to be Seshat?"

"Why are you pretending to be..." He sized me up and down. "Whatever the hell *this* is?"

My cover was blown. I dropped the book and made a run for it, but he nabbed me and yanked off my sun-spectacles and Kangol, revealing my true identity.

"So you have finally uncovered my true form," I said to him. "Yes, I am the same child of the Indigo Light. I have penetrated the walls of the temple. Tell me, old man, if a woman built this temple, why did you refuse my entry the first time? Speak quickly!"

"Of all the loose marbles that used to roll into this place, you are by far the strangest."

"Why did you pretend to believe that I was a man?"

"Hey"—he threw up his hands defensively—"*you* showed up dressed like one. If that's how you identify, then who am I to question that?"

I studied his face. He was telling the truth.

"So you are the librarian here?" I asked him and he nodded. "So then you are the one who stretched the cord?"

"Stretched the what?"

"Are you the one who measured and designed this temple?"

Before he could answer, I saw on his finger a ring bearing the sign of the compass and the square. He saw me noticing the emblem. Right away, the look in his eyes suggested that *his* cover was also blown. The easiest person to trick is the trickster.

"Are you a student?" he asked, relaxing his body language.

"Yes," I answered.

"Of?"

"Everything."

This answer not only pleased him; it surprised him. He turned, walked away and locked the door. Apparently, the library was now closed. He came back and motioned with his hand for me to sit, then took a seat next to me. He showed me the ring on his finger.

"I received this a long time ago from a man who saw me sitting at a café with a half dozen books around me. He asked me what I was studying and I gave him the same answer you did. That's when he invited me to join a secret society he belonged to."

"Where did they meet?"

"Here," he answered and looked around. "It wasn't a library at that time. It was a temple for our members."

"Where are they?"

"Dead. I'm all that's left. Me and the books they left behind." He swayed his arm to showcase the thousands of old books that surrounded us.

"The architect of this temple... Is he dead too?" I asked.

"Probably. Either that or he's like me: an old man lingering around from the past."

"Like a ghost?"

"More like an anachronism," he said with a soft smile of resignation. He saw in my eyes that I didn't recognize this word, *anachronism,* so he explained it to me. "Anachronism means when something or someone is out of place, because they belong to another time."

"Like me."

"Like us," he nodded.

This brought me to smile.

"You know," he continued, "the architect they hired didn't even know he was building a temple for a secret society. He thought he was building a house. He was young then, so if he's alive, I doubt he even knows that it's now a library. These days libraries are also an anachronism," he said while looking around at the vacancy that surrounded us. "Knowledge is power," he concluded. "But not the kind of power that attracts men."

"What about women?"

"The tradition of the Secret Temple was created by a woman. She made it for the betterment of men."

"Seshat," I said and he nodded.

He kneeled to pick up the book I dropped and opened to the first pages, pointed to Fu Xi and Nu Wa and passed his finger along their dragon tails.

"Seshat believed that knowledge would curb men's aggressive nature. Unfortunately, it only made him more arrogant." He tapped the dragon tails. "The Dragon is a symbol of man's aggressive nature. He is a most fierce creature. It shows in his eyes—the look of the beast, acting without reason, only on the impulse of hunger. But what happens when such eyes see an image of itself in the mirror? When the Dragon turns his appetite towards himself? He cannot eat himself, and this is the first step towards taming the impulse to devour everything. It is the first step towards enlightenment. Hence, the word 'dragon,' which comes from the Greek *derkesthai*, 'to see clearly.'

"The Dragon is first and foremost a form of the Snake," he continued. "When he learns to tame his impulses, he sheds this self-destructive identity, just as a Snake sheds its first skin."

His finger flowed up the illustration of Fu Xi and Nu Wa to where their dragon-bodies morphed into human form. He tapped his finger here.

"When the Dragon has shed his skin, he takes the form of a man—a creature capable of taming his wild nature with reason."

"The tools in their hands?" I asked, pointing to the compass, square and plumb line.

"For building the temple," he answered.

I thought he was referring to the library, but he pointed to the temple at his head and repeated his words.

"For building the temple."

His eyes were strong and piercing as he looked at me. When he finally saw my eyes light up, he bade me to stand and follow him. He led me to the stairwell, but before we descended, he looked back at me.

"You know, I am not supposed to tell you any of this," he said. "The name Seshat means *'Lady of the Books,'* but it also means *'Secret.'*"

"Then why are you telling me?"

"Because you asked," he said, but then paused as if second-guessing his decision. I watched him as he deliberated with himself, then his eyes blinked with a certainty that assured me his verdict was final.

"Voltaire said, *'Judge a man by his questions. Not his answers.'*"

With those words, he hit a light switch. And together we descended into the closed stacks of the temple.

*

The Concierge stopped the player. The Gods looked at each other, exchanging an eye opening silence. When words fail, the eyes pick up the baton of communication, and blinking works as syllables. A single blink means "!" and any number of rapid blinks means "!!!!!!!!!!!" Three blinks means "WTF" and three slow and measured blinks means "OMG." The Gods mostly did the last, except for Sirius, who let out a gaping yawn, entirely unaffected by the news. It took Clarence to break the blinking silence.

"So, basically, I wandered into the head of a New Age nutcase."

"Kyllä." Väinämöinen nodded. "It appears we all did, ystäväni."

"Hai," Omiokane agreed, "but at this very moment, I would surmise that we are in the head of the librarian, not the crazy woman."

"Why do you say that?" Clarence asked.

"Recall the condition of this town and this library, Clarence-san. It is as dilapidated as an old man's memory. The New Age woman may be crazy, but she is, at least, younger. If we stay here too long, we will die here."

"But we're not finished," Clarence objected. "We have to find out more about Seshat. She can help me build the temple."

"Perhaps you were not listening as carefully as you should have, Clarence-san. The librarian said that Seshat's name means Lady of the Books and *Secrets*."

"What the H!" Clarence rolled his eyes. "So you're saying she'll clam up just like the Barkeep. Is there anything in this world that isn't a secret?"

"In Nature's world everything is a secret, Clarence-san."

"But I thought we were in the world of the Mind."

"Hai. And what better key to unlock Nature's secrets than with the Mind?"

"Mister Omiokane is right, Mister Clarence," Shiva cut in. With all four of his arms, he held up the **Creation of Adam** and tapped the empty space where God and Adam fell short of a synaptic contact. "Some clever man is proposing that the shape of this deity's shawl approximates the shape of the brain. He is suggesting that God is a figment of the human imagination. Or," Shiva continued, turning his head to a second book, "perhaps the artist is illustrating the point made in this other book. Listen to this:

'Atum is the Great Mind of the Cosmos. The invisible may only be seen with our thoughts, which are as invisible as the Mind. If you can't see thoughts, how can you expect to see Atum? But if you look with the Eye of the Mind, the thoughts of the Cosmos will appear to you.

'But if you wish to see Atum with mortal eyes then watch the world around you, where the invisible laws of the Great Mind assume a multitude of Forms.' "

"Who wrote that?" Clarence asked.

"Who wants to know?"

Every head turned in the direction of a firm, feminine voice that came from the top of the stairwell and was followed by the sound of slow descending steps. Sirius jumped to her feet at the approaching sound, but her light, which had dimmed from sleepiness, failed to reach the stairwell. Darkness protected the form of the stranger, who stopped at the edge of the shadows. Her eyes glowed iridescently.

"Who are you?" Clarence asked. "Come out so that we can see you."

She agreed. With one paw followed by the other, she stepped into the light. Clarence froze up as a large Cheetah emerged.

"Sekhmet!" Väinämöinen gasped. "Quick! Hide the beer!"

"I am not Sekhmet," she hissed.

With the slow steps of a master hunter, she advanced towards Clarence and stopped when her muzzle was only a breath away from his face. She recognized his scent and sinuously swiveled in a half circle until stopping to offer her backside. She looked back and meowed.

"Would you mind scratching my back again, handsome?"

Again? Clarence blinked absently, but then he remembered. He had heard these words before. His eyes were in a daze as he reached out to satisfy the request. She arched her back approvingly while Clarence scratched. He stopped as she began to stand up on her hind legs and straighten herself. Her fur began to recede into flesh while other parts took on the form and fabric of a spotted robe. Before Clarence knew it, he was staring into the slender back of a tall, hazel-brown Ethiopian woman.

"Don't stop," she purred. "To the right, please. Just below the shoulder blade." To help him, she pulled aside her Cheetah's robe to expose more of her back. "Don't be shy. Really get in there. In fact, why don't you try with your cane?"

In perplexed silence, all the other Gods looked on as Clarence's cane—his katana, his staff of power—had now found its true calling as a back scratcher.

Satisfied, and without so much as a thank you, she returned her Cheetah's robe to its previous position and went back the way she came—up the stairwell. Seconds later, they saw a light burn and glow from the top of the stairs.

"Sirius is tired," she said, returning with a lantern in hand.

The direct light on her face gave Clarence a chance to appraise her identity. She had a seven-petal plant emerging from the roof of her head, identical to what Toby described.

"Now"—she looked around the room—"one of you asked a question."

"I did," Clarence raised his hand, somewhat timidly.

"Oh"—she smiled—"well, you of all people deserve an answer, don't you? What was your question, handsome?"

"I wanted to know the author of this passage. Shiva, read it again."

Shiva nodded and obliged: "*Atum is the Great Mind of the Cosmos—*"

"The writer's name is Hermes Trismegistus," the Cheetah-Goddess cut him off. "He is known as *Thrice-Great* Hermes. However, in Egypt we knew him as Djhuti."

"Are you... *Seshat*?" Clarence asked.

"Yes. I am the Lady of the Books and the Keeper of Secrets."

"Splendid!" Balaam blurted. "Then you can help us find what we are looking for. In addition, you can assign us with library cards so that we can check out our books with the mandatory due dates noted on the back, and then we'll be on our way."

"Hold on just a minute, Mister Balaam," Shiva cut in. "Before we cut to the chase, I am very curious about what Mister Hermes has written here. Madam Seshat could you perhaps explain what it means? For instance, who is this Mister Atum?"

"Atum is the paradox of existence. His name means *to be*, but also *not to be*."

"Oooh, like Mister Shakespeare?" Shiva whispered with wonder.

"Something like that," Seshat equivocated with a bob of her head. "Atum

178

is the Void, which humans consider to be absolute nothingness, but it is, in fact, the source of everything. The Void itself is Mind, which is utterly empty, taking form only in what it imagines. Having no form, no shape, and existing in neither the dimensions of time nor space, it is the pure darkness out of which emerges the primordial light of thought."

"Fascinating..." Shiva's eyes glowed. "And your decrepit library is most exhilarating, Madam Seshat."

"Yes, even if a bit dusty," Balaam wryly added. "Anyway, back to the big question at hand. Can you help us locate a book?"

"What is it that you are searching for?"

"Firstly, this brick-boffin here is pursuing a promising career in architecture." Balaam placed his hand on Clarence's shoulder. "Specifically, he is keen for books on how to build temples. If you could point us in the right direction on this puzzling project that would be most productive, indeed."

"Has he not already found what he is searching for?" Seshat answered, noticing the books they had been looking at.

"Yes, but as you are, no doubt, acutely aware, the titles in your closed stacks are in exceedingly poor condition, so we were wondering if perhaps you could direct us to your more carefully preserved selections, perhaps second or third editions."

"There are no recent books written on building temples. The art of temple building is very ancient and, alas, lost to the modern world. All that survives are fragments written by the ancient priests. The only complete and surviving book on temple design was written by Hermes himself."

"Where do we find him?" Clarence sighed. "Or, at least, where do we find his book?"

"Upstairs. Follow me."

She lead them up the stairwell, with Clarence and the rest of the Gods closely behind. They re-entered the open stacks room and stood among the same titles that Omiokane had dismissed before as pedestrian. Clarence glanced back at the blind God with a look of mild reproof.

"The real treasures are kept away from the eyes of the vulgar, huh?" he

threw the old man's words back at him, with a little salt for good measure.

"He is correct," Seshat defended. "True treasures of knowledge are hidden from the eyes of the vulgar. However"—she paused as they left the library and returned to the open air—"they are usually hidden in plain sight."

She turned to Clarence and pointed to the sky, directing his gaze into the vast dome of the night for his eyes to pan across a sweeping canopy of stars.

"*This* is the Book of Hermes?" Clarence asked, somewhat incredulously.

"Yes." Seshat smiled, then quoted **The Enneads**. "'*We may think of the stars as letters, perpetually being inscribed on the heavens once and for all.*' You'll learn to build our temple with the stars."

"Splendid! Brilliant!" Balaam clapped his hands. "You've proven the inimitable value of librarians and the public library system, for which We are all eternally grateful! Now, with this matter behind us, we can all chivvy along to the local tavern for a victory cele—"

A distant rattling disturbed the air. It was faint, but against a noiseless night, it was still conspicuous enough to break up Balaam's victory speech. They all turned their heads to the approaching sound, which their ears made out as rumbling rocks and old wagon wheels treading through the Earth. Quietly, the Concierge sang cryptically.

♪ *Then the door was open and the wind appeared*
The candles blew and then disappeared
The curtains flew and then he appeared... ♪

"Who appeared?" Clarence asked.

"Ankou," he whispered. "By the way, that was Blue Öyster Cult's song 'Don't Fear the Reaper.'"

"Don't fear the re—" Clarence nearly shouted, but stopped when he heard the wagon getting nearer. "Why is he coming here?" he whispered.

"To collect."

"Collect what... or *who*?" Clarence asked, but his face collapsed when the answer hit him. "Oh S. It's the librarian. He's dying. Ankou is coming for the librarian, right?"

"No," Omiokane interjected. "Ankou is coming for *you*."

180

"Me?!?"

"Hai. I believe..." He hesitated. "You may have missed your trial."

"I missed my tri— When was my trial?"

Omiokane shrunk at the question.

"Today. It slipped my mind. I am sorry, Clarence-san."

"I'm going to kill you." Clarence actually went for his jugular with his katana, but Väinämöinen stopped him.

"No, ystäväni, Ankou has a keen nose for death. You will have to kill your lawyer later. Right now we have to run. *Sillon liikkuu!*" Väinämöinen turned tail to haul ass, but Clarence grabbed him.

"Wait a minute, wait a minute. Let's not overreact. Maybe he just wants to bring me back to the trial."

"I'm afraid your trial has come and gone, ystäväni. Your case is forfeit. Ankou isn't coming for an innocent man. He's coming for a dead man."

"Man alive! Ever since I got here, there's been nothing but Gods trying to eat me or kill me! And how the H. did he find me so quickly?"

Clarence's question was answered with an audible yawn and a whimper from the ground. Everyone looked down and saw Sirius prostrate, struggling to stay awake while flickering like a shorted strobe light.

"Are you kidding me?" Clarence flapped his arms.

"Maybe it's an S.O.S. signal," Omiokane suggested with feeble optimism.

"Okay, you're a terrible lawyer, let's just get that out in the open," Clarence replied. "But you're a God of Wisdom, right? So what should we do?"

Omiokane didn't answer. His eyes were indifferent to the darkness, but his ears, sensitive as ever, twitched twice at the percussion rippling through the air. He nodded as if the disturbance was a voice talking to him, advising him and the others to run, but it was too late for that. Fate had found them. They were all still waiting for an answer from the old God, though they knew what words restlessly waited at the edge of his lips.

"It is too late to do anything, Clarence-san. He's already here."

Chapter 9

They all darted back inside the library, tumbled down the stairs and scattered in the closed stacks—all except for Seshat, who watched quietly as the wagon appeared on the edge of the horizon, pulled by four ebony horses. They slowed their charge as they drew nearer and brought the wagon to a creaking stop. Ankou dropped the reins and emerged as a gangly shadow with a silver-white beard. He made no sounds as he slithered to the wagon's rear.

In his trailer, he carried a strange cargo of small stones, hundreds of them. Seshat, being a true librarian, knew their significance. They embodied souls collected by Ankou from the deceased. The number of stones he grabbed on any given errand was an indication of the number of souls he had come to collect. In this case, Seshat saw him reach in and fetch only one, which he gripped tightly with his left hand. With his right hand, he grabbed his scythe.

Having no concern or quarrel with Seshat, he glided past the librarian, exchanging no words, not even so much as a gesture, while making his way inside the library. He moved as dispassionately as death itself, a dark shadow dissolving into darkness.

*

The closed stacks room was a wide-open space of rigidly arranged shelves, terrifyingly limited in options for five Gods and one old man to hide. The best Clarence could do was clear the books and cram his stiff bones into a small cavity. Several books struck and scattered across the floor. The noise betrayed their location. Worse yet, the fire from Seshat's lantern pointed the way.

"The lantern!" Clarence whispered forcibly. "We forgot to put out the lantern."

The lantern's light coruscated hypnotically, soundlessly. The hush was broken by the sound of the library door opening. They listened for footsteps and floor creaks, but there was no sound. Ankou moved as silently as death itself. He drifted inside and waited. The prey will always leave a trace for the predator. Always. A book fell from the shelf and slapped the floor. His head turned in the direction of the disturbance. It came from down the stairwell. They always leave a trace.

Väinämöinen volunteered to play the hero. He wheezed and grunted as he wrenched free from the tight cavity of the shelves, hustled over to the lantern and extinguished the small flame with a single sharp puff.

His eyes widened with dismay when he realized the light hadn't gone out. A second light was still glowing and fluttering. He looked down. It was Sirius.

Like a light bulb on its last leg, the fatigued light of the Lapphund was flickering at the base of the stairwell as she fought the urge to fall asleep. Väinämöinen darted off for her. It was a brave and noble effort, but futile nonetheless. She watched with her head tilted, confused by his rabid gesticulations commanding her—begging her—to put out her light, or even to just go to sleep. But he only succeeded in eliciting the opposite. Her light shined brighter and her tail wagged as she tried to understand the game he was playing. With no time left, he surrendered.

"You're the only one who can save us now," he whispered. "Get him, girl!"

He turned to run, but Ankou was already there, as steady as the stone in his one hand and his scythe in the other. Face to face, Ankou took a long, penetrating moment to suss out his first prospect and study his fear. Finally, he held out the stone and gauged it as if it were a compass. Whatever the stone told him, its needle pointed some other way. With chilling indifference, Ankou moved on, noiselessly gliding past Väinämöinen to continue his hunt.

Clarence saw the whole thing from between a small sliver of shelf space. He held his breath, trying to withdraw even the faintest noise, but also trying to withhold the chilling realization that he was being hunted by a shadow—a predator impossible to detect by sound.

Clarence's lungs gave out and he heaved an audible exhale. Ankou's acute ears discovered the sound, and his eyes locked in on his target as he swiveled his scythe in Clarence's direction.

Sirius began barking rabidly, shattering his concentration. With her muzzle peeled back and her fangs flashing, she blocked his path. Sirius was serious.

Ankou, on the other hand, was only curious. He peered down at her, looking her over like some sort of specimen in a lab. As he reached down to touch her, she lashed forward and snapped. Her teeth sunk into his fingers and clamped down into a dense dark fog that fumed apart and reconstituted within seconds.

Ankou lost interest and clutched his scythe with the intent to quiet this cacophony with a single slice. Clarence struggled to see what was going on, but they were now beyond his view. He could only hear Sirius' aggravated barking and her electric buzzing, which, to the dismay of everyone, abruptly extinguished. Dense darkness now claimed the room.

As the light of Sirius went out, Clarence's heart sunk from grief, but it also swelled with anger. Violent visions of swift retribution flashed through his mind. Omiokane once advised him to think like a samurai, a ludicrous suggestion then, but entirely relevant now. The samurai's path is fixed and without detour, for its way is that of death.

Clarence's fist tightened on his katana.

He came out of hiding, though the blanket of darkness continued to conceal him. Only his voice could make his location known.

"Here I am."

That was all he needed to say. The rest would take care of itself.

At the sound of his voice, a light came on. He looked down and saw his own shadow stretching across the floor. In his shadow's hand, however, was not his katana, but a scythe. He spun around and found Ankou holding the rekindled lantern and standing behind him.

"There you are," Clarence said, sizing up the shadowy figure, surprising even himself with a sudden spurt of cockiness. "I'm too old for running, too tired and, quite frankly, too busy. I don't care that I missed the trial. I don't need forty-two Judges to tell me what I already know—I'm innocent! And I'm an architect. That's right, you SOB, looks like we're both coming out of retirement. You've got a job to do and so do I. One way or another, I'm building that GD temple. So if you want me, here I am. But know this and know it well: If I gotta die today, I'm taking you with me."

Clarence spat to the side and squatted into a samurai's stance, wielding his katana. His little speech bolstered his self-confidence, but, unfortunately, his arthritis would have the last word, which came out with a groan as his bones buckled. He dropped his katana. Ankou just looked at him. Another curious specimen.

He studied the strange old man for a short while until his curiosity was sated. Then he raised his scythe and reverted back to his resolute machine-like mannerisms, moving and acting with cold ambition. He advanced forward to make his claim on Clarence but was interrupted again, this time by a troll-like British fellow, who, though noticeably perturbed, still displayed impeccable manners.

"I beg your pardon," Balaam interjected as he stepped between them. "First, let Us commend you on your due diligence. You seem to be quite the perfectionist and very dedicated and determined, which can only be applauded. Whomever your employer happens to be, he or she is quite lucky to have you in their employ, and We have no doubts that you have a bright future ahead of you. No doubt, you will move up in what must be a profitable and promising organization. Having said that, this little fish you caught today will, unfortunately, have to be thrown back. You see, just as the ol' chap has informed you, he's *Our* architect and his swan song is reserved, exclusively, for Me and my Father who art in Heaven. And while We are sure you do not wish in any way to disappoint your employer, We can also assure you that the last thing you want to do"—Balaam stepped forward—"is piss off my Father."

The gauntlet was thrown down. From here on, British etiquette was out the window. Balaam raised his fists and jerked his head in one direction to pop his neck before cracking a sinister grin that dared Ankou to make his move.

"You're outnumbered, ol' chap," Balaam sneered. "*Three* against one."

Ankou peered over his shoulder and saw that Balaam was right. Standing with the perfect poise of a master warrior was Shiva with four fists clenched for battle.

"Make your move, Mister Ankou," Shiva quipped. "It is Death versus Total Destruction."

The rest of the cavalry found their courage and came out of hiding. Väinämöinen, and the Concierge joined the other three to enclose Ankou in a circle. Omiokane also took a stand, although he was facing the wrong way.

The God of Death was outmatched, but not for long.

A deity duo donning complex carnival robes suddenly slid down the stairs with amazing acrobatic skill. Simultaneously, they somersaulted in the air and landed in the poise of Shaolin warriors. One arched a jet-black axe over his head while wielding a broad sword at waist level. His partner stood nearby clenching a long javelin that terminated into a hooked spear.

Clarence recoiled as he looked into a pair of white-hot eyes flashing from behind a scowling yellow mask. The second God was just as terrifying in his blue mask that ended with a strange beard shaped like a fish tail.

"Who the H. is this?" Clarence exclaimed.

"Shentu and Yulei," Väinämöinen answered. "Also Gods of Death."

"You forgot to mention them?"

"No, ystäväni," Väinämöinen replied. "I was hoping I would never have to."

Shentu and Yulei moved in tandem, making slow side steps with one leg crossing over the other. Each time, their arms swiveled and stopped, wielding their weapons in a different position. Clarence and the others looked on in terror. Whatever advantage they had in numbers was now lost. Though they still surrounded him, Ankou's ultimate ally, the darkness itself, surrounded them. Ankou looked at his lantern and with a single huff, he put out the lights.

No one could see Ankou's next action, but they heard it. The God of Death slowly reached out his clenched hand and opened it. The stone fell from his palm, plummeted a short distance and struck the ground with a dull, rolling thud that terminated at the tip of Clarence's feet. The compass pointed out its target.

Clarence heard Ankou's scythe slice through the darkness with a sound as sharp as his blade. He screamed. It was an old man's shriek, weak-willed and riddled with terror. But the scythe did not make the sound of dicing through flesh; rather, it clanged from the impact of a second blade intercepting the blow.

A delay followed, as if a strategy was being rethought. The metal whizzed through the air and clashed again. The chinks and clashes came one after the other in quick succession, echoing off the walls. It was enough to awaken a sleeping light, which winked slowly at first, but was soon blinking rapidly. Sirius was alive and awake. Her light, though still a bit jittery, especially as she yawned, allowed Clarence to see that Ankou was engaged in a vicious battle against Shentu and Yulei.

186

They were equally matched, which gave everyone the window they needed to run. Or, at least, it gave the Concierge, Shiva and Balaam the opportunity to run; Clarence, Väinämöinen and Omiokane were only able to manage an old man's retreat, which consisted of making one steady step at a time. They plodded in slow motion across the room and labored up the stairs with feeble grips on the rail. This wasn't an action-packed escape by any estimation. But that didn't matter. The point now was to simply get away.

They made it upstairs and were only seconds away from freedom when a thick smoke smoldered from the stairwell and clouded their view. They fanned the fog with their hands, but much to their dismay, as the smoke cleared, they found Shentu and Yulei blocking their escape. Ankou had been defeated by the duo. Or so they thought.

Shentu looked up and saw a shadow travelling fast across the ceiling. A stone dropped and fell near Clarence's feet as if advising him, *Stay put, I'll get back to you shortly.* The travelling shadow descended like a dark cloud, spun into a tornado and spiked the floor. From the windy pillar emerged Ankou's scythe, which came with a thunderous blow that struck the axe and spear of his foes with a force so strong that the library quaked. The rumbling refused to quit. The trembling toppled the shelves, barricading any retreat in the opposite direction. There was simply no way out. The runners would have to wait and see who would succeed to claim Clarence as their prize.

"Death has an insatiable appetite, ystäväni," Väinämöinen whispered. "And it appears they are fighting over who gets the kill."

It was to be a fight to the death, one that would be decided in a single blow. Shentu and Yulei made theirs: They exchanged weapons by tossing them in the air and reclaiming them mid-somersault. Shentu landed and struck for Ankou's feet while Yulei made a roundhouse slice aimed for his neck. Ankou dodged the blow by dissipating, then reappeared behind them and swept his scythe in a circular motion that felled both their heads. With their bodies still standing, their heads struck the floor and rolled in Clarence's direction, as if hoping to take a last-minute bite at his ankles.

Immediately, Balaam, Shiva, Väinämöinen, Omiokane and the Concierge formed a wall to protect their friend. Ankou, unfazed, advanced forward, gripping his scythe as if promising to sever their heads too.

"Ankou!"

A firm feminine voice called out from outside, arresting Ankou's agenda. As Clarence looked over the shoulders of the headless Death deities, he spotted a scarlet light that flashed through the windows and consumed the room. Ankou threw up his arms to shield his eyes. Shentu and Yulei, despite having no heads, did the same. As the powerful light retreated, Clarence saw the pleasantly plump figure of a winged angel wearing a crimson dress, confidently flaunting her wide, womanly curves.

"Lucifer," he whispered.

"Luci," she corrected, strutting like a mob boss. She walked right up to Ankou, grabbed him by his beard and chastised him with rapid-fire sass: "What the *Hell* are you doing, Ankou? I don't remember putting out any contracts or even circulating a memo for anyone to be whacked— especially not one of my new business associates. I'm trying to run a business here, and you're trying to run it six-feet into the ground. On top of it all, you're killing my brand with this funeral-fashion you've been trying to pull off for Gods know how many millennia. When was the last time you've seen a fashion photographer at a funeral? Never? Exactly. It doesn't work, okay? Black is cool and sexy, but not when you're walking around with kitchen cutlery. Then it's just creepy. And for Heaven's sake trim the beard. You've gone from gothic grungy to morbid and mangy. Think half-shaven, hipster, sleek and sexy in a slender kind of way. When you show up to do your job, people should want to run *to* you, not *from* you. Now go wait by your wagon or something and let the big girl work. I'll deal with you later. I may have to feed you to put some meat on that bone. But first, don't forget to handcuff and take these two fashion felons with you." She wagged her finger at Shentu and Yulei. "Lock them up in an empty closet so that they never dress themselves again."

Ankou obeyed the order and handcuffed Shentu and Yulei before grabbing their heads, tucking them under both arms and escorting the them away.

"You forgot this," Clarence called after him. He kneeled down and picked up the stone that was made for his soul. He was slightly taken aback to discover that it was surprisingly warm.

He tossed the stone to Ankou. As he threw out his hands to catch it, Shentu and Yulei's heads slipped away and rolled across the floor. Ankou scrambled after them, cursing from behind his mangy beard. He secured the heads under his arms again, looked back at Clarence with a scowl and slithered out the door.

Clarence practically deflated his lungs from a single exhale. Relief was not the word. The look on the Concierge's face suggested that the better word was *repent*.

"The Grateful Dead warned you about 'Loose Lucy,' bruh." He chuckled and then sing-cited a verse.

♪ *Don't shake the tree when the fruit ain't ripe* ♪

He stopped to re-asses Luci's *over-ripe* age and changed his tune.

♪ *I need a woman 'bout twice my age...*
I need a woman 'bout twice my height,
Statuesque, raven-dressed, a goddess of the night...
I need a woman 'bout twice my weight...
I need a miracle every day. ♪

"He's right, ystäväni." Väinämöinen shook his head in agreement. "Made a deal with the devil, did ya?"

"Business deal," Luci answered before Clarence could. "Now I know what you're thinking: *same difference*, right? Corporations are the new Satan like Orange is the New Black. I get it, but here's the difference: First of all, I've never had to wear orange and I don't even wear red. My shade is the *cherry* on the icing on the cake, and I want every calorie in that cake to count. I don't want to eat to regret; I want to eat to live, love and lust. That brings me to point number two: We don't want to lock girls up; we want to set them free. And freedom is embracing your self-image, not starving it. I'm not saying that we need to keep feeding the ego, but a woman's ego should expand with her waistline, just like a man's eyes expand with his stomach, and we all know the quickest way to a man's heart, don't we?" She pronged Väinämöinen in the belly three times. He looked at her and melted.

"Will you marry me?" he proposed.

"You're taken." She tapped his nose with her finger, then threw her arm around Clarence. "And so am I." She looked at her new business partner. "Why were they trying to take you, anyway?"

"I missed my trial."

"Oooh, the lawyer thing. Well, I'm going to tell you right now that if you're ever late for a meeting with me, I'll kill you myself. I need you to

189

be on point and on time. Business is money is time is money is business, so be on time, got it? Now what time was your trial?"

Clarence looked back at Omiokane for the answer.

"*He's* your lawyer *and* your time-keeper? Oh God, no. Let me show you a real time-keeper." She escorted them out of the library and called out: "Bezazel, honey, could you come here, please?"

On call, a young Angel ran with heavy footsteps and stopped by her side. Right away, Clarence and the rest of the group noticed there was something *unique* about Bezazel. Though he was standing right there, he didn't seem to be present. His eyes were off in some other world and showed zero affect even as Luci doted on him.

"This is Bezazel," Luci said with a sweet, saccharine voice. "He's my little angel and he's autistic. Bezazel is a special soul with a special ability. He keeps time better than any watch or Watcher. I tried getting him a job as a Watcher because he would absolutely excel at that profession, but they keep ignoring my calls, which is a real problem with typical Gods. They are a tight-knit circle. Nobody gets in, so you can imagine how difficult it is for demons with disabilities. But Bezazel is very gifted and he works with me, helping me with my schedule and all kinds of knick-knacks at the office, and we at Pentagram Plus Enterprises just absolutely adore him. Don't we, Bezazel?"

"Yis!" Bezazel's voice was sharp and spiked so high that it turned his e's into i's.

"Oh, I just love him," Luci melted.

"Nice to meet you, Beza—" Clarence reached out his hand, but Luci smacked it away.

"Oh no, don't do that. He doesn't like to be touched, except by animals. Don't take it personally; it's a sensory thing. Now, when did you say your trial was?"

"Uh, I didn't," Clarence looked back at Omiokane.

"It was when the last Decan went down," Omiokane answered solemnly. He turned and looked westward. "An hour ago, by the looks of it."

"By the *looks* of it?" Luci intoned. "Bezazel, please tell the blind old man what the *real* time is."

190

"BEZAZEL! BEZAZEL! BEZAZEL!" Bezazel began jumping up and down.

"See!" Luci smiled. "This boy is a friggin' genius."

"A genius? All he's doing is shouting his name. What the H. is he talking about?"

"Do you see that star, honey?" Luci pointed to a single star hovering over the crimson West horizon line. "That star is a Decan. They are stars that follow the path of the Sun. The last star that sets after the Sun starts the night hours. But today you have to go back one star—to the star *Bezazel*. My little muffin is a star."

"Go back one star? That is non-sensical." Omiokane huffed.

"Daylight savings time, honey!" Luci huffed back. "You forgot to set your clock back."

"What is that? Some modern invention?" Omiokane snapped.

"Yes," Luci snapped back. "Like modern fashion, which you obviously know nothing about."

"Never mind that," Clarence cut in. "Is there still time for my trial or not?"

"There's still time, honey, but not a whole lot of it. And you'll never make it on foot."

"Can you take me?"

"I'm running a fashion agency, darling, not a travel agency."

"What? I'm your business partner! If I miss the trial, I'll be condemned to death," Clarence exhorted, but Luci looked the other way, demurring. "Luci, if I'm terminated, our contract is terminated. If you don't care, why did you even bother to come here? You might as well have let those guys kill me!"

Ankou looked alive and raised his scythe. Shentu and Yulei raised their cuffed hands to refasten their heads to their shoulders, readying themselves for round two. But before the bell could ring, a thunder roared, and from the sky emerged five Gods excessively robed in pure white.

"Finally, the fashion police," Luci quipped, then looked at Ankou. "You better hope they're not coming for you too."

She and the others watched as the five Gods whisked through the air. Behind them was an exotic chimera with the body of an ox, the face of a three-eyed tiger and a sharp horn growing from its head. White lightning flashed as they landed, striking the Earth with tremendous force. Even on the ground, their white linens fluttered endlessly as if powered by their own wind. The chimera shook his body of the rainwater collected from the clouds and prowled over to Shentu and Yulei, both of whom cowered into an obedient bow.

"There you two are! I've been rooking ewerywhere for you!" The creature scolded. "What the hell is wong with you? I turn my back for one minute and *poof*—you gone! Hunting after the first game you see. Bow you heads in shame!"

Shentu and Yulei did as ordered. Satisfied, the chimera turned to Clarence, who flinched at his blood-shot gaze. But despite the ferocity of his face, the creature was quite courteous.

"My name is Hontu. Prease excuse my overzealous colleagues," Hontu said formally. "It has been a rong time since they have been able to hunt and, I am afraid, their hunger for a kill has clouded their judgment."

Hontu turned to Seshat and directed her attention to the five bearded Gods that accompanied him.

"Prease accept the volunteer assistance of Fuxi, Yandi, Shaobao, Zhuanxu and Huangdi, Gods of the East, South, West, North and Center, as compensation for any damages you may have incurred."

"Good! They can help clean up the mess those two morons made," Seshat snapped. "But what about all the busted book shelves that need to be replaced?"

"In thirty days you will receive a check in the mail—with my aporogies, of course."

"Apology not accepted!" Balaam stepped forward. "We've just been hunted by Ronald McDonald's Yardies and all you have to offer is an *'aporogy'*? Well, *we're sorry* to inform you that your contrived contrition is as unsatisfying as it is inadequate. We've suffered a severe and acute psychological stress from these two yobbos. You'll be hearing from Our lawyer concerning punitive damages." He grabbed Omiokane by the sleeve, pulling him closer. "If I were you, Mr. Hontu, sir, I'd expect to put *two* checks in the mail."

"Actually..." Clarence jumped in front of Balaam. "If you can give me and my companions a ride, we can call it even."

"There are six of you," Hontu replied. "My men only make five."

"And *you* make six," Clarence rebutted. "I'll ride with you."

"Aporogies. But I have to escort Shentu and Yulei back to *Taodu*, our mighty mountain in the East, where they will be duly punished."

Clarence puckered his lips at the prospects of trying to get a creature that was part ox, part tiger and part unicorn to reconsider. He looked at Luci and decided he was better off striking another deal with the Devil. Luci saw the look in his eyes and reflexively looked away.

"C'mon, Luci," he pleaded, but she raised her nose and snubbed him. "Luci, please," he exhorted, but she wrapped her arms under her heavy breasts and stood her ground. He walked up to her and whispered in her ear.

"I need you to fly, baby."

She shifted her head his way, but only slightly. Still, it was enough to see that his words were working. Of course, these weren't exactly *his* words. They were hers. From the *Big Girl's Bible*.

"*Spread your wings and fly for me, baby, full-figured and fertile,*" he recited.

Enraptured by her own poetry, she slowly turned the rest of her body towards him. He had her hooked. All he had to do now was reel her in.

"*Big Girl, Big Girl, spread your wings and flap those curves!*" he continued. "*Get off the ground, come on, baby, you can do it. Flap hard... and fly.*"

The Big Girl's ballad resounded in her head like trumpets on the battlefield, rallying her into service. Three simple and seemingly unassuming letters had sent her imagination skyward: *FLY*.

She saw herself, a scarlet starlet once more, beating her wings and soaring amidst stars and spangles. Cameras flashed and followed her as she flew far and wide before finally floating down like a fairy into the spotlight. A fire ignited in her ember eyes, casting a strong glow across her face.

She straightened her stance and threw her hands on her hips, assuming the poise not of a superman, but of a supermodel.

"Make up!" She clapped her hands, summoning her make-up crew, who zipped in from both sides to powder her nose and touch-up her face, then zipped away leaving her refreshed and regal. She turned to Clarence.

"Are you afraid of heights?"

"Yes," he whimpered.

"Too bad. Hop on these hips and hold on." She patted her backside. "Bezazel loves dogs, so Sirius will fly with him."

Sirius, as if understanding these words, barked and leapt into Bezazel's arms. The boy's wings shot out from behind his shoulders and struck the air until they lifted him and the Lapphund off the ground. Väinämöinen, Omiokane, Balaam, Shiva and the Concierge followed suit by walking into the embrace of Fuxi, Yandi, Shaobao, Zhuanxu and Huangdi. Like a hundred silk scarves beating in the wind, the robes of the five Cardinal Gods began to flap and wave, vigorously fluttering against a blustering current that lifted them and their passengers high into the air.

Clarence blocked the small hurricane with his arm as he struggled to locate Seshat through all of the whirling debris. She felt his eyes searching for him and stepped through the wall of dusty mist to wave.

"When you're ready to build another temple, come see me," she yelled.

Another temple? Clarence thought and then realized she was referring to the library. He looked at the leaning hovel and realized that this had been his handiwork from long ago. He was the architect.

"It will be just like old times in the days of the Pharaohs." She smiled. Clarence nodded, smiled back and watched as she disappeared inside the library.

Still shielding his eyes, he turned back to find Luci, but she was gone. Before he had a chance to panic, he felt a hand reach down, latch hold of his walking stick and whisk him upward. Instinctively, he threw the cane around Luci's wide waist and put a chokehold on her stomach. His cane became his handlebars. He tightened his frail fingers around them and watched as the ground rapidly receded from his feet.

Ankou witnessed it all from below, but with little interest. Silently, his shadowy form slithered to his trailer and returned the lone stone for Clarence's soul to his stash of hundreds. He glided to the front of his wagon and, with a surprising show of affection, rubbed his hand across the long faces of his horses, which appeared to be quite fond of him. He took his seat and the reins and prompted his four steeds to gallop off, leaving only a trail of dust.

Clarence was no thrill-seeker, not even a thrill-*peeker*. The sight of the world swiftly scaling down was too much for him, and he wrenched his eyes shut, wondering how he was going to get through this. *Best to keep my eyes closed*, he decided, but the winds overruled him and filled his ears with a deafening whoosh, urging him to look again and see the world from the view of the Gods. *You don't want to miss this,* they whispered. Slowly, reluctantly, Clarence pried open his eyes and dared a second look down.

The winds were right. From Heavens' view, he saw an organic grid of glowing synapses that could have easily been mistaken for a circuit board or a sprawling, sparkling cityscape as seen from space. But this wasn't a view of the Earth; it was a view of the Mind, and each amber synapse was like a star, bound to its neighbor and streaming thoughts of attraction across great darkness and vast distances.

Rapid flashes of electric activity exploded and faded like a festival of fireworks, fizzling into a colorful spectrum of consciousness. Perhaps he was witnessing new thoughts being born, buzzing with exciting novelty. But even the most novel of thoughts age and mature, and are weathered by time. New knowledge becomes old knowledge. They become unremembered ruins, where forgotten wisdom lingers.

This was the mental landscape of the librarian. Clarence thought back to the desolate strip that he and his companions passed through and were now leaving behind. Omiokane was right: The old librarian was in his final hours of twilight.

There was a strange stasis in the air and many areas where the light of the mind was burning out as if deforested. *What was it?* Clarence wondered. What would cause ideas to die? Had imagination itself atrophied? Was creativity collapsing under the weight of too much logic and symmetry? Why was imagination derided as if the power to dream were only a dream, as if everything engineered hadn't once began as a dream? To dream and deduce, to create and calculate, to invent and imagine—that was the power of the Great Mind that was all minds. Whether God invented the mind or the other way around, regardless of who created whom, the two were compatible, like the human mind and the grand Universe, which is comprehensible precisely because it is compatible to our thoughts—compatibility made possible by numbers.

Clarence tightened his grip as they encountered a bit of turbulence. Suddenly, the skies had turned against them. The geography became violently active with quakes and eruptions, sweeping winds and crashing torrents. Luci's big bones held strong against the currents. Added comfort came from his peripheral, where he saw Shiva using Shaobao as a hang glider and enjoying every second of their dare-devilling. He spotted Clarence and threw out a thumbs up, assuring him that a crash landing was unlikely, but even if it weren't, how cool would it be to scream helplessly while being sucked into the cycle of swift destruction and eventual renewal.

"Flight attendants, prepare for our descent," Luci called out. "Passengers hold on tight. We're going to make this a fast one."

For a moment Clarence thought they were falling, but it was a controlled drop, like skydiving. To get his mind off the sight of the ground rushing towards him, he thought about numbers. Luci must have read his thoughts because she proceeded to do a countdown.

"10...9...8...7...6...5...4...3...BRACE FOR IMPACT! BRACE FOR IMPACT!"

Chapter 10

♪ Feels like flying
I close my eyes, oh God I think I'm falling
Out of the sky, I close my eyes
Heaven help me ♪

The Concierge bopped and sang Madonna's 'Like a Prayer' while Clarence lay on the ground as a big ball of sweat, gripping his heart.

"Sorry, honey," Luci wheezed as she tried to control her laughter. "I couldn't help myself."

The rest of the gang chuckled with her, including Shiva, who walked over with a broad, affectionate smile and extended four arms of assistance. Clarence reached up to grab the helping hands. Once he was on his feet again, Shiva handed him back his staff of power, which Clarence definitely needed as he couldn't stop his knees from jittering. He turned to walk away and nearly tripped over Väinämöinen who was still on the ground, passed out. The Concierge hovered over him, fanning him for air.

"Judging from the look of the ol' chap, it would seem he's already had more than his share of fresh air, wouldn't you say?" Balaam suggested.

"How's he going to get home?" Clarence asked, and the Concierge answered with a song:

♪ Whoa, I know you feel like you wanna die
But try pretending that I'm your guy
And don't worry, I'll take him home ♪

"The Drifters," the Concierge noted with a snap and smile, then pointed. "Your trial takes place over there."

Clarence looked up at a larger than life statue of Lady Justice. She was blindfolded, and in one hand she clenched a sword, in the other a scale. Clarence took a deep breath and began to stumble towards her feet.

"You're forgetting something, Mister Clarence," Shiva said and held out his hand. Clarence looked down and saw in Shiva's palm the Heart of the Pole Star. "It fell from your pocket while you 'crash' landed." He chuckled.

Clarence nodded silently to say thank you. He grabbed the evidence of his innocence with both hands and hobbled over to Lady Justice. He stood there for a moment, looking up at the silent dignity of the stone structure. It was carved and chiseled with such animate detail that it appeared to be alive. Indeed, for a moment, he could have sworn that he saw her right arm rise up and lift the corner of the blindfold, so as to offer him a wink. His face dropped and he quickly turned around to confirm with the group what he saw, but the look on their faces told him that it was an illusion. He looked again and Lady Justice was back in her original state, demanding with all her monumental weight that the law be fulfilled. Clarence felt the demand ripple through his body, causing his legs to give out. He fell to his knees and pleaded.

"My Lady," he began, almost weeping. "I come before you broken and humble. I have travelled far to carry out a great mission that has been assigned to me. It is my wish to fulfill this mission, but there has been a misunderstanding which keeps me from my holy duty, and this is why I am kneeling before you today as the old man that I am, with acute arthritis and not many years left to me. Unknowingly, I have broken the law of this land and was accused by a God who knew not that I knew not what I was doing. I have evidence of my innocence, My Lady." Clarence held the Pole Star in his trembling hand. "It was given to me by Charles, a great Little Bear, who ate me and scared me, and now I'm confused, My Lady, because my accuser isn't that bad of a guy. He's a bit aggressive, but deep down he's crying out like me for help because he's retired and he's lost his purpose, but does that mean he has to lose his life?"

Clarence sobbed almost uncontrollably, until a gentle hand extended and touched his shoulder, assuaging his pains. He rubbed his sleeve across his eyes, almost too ashamed to look up, but a hand cupped him under the chin, bidding him to lift his head and open his eyes. The view was a bit fuzzy, but through his tears he saw Luci.

"Get up, get up!" she whispered hastily, looking over her shoulder to see who was watching. "You're ruining your own image and killing my brand with this crazy talk. This is just a statue, honey! The door is right there—at the base of the statue."

She helped Clarence to his feet and gave him a hankie to blow his nose.

"Make up!" She clapped twice and this time her assistants flocked to Clarence to powder his nose and touch up his face. Then they dashed off leaving the old man looking as good as new.

"Don't. Screw. This. Up!" Luci ordered and, like a true lady, opened the door for him.

As Clarence started to move, he felt a tug on his arm. He looked back and saw Omiokane.

"When we get down there, perhaps it would be wise to let your lawyer do the talking."

"We're going down *there*?" Clarence hesitated while peering through the doorway and frowning at the abject darkness that awaited them.

"Hai. We are." Omiokane hooked Clarence by the arm. "And who better than a blind man to lead you into the underworld?"

Wise words, perhaps, though not exactly consoling. But it was too late for that. The way was set and, with a hard swallow, Clarence followed Omiokane to the edge of darkness.

The moment they stepped into the abyss a deep, harrowing gong sounded. It was more than just for effect. Like a pond rippling its reflection of the moonlight, the low tone created visible vibrations in the air. Light broke into thousands of small particles and danced before dissolving back into the darkness. The gong sounded again, cuing the light to reappear, to ripple and to dance. Clarence stood in rapt fascination, as did Omiokane, who, for the first time in ages, could *see*.

Another gong brought on more dancing light. Omiokane's sharp ears could hear the sound splintering into overtones before settling into silence. The gong sounded once more, this time shimmering into chaotic patterns of pink lavender. Once again the reverberations decomposed into tiny wavelets that eventually ceased vibrating, leaving only what appeared to be cherry blossoms gently drifting in free space. Omiokane waited for a fifth gong, but it never came. With his rediscovered sight, he peered closely as the ripples came to a rest and a lake of air reflected the dark fractal limbs of a Sakura tree rooted on a small mound rising from a vast plain.

The Sakura tree was the living symbol of wisdom. Its ephemeral nature meant that it bloomed briefly, sharing its sweet-tempered colors for only a short season before shedding into a rainfall of bitter-sweet tears. The resulting view was like a fusion of art and folklore: pink petals splashed across a canvas of green, painting the real world in the hues of myths. A fallen world teeming with Kami.

It was customary to sit under the Sakura tree and reflect. Nobles, samurai and even poor poets took to the fugacious tree for meditation and solitude. It was here that Omiokane would meet them, making subtle steps in their minds, finding his way around their thoughts in the dark by reaching out his arms and feeling here and there until a window of inspiration was discovered. That's how insight and ideas were always found: a muse sneaks inside the mind and opens a window, allowing light to pour in.

Many came to this hill, to this tree, to commune with the Gods in thought, but not anymore. That season had passed. Omiokane sat beneath the naked limbs of the Sakura tree waiting for it to bloom again, but it never did. Like a lover who waits for lost love to return, Omiokane had to accept that his disciples were not coming. They had all moved on. Wisdom retired from this hill, but many said it had died that day, leaving no body and no remains. It evaporated with a gong.

"What was that?" Clarence asked.

"A warning," Omiokane answered, snapping out of the ancient memory.

"A warning? Of what?"

"That wisdom is lost. And justice with it."

"Don't be so dramatic."

The reply didn't come from Clarence. His voice was soft and deep, while this third voice was rough and crunchy. A light turned on and revealed that the coarse voice belonged to a bipedal dog.

The gongs having ceased, Omiokane was blind again, and the only way he was going to know who had just addressed him was with his hands. He reached out, giving his fingers an open invitation to walk across the long, jet-black face of the canine. Like tame dogs so often do, he waited out the annoyance with immeasurable patience while the blind old God fingered his lips, tinkered with his teeth and practically gave a hand job to his erect ears, which were permanently and attentively spiked.

"Is there a name we can put with this face?" Omiokane asked.

"Anubis," the dog answered. "Now, if you don't mind..."

Anubis reciprocated Omiokane's intrusive interrogation by extending his nose and sniffing him out, beginning with his face and working his

200

way down to his crotch. Moving around on all fours, he trotted around to Omiokane's butt, lifted his kimono with his muzzle and took a big whiff.

"Interesting," Clarence said.

"What?" Anubis asked, making his way now to Clarence.

"I heard that dogs do this because they are looking for some lost legal document."

"Oh, yeah, that," Anubis said, sniffing Clarence's crotch. "You haven't seen it, have you?"

"No. I only just recently heard about it from a friend. I thought it was a just a myth."

"It's not a myth, Mister...?"

"Moody. Clarence Moody."

"It's not a myth." Anubis circled around to Clarence's butt. "We're still searching. Someday we'll find it." Finished with his canine version of a security pat-down, he straightened himself and stood on two human-like legs. "Okay, so if you're Clarence Moody, you must be Omiokane, his lawyer. Correct?"

"Hai." Omiokane bowed.

"Good. Follow me."

Anubis picked up a mallet the size of his body and struck an enormous bell that moaned with an ominous gong. It triggered a succession of candles that somehow ignited all on their own, revealing a private courtroom of two desks, each with a pair of chairs, placed parallel to each other and positioned before forty-two chairs that were elevated on a high-rise platform.

Clarence recognized Ptah sitting at one of the tables. Omiokane recognized the man sitting next to him, although not by sight but by his *smell*.

"Ahura Mazda," Omiokane said. "I should have known."

"How did you know?" Clarence asked, completely befuddled.

"I can smell the labdanum in that beard a mile away."

"Yeah, me too," Anubis confirmed.

"You should consider using it," Ahura Mazda replied, standing up from the table. "Because I can smell your odiferous old person's smell *two* miles away."

"Okay, you two, settle down," Anubis said. "Save it for the Judges."

"Judges?" Clarence exclaimed. "What Judges? I see forty-two *chairs* on that stage and every one of them is empty."

"Of course they are empty. They are the unseen Gods."

"Unseen Gods?" Clarence raised one dubious eyebrow. "You're joking, right?"

"No, I'm not joking."

"This is madness. If they are 'unseen,' how can we know if they are even there?"

"Did you happen to see the New Moon tonight?"

"Of course not."

"Right. And yet you know the Moon is there," Anubis curtly countered. "The same goes with the Judges. Now take your seat, so we can get started."

Ahura Mazda gave Omiokane a sinister smile that promised to put an end to their feud right here and now. Clarence and Ptah's silent exchange was nowhere near as menacing. In fact, the look Clarence took from Ptah was one of indifference. The old African God seemed at peace with the whole procedure, albeit just beneath the stoic exterior Clarence could detect that he was disquieted. He had to be, since standing ominously in a corner, like some kind of court bailiff, was none other than Ankou. He brazenly brandished his scythe while tossing and catching a stone, eagerly anticipating a guilty verdict—or an innocent verdict. It didn't really matter. Either one would render him a quick and easy kill.

Finally, everyone took their seats and sat silently before forty-two empty chairs ostensibly occupied by deities. Whoever these Gods were, they were stubbornly silent—they gave no word or sign for the proceeding to begin. Everyone waited for a signal. Clarence uncomfortably cleared his throat and shuffled restlessly as his butt disputed with his disagreeable chair. This only made him more impatient, and after only a minute, he turned and looked at Anubis.

"Well?"

"Well what?"

"When do we begin?"

"Hopefully, right now," Anubis snapped. "I'm waiting for one of you guys to say something."

"Aren't the Judges supposed to cue us?"

"The Judges are here to listen. It's up to you guys to decide who goes first."

"That's all the Judges do? Listen?" Clarence replied indignantly. "Do they even decide who wins, or do we have to do that too?"

"The Scale of Truth will decide that," Anubis answered irritably.

"What scale? I don't see any scale."

"Oh, that's right." Anubis sighed and looked over at the bailiff. "Ankou, do you mind getting the..." He flickered his finger towards a back room where the scale was kept.

Ankou sighed irritably as he set down his scythe and the stone and complied. He slithered away and returned with an industrial-size scale that he could barely handle. He set it down at the head of the stage. For all his impatient crankiness, Anubis had a touch of OCD. Several times, he instructed Ankou to shift the scale a little this way and that and then a little more the other way, and to make sure it was perfectly parallel to the stage. Ankou wasn't one for words, but he hissed like a snake as he obliged Anubis' prissy attention to detail. Finally, a self-satisfied nod from Anubis confirmed that it was perfectly centered. Ankou contemptuously forearmed his sweaty brow and hissed as he slithered back to his place.

"Okay," Anubis flapped his arms against his side. "Start the trial. And keep it clean. No foul language or foul play, okay?"

"You mean you don't even have a holy book that we have to swear on? What kind of courtroom is this?" Clarence objected.

"The prosecution agrees," Ahura Mazda chimed in. "I don't trust the defense to be true to their word."

"The Scale of Truth will weigh the truth," Anubis sighed. "But fine. SANCUS!" he shouted. "Could you please get out here and do oaths so that we can get this show over and done with?"

A young, good-looking God with golden curls and a perfectly proportioned Greek figure emerged, butt naked, holding a large stack of legal papers, which he slammed on their tables.

"What the—" Clarence exclaimed, censoring the nudity with his forearm.

"Don't complain. You all wanted this," Anubis hounded with hands on his hips.

"Who the H. is this naked man?"

"Excuse me, I'm right here. You can ask me, okay?"

"Who the H. are you?"

"I am the Roman God of Oaths," Sancus answered in a snobbish voice. He sorted out his papers on Clarence's desk, then planted his finger on the top page.

"What the H. is this? Am I'm supposed to put my hand on this?"

"You're supposed to put your *name* on it," Sancus answered.

"Can't I read it first?"

"Maybe you should have your lawyer read it."

Clarence looked at his blind lawyer, who shrugged his shoulders.

"Fine. Just tell me what it says," Clarence conceded.

"It says that you swear to tell the truth, the whole truth and nothing but the truth, and that you swear to not swear in the courtroom, not even in acronyms, and that if you violate this oath, you agree to have your tongue divided in two like the forked tongue of the serpent."

"All of *this* says *that*?" Clarence gazed at the huge paper stack. "You could have just said that in one paragraph."

"I just did," Sancus replied. "Now, if we can get on with this... Please print and sign your ridiculous name here."

"And make sure his lawyer signs too!" Ahura Mazda shouted. "I want every word he says to be bound to the law!"

Clarence looked on with horror as Sancus reached behind his lower back and shuffled his hand as if he were scratching an itch. Seconds later, his hand re-emerged holding a pen, which he offered to Clarence.

"Please tell me you didn't just pull this out of your—"

"Your language, *Clarence*," Sancus reminded him. "Unless you plan to testify with a forked tongue."

With a look of repugnance Clarence accepted the pen and signed his name. He tried handing the pen to Omiokane.

"No, thank you," he politely declined while pulling a brush and a small jar of black ink from the sleeve of his kimono. He inked his name next to Clarence's.

The drill was repeated with Ptah and Ahura Mazda, who signed his name as quickly as if making a single stroke of the pen. This was the moment he waited for. Judgment day had finally arrived. With no delay, Ahura Mazda sprung from his table and marched over to the defense, where he stopped in front of Clarence, folded his hands behind his back and bullied him with an aggressive stare-down competition. It was too intimidating for Clarence, who had no idea what to do with his eyes, so he averted them to the floor, waiting for the interrogation to begin, but it never did, at least, not for him. When Clarence finally looked up, wondering about the delay, he saw that Mazda was no longer peering at him, but at his lawyer.

"Omiokane," Ahura Mazda finally spoke, completely by-passing Clarence. "Are you familiar with the *Mazda. Motor. Company*?"

It was the way Ahura Mazda said *Mazda Motor Company*, as if each word were its own sentence, that made Omiokane roll his leaden eyes and groan. It wasn't a trick question, but a *trap* question, and though he knew where this was going, he also knew from experience that resistance was futile. He reluctantly took the bait.

"Hai," he sighed. "I am familiar with them."

"Excellent. Please tell the court what you know about the *Mazda. Motor. Company.*"

"They were founded in 1920."

"They were? That's very interesting, Omiokane," he patronized. "You seem to know *sooo* much about them. What else can you tell us about the *Mazda. Motor. Company?*"

"They began as a maker of machine tools."

"Keep going." He paced in front of their table.

"And now they make cars."

"Yes. And?"

"And I am told that they make top quality cars, Mazda-san. Especially, their latest model, which features a four-cylinder—"

"Ahem," Ahura Mazda interrupted with a cough. "Omiokane, even if this court was not already aware of the *fine* vehicles manufactured by the *Mazda. Motor. Company*, I can assure you that *I* am. However, I am also sure that this court is very interested in knowing where the *Mazda. Motor. Company* is based."

Omiokane hesitated. He knew what Ahura Mazda was fishing for.

"They are based in Hiroshima," he relented. "They are a Japanese car company."

"Wait!" Ahura Mazda stopped pacing. "I'm confused. A *Japanese* car company with the name... *Mazda?*"

"Hai."

"Let it go on court record that *my* name is Ahura *MAZDA* as documented under oath. Now, Omiokane, can you explain how a Japanese car company goes about naming itself after... *me?*"

"No."

"Oooh, but I thought you were the God of Wisdom."

"Wisdom is not the same as information, Mazda-san. However"—Omiokane raised a finger and mimicked Ahura Mazda's inflections—"I do have some information for you: Before the *Mazda. Motor. Company.* was named after you, it was first named after Jujiro Matsuda—the founder. It was not *re-named* to Mazda until its partnership with the *Ford. Motor. Corporation*—an *American* company!"

"Oh sure, let's blame everything on the Americans. Very predictable."

"Also, very *factual*, Mazda-san."

"So the Japanese God of Wisdom is also an American History enthusiast," he mocked. "I had no idea you were so *occupied* by the Americans."

"I like to see myself as a student of all histories, Mazda-san."

"Good. Then maybe you can enlighten us on why an American car company would persuade a Japanese car company to rename themselves after a Persian God."

"Perhaps you should ask the Americans."

"Perhaps I will." His head swiveled towards Clarence. "Oh, look! There's one right here. Tell us, Mr. American, is what your lawyer said true?"

Clarence blinked absently. He had heard many bizarre things attached to the divine will of the Almighty, like which country will win a war or which team will win the Super Bowl. But two Gods hijacking a court proceeding and arguing about automobiles trumped all of that. His eyes yo-yoed between them until finally Mazda snapped impatiently.

"Well?!?"

"I— I... don't drive," Clarence stammered. "And how is this relevant to my trial?"

"Because *he's* a thief." He pointed to Omiokane. "And so are you."

"*Oh sure, let's blame everything on the Americans,*" Omiokane parroted.

"Your honors"—Ahura Mazda turned to the empty chairs—"this is a case of theft pure and simple, and what I'm trying to establish is that the defendant, a no-good thief who stole from a God, has hired as his lawyer a no-good thief who stole from a God."

"Objection!" Omiokane shouted. "This is all conjecture."

"Conjecture?" Ahura Mazda laughed. "Allow me then to call to the stand our first witness—VERITAS."

"Oh S." Clarence muttered. He had forgotten all about her.

Ahura Mazda saw the disturbance in Clarence's face, walked over to him and sneered as he waited for Veritas to take the stand, but after an interminably long minute, he turned around and realized she was a no-show.

"Uh, is Veritas here?" he asked in a loud voice, but there was no answer.

"It would seem that the Truth has abandoned you, Mazda-san."

"Your honors," Ahura Mazda rushed back to his table, fumbled through his papers and came back with a written document, which he proceeded to read. "I have documented here that the defendant brazenly entered the room of Veritas—the Goddess of Truth—while she was naked. According to the reports, he failed to knock, your honors."

"Reports? From who?" Omiokane objected.

"From key eye-witnesses who were there."

"So you have plenty of testimonies—but not the Truth."

Ahura Mazda briefly recoiled at Omiokane's nimble intellect, but being a wise God in his own right, he quickly recovered.

"The reports that I have collected from key eye-witnesses corroborate with the testimony of my client that Mister Clarence Moody entered the sacred sanctuaries of not one but *two* Goddess, both times without knocking. We are dealing with a repeat offender. Correction: repeat *offenders*. Two peas in a pod, or, as the expression goes, *as thick as thieves.*

"Omiokane," Ahura Mazda continued, "since you are an American history buff, maybe you—or Mister American, himself—can tell us what they used to do to horse thieves in the old West." He paused and waited for an answer. "No? You don't know? Okay, I'll tell you. They'd hang them. Interestingly, while the Japanese like to name their cars after, well, *me*, many American cars are named after horses. *Mustang, Pinto, Bronco, Ranger.* I think this is more than just a coincidence. This is the automobile industry advising us to deal with car thieves in the American way." Finally, he turned to face the Judges. "Your honors, it is the recommendation of the prosecution that Clarence Moody *and* his lawyer both be sentenced to death for the crimes of larceny."

Clarence couldn't believe what he had just heard. He looked to his right and saw Ankou's hand tightening on his scythe, excited by this good news.

"Mazda-san!" Omiokane pleaded.

"Too late to deny it now," Ahura Mazda cut him off. "You're a wise God, but when it comes to choosing your clients, you're a fool. One thief steals a God's name and the other steals their food. If you are truly a God of Wisdom, then you should have known better than to represent thieves."

"Mazda-san," Omiokane said quietly. "I did *not* represent the Mazda Corporation."

"Pffft," Ahura Mazda motored his lips. "Are you or are you not the Japanese God of Wisdom?"

"Hai. I am."

"And yet you're going to sit here and tell this court that the good people of the Mazda Motor Corporation failed to consult you—their God of Wisdom—in their branding strategies?"

Ahura Mazda leaned and pillared his arms to dump every pound of his intimidating weight on their table. He waited for their defense. Omiokane parted his lips to say something, but the words retreated. He tried a second time and a third, but each attempt ended with a constipated silence. This surprised Clarence. Omiokane may have been a God of few words, but he was never at a loss for them.

With the wise God by his side and Mazda still breathing fire in their faces, Clarence had a chance to compare the convictions of the clashing Gods. If there were burning embers in Mazda's pupils, then behind Omiokane's, Clarence could see only gray ashes. But he also saw that there was still life, if not light, in his sunless eyes. Ahura Mazda noticed it too. He inched closer and saw that from the ashes of wisdom a spark rekindled, flashing the fleeting color of cherry blossoms. He pulled back, the fire in his eyes having abated.

"They never consulted you," he whispered.

"No, they did not," Omiokane answered wistfully. He finally found his words or, perhaps, the courage to speak them. "I waited for my disciples under the Sakura tree, as had been customary, but they elected to meet in a boardroom instead. The Age of the Gods had long since passed, Mazda-san."

Ahura Mazda slowly and silently stepped away from the table and looked into the face of Omiokane. He could have sworn that the old God was looking back at him. He turned to look at his client, Ptah, and saw him sitting quietly at the table, staring straight ahead as if detached from everything. However, his was not an aura of dejection but resignation to the truth of Omiokane's words. Ptah felt Ahura Mazda studying him and looked back to advise him with only a glance that it was time he resigned himself to the truth as well.

In fact, it was best that they all conceded to the truth, even Clarence, who now understood why he had arrived in this world. He was one of them—a creator whose time had come and gone.

Ahura Mazda suddenly found himself studying his sun-smitten, leathery skin. Every groove and wrinkle was a true token of time, like the rings of an old, fallen tree. Mazda had stopped counting the days of his life a long time ago, but just now, as he gazed upon the time etched into his hands, he suddenly remembered the number of years that had passed through these old fingers.

He turned his hands over and noticed a thick layer of dust on his palms. It was obvious where the dust had come from. He peered up and saw the spot where his hands left an impression on the defense's table, which, apparently, hadn't been cleaned for ages. His eyes panned around the courtroom and saw that it was in no better condition. It had the appearance of a barren cave, and only on close inspection would anyone notice that beneath the mire of dirt were elaborate relief inscriptions of the Gods. But they were covered now, buried by time and neglect.

He took a deep breath and sighed as he directed his last question to Clarence.

"Just tell me—tell us—did you steal from the House of the Gods?" he asked quietly.

"No," Clarence answered in a low voice. "Big Momma's house was empty. There was nothing there to steal."

Ahura Mazda nodded and faced the empty chairs.

"No further questions." He turned to walk away but Clarence's voice brought him back.

"I think you have one more question for me."

Mazda turned and looked at Clarence with complete puzzlement. His lips moved as if wanting to ask, *What are you talking about?* Clarence read his mind and answered:

"I did not steal from the Gods, but ask me if I have given anything to them?"

"Have you made any offerings to the Gods?"

"No," Clarence said flatly. "Where I'm from there are no Gods. Only accidents. Sometimes happy accidents, but in the end we believe that life was just one amazing accident. But I happen to believe in ideas," he continued. "One of my favorite books is **The Fountain Head**, which is about a young architect who refused to compromise his ideas. I tried to be that person, but in the end all I did was compromise. Now I am old and my only claim is to having become a mediocre architect, at best. Most of the stuff I built was pretty bland, uninspiring. I don't know." Clarence sighed. "Maybe it's a mistake to compare yourself to a fictional character. But if there was a real life architect that I looked up to, it was Louis Khan. He was a lot like myself, short and ugly, scarred. But, man alive, did he build some amazing buildings. Most architecture borrows language from modern art to dignify itself, but Louis Khan's buildings didn't need those stuffy words. His buildings invoked silence and a feeling of sanctity, like stepping into a temple. Louis Kahn made modern ruins, and he only made a handful of them. What was it? Four, maybe five buildings materialized from his imagination for the world to see. The rest were rejected ideas. If only we could have seen what else was in his head. Anyway"—he sighed, before continuing—"those buildings were Khan's offerings to the Gods. I have a building in mind that will be my offering. And for the record, the Age of the Gods may be over, but the Gods are not dead. I'm here to build a retirement home, not a cemetery."

There was a look of admiration in everyone's eyes, especially Ptah's, who made no attempt to contain his swelling pride at being the one who initiated this young man.

"If the prosecution will rest, then I will begin our defense." Omiokane turned his head to Ahura Mazda. "Is it my turn?"

"Yeah," Ahura Mazda nodded and quietly took his place next to Ptah, who placed a reassuring hand on his counselor's shoulder.

Omiokane pushed away from the table and used his hand to guide him along its side, around its corner, until he stopped somewhere in front of Clarence. He rubbed his hands briskly together to remove the dust, then cleared his throat.

"Clarence-san, I have only two questions for you," he began. "Repeat for the court again: Did you steal from Big Momma's house?"

"No, I did not."

"Hai. My second question is: Can you prove it?"

Clarence glanced over at Ptah, who kept his eyes forward. He looked up at Omiokane, who waited for the answer.

"I can," he whispered.

He stood up, removed the Heart of the Pole Star from his pocket and made his way to the Scale of Truth, which had a single feather resting in the left pan. The opposite pan was empty, but not for long. He took a deep breath and deposited the iron ball. Immediately, as Clarence expected, the scale tipped.

Flustered, he looked around at all present, expecting to be called out as a liar. But everyone remained poised, as if they had expected this all along, or perhaps because there was more to the proceeding.

"And now," Omiokane continued, "please repeat for the court one more time: Did you steal from Big Momma's house?"

Clarence opened his mouth to answer but stopped after he saw a figure up against the far end of the wall, lurking in the shadows. Though it didn't so much as stir, Clarence felt the presence of life, similar to the life-like aura of dolls. As Clarence's eyes refocused, he realized that the entity in the room was a graven image of a man seated on a square throne with his hands resting in his lap. It was a wall engraving of the Egyptian God Osiris.

The eyes, so realistically etched, appeared to be looking across the room. Clarence turned, followed the direction of his gaze and found that sitting against the opposite wall was an engraving of the Goddess Isis. Nested in her arms, like the Virgin Mary cradling the infant Christ, was a child. Clarence's eyes widened with shock when he realized that the image of the boy in Isis' arms was none other than the Barkeep. The likeness was unmistakable, and he even held a single finger to the edge of his lips, as if saying *shhhhh*.

"We are all waiting for your answer, Clarence-san," Omiokane broke the silence. "Did you steal from Big Momma's house?" Omiokane repeated the question, to which Clarence answered with sureness of tone.

"No."

The scale moved. Clarence heard it and turned. However, as if taunting him with a game of peek-a-boo, it was now as still as the etchings on the wall.

"No," he repeated and the scale shifted again.

"Noooo," he elongated the vowel for a few seconds, and the pan visibly trembled.

"Nooooooooooooooooooooooooo." This time he stretched the vowels long enough to confirm that it wasn't the pan moving; it was the Heart of the Pole Star. It was resonating with his voice. He took a deep breath, sucking in the full capacity of his lungs, and after a split-second delay he exhaled a deep, almost melancholic tone.

"Ooooooooooooooooooooooooooooooooooooooo..."

His eyes widened at what he saw. The heart was losing its weight, returning the scale to a state of balance. But there was also something cathartic taking place. Like a good cry or even a good scream, Clarence could feel his heart purging itself of clutter. Thoughts of inadequacy and regrets of a long life still incomplete and unfulfilled were released. His heart needed the reprieve, and his lungs obliged by supplying as much air as needed to exhaust the heart's heavy burden.

"...ooooooooooooom." After a long and lasting minute, his voice faded as he completed the invocation. The last of Clarence's breath was expended, like exhaling one's last breath before death.

And then he inhaled, drawing in new breath and new life. The Heart and the Scale returned to their previous state, as did his heart, which reclaimed its heavy luggage to continue his life's journey. This almost brought Clarence to weep, wishing that his life could go on weightlessly.

He turned to look at the Judges for their verdict, but they were as silent as their chairs were empty. Perhaps no words were needed; what transpired spoke for itself. Omiokane smiled as if his blind eyes had somehow seen it all, and Clarence wondered if by some miracle he did.

"You saw it?" he asked.

"Of course not. But I heard it." Omiokane nodded approvingly.

"As the Ancient Egyptians used to say"—Anubis stepped forward—*"you are true of voice, and, therefore, innocent."*

A feeling of relief should have followed, but Clarence immediately turned to look at Ptah, who was, by default, guilty of trying to kill an innocent man. He wanted to object, but Ptah had already resigned himself to the verdict and stood up to accept his fate, which emerged not from the shadows, but as one—Ankou. From a secluded corner of the courtroom, the Grim-Repo appeared with scythe and stone ready.

Unfazed, Ptah reached under his table to grab an old wooden chest. He managed to muster up a smile as he approached Clarence, holding it close to his breast.

"From one Architect to another," he whispered wistfully.

Clarence accepted the box and opened it slowly. A hammer, a ruler, a compass and the infamous T-square were all inside. Clarence gaped at the would-be murder weapon with a strange and unexpected nostalgia. He looked at Ptah and reminisced about the good ol' days of almost being bludgeoned to death. Almost being... *killed?*

"Wait!" Clarence threw out his arm to stop Ankou's advance, then looked at Ahura Mazda, Omiokane and the Judges.

"I know what these are. These aren't tools—I mean they are, but in this world, what good are these tools? They're useless." Clarence walked over to his table and shook it. Next he ran his finger along it, collecting the dust. "The Mind is not a world of matter. Everything here exists as an idea in someone's head." He turned and looked at Ptah and then corrected himself. "In *everyone's* head. These aren't tools." He turned back to the Judges. "They're symbols."

Ptah smiled. Finally, the old boy got it.

"Symbols of what?" he asked.

Clarence picked up the ruler.

"This signifies lines and distances." He held up the compass and T-Square. "These signify circles and squares." Last, he held up the hammer. "And this signifies force and weight. All measurable by numbers. Your honors," Clarence continued, after turning to face the forty-two Judges. "Ptah wasn't trying to kill me. He was trying to *initiate* me!"

"No, actually, I was trying to k—"

Clarence hushed him with a swat from his cane. "He *was* trying to initiate me, which begins with a symbolic killing."

Once again, the courtroom fell silent. No one said a word because, quite frankly, they were all confused—Ptah most of all. He had never anticipated that the man he accused of theft would accuse him of being innocent. Clarence scanned every face in the room, waiting for someone to give the verdict, then he looked to Ankou, who could do nothing else but shrug his shoulders.

"You know I'm right!" Clarence pointed at him, then turned to the Judges for their ruling. "Your honors, as everyone can see, I'm alive and well and I'm ready to build your temple. Ptah is innocent."

For a long minute, everyone stared at the empty chairs, waiting for the Judges to finish what had to be a silent deliberation. Ankou most of all was antsy. He preemptively raised his scythe above his head, readying himself to drop it like a guillotine on Ptah's neck. All he needed was the word. He waited. Clarence waited. Ptah waited. They all waited.

"Well?" Clarence blurted.

"What was that?" Anubis cupped his hands around his ears. "Did you hear that?"

"Hear what?"

"The Judges have spoken!" Anubis threw out his arms to make the announcement. "They have ruled that Ptah is NOT GUILTY."

"I didn't hear anything."

"Yeah, well, I'm a dog and you're a human. Your hearing sucks. The ruling was not guilty. Unless you want to dispute that."

"No, no." Clarence backed away. "I'm cool with that. Is everyone else cool with that?"

"Hai," Omiokane agreed, as did the others who looked at each other and nodded.

"Perfect." Anubis clapped his hands. "Ankou, would you mind returning the Scale of Truth to the back room?"

That did it. Ankou threw down his scythe and threw a tantrum. They all ran for cover as he turned over tables, kicked over chairs and punched the air for want of more things to trash. With the wild eyes of a madman, he scanned the room for a victim. He was not leaving without a victim. His eyes locked in on the scale. *That damn scale.* With both hands and with every iota of strength, he flipped it over and sent it crashing to the ground. He kicked and punched it and even stabbed it several times with his scythe. By the time he was finished with it, he was heaving violently. But he wasn't done yet. He fixed his raging eyes on Clarence, who reflexively clenched his katana, but before he knew it, Ankou hurled his stone at his head. Clarence ducked, dropping Ptah's chest. The tools spilled out scattering across the floor.

"Ankou!" Anubis barked.

Ankou was done taking orders, especially from him. He flipped him the bird, spiraled into a pillar of smoke and, quite literally, *stormed* out of the courtroom, leaving everyone coughing, wheezing and chasing away the aftermath of dust and debris with their hands.

As Clarence fanned away the fog, he noticed that a *fifth* tool, one he hadn't noticed before, lay scattered on the floor. Next to the ruler, compass, T-square and hammer, it seemed out of place. With the help of his walking stick, he kneeled down to retrieve it and stood up holding in his hand not a tool for architects or for a draftsman. It was the tool for a musician.

"A flute?" Clarence muttered to himself, but his many questions were chased away by the coarse, curt commands from Anubis.

"Okay, the drama queen is gone. The show is over and so is the trial. You don't have to go home, but you're not staying here."

Ahura Mazda was the first to take the cue. He made the obligatory professional handshakes, starting with Omiokane and then Clarence, but to Ptah he gave a congratulatory pat on the back. The three followed behind him, but on their way out Clarence stopped and pulled Anubis to the side, making a gesture with his eyes that indicated he wanted to ask a question in private.

"What about them?" Clarence whispered.

"What about who?"

"The Judges?" He thumbed to the stage.

"Oh, *them*." Anubis shook his head at Clarence's naiveté. "Those are just empty chairs. The Judges retired from this gig years ago—for obvious reasons," he made sure to add.

"What? You mean we've been talking to… *nobody?*"

"Hey, it works." Anubis shrugged. "As long as everyone thinks they're talking to the Judges, they're usually able to sort out their petty quarrels for themselves."

"What about the Scale of Truth? Was that all a lie, too?"

"Those were your words up there, not mine, so you tell me."

Anubis gave Clarence a farewell pat on the back and nudged him towards Omiokane, who waited for him. The blind God hooked his hand under Clarence's elbow and the two began walking the way they came.

Anubis turned to look at the empty courtroom, the empty chairs and the wall engravings of Osiris, Isis and Horus. He picked up his mallet and struck the bell once. The gong rippled throughout the room and the light of every candle went out.

*

The door opened and Clarence and Omiokane were met with the soft light of every star shining overhead. Omiokane couldn't see the diamond-studded sky, but he could feel the rays of the celestial lights and how they softened the darkness. He tilted his head back and smiled as he breathed in the cool evening atmosphere.

While Omiokane basked in the moment, Clarence watched Ahura Mazda who was already a distant figure as he made his way back to the retirement home. He was surprised when he saw that Ptah had also left without saying so much as a goodbye. Ptah must have read his mind because he took a short second to turn around, look at Clarence and give him an approving nod. Clarence firmed his grip on the chest and raised a hand, bidding him farewell.

He reopened the chest and gazed at the flute resting on top of the architect's tools. He pulled out the flute to study it, counting the number of holes along its short neck. He had never played a flute before, but at this point he knew it didn't matter. Like the other tools, it was there only as a symbol. He raised the flute to his lips and blew, creating a dissonant whistle that broke Omiokane from his trance.

"What was that?" Omiokane asked.

Clarence pulled the flute from his mouth and answered with quiet revelation:

"This is how I'm going to build the temple."

Chapter 11

Rudely hammering in the middle of the night was flat out discourteous, even in a town with no one to hear it. But government types, who aren't known for their decorum, have no patience for doing things in a round-a-bout way. They think and act in straight lines, and expediency is emphasized, often at the expense of etiquette. So it didn't matter to 007-2 what hour it was when she went about the business of hammering an official notice on the door of the tavern. One nail in the top center would have sufficed, but her clock-like compulsive nature compelled her to pound a nail in each corner, quadrupling the ruckus.

The repetitive rapping travelled across the street from the tavern to Väinämöinen's home, where Triglav, the three-headed ocular idol, swiveled its head like a submarine's periscope to locate the disturbance. His eyes dilated into an extreme zoom-in on the bulletin.

CLOSED AND CONDEMNED

For violation of town ordinance LXX : Article XXII : Line XII
Peddling of alcoholic beverages by a minor

Panic pulsed through Triglav's pupils. They blinked and pulled away. Seconds later, Väinämöinen exploded out the front door, dressed in nothing but pajamas and his wife's pink bunny flip flops. He waved his arms as he railed.

"Sweet hops from Heaven, woman, what do you think you're doing?!?"

007-2 spun around, wielding a long chain fastened to a bullhorn. She snapped the chain like a horsewhip, and the horn whizzed upward, allowing her to snag it mid-air. Väinämöinen stumbled backwards. His eyes squinted at the three words inscribed on the horn's neck: *Chain-of-Command*. A fitting pet name for a woman who roared through the mouthpiece like a drill sergeant.

"BY THE POWER INVESTED IN ME, I HEREBY CONDEMN THIS TAVERN FOR VIOLATION OF ORDINANCE SEVENTY, ARTICLE TWENTY-TWO, LINE TWELVE, WHICH PROHIBITS MINORS FROM PEDDLING ALCOHOLIC BEVERAGES."

The hollering, worse still than the hammering, awakened the others. Väinämöinen's front door swung open again, and this time out came the Concierge, Balaam and Shiva, stumbling from the stupor of sleep. Even

219

Väinämöinen's wife joined the fray, hissing as stray stones and pebbles nipped at her bare feet.

"Matylda," he said and smiled at his wife's approach. As far as he was concerned, she was the true cavalry. He looked back at 007-2. "Oh, you're in trouble now."

Not quite. Unfazed by their numbers, 007-2 raised the bullhorn to her lips and blared: "THIS ESTABLISHMENT HAS BEEN ORDERED TO CEASE ALL OPERATIONS, AND ALL OF ITS ASSETS AND INVENTORY HAVE BEEN SEIZED."

"What does that mean?" Väinämöinen whispered over his shoulder.

"It means," Balaam began, "this hard-boiled heifer has mooched the moonshine."

This was all Väinämöinen needed to hear. He rolled up his sleeves to attack, but 007-2 cracked the air with her chain, keeping him at bay. It was only a warning shot, but it still sent Väinämöinen toppling backwards. The flip-flops flung from his feet and landed right at the tips of Matylda's toes. She happily stuffed her feet back into what was rightfully hers and, having no further concern about the tavern, waddled back to her home to finish her beauty sleep.

"Coward!" Väinämöinen shouted to her back. He then returned his attention to 007-2, who spun the horn and chain, revving up for a second attack.

It was four against one. The Concierge, Balaam and Shiva rushed to Väinämöinen's side. They gripped him by both arms and pulled him back to his bare feet. Shoulder to shoulder the four of them took to a battle stance.

"Careful, men." Väinämöinen threw out his arms to stop their advance. "I think she may have had more than a few sips of our ale."

"I'M ORDERING ALL OF YOU TO DISPERSE NOW, OR I WILL ARREST YOU FOR DISTURBING THE PEACE."

"Disturbing the peace! You curmudgeon of a woman," Balaam objected. "We were all *peacefully* asleep until *you* disturbed *us* by babbling through your bloody bullhorn."

"I REPEAT! WITHOUT A LICENSE, THIS IS AN ILLEGAL PROTEST.

DISPERSE NOW, OR YOU WILL BE ARRESTED FOR DISTURBING THE PEACE."

♪ Fight the Power! ♪

The Concierge pumped his right fist while chanting the Public Enemy song.

♪ Fight the Power!
We've got to Fight the Powers that Be. ♪

He looked around for the others to join in, but they only looked confused.

"So now this illegal protest has become a riot," she said, still whooshing the chain through the air. "That's not a problem. I'm real good at riot control."

She splayed her legs, anchored her feet like a master warrior and spun the weighted weapon over her head. The so-called chain-of-command was now a long-range chain and sickle. Väinämöinen's eyes darkened into that of a gray and beleaguered old wizard as he gauged the threat looming in the darkness.

"This foe is beyond any of you," he grumbled and turned to face his friends. *"Run!"*

They scattered like roaches. Within the hair of a second, she attacked.

The chain spiraled twice like a gust of wind. On the third swing, she let it rip. Like a planet that had suddenly been knocked out of its orbit, the horn fired in a new trajectory aimed for the protestors. Väinämöinen, the Concierge, Balaam and Shiva scrambled, toppled and tumbled like a row of bowling pins. No sooner had they regained their footing, the horn and chain struck again, and once more. From their hands and knees, they made small, evasive leaps and clumsy somersaults. The spiraling winds of the chain generated the force of a tornado. Clumps of dirt and debris were ripped from the Earth and sucked into the orbit. From out of the vortex the horn rocketed like a projectile. Väinämöinen, the least nimble of the four, was the easiest target. This time it was a direct hit. The horn struck him in the center of his forehead, knocking him senseless.

The Concierge jumped in front of Väinämöinen and threw out his arms to protect his friend. Wide open and vulnerable, he began a freedom song.

♪ We shall overco— ♪

221

But it was cut short by the next attack. The chain cracked in the air, aimed for him. He tumbled in the mist, narrowly dodging the blow.

Levitating on his hands and knees, he heaved in heavy breaths. But there was precious little time for his lungs to recover. He looked up and saw that the horn was already cycling around in a broad Saturn-like orbit. Shiva ducked and Balaam dived to the ground to avoid it. But for the Concierge, who helplessly buoyed a foot from the ground, ducking or diving would not be so simple. With his legs too weak to springboard off the air, he was a sitting duck. His eyes widened and he threw up a protective arm as he braced for impact.

The blow sent him skyward. His body paused for a split second at the crest, then cascaded back to Earth, as if he had just tripped and tumbled down a stairwell. He smacked a layer of air, only knee-high from the ground, and lay there unconscious.

Without pause, she made her next mark. The horn whooshed through the air and crashed into Shiva's barrel chest, but he caught it with his four hefty arms. It was like catching a 79-yard Hail-Mary touchdown pass, but without the standing ovation. There was only Shiva's scream as the chain swung him into a reckless orbit. The poor guy barely made it through one cycle before he finally let go of the horn and went hurdling into space, then came crashing down like an asteroid into the Earth. The small explosion from his crash swept Balaam off his feet and blew him backwards.

007-2 had won. She snapped the bullhorn back into her hands and stood triumphantly, surveying the aftermath of four fallen Gods who lay flat on the ground, defeated. Hers was the look of a completed duty. Satisfied with the restoration of order, she marched back to the retirement home.

*

"I don't see her behind the lobby desk," Clarence whispered to Omiokane. The two covertly probed through the glass door of the retirement home's front entrance. "But she might be doing rounds or something. Wait here and I'll go check it out."

Omiokane took refuge behind a row of hedges while Clarence casually strolled through the front door, conspicuously whistling to announce himself. He stopped at the center of the room and looked again at the completely naked walls. 007-2 hadn't even bothered to at least cover them with bad paintings. Not that he should have expected otherwise; government buildings are notoriously neutral.

The last time he stood in this very place, she came bursting through the door, evicting Balaam and Omiokane by the collar. He waited a short while to see which Gods she would evict this time. There was no lobby bell to get her attention, so he resumed whistling, amping up the volume. He paused and listened for her approach, but there was only silence.

He checked the doors behind the lobby desk. 007-2 was nowhere to be found, but the effect of her commanding presence was still there. The hallways, normally bustling with bodies, were empty, as if a curfew had been decreed and strictly imposed. *She must be here somewhere*, he thought and closed the door. His first instinct was to hurry from behind her station, but as he turned to retreat, he caught sight of her computer or, at least, what was left of it. Computer limbs and guts were still scattered across the desk, beyond any hope for repair. This was Shiva's masterpiece, appropriately nested near a trove of unguarded office supplies.

Clarence hoarded all the free stationary his arms could handle. Paper, pencils, pens, post-it notes—whatever he could find was stuffed into his green sweater, creating a potbelly of plundered products. Stray items fell from the seam as he hobbled out of the front entrance for a fast getaway.

"Come on, come on!" he hurried Omiokane.

"What is wrong, Clarence-san? Is she coming?"

"I don't know. Come on, let's go!"

With his one arm feebly cupped under his belly full of booty, he used his other arm to stick out his cane for Omiokane to find and grab and helped the blind God to his feet. Together they made a run for it.

"No, no, no!" Clarence whispered, as Omiokane instinctively moved for the front entrance. "We might run into her in there. I know another way inside."

With surprising stealth, they prowled along the perimeter walls until they found a large impression of a body, leftover from Clarence's nosedive from his apartment window. Thankfully, as Clarence suspected, the window was still open. Omiokane heard the rustling of extra baggage as Clarence removed his sweater and turned it into a satchel for his stolen goods.

"What is that, Clarence-san?"

"Supplies. For drawing," Clarence answered, then stopped when he remembered something. "The chest? Where's the chest?"

"We left it behind the hedges, where I was hiding."

"Crap! Okay, okay." Thinking fast, Clarence quickly hurled his stuffed sweater through the window, then proceeded to smuggle the evicted Omiokane into his room. "Wait here. I'll be back."

Clarence moved as fast as he could, but as he turned the corner, he saw 007-2 stopping at the mouth of the front entrance. She jerked her head in Clarence's direction. Reflexively, he recoiled and held his breath. She had spotted him. He was sure of it. He could hear her feet marching for him. With his slow feet, there was no chance of a fast getaway. He raised his katana and prepared for battle.

He waited. And waited. This was taking too long. He heard the hedges rustling and peeked around the corner. She was there, but she was kneeling over and muttering complaints about the stray pens and pencils littered on the campus grounds. Clarence's heart dropped when he realized that the stray articles were like bread crumbs leading her directly to the chest. Silently, he cursed himself and moved to smack his head with his own cane, but his fingers fumbled and the cane dropped. It made a small sound as it struck the ground. Her head snapped upward and she looked around. Clarence pulled back and held his breath again. He counted the seconds before finally letting out a silent exhale. Cautiously, he peeked again around the corner one last time. She was gone.

Ignoring the objections from his limbs, he darted back the way he came. When he reached his window, he looked back to see if he had been spotted or followed. Thankfully, the coast was still clear. He anchored his hands on the window sill and sounded off a great cacophony as his feet grated against the wall, all in the nearly impossible effort of pulling himself through his own window. He made a loud audible groan as he made a final effort and successfully lunged one half of his body through the open cavity, allowing Omiokane to aid him in pulling in the other half. He struck the floor with a resounding thud.

"Are you okay, Clarence-san?"

"The window," Clarence groaned and pointed. "Close the window."

"You have not been evicted. Why did you not just go through the door?"

"She found the chest," Clarence grunted as he picked himself from the floor. "The first person to walk through that door would have been held for interrogation."

"So what now?" Omiokane asked.

"Well, I'm officially harboring a stowaway, so I think now you have to lay low. We'll sneak out of here before dawn. The bed is right behind you."

"But where will you sleep, Clarence-san?"

"I won't." Clarence unfastened his satchel and pulled out his looted paper and pens. "I'm going to get started on the temple design."

*

I am all that has been and shall be...
And no mortal has lifted my veil.

Clarence gazed at the door sign and shook his head, wondering why it couldn't just read *please knock before entering*. Not that he would have noticed it amidst the chaotic frenzy of before. He looked to his left and right, still unable to believe the quiet discipline of the hallways. It made him painfully self-conscious of even the slightest noise he made. He raised his fist to the door, took a deep breath and knocked. Though he did so delicately, the sound was amplified by the dense silence. He looked around again in a slight panic, convinced that he had awakened the Gods. But there wasn't so much as a stir, not even from behind Veritas' door.

He raised his fist to knock again, but stopped. Instead he pressed his ear against the door and listened. He heard nothing, but somehow he had a hunch that directly on the other side was Veritas doing exactly the same.

"Hey. I knocked this time, just so you know," he whispered to the door. "I just want to say thank you for not testifying against me at the trial. I..." he paused and sighed at the prospect of babbling to a door, but fought back the doubts and continued: "Before the trial, I made a stop at the library and did some research on temple design. I have to be

225

honest and tell you that most of it went right over my head. But I saw something about you. It was a drawing of a woman who looked just like you. She was standing with the world in her hand, against a backdrop of stars and an oval frame with the signs of the Zodiac. Your quote about no mortal lifting your veil was printed just underneath. The Concierge told me you were the Goddess Veritas, but this book said that your true name is *Tetrad*, and that your body is named *Gnosis*, which means *knowledge* or *truth*. This book said that the stars of the Zodiac were seen as temples, but you were seen as the grand temple—the Temple of the Cosmos.

"You know, when I was a kid, I used to make photocopies of the stars and re-connect them into my own buildings. They didn't look anything like temples, more like crazy, random shapes, but to me they were legitimate houses. I called this starchitecture. A little gimmicky, I know, but I was a kid, so there you go.

"Anyway, apparently I'm here to re-do the temple of the Gods. Don't worry, I'm not going to do starchitecture. I have something else in mind. I was thinking maybe I would model the temple after you. I mean, I was wondering if you would be a model. Not a fashion model; conceptually, I mean," he began to stammer but took a deep breath to recompose himself. "What I mean is, I want the temple to be based on you. But I have to unveil you so that I can draw you. Basically..." He finally just spat it out: "I want to know if I can see you naked?"

There was no reply.

"Please knock or tap or something, so that I can know that I didn't just ask this door to strip for me."

After a brief delay, Clarence heard the sound of a latch turning. He stepped back and watched as the door opened slightly with Veritas sizing him up through the open cavity. She pulled open the rest of the door, inviting him inside. The room was brewing in a mist of shower steam, just like before. He couldn't help but blush as he bashfully looked around for a place to sit. There was no prayer desk or even a chair like he had in his room. He looked to her for direction and she pointed to the bed. This made him sweat profusely, but he didn't argue as he stumbled past her and placed his bum on the extreme edge of her mattress. He lifted both hands, to show that he had brought paper and pen with him, confirming his intentions.

Now came the tough part. Watching her strip.

Or maybe not watching her was the least awkward way to go about this. His eyes wandered in every direction except where she was. He took a forced interest in ceiling fixtures. She saw how much he was struggling and decided it was better to just cut to the chase. She whipped off her white towel and flung it across the room so that it draped on Clarence's face. Slowly, he raised his hand and removed the towel. Standing before him was the naked truth.

"Oh my God," he whispered. "You're beautiful."

*

The finished drawing looked like a bloated stick figure. Rigid but rickety pencil lines sketched out the rotund contours of a stay-puff marshmallow woman with thick robot-like arms and pudgy fists punching into her heavy hips. The legs seemed to lack knees and maybe on purpose—the two stout pillars were specifically drawn to never so much as bend while holding up the shaky weight of a blocky body. The crude drawing terminated with a balloon head bloated with two chins and a maniacal smile that wrapped across one half of the face. From the corner of the mouth, of all things, hung a briar pipe.

Matylda hovered the drawing over Väinämöinen's head, waiting for him to wake up. She tapped her foot, which made the pink bunny flip-flop appear as if it were alive and hopping impatiently. Finally, she gave him a swift kick to the top of his head, bringing his eyes to flutter open. He reached up, touched the bruise on his head and winced.

"Maniac maidens of mayhem! What happened to me?"

"What happened is that woman knocked you out cold. Serves you right," she snorted. "A man your age getting into a bar fight. And who do you think had to drag your heavy hump home and up the stairs?"

"And then you leave me on the floor?"

"Would you rather I left you outside, which is probably where you belong anyway. At least you were able to get some sleep. I haven't gotten a wink listening to you and those clowns clash with that woman. And now I've got this old man, who doesn't know dung about door manners, knocking on my door in the middle of the night looking for you."

"It's my door too! And what are you yappin' about anyway, woman?"

"I'm yappin' about the *architect*. At least, that's what he claims. He sure as shinola isn't much of an artist." She looked at the portrait.

"He drew that?"

"Yes! As 'evidence' of his story. He claimed he just finished *drawing* the temple based on some harlot at the retirement home."

"*That's* the temple?" he murmured and pointed at the legs. "I guess these are the columns. This must be the *expanded* home. Is this a head or a chimney?"

"No, you idiot, this is *me*. Or, at least, it's supposed to be. I made him draw me as proof of his story." She crumpled the drawing and tossed it. "Absence of evidence may not be evidence of absence, but it sure as shinola is evidence of the absence of talent. Why are you still laying there? Get up, already!" she demanded. "Go see what he wants, so that he can get out already."

Väinämöinen groaned as he lifted himself only as far as his elbows.

"Where are the others?"

"The same place where I should have left you. Now get up!"

"Outside?" Väinämöinen shot up and ran to his window, where he saw Balaam, the Concierge and Shiva sprawled out, still unconscious. "Oh, for the love of ale, why didn't you bring them in, woman?"

"Because the property value on my home is already low enough having you around. I don't need those transients hanging around making it even lower. There's going to be some changes around here, beginning with those drifters who've been sleeping in my home. Then we'll talk about your unemployment status. The tavern is closed! Time to stop belching beer and start looking for a job."

"Where am I going to find a job around here, woman?"

"If you can't find a job, then make one. Ask the 'architect' downstairs to build you a homeless shelter. You can make those three vagrants out there your first customers. In fact..."

She grabbed Väinämöinen by the collar and dragged him out the door, down the stairs and past Clarence and Omiokane, who waited in the living room. They watched as she marched Väinämöinen outside and ordered him to help clean up the body count littered in front of her home.

"C'mon, get up already! Get up!" She kicked the Concierge, Balaam and Shiva, then swatted Väinämöinen across the head. "Lift them up! Get them on their feet."

"Did we get her?" the Concierge grumbled.

"Ha!" Matylda huffed. "If you 'got her,' you wouldn't be laying out cold *in* the cold. Let that be a lesson to you: A man can knock *up* a woman, but he can't knock her out. Better keep that in mind the next time you split hairs with the wrong gender. Now, I want all of you off my property before I'm forced to put it on the squatters' market."

"You heartless heathen!" Balaam groused. "Where do you expect Us to go?"

"Try a church! They should take *you* in with open arms."

"When was the last time you read your Bible?"

"Never!" she snapped.

"Well, let me refresh your memory. Luke Chapter nine, verse fifty-eight, and I quote: *'Foxes have dens and birds have nests, but the Son of Man has no place to lay his head.'* "

"Then go lay your head with the foxes and birds. If they'll even have you."

"FOOL!" Balaam boomed. "YOU DARE DENY MY SON COMMUNITY HOUSING!"

"Oooh..." Matylda rolled up her sleeves. "So your first ass-whoppin' wasn't enough, is that it? Time for mommy dearest to teach you what your deadbeat daddy wouldn't."

"Namaste, Madam Matylda." Shiva jumped up and bowed to Matylda to assuage the conflict. "We thank you for letting us stay in your humble abode. We do understand that you now desire privacy, so we will be on our way taking with us our deepest gratitude for your kindness and hospitality. However, before we go, we beseech you: Please spare some change for a hot meal."

"No!" she snapped.

"Damn, girl, you could have at least thought about it," the Concierge inserted. "What about some cereal then? Before you give us the boot, you can at least hook us up with some breakfast."

She glowered at the request, but in the end she conceded with a grumble as she stomped back into the house. The fact is, what Väinämöinen had said before about his wife was true. Matylda did have a weak spot for chocolate, and the Concierge was too dark and sweet to resist. However, this hankering for a hazel hunk did not include Clarence, who, along with Omiokane, was promptly ejected from the home as she returned with an unopened box of Rice Krispies. She flung the package to the Concierge and didn't even wait for a thank you. Any obligation for charity was duly satisfied, and the matter, along with her front door, was officially closed.

"Well," Väinämöinen said after a long silence. "We're all homeless now. If any of you have any experience with panhandling, now would be the time to speak up."

"Nobody is going to panhandle." Clarence stepped forward. "And we're not homeless. Not for long, anyway. Or did you forget that we have a temple to build?"

"No, we didn't forget, ystäväni, but I'm thinking maybe we should. No offence, but my wife showed me some of your work. Are you sure architecture is your thing? Have you thought about a career in sales?"

"I'm rusty, okay? I admit it. And I have arthritis, so my hands are a bit shaky. But I have a plan." Clarence paused as his eyes panned across the group. They all waited with eager eyes and open ears to hear *the plan*. "We're going to evict all the Gods from the retirement home," he began. "All thirty-three million of them."

These words were swallowed by a droning silence. Väinämöinen, the Concierge and Shiva sized Clarence up as if he had just unmasked himself as Judas. Balaam, on the other hand, had the wide-eye gaze of a disciple who had just met his savior.

"Dear man, We underestimated you," Balaam's voice cracked as he whispered. "Please forgive Us and instruct us on how to help you in this holy crusade to remove the refugees from Our holy land."

"I need you to make wine, Balaam. Lots of it."

"It shall be done."

"But why, Mister Clarence?" Shiva asked, completely confused.

"Because I can't build the temple with the Gods still in it. And I doubt I can get the Gods out on my own."

"What he means, ystäväni, is why are you taking the side of this treacherous troll?"

"Do you have a better idea on how to get the Gods out of the temple?"

"I do." The Concierge raised his hand and straightened his shades. "1984. Rockmaster Scott and the Dynamic Three. Who remembers them?"

He actually searched their faces, looking for a spark of familiarity, but they just stared at him blankly as if he were crazy. To explain, he began bobbing his head and busted into an old-school rap song.

> ♪The roof, the roof, the roof is on fire.
> We don't need no water, let the— ♪

He stopped at the end of the hook and looked around.

"Let it burn!" The Concierge snapped his finger and pointed. "That's how we'll get them out."

"I am not familiar with this song," Shiva injected, "but if I am understanding this correctly, it sounds as if you want to burn down the temple. While I am capable of producing fire, this does not sound very practical to me."

"No, not fire," the Concierge smiled. "A fire *drill*. We just pop the latch, kick back and watch them as they all walk out—except the Fire Gods. The sprinkler system will probably drive them out."

"Brilliant strategy!" Balaam said. "Except for the part where we have to get past that bullhorn bludgeoning bulldog of a woman to 'pop the latch' in the first place, or did the thorough thrashing she administered to all of us already slip your mind?"

"It's okay," Clarence cut in. "We won't need a fire drill. But we will need that government lady's help." He turned to Balaam. "And we'll need that wine."

"Wine for what, ystäväni?"

Clarence smiled and, without saying a word, turned to Omiokane, who could feel that the answer had been delegated to him.

"So that 007-2 will evict all thirty-three million Gods for the same reason she evicted me: drunkenness."

"Whaddya say?" Clarence patted Balaam on the shoulder. "Think you can throw a wine tasting party for a bunch of 'derelict deities?'"

"Indeed and indubitably," Balaam boasted. "You provide the water and We will provide the wine. And please allow Us to add that We have many other talents that may also be of later use, including turning sin into salvation, but We'll circle back to that later. More pressing to this point is that while artisan wines are a feature forte on our *carte du jour*, if you'll forgive Our French, it would be remiss of Us to not inform you that converting water to wine for thirty-three million heathens—I beg your pardon, but that is what they are—might be a bit taxing, even for Us."

"Not to worry, Balaam-san." Omiokane raised a single finger. "We will also serve premium beer at this festival. I know just where to pick it up. However, there is the *small* issue of transportation."

Omiokane's wizened visage rolled into a devilish smile. "Are there any volunteers for a designated driver?"

*

The Mazda T2000 model was a three-wheel wagon truck of gargantuan size, belied only by its gentle pastel-blue color. It looked as if someone had taken a typically good-natured, reliable farm truck and bred it with a rebel motorcycle. The result was the automobile equivalent of a mythological chimera. At the South end of the temple was a stretch of plain land resembling a parking lot. It was here that the chimera rested.

Omiokane approached the strange metal beast surreptitiously, as if he were tip-toeing around a sleeping dragon. His companions, lacking the old man's nerve, kept their distance, watching as he navigated through empty space with his arms as his only compass. Everyone breathed in deeply when his hands made first contact.

Shiva stuffed all four hands into his mouth and gnawed at his nails, certain that the metal dragon would awaken, breathing backfire and smoke. To his relief, the creature remained idle, though surely by now it was awake and could feel its hide being touched. Thankfully, the soft-hued she-dragon kept her repose, perhaps enjoying the caress of a brave admirer.

"A beauty," Omiokane whispered as he passed his old hands along the creature's industrial contours, creating a fresh image of the truck in his mind.

"Don't talk!" Shiva whispered back. "You will awaken the Dragon!"

"Awakening it is exactly the point, Shiva-san. And it is not a Dragon; it is a *Nue*, a Japanese chimera. That is what I would have named it, had I been the brand consultant for the Mazda Motor Corporation. But the creators of this fantastic monster named this gentle giant—"

"Mazda," Clarence completed his sentence and shook his head. "So you're stealing his name after all."

"Not his name, Clarence-san"—Omiokane reached into the long sleeve of his robe and pulled out a single key—"only his car."

They all flinched from the sound of a latch popping and the door making a metal whine as Omiokane pried it open. The sage God of Wisdom was now a God of Grand Larceny. They watched him through the windshield as he fumbled around to find the ignition. With only two attempts and a forward turn of the wrist, the chimera she-dragon was alive.

*

Omiokane sat upright, as straight as a weathervane, while enjoying the crisp temperature that streamed through the passenger-seat window. He said little during the drive, though not from the mere golden virtue of silence. He could tell that Shiva was a nervous wreck behind the wheel. He was, after all, riding a rather large and cumbersome metal dragon—for the first time. This task demanded two things: one, a non-drinking designated driver and, two, complete concentration.

It took a while for Shiva to break her in. At first, the dragon resisted with a series of violent bucks and thrusts, stopping abruptly and then zipping off as if to take to the sky only to stop again. Shiva had to regularly rotate his sweaty hands to hold the reins, but at least having four arms at his disposal gave him the advantage. Eventually, the dragon had no choice but to concede the fight. She stopped rocking the wagon and before long they were all flying on the ground along a road as wide and open as the air. Shiva's she-dragon now cruised at the soothing pace of a mother's hum.

The rest of their party rode in the trailer wagon, and the hum of the engine lulled them all to sleep. All except for the Concierge, who had to focus on levitating fast enough to keep pace with the metal beast. Once he got into the rhythm, he relaxed and gazed. He heard a body shift, looked down and saw that Clarence wasn't sleeping but stargazing.

"You're in love, aren't you?" the Concierge teased.

"In love?" Clarence blushed. "With who?"

"With Big Momma."

"That's ridiculous. How could I be in love with her—I just met her."

"Love at first sight, homie. That's why you tried to feed her, isn't it? You were trying to get on her good side."

"She looked hungry."

"Hey..." The Concierge chuckled. "The quickest way to a woman's heart is through her stomach."

"That's the saying about *men*," Clarence irritably rebutted.

"Yeah, but women need to eat too. You just have to take them out for the right food: Greek yogurt parfaits, Thai salads, gluten-free breads."

"Whatever."

"You can't hide love, my brotha. It's okay to fall in love with Big Momma. How can you not?" The Concierge looked out at the rolling landscape. "But don't think you're the only one who got eyes for her. You have some competition."

"Who?"

"The Night Sky." The Concierge pointed up. "They were a pair at one time. That's what all the ancient myths say. Two halves of a whole. But human beings came along and pried them apart so that they could have the Earth to themselves. This pissed off the Night Sky, and he took the form of a fire-breathing Dragon and swallowed civilization with an inferno. Big Momma took pity on people and saved them by turning him into a Bear. It broke her heart to do this—and his. But he left a token of his love in the starry sky by placing his heart in the center of the stars, where Big Momma could always see it. Ever since then, his heart has been the link between the two worlds." He finished the tale by pointing at Clarence's pocket, cuing him to reach in and pull out the Heart of the Pole Star. The Concierge smiled and nodded.

"Great story," Clarence said. "But when I'm done here, she's more than welcome to have his heart back." He returned the Pole Star to his pocket and, having had his fill of Bears and Dragons, resumed his reclining position and turned away from the Concierge to finish stargazing.

*

At the hours before dawn, the liminal horizon suffers severe mood swings: dark and morose at one hour, deep blue and pensive at another and burning with passion at the last. Like clockwork, the passion of the sunrise is strong enough to rouse the rooster to crow.

"WAKE UP!"

Clarence snapped out of his sleep. Väinämöinen and Balaam practically leaped from the seat of their pants and came down with a rude thud. With their sleepy eyes, now wide awake and burning, they peered angrily at the Concierge, demanding an explanation for the crude prank. He explained with a Brand Nubian rap song and the Roy Ayers sample.

♪ *Wake up, wake up, wake up*
Everybody loves the sunshine
Wake up, wake up, wake up
Folks get down in the sunshine ♪

This was still too cryptic for the rudely awakened, but the answer was decoded in the dark mirror of his shades, which reflected the first sign of a fiery dawn.

They all turned their heads eastward and watched the morning spectacle at the horizon. All the bustling of a city could never compare to the lively buzz of Nature herself, especially when she was just opening her eyes at dawn. But the approaching overcast suggested a murky morning temperament. As they passed under a short stretch of grey clouds, rain began to fall, though not in any heavy downpour.

235

It came down innocuously, like a drizzle, and in the few short minutes it took to pass from under the nozzle, the passengers were no wetter than children running past a sprinkler. Even Balaam's prickly personality had finally relaxed its pins as he held out both hands to catch the hazy drops of rain. It was the first time that anyone had seen him behave so innocently, as if the soft rain had washed away his usual British arrogance. But the fact was, the Sun had a noticeable effect on all of them. No matter how many times it rose in the morning, they gathered to watch it as if they were seeing it for the first time.

Even Clarence was moved by the solar spectacle. But he also marveled at watching the Gods in their moment of quiet reverence. Just as he did at the retirement home, he stood on the sidelines as a silent observer, studying their enraptured faces, which seemed to have forgotten that this was the same respect that had once been paid to all of them. When the Sun shone at dawn the Gods became the worshippers. Even if humans had abandoned this post, the Gods held fast to it.

This was both their divine virtue and their tragedy. Not that the Gods should die, but that they should be forgotten. Such abandonment shone in all their faces, but none more than Balaam, whose eyes were especially poignant. The same frowning features that made him appear a troll now rendered him a child.

Balaam brought his palm closer to his face and extended his forefinger to touch the rain droplets, turning them to wine. He inclined his hand to his mouth, allowing them to roll from his palm to his tongue. He licked his lips refreshingly, which only made Väinämöinen scoff with jealous frustration.

"Turn it into an amber ale," he said. "Then you'll impress me."

"You, sir, have the aesthetics of an ogre," Balaam retorted. "I imagine the only way to impress you is with a caveman's club over your head."

"Nay, a caveman's club over *your* head."

And just like that, the charm of the moment vanished in a poof. The old Gods were back and bickering like two best friends believing themselves to be rivals. Clarence shook his head and bemoaned the thought of managing over thirty-three million more just like them.

"Better get used to it." The Concierge grinned and opened his cereal box to start his morning breakfast. "We've got a long road ahead of us."

Just as the Concierge said this, the truck jerked slightly to the side and then snapped back into place. Clarence instinctively gripped the edge of the trailer bed and peered up at the Concierge with worried eyes.

"That's assuming we'll even stay *on* the road," Clarence rebutted.

"Boombayala!" the Concierge blurted with a snap of his fingers. "I know what you need to relax you, my man—travelling music. Every open road wants a soundtrack."

He snapped his fingers to turn on the radio. The radio, of course, was him. He began singing Cole Porter's "Don't Fence Me In."

> ♪ *I want to ride to the ridge where the west commences*
> *And gaze at the moon till I lose my senses* ♪

Clarence tried to smile confidently, but as he looked over the edge of the trailer at the passing road, he could feel the wheels of the truck struggling to keep equilibrium. The truck skipped and rattled over a pothole, and Clarence swallowed hard.

The smooth ride was over. Clarence felt every bump as if the truck were colliding into small mountains. He tried to hold on to the side of the trailer, but his sweaty palms offered only a feeble, sliding grip. He looked over the edge again and his eyes shot open when he saw the wheels hugging the road's shoulder. This could only mean one thing.

"Shiva's asleep," Clarence said to the Concierge, then turned to the front of the truck and yelled: "WAKE UP!"

"We are up!" Balaam shouted back. "Enough with that prank. It's getting old."

"No… Shiva— The truck," Clarence stuttered in a panic.

Before he could reorganize his words, the drifting vehicle hiccupped and heaved. This sent Clarence, Balaam and Väinämöinen careening into the side of the truck and soaring over the edge. Omiokane went somersaulting out of the passenger's window. He would have gone soaring into the pavement, had he not managed to clench the side view mirror. Only the levitating Concierge was spared. Lost to the music in his mind, the fool had his eyes closed while snapping his fingers and singing the Cat Stevens song "Bad Brakes."

> ♪ *Bad brakes whole car shakes*
> *Looks like I'm heading for a breakdown*

237

Black smoke engine beginning to choke
I must be heading for a break— ♪

The screams of the others skipped the needle. He turned around, snatched the sunglasses from his face and saw that his friends had all suddenly vanished. He saw no signs of bodies or faces, only rows of wiggling worm-like fingers, haplessly clinging to the ribs of the runaway dragon while they all helplessly screamed for dear life.

To Shiva's ears, the howls for help were all part of the dragon's hum. He slipped deeper into his coma and slumped on the wheel, giving it a tug in one direction. The truck steered away from the shoulder, but the muted screams duly continued.

Clarence's sweaty grip was already threatening to give out. The Concierge scrambled to make the rescue. Thinking quickly, he grabbed Clarence's walking stick, hooked it into his shirt and fished him back into the trailer bed. He repeated the same with Balaam. Väinämöinen, however, who was much heavier, would require a more robust strategy. Together, the three reached over the ledge to grab at him, but even with their combined strength, the big man's weight was too much.

The truck passed over another pothole, rudely awakening Shiva, or, at least, it jolted his right eye to open. His left eye stayed shut and his mind remained as foggy as the horizon just ahead of him. But one open eye was still enough to get his arm to pull the wheel, which it did haphazardly. The tires screamed. Everybody was screaming. Except for Shiva. He was snoring.

"PLEASE FATHER SAVE US... AND SAVE THEM TOO," Balaam pleaded.

His prayer was answered. The truck tipped the other way and made a thunderous pound against the pavement, somersaulting Omiokane back through the window. But it also shook loose the grip of Väinämöinen's rescue party. He slipped away, smacked the pavement and tumbled off down the road. Clarence blinked in disbelief. If there was ever a time to curse, it was now.

"Holy S—"

"SHIVA!" Omiokane implored the dozing driver to wake up. He grabbed him by the shoulders and shook him with as much force as his old limbs could muster.

238

Shiva's brain finally came out of sleep mode, and after a few painful seconds of rebooting, he was back online. He slammed on the breaks, causing a tire to blow.

The truck came to a screeching halt. Clarence toppled forward. Balaam flipped over the cabin roof and vanished. He reappeared after smacking the hood of the truck and rolled off into the pavement with a loud gravel-like thud.

"Oh dear," Shiva whispered.

Adrenaline catalyzed by anxiety, or perhaps anger, worked as an instant panacea for Balaam's injuries. He was already on his feet and darting off down the road. No one expected this. He had always been the arrogant antagonist of the Gods, but now there he was, rushing off to save one. Perhaps it was the call of duty—his covenant as a savior—that sent him off to see to the soul of the fallen, be they friend or foe. Whatever the case, Balaam lead the way with the others limping behind him. Each labored step brought them closer to the unthinkable. They huddled over Väinämöinen's body and leaned forward, scavenging for even the smallest grain of evidence that the big guy was still among the living. If he was, he made no effort to show it.

"He's dead," Clarence declared.

"No." The Concierge leaned in closer. "I just saw his eye twitch."

It was more like a spasm, which was not a good sign. A twitch signifies life hanging on by a thread. A spasm, on the other hand, meant that life was dangling.

There was a small cavity, no wider than a hairline, through which Väinämöinen could see his companions hovering over him. His mind was also going into spasms as his consciousness erratically flickered. He lapsed in and out, and between each lapse, he could hear them.

"We need to call for help?"

"Call who? And how? We're in the middle of nowhere."

"We have to do something NOW!"

"YES!" a British voice boomed, commanding immediate silence. After a chilling hush, the voice issued a verdict. "We must *resurrect* him!"

239

That meant mouth-to-mouth resuscitation. Väinämöinen's cloudy eyes went into another spasm at the sight of the unsightly ogre diving into him, as if to kiss a sleeping beauty.

It was enough to send his mind retreating into the darkness.

Chapter 12

The dreadful noise of hundreds of stones rattling together was Ankou's signature sound for summoning the dead, but this time it was an alarm for awakening them. The clattering rocks were accompanied by the familiar drone of old wagon wheels grinding on the pavement.

Väinämöinen opened his eyes at the creaking disturbance and immediately felt a stiff pain in his back. His hands patted around and reached under his backside to confirm that he had been sleeping on a mattress of rocks. He held one of the stones directly in his line of sight, but it was a bit fuzzy, a problem he easily remedied by rubbing the sleep from his eyes. Finally, he could see. Beyond the stone, the overweening welcoming face of his savior-ogre came into focus.

"Are you dead too?" Väinämöinen asked with a congested voice.

"No, my child," Balaam answered softly. "We are alive."

"You mean *we* as in you and the other yous? Or you and *I*?"

"Yes, my child. *We* survived."

"Am I alive too? That's what I'm asking."

"Yes, my child."

"Wait… You saved me?"

"Indubitably," Balaam smiled. "I am, and always will be, your personal savior."

Väinämöinen rolled his eyes and struggled to get to his feet. He flayed his arms to keep balance on the rocks as he looked up and was immediately struck by a sweeping landscape of green and golden hues, nested under a sky that had gone from dark and dull to a rich cobalt blue. The fog was still there, but now it hugged the peaks of rustic snow-topped mountains. A heavenly view. In fact, it occurred to Väinämöinen that he was being ferried to paradise. He stumbled to the edge of Ankou's wagon for a closer view.

"Please, my child. Do not fall again."

"Stop squeezin' your skivvies, I just want to see where I'm at."

"Better to know where We are going, my child."

"Again, when you say *we*, you mean..." his voice trailed off, hoping that Balaam would just answer the question directly.

"Yes, I mean Us," Balaam confirmed. "And also *our* companions over there." He pointed beyond the wagon's head where Väinämöinen's sore eyes were met with the grateful sight of the familiar pastel-blue Mazda T2000 leading the way for Ankou's wagon. Clarence, Omiokane and Shiva sat in the rear of the truck, taking in the view. The Concierge, apparently, had become the new designated driver. He was much better than the previous one and sailed the blue dragon with smooth finesse.

"If we're not dead, why is Ankou here?" Väinämöinen asked Balaam.

"Who knows? Perhaps the ol' bugger thought you were as good as dead. We all did, really. Or perhaps he was going about some other business when he saw the six of us stranded on the side of the road with a flat tire and a stiff body. Either way, it was most fortunate that he chanced upon us. Dead bodies We can handle on Our own, but We admit to being completely inept in the vocation of automobile repair. Ankou, on the other hand, demonstrated remarkable proficiency on the subject. One could rightly assume that he's had more than one wheel fly off this old wagon of his." Balaam patted the jittery wood affectionately, but then something else soon grabbed his attention. He stood up and smiled.

"My child, it appears you've awakened at precisely the right moment. We have arrived at our destination."

"How can you tell?"

"How could We not?" Balaam breathed in deeply. "The spirituous smell of grapes fermenting in fresh air. The sound of tractors frolicking along acres of green and golden hue pastures. Oh, I'd recognize those soft parallel lines of autumnal harvests from any distance. However, the surest sign that one has crossed the borders of wine county is the sign itself, elegant in its vintage vineyard calligraphy." Balaam threw out his arms. "My child, I give you... the inimitable... Elysian Fields."

Balaam's description was a bit puffy, but on-point nevertheless. Elysium was a paradise of sprawling spring and autumnal colors, as if the two seasons had agreed to meet over a glass of wine. This made the view alone intoxicating. But the air also played its part in inebriating the visitors. They all dismounted their wagons and took several long minutes to inhale and imbibe the heady fragrance.

The Concierge removed his sunglasses and floated over for a closer view of the welcome sign. Next to the sweeping strokes of calligraphy was a marble relief of a dashing Grecian man, whose poise was as refined and elegant as the contours of his lean body. His effeminate face was as full and fresh as the fragrance lingering in the air. The creator of the sign had no qualms with exhibitionism. With the sole exception of fig branches and leaves twining around his waist to conceal the lower half, the relief sculpture was brazenly naked.

"Dionysius," the Concierge read the name printed next to the relief. A truly romantic welcome statement was printed underneath:

Welcome to the Elysian Fields: A Winery Company.
We are artisans of the vine.
Our oeuvre of fine wines is diverse yet refined;
Our aesthetics, firm and passionate; our scents, sensual;
Our flavors, ancient and memorable.

The description was all so very Italian, but when the Concierge gazed out over the fields, where men were hard at work, he saw a fraternity of...

"Mexicans?" he mumbled. A master counter, he numbered them at four hundred, with each one donning a large, elaborate Aztec-style tattoo of a rabbit emblazoned on the whole of his back.

"Welcome!"

A hearty, warrior-like man with an enormous handlebar mustache that arched into a full beard marched towards them. They all peered at him, wondering how and why an obvious Viking was wearing a banker's business suit. Standing next to him was a younger, flamboyant version of himself: a broad-shouldered, strapping young man with long Norwegian-blonde hair. He too was in a suit, though, for some reason, he carried an industrial-sized hammer in his hand.

"Welcome!" the older gentleman announced again. "I am Odin. Tell me, what brings you all here? Oh, and this is my esteemed son, Th—"

"Father," Thor interrupted and whispered into Odin's ear. "Asking *'what brings you all here'* sounds unwelcoming, as if they have no business being here. Perhaps it would be more inviting to new customers to thank them for taking the time to visit our establishment and then ask, *'How might we assist you today?'"*

"Welcome!" Odin announced again for his second take. "Thank you so much for visiting our warm, welcoming establishment. We invite people of all race, creeds and colors to join in the festivities of our wines and ales. How might we—"

"Father?"

"That was too much, wasn't it?" Odin whispered back.

"Yes. And it was transparent. You don't need to mention issues of race and ethnicity unless they do it first. Try it one more time."

"Uh, actually"—the Concierge raised his finger, overhearing them— "I do have a question about race and ethnicity."

Odin plastered his face with the most politically correct smile he could muster.

"This is the Elysian Fields, right?" the Concierge asked.

"Absolutely. And Welcome!" Odin answered earnestly.

"But the Elysium is from Greek mythology. You two are Nordic."

"Excellent question!" Odin clasped his hands.

"Father, that wasn't a question."

"What is your question?" Odin asked the Concierge.

"My question is…" the Concierge began, but was soon distracted by the sound of the Mexican workers. He thumbed in their direction. "How did you immigrate Mexican workers into Greek mythology? Who are those guys?"

"Them?" Odin nervously twiddled his fingers. "They're called— What are their names again, son?"

"*Centzon Totochtin,*" Thor answered fluently, though it was evident that this was from some practice. "They work here," he added with an assuring smile.

"Are they *documented*?"

"Great Ragnarok! I knew it!" Odin grabbed his son and spun him around. For a moment everyone thought they were going to make a run for it, but instead they convened into a private meeting with their backs turned.

"They're with the government," Odin whispered a little too loud. "You distract them. I'll set everything on fire."

"We're not with the government," Clarence interjected.

"You're not?" Odin turned back. "Are you with the IRS?"

"No."

"Are you sure?" Thor asked, holding up his hammer as he approached the Concierge. "Because a short, plump government lady came through here making all sorts of accusations and asking questions similar to yours."

"Nah, nah, nah, homie. That woman is why we're here."

"So then you *are* in cahoots with this woman!" Odin shouted.

"No, we're in cahoots *against* her," the Concierge raised his voice. "She's the reason that we are all homeless. Now could you tell your homeboy here to put down his hammer? Increase the peace, homie."

"This hammer has a name." Thor inched forward. "*Mjölnir*. And if I must, I will use it to pound every pinch of slang from your plebeian vocabulary!"

"My word! I like this fellow," Balaam exclaimed.

"Sorry. This is my son, Thor. And this"—Odin prompted Thor to lower his weapon—"is his grammar hammer."

"It's called *Mjölnir*, Father."

"Whatever," Odin snapped and rolled his eyes. "Ever since we got into the wine and ale business, he insists that we be more refined for our customers. I've taken more than my share of lumps from… 'Mjölnir.'" He mockingly made air-quotes.

"Wait!" Väinämöinen chimed in. "Did I hear you just mention that you are in the business of wine *and* ale?" Odin and Thor nodded. "Oh, thank the Heavens. We'll tell you everything you want to know about what brought us here"—Väinämöinen threw his arms around Odin and Thor—"over a beer!"

*

Odin and Thor escorted them to an old but renovated amber-colored chalet, situated on a small hill right outside the vineyard. Inside, with its combination of stonewalls and wood enclosure, was a temple for libations. Ankou, aloof as always, parted from the group and took a lone seat at a corner bar for wine tasting.

The rest of the group went to a separate room for beer, where the bartender acknowledged them with a silent, unsmiling nod—just like the Barkeep back home. Expressionless, he stood behind the bar, drying glasses with a fresh white towel. He wore no white shirt, no tie—not even pants. His fashion consisted of a waist tunic, an elaborate gold breastplate and a headdress of standing streamers and confetti. When he turned around to stack his cleaned glasses, the Concierge noticed that he, too, had the same rabbit mural on his back.

"Tepoztecatl," Thor summoned the bartender as they all took their seats. "A round of Kvas for everyone, please." He looked down the bar at the group. "This is our house label. Is everyone okay with that selection?"

"Kvas," Omiokane said, smacking his lips, "is why I brought them here."

"None for me, Mister Thor," Shiva declined. "I will pass."

"Glass of water this way, thank you very much," Balaam added.

"Water?" Odin asked.

"He turns it into wine," Väinämöinen answered and then whispered: "Show-off."

"Ah, well, if you're tired of drinking your own wine, we've got plenty here."

"What do you have?" Balaam asked, considering the offer.

"Beats me." Odin shrugged. "I don't drink wine. Neither does my son."

"But you run a winery," Clarence said.

"Ah, we just got into the business as a way to postpone going into that retirement home."

"So you bought this place from Dionysius?" the Concierge asked.

"Nah. We *took* it from him. That was back in the good ol' days when my son used his hammer for conquering, not correcting people's grammar."

"Wait!" the Concierge stopped him. "Did you say you *took* it from Dionysius?"

"That's exactly what I said. I only wish I could find him and give it back. Awful profession, this business of grapes," Odin lamented. "It turned my son into a fruit and me into a failure!"

"Father, please," Thor protested with two pinches of sugar in his inflection.

"I tried expanding this into a brewery, hoping that would re-make him into a man, but just look for yourself." Odin gestured at Thor who rolled his eyes effeminately.

"Perhaps a better explanation is that the apple doesn't fall very far from the tree," Omiokane suggested.

"I don't know what that means. Besides, we don't make our wines from apples." Odin rapped the bar. "Tepoztecatl, where are those beers?"

Tepoztecatl was unresponsive. With his signature stoicism, he took his time pouring the beers, angling each glass so as to even out the head of foam. Only after such perfection was achieved did he line them up on the bar. Väinämöinen skipped all tasting etiquette and dove beard first into Tepoztecatl's craftsmanship. Odin saw his eyes light up at the first tang of flavor.

"Aaah," Odin roared approvingly. "That look right there is why they call it the *Mead of Inspiration*!"

"I've never tasted anything like this," Clarence added after imbibing a mouthful. "How do you make it?"

"We begin by taking all the Gods of the *Aesir* and all the Gods of the *Vanir*, and all at once, we have them spit into a bowl."

The repulsive description immediately made Clarence spurt.

"Yes! Just like that," Odin roared again. "Except human spit only makes a mess; the spit of the Gods created a new God named *Kvasir*. Then we hire two dwarves to drain the blood of Kvasir and mix it with honey. After that you just have to let it ferment for a spell and then"—Odin slammed his hand on the bar—"KVAS! The beer so strong that three glasses makes even the giants a little tipsy."

"This is perfect!" Clarence exclaimed.

"Thank you, kind man. We try." Thor smiled humbly.

Stoically, Tepoztecatl began cleaning up the splattered beer heaved out by Clarence. He made no reactions to Clarence's apologies. He simply swabbed the deck and walked off.

"The ol' chap doesn't strike one as too terribly happy to be here," Balaam noted.

"Bah!" Odin grumbled and dismissed this with his hand. "He's not 'terribly happy' to be anywhere."

"What's with the rabbit tattoo on his back?" The Concierge pointed as Tepoztecatl walked away. "I noticed the others have it too."

"It's the symbol of the Centzon Totochtin, which means *four hundred rabbits*," Thor answered. "It's the name of their fraternity. Gods of Drunkenness."

"Gods of *Destruction* is more like it," Odin added. "I swear to you, every weekend there's a frat party and they make a wreck of everything, completely defeating every purpose of cheap labor—" Odin quickly stopped himself. "You did say you're not government spies, right?"

"Right," the Concierge nodded.

"Gods of *destruction* through *drunkenness*?" Shiva shook his head. "I have never approved of artists who require drugs or alcohol to inspire their creativity. The impulse for destruction should come from the heart. Mister Odin, these men of yours are amateurs."

"Yeah?" Odin rejoined. "Come back and look at this place on Monday. Better yet come on the weekend. See if you don't go crazy listening to them jump up and down from the roof. Blasted bunnies can jump as high as the Moon, I tell ya."

"All part of the re-management process," Thor hurried to add. He winced when he saw his father washing down one half of his glass in a single gulp. "Tepoztecatl? A glass of water for father, please."

"See?" Odin said, looking at the Concierge. "This is what wine does to a man."

"Maybe we can help you with that," Clarence butted in. "We'd like to take some of your wine and Kvas off your hands."

"How much of it?" Odin asked.

"All of it."

Thor and Odin looked at each other, blinking and bewildered.

"All of it?" Thor asked and Clarence nodded. "Why do you need *all* of our merchandise?"

"To throw a party."

"Great Ragnarok, not another party." Odin palmed his face.

"It won't be here," Clarence clarified. "It will be at the retirement home. And there will be thirty-three million Gods there. Maybe more."

"Well," Odin thought it over. "That might certainly put us out of business, which wouldn't necessarily be a bad thing."

"Father, you can't be serious," Thor protested. "This is our business—a family business. And contrary to the popular expression, yes, this business *is* personal. It is personal to *me*."

"Oh boy, here comes the Drama Queen."

"Excuse me, *your majesty*!" Thor popped his lips, rolled his eyes and rotated his neck. "You are not going to tell me how to live my life. I may be your son, but I am *not* a little boy anymore. I am a grown man and I've finally found an occupation that I enjoy and I am not—I repeat, NOT—going to let you take it away from me! I hate you, I hate you."

Thor's stool knocked over as he pushed away from the bar and ran off sobbing. Odin was expressionless as he watched his son storm away.

Then he looked at Clarence.

"Just in case you really are with the IRS, if we make this a donation, it would be tax deductible, right?"

"Absolutely," Clarence nodded. "But no, we're not with the IRS."

"Done!" Odin slammed his hand on the bar. "We'll drink to it. Tepoztecatl, bring us another round."

"Oh yeah, that reminds me," Clarence added. "Do you think we could also borrow the 'Centzo–whatchamacallits?"

"The Cinco de Mayans? Sure. But what do you need them for?" Odin asked.

Clarence looked down the bar at all of his companions and smiled.

"To help us throw the party, of course."

*

007-2 wiped the weary from her face and decided that after a full week of restoring order to the retirement home, she deserved a drink. She pushed away from her office desk, which was still soiled with the remains of her disemboweled computer, and made her way to the water cooler. She was still on the job, so a "drink" meant a glass of water.

The break room was completely vacant. The long lunch tables were unpopulated and the proverbial water cooler, which looked lonely in the corner, longed for the old days of hosting an idle congregation of gossipy Gods. This was all part of the new government regime that restricted the Gods to their own stations and kept them at a due distance from any and all government offices—including the break room.

She grabbed a clean mug from the cabinet and poured herself a glass, then hovered alone around the cooler, enjoying her own company and savoring the feeling of shaving off a few minutes of company time. She even leaned her elbow on the top of the cooler, making it clear that she was, indeed, slacking.

There was no office or elevator music playing to fill the dead silence, so she made it up by whistling a tune from the '80s, humming at certain intervals and snapping her finger at others. Then she looked at her watch, the only proper way of reckoning time as far as she was concerned, and decided that she didn't want to overdo it with the whole slacking thing.

She finished the last of her water and dutifully made her way to the sink to clean it. There would be no dirty mugs sink-squatting on her watch.

She turned the sink knob and the faucet made a coughing sound, then went into a short, violent convulsion. She didn't flinch at this, but blinked suspiciously. She turned the knob a second time, and the faucet repeated the action, only this time it worked harder to give her what she wanted. After a long minute of choking, it finally heaved up the goods. A single drop fell from its mouth, and then another.

The faucet offered no more than a succession of continuous drops. But this wasn't the only thing that was wrong. She shifted her angle to allow the light to hit the drops and leaned in forward for a closer look. She held out her hand and allowed one droplet to fall into her palm. Just as she suspected, it was rust colored. Just before concluding that the piping system had rotted, her nose caught a scent coming from the faucet. The smell was unmistakable.

She gave the knob another turn, which finally brought the faucet to drool a small quantity into her mug. She had to be sure and there was only one way for that to happen. With no reservation, she poured what could have been rust-water into her mouth and swished it around from cheek to cheek. She swallowed and sighed. Her blood immediately turned warm, not from the drink but from the realization that contraband had been smuggled into her retirement home. Even worse, it was surreptitiously filtered into the water system. The word banged in her head like a hangover: *Beer!*

She stormed out of the break room with a trail of smoke practically steaming from both ears. The door slammed and came off its hinges as she exited. After a few short seconds, she was back to appraise the damages, but also to follow up on a second thought that had occurred to her.

She was back at the faucet. This time, she turned the other knob and placed her mug back under the nozzle. It hacked and heaved until finally dribbling from its mouth a stream of blood-water. She did another taste test, and it was as just as she expected: *Wine!*

She exploded into the hallway, which, much to her surprise, was empty. *No, of course it's empty*, she immediately thought. *If they had been partying in these hallways, I would have heard it.*

She went to the first door and knocked, but there was no answer. The second door was the same. She stopped at a third door and stared intently at a sign emblazoned above the knob.

I am all that has been and shall be...
And no mortal has lifted my veil.

This time, she didn't bother to knock. Like a suspicious mom trying to catch a substance-abusing child red-handed, she bolted in with such force that she almost toppled to the ground. The room was empty.

All rooms were empty.

Marching back the way she came, she passed through the lobby and out the front door, where she was greeted by, of all people, a pizza delivery boy. With a flat face and even flatter eyes, the kid checked the address on a small notepad, then looked at 007-2.

"Is this the Golden Age Retirement Home?" he asked. Dumbfounded, she didn't answer. Reading from his notepad, he continued. "I've got an order of three million thick crust, extra cheese, triple anchovy, no pepperoni pizzas. Oh, and one veggie pizza on thin, gluten-free crust. Will this be cash or credit?"

Speechless, 007-2 stepped past him and gaped at the huge delivery truck loaded with three million boxes of pizza.

"The pizzas are getting cold, ma'am."

With those words, the sky was suddenly set ablaze as a comet rocketed down from the sky leaving a smoldering trail of white smoke. It crashed and detonated into the delivery truck, exploding into an apocalypse of flaming cheese and stray feathers. 007-2 and the delivery boy flagged their arms vigorously to clear the aftermath. Any human would have liquefied from the impact, but this was a world full of Gods, and 007-2 immediately recognized the winged woman wrapped in a smoking-hot, cheese-covered crimson gown.

"Lucifer," she growled.

Only half-conscious, the fallen angel lifted her head slowly and pointed to the sky.

"The roof... is on fire."

007-2 looked up. Her eyes swelled. The roof *was* on fire.

She bolted back into the retirement home and slammed the fire alarm. She reached under her desk to grab the Chain-of-Command. Red lights flashed and coruscated as she darted for the stairwell. She stopped at the base of the stairs and looked up. Her eyes spun from vertigo at the overwhelming sight of thirty-three flights of stairs.

By the time she reached the top floor, she was a sweaty mess. The beehive get-up on her head had cracked and splintered apart into scattered threads of hair. She panted so hard that her lungs threatened to collapse. But somehow she found the strength to keep going, one shaky step at a time, until she finally reached the roof door. She could smell the smoke. She could also hear music: a rap song. About a roof. And fire.

She felt a second wind gusting through her and fanning the flames of outrage. She trembled violently and combusted with a single foot that fired into the door. It exploded open and came off its hinges. She stood in the smoky debris with one fist clenched and the other spiraling her deadly horn and chain.

But nobody cared.

Thirty-three million Gods were somehow jammed packed and jamming away on the retirement home's rooftop, dancing in a bed of flames and wasted beyond all belief, religious or otherwise. They were having the time of their retired lives.

Behind a set of turntables, as the DJ of the rave, was none other than Tepoztecatl. Leaping around in the center of the dance floor was a fraternity of four hundred Mexican rabbits.

"OUT! OUT! EVERYBODY OUT!!!"

She shouted and bulldozed the Gods from the roof of the building. Those who escaped the demolition ran for the doorway, but she was soon after them too, punting them down all thirty-three flights of the stairwell before ejecting them out of the front door. Without pause she turned around and stormed back into the retirement home to repeat the process again.

This eviction rampage lasted well through the night as she hurled Gods off the roof. Some of the Gods were natural thrill-seekers and didn't bother waiting for the boot. They just jumped, with arms spread as if their feet were attached to a bungee. It took less than a minute for them to smack the ground, usually with a thud but sometimes with a tremendous thunder.

Actually, it was the sky that was thundering. As millions of drunken deities rained down from the roof, storm clouds gathered, promising a long night of heavy rain. If nothing else, the downpour helped to extinguish the rooftop fire.

From a far-off distance, Clarence, the Concierge, Väinämöinen, Balaam, Omiokane and Shiva rested on Omiokane's private hill, under a lone tree protecting them from the deluge. They listened to the chimes suspended from the branches as they danced and sang in the rain, but also to the far away voice of 007-2 as she blared through her bull horn, continuing her eviction rampage.

By morning, the purge was over, and the Sun was casting its rays through the abating smoke and shining its warmth on a wasteland of wasted Gods.

Chapter 13

"Strange numbers," Matylda brooded. "Very strange numbers."

She made three attempts to blindly stuff her feet into her flip-flops, each time missing her target. Her attention was locked on a book splayed across her lap, which she studied intently while lighting her briar pipe. Her face glowed as she fired up the tobacco leaves. Finally, her feet made contact with the pink bunnies. She looked up and under-hooked the pipe in her palm, ruminating on pages filled with hieroglyphic numbers.

Deciding she would figure the matter out later, she flapped the book shut, shoved it down her bosom, waddled across the room and opened her bedroom door to find Sirius eagerly waiting for her. The loving Lapphund pranced around in a small circle, then followed her as she plodded through a living room so littered with cultic knick-knacks that one could have easily mistaken her home for a flea market. The floor was full of random trinkets waiting to be stepped on, like landmines. But Matylda and Sirius both navigated the hostile terrain with staggering instinctual skill, avoiding every stray article on the floor until they reached the kitchen. There, seated silently at the table and propped up on two phonebooks, was the child Barkeep, Harpocrates, a.k.a. Horus.

"I'm assuming any boy who works at a bar serving beer won't be offended by a little pipe smoke," Matylda said with about as much maternal instinct as she could muster. A haze of smoke followed her as she went from one part of the kitchen to the next, retrieving two bowls, a spoon, a box of cereal and some almond milk. She prepared a serving for Sirius, who was practically ingesting it before the bowl was set on the floor. Everything else was placed on the table for the boy.

"I know what you're thinking," she claimed. "My hospitality leaves a lot to be desired. But if I bother asking you what you want to eat for breakfast, you probably won't answer until it's time for dinner, so here." She poured the cereal into his bowl. "Eat as much as you want. Oh"—she remembered something, went back to the cabinet drawer and came back with a pair of chopsticks—"just in case you're like the other weirdo. He's cute, but still a weirdo. Not that either one of us is the poster child of normalcy, but this neighborhood is full of nutcases, if you haven't noticed. Not sure what it says about me that I married one.

"You're probably wondering how we even got married in the first place." She blew smoke from her pipe. "Everybody wonders how a

Polish Goddess gets lassoed in by a Finnish God. Well, he wasn't my first pick. I was travelling abroad and got a bit of the jungle fever. I fell in love with an African God. But it didn't work out. So I stopped at a bar in Helsinki on my way home and saw that old fool watering down a perfectly good beer with his tears. Some blonde broad named Aino broke his heart. Next thing you know, we got drunk and woke up the next morning in the same bed. He had a job back then, so I so figured what the Hades and married him.

"People say love is blind, but it isn't true. Love has twenty-twenty vision—it sees everything but chooses to ignore what it sees. He ignores that I'm fat and I ignore that he's a drunk. And that's the trick. The secret to love is to lie. Lie to yourself. And lie to your lover. If you do that, you'll stay married. Nothing kills a marriage quicker than the truth. Women don't want the truth; we want a lie that sounds like the truth. Exhibit A: every fat woman knows that she's fat. Show me a woman that doesn't have at least five mirrors in her home. Trust me, we know that we're fat, but we want to hear that we're not and we want to hear it in a way that is convincing. So if you ever grow up and marry a fat woman, and she asks if she's fat, you give her exactly this answer: 'Sweetie, you're the perfect size for me.' She'll know you're full of it, but she'll fall for it anyways.

"Exhibit B—" She was interrupted by a door knock. "To be continued. In the meantime, prepare your own cereal. What do I look like, your mom? That's another thing: Your woman is not your mom. Your mom is your mom. Your woman is your woman. Know the difference. I'll be back with Exhibit B."

Matylda waddled out of the kitchen and to the front door. She had no peephole to help her see who was bothering her at this early hour, but she did have Triglav, her three-headed totem overlooking the doorway. From the inside, it worked like a submarine's periscope. She grabbed the cross handles and peered inside the ocular lens to discover Clarence waiting outside for her to answer.

"Him again?" she groaned. "What does he want?"

Reluctantly, she opened the door and Clarence tried his best to greet her with a warm smile.

"Good morning," he announced.

"I know you heard me through the door, so don't bother trying to butter me up with pleasantries. Just tell me what you want."

The palpable thought of buttering her up at all made him wince. She saw his face recoil and read his thoughts.

"Okay, so I'm not exactly a Barbie doll. But the question still stands. What do you want?"

"Is the Barkeep here?"

"He's eating."

"I need to talk to him."

"I said he's eating."

"Please?"

"Oooh, now we've found our door manners."

"I said good morning!"

"True"—she anchored her pipe into the corner of her mouth—"but I couldn't care less about how good the morning looks. A girl wants to hear how good *she* looks!"

"Maybe the morning is good because it's good looking at you this good morning."

"Hmm..." She curled her lips while deliberating Clarence's crock. Meanwhile, he summoned as much sincerity as he could into a smile.

"I guess that's good enough," she said and stepped aside, but as Clarence tried to enter, she blocked the way with her arm. "One more question, sweetie. Am I fat?"

"You know the good thing about fat?" Clarence answered without missing a beat. "*It sizzles when it's hot.*™"

"Good man." She lowered her arm, and though her apartment was a cluttered mess, she still had the nerve to demand him to: "Take off your shoes!"

Fortunately, Clarence was getting around on three legs, and his cane managed to give him advance warning of every landmine. Despite the obstacles and his old age, he moved quickly and found the boy already pouring his second bowl of cereal when he entered. Sirius jumped and barked with joy at the sight of Clarence, who leaned down to let the Lapphund lick him as he took a seat across from the boy.

"First and foremost, sorry to hear about the bar," Clarence began. "We have a plan underway to overthrow the government. Hopefully you'll be able to reopen in a day or two, and I will, of course, pay my tab just as soon as you tell me what it is. That brings me to why I'm here—I don't mean the tab—I mean, I think I know why you won't tell me what my tab is or why you won't say much of anything. I saw your image on the courtroom walls. I now know who you are."

Clarence paused and looked the Barkeep in the eye. The boy remained expressionless as he waited for the answer. Clarence dug into his pocket to retrieve the Heart of the Pole Star and held it out for him to see.

"At my trial, when I spoke, I was able to move this," he continued. "Omiokane said you are the God of Silence. But I think the opposite is true: You are the God of Words. Words matter. They *are* matter."

He paused and waited for the boy to say something, but, of course, he didn't.

"Anyway, I think the reason you stayed silent about the temple is because you knew I wasn't ready for the truth, but I think I'm ready now." Clarence studied the stoic look on the boy's face. This time he could tell that he was waiting for him to ask the question. "I can't build the temple, can I?"

"No," the boy answered flatly and without hesitation.

"Right." Clarence nodded. "But *you* can."

Clarence looked at the boy for confirmation. After a brief delay, he nodded. Clarence had the answer he needed. He returned the Pole Star to his pocket, stood up and turned to leave, but then stopped with one last question.

"That's what I thought. But before I go, I need to know one more thing: Why haven't you charged me for my beer?"

"Because," the boy began, "employees drink for free."

*

The Concierge, Balaam, Omiokane and Shiva sat atop the private hill, looking proudly at the aftermath of the Great Government Eviction. Only Väinämöinen sulked throughout the whole ordeal as a lovelorn beer lover.

"Free and unlimited Kvas," he scoffed. "If they only knew how good they had it."

"Say what one must about that crow of a woman," Balaam quipped. "She is, at the very least, effective."

"Looks like she's done too," the Concierge added.

"Good. Maybe there's still some Kvas left over." Väinämöinen stood up. "Time to claim the spoils of war."

"No. We cannot do that." Shiva jumped up and blocked him with all four arms.

"No, *you* can't do that because you don't drink. But I'll gladly take your share."

"I must insist that you resist. Mister Clarence says that he needs all of us sober, especially you and the Concierge."

"Well, as you can plainly see, the captain is AWOL?" Väinämöinen sat back down.

"Mister Clarence is meeting with the Barkeep."

"Exactly! They're reopening the bar as we speak, and I'll bet the bottom of my butt and boots that he's sneaking more than a few sips and samples while the rest of us sit here wasting away in sobriety."

"I am sorry, but you are most certainly wrong about Mister Clarence."

"And how would you know?"

"Because he is on his way here now. Look!" Shiva pointed the way and Väinämöinen turned to see Clarence making hurried steps to rejoin the group.

"Splendid!" Balaam leapt to his feet. "Let's hope he brought bottled water with him. We're dreadfully dehydrated."

"Oh no, you don't," Väinämöinen protested. "It's one for all and all for one."

"Hence, the operative words: *We're* dehydrated."

"Nice try," Väinämöinen sneered, "but if we don't drink, *We* don't drink."

"We were referring to drinking a glass of water, you tyrant."

"Which you can easily turn to wine when the rest of us aren't looking. Forget it. You don't drink a spit until the rest of us can. And don't try sneaking the Kvas when we're not looking. Whatever is left belongs to the lot of us."

"Surely, you are mistaken, sir. Whatever is left belongs to Us."

"Here we go." The Concierge rolled his eyes.

"My dear man, was there every any question about this?" Balaam continued. "Need We remind you that We've been petitioning for the two of you to purge this place of its heathen trash for years, and you failed miserably—both of you. Now that the task is done, We'll be moving in straightaway. All assets are hereby appropriated, and yes"— Balaam turned to Väinämöinen—"that includes the wine and ale."

"Don't you threaten me!" Väinämöinen grabbed Balaam by his collar.

"Mister Balaam"—Shiva jumped between them—"you don't even drink ale."

"And you don't even drink," Balaam retorted, "so stay out of this!"

"Kyllä," Väinämöinen agreed. "I want to see this British troll turn his other cheek after I punch the first one."

"My friends," Omiokane intervened. "Clarence-san is almost here. We have plenty more work to do. Surely we can bicker when this is over."

Reluctantly, Väinämöinen relaxed his grip, prompting Balaam to swat away his hand. They all turned to find Clarence, huffing and wheezing as he finally made his way to the peak of the hill. He paused to catch his breath as he looked over the landscape and at his plan that had pulled together as perfectly as a jigsaw puzzle. Of course, all the pieces were now scattered across the vast lawn waiting to be assembled. But still, the work that would have taken Clarence and his companions days to do had just been pulled off over the course of a single night.

"So what now, ystäväni?"

"Now comes the hard part." Clarence wiped sweat from his brow. "We have to evict the last occupant from the retirement home: 007-2." These words were immediately demoralizing, and everyone released a collective groan. "I know," Clarence conceded, "it's going to take all of us to pull this off."

"It's going to take more than that, ystäväni. Even the four of us couldn't—" Väinämöinen stopped mid sentence. He muttered suspiciously as his eyes scanned the group. His lips moved noiselessly as he bobbed his finger up and down, taking inventory. Despite their small number, he did three re-counts to be sure.

"I knew it!" he said. "Where's the troll?"

These words had everyone pivoting in place, searching over their own shoulders only to reach the same conclusion: Balaam had inexplicably disappeared.

"Perhaps he ascended," the Concierge shrugged. "I heard he can do that."

"No," Omiokane said, his antennae-like ears having detected him. "Judging from the sound of feet hastening through the grass, I would say he's running from something."

They all turned in the direction Omiokane pointed out and saw the distant figure of Balaam sprinting away. He was headed for the retirement home.

"Mennä tuli hännän alla. He's got a fire under his rump," Väinämöinen scoffed. "What did I tell ya? Soon as we turned our backs, he's off to claim the ale for himself."

"No," the Concierge shook his head as if he knew this was going to happen. "He's going to claim the temple."

*

With one hand holding her bullhorn tight to her waist, 007-2 patrolled the hallways, one by one, checking each apartment. A graveyard shift of evicting over thirty-three million Gods had taken its toll. Her clothes were as baggy as her eyes and as wrinkled as her tired face. Still, she showed no signs of letting up. She was even whistling as she completed the last of her rounds and made her way back to the lobby.

261

But the whistling stopped at the sight of a shadow stretching across the lobby floor and terminating at the sandaled feet of a lone figure standing defiantly in the doorway with his back to the Sun.

"You again," she whispered.

"Yes," Balaam whispered back. "I've come to fulfill the prophecy."

"What prophecy?"

"Of my return." Balaam tightened both fists. "In other words, *I'm back.*"

"Not for long."

She anchored her feet into a battle stance and began twirling the bullhorn by its long chain. With a single forceful whip, the chain snapped and sliced through the air with Balaam's head as its target. This time, she underestimated the troll. He wasn't fighting for a tavern like before; this time he was fighting for his home—if fight was even the word. This was a crusade.

Balaam dodged her attack with a duck and effortlessly leaped into the air, where he somersaulted and came down with an arrow-like kick.

She eluded the blow by leaping to the side and snapping her chain so that it hooked and raveled around his feet. She pulled again sending him toppling to the floor. Before he knew it, the bullhorn was already arching through the air, leaving him with only a split second to roll to the side and avoid its crushing blow. This gave him his chance for a counter-attack. He grabbed the horn and pulled it with such enormous strength that it yanked her off her feet and sent her tumbling through the air and crashing into the lobby desk. Her computer parts scattered across the floor.

She stood up and shook the cobwebs from her head. Surprisingly, despite the impact of the crash, she hadn't released her end of the chain. Balaam held tightly to his end, gripping the bullhorn. The battle for the Chain-of-Command had now escalated into a tug of war as they took turns jerking on their respective ends, hoping to pull the other off their feet.

"Give it up, Balaam. This is the end."

"No, this is only the beginning. And in the beginning was..." He took a deep breath and finished with a blasting roar. *"THE WORD!"*

The force of his voice amplified through the bullhorn, whisking her off her feet and sending her cracking into the wall where she left a permanent impression. In slow spurts, she peeled away from the wall and plopped to the floor, beaten and unconscious.

"Now that's what I call a Big Bang," he quipped with cocky victory.

Breathing heavily, Balaam claimed his prize by whipping the chain at himself to catch the other end. The retirement home was now his, and his alone, though the lobby was almost completely destroyed.

"A masterpiece!"

Balaam spun around at the sound of Shiva's voice and found the four-armed God marveling at the aftermath of dust and debris. Clarence, the Concierge, Väinämöinen and Omiokane didn't share in this sentiment. Though 007-2 had been duly deposed, they now had a more formidable tyrant to deal with.

"You and you." Balaam pointed to the Concierge and Väinämöinen. "You're both fired. You and you"—he pointed to Shiva and Omiokane—"are no longer welcome here. And you..." He pointed to Clarence. "You are the new Concierge."

Väinämöinen and the Concierge flapped their arms and groaned.

"Ignore them," Balaam ordered. "It should be easy enough for you to keep count of the tenants now."

"It will," Clarence answered. "Every day I'll count one. Is that really what you want?"

"You'll count *three*, and yes, this is precisely what *We* want."

"And now you have it. Sounds like a lonely life. Who will you talk to, Balaam?"

"To Us!"

"Right. To yourself."

"Me, myself and I."

"Should make for a rich conversation."

"You're quite welcome to join Us."

263

"No, thanks. I don't want to live in a world where there is only one idea, one truth, one lie and one answer to every question. I believe in diversity. But if it's monotheism you want, then cut the BS and work with us, all of us, as *one*."

"Compelling, sir. But, unfortunately, also a bit corny. We're terribly sorry, but We're afraid We'll have to pass."

"Balaam, listen." Väinämöinen stepped forward. "I know we've had our differences. I've always blamed you for losing my job. I don't know how many beers it's been since I last stepped foot in this lobby." He looked up and around at the empty and now tattered walls. "Brings back memories. I was a singer, ya know, and a counter. Sometimes I was able to do both at the same time. I had all the Gods numbered until you came along and messed me up. Couldn't tell how many of you there really were. Were you three or were you one? But after hearing the wise words of ystäväni, I realize you're both. The lot of us can be six *and* we can be one. What I'm saying is: Two numbers can occupy the same space at the same time. For instance, my mother never looked a day older than sixteen, even when she turned one hundred sixty-one. People would ask her all the time where the fountain of youth was, and she'd raise her beer and say 'right here.' And because I know you're itching to ask, I'll just tell you now that she passed her genes and her beer over to me, and I don't care what anyone says, somewhere underneath this friendly fat and thicket of whiskers is a Mister Olympia of the new millennia. I'm sure of it."

Väinämöinen's eyes went skyward, but why he was also rubbing his belly wasn't clear to the group. They just stared at him, mentally lock-jawed.

"Splendid story," Balaam said. "The part where you went completely past the point was especially brilliant."

"Balaam, if you do this, I won't be your concierge," Clarence threatened. "It will be you and only you. Make a decision."

"Decision duly made—you're fired."

"Tough break, ystäväni. You can crash and cry on the couch when this is over."

"Mister Balaam," Shiva pleaded, stepping forward, "please take me as proof of Mister Clarence's wisdom. I am one God, but I have four arms. I can't imagine what I would do with only two, much less one."

"Great," the Concierge frowned. "That makes us all feel real adequate, Shiva, thanks."

"Oh, come now, sir. Surely you're not slighted by this quadruped"—Balaam pointed—"or are We supposed count the legs too? Hard to know how many limbs this loon really has. However, We're fairly certain that it only takes two arms to steer an automobile, and Sir Shiva here couldn't do it with even four."

"I was driving a Dragon. It is a very difficult occupation."

"Sorry to bust the old bubble, Shiva, but you were driving a wagon not a Dragon, though in either scenario, one could hardly call that driving. Next time, start small and try 'driving' a tricycle. But if that doesn't satisfy your completely delusional imagination, you can try investing in a mule and pretend you're riding a unicorn."

"See, now that's just wrong, Balaam," the Concierge cut in. "You can bust bubbles, man, but don't diss dreams."

"It's okay." Shiva shoved aside his comrades and stepped forward with his chin up and his chest inflated. "The Dragon is real. But if it is proof he wants, then it is proof he shall get."

Shiva ignited a fire in his hands. Balaam had awakened and angered the Dragon.

"Are you threatening Us? Do you not know who We are? I, sir, am the Lamb of God."

"And *I*, Mister Balaam, am in the mood for lamb curry."

"Whoa, whoa, whoa!" Clarence jumped in between them. "Shiva, what are you talking about? You're a vegetarian."

"Bugger off. Clearly, this heathen is hungry for a thrashing. By the way, Shiva, We must say that We find your witticism quite amusing, but unfortunately for you, the last laugh is reserved for Us."

Balaam released a heinous laugh through his bullhorn, creating a vibration so violent that it shook the walls, causing them to splinter apart. The tremor erupted into a massive quake and broke the lobby in two. The ceiling collapsed on Clarence and his companions, but Shiva made the save by throwing up all four of his arms and intercepting a massive chunk of wall that would have crushed them. His knees buckled from the pressing weight, but he soon found his footing and his strength and hurled the rock directly at Balaam.

Balaam panicked. He had no other defense except to shriek through the bullhorn. The force of the sound wave pierced through the rock and shattered it into sand. Once again he laughed, creating a second tremor even stronger than the first. Shiva threw out all four of his arms to hold his balance, but eventually he and the others lost their footing and fell to the ground—except for the Concierge. He floated in free space, and the look on his face showed that he had enough of keeping his cool. The debris had cracked one lens on his shades. Slowly, he removed them. They were useless now. He flung his arm and tossed them. Balaam lowered his bullhorn. It would take more than earthquakes to topple this one.

"Clever boy," Balaam said. "Do you have any other tricks you'd like to show Us?"

"Actually, I do, homeboy. Ever heard of the Twelve Foot Ninja?"

"Can't say that We have, though judging by the name it's probably safe to assume that this tall ninja has never heard of the metric system."

"Twelve Foot Ninja is a band, homie. They have a song called 'Shuriken.'

> ♪ The bird slips out of my hand
> and into the heart of the enemy
> The bird slips out of my hand
> plunges into the heart ♪

"Not quite sure We understand."

"A shuriken is a small-blade used by Japanese warriors. Usually, it's concealed in the hands." The Concierge held up both hands to show that they were empty.

"You certainly are a cultured one, aren't you? Though We never would have pegged you as the Japanese military type."

"I'm not," the Concierge rebutted. "But I love their food."

With lightning speed, the Concierge reached into his dashiki, pulled out his chopsticks and rocketed one at Balaam. It shot through the air like a shuriken. Balaam haphazardly stumbled to the side. He saw a blur whistle past his temple as he barely avoided the fatal blow. The

Concierge arched back his arm ready to launch the second shuriken.

"Sorry, ol' sport, but you missed."

"That was a warning shot, brotha."

"Good. Because this one isn't, *brother.*"

Balaam inhaled deeply, preparing to release a thunderous sound that would send the Concierge crashing through the wall. Quicker on the draw, the Concierge fired his second chopstick. This time, he didn't miss. It shot right through the mouth of the bullhorn and into Balaam's throat, hitting him at his most powerful and vulnerable point.

The ogre collapsed to his knees, clenching his throat and coughing violently. He was down and open for attack. All at once, they rushed in to tackle him, but Balaam proved yet again that he was not to be underestimated. He gagged himself with a finger, inducing a heave and a hack that sent the chopstick rocketing back through the air. Everyone ducked. But it didn't fire with as much force as they expected. In fact, it fell on the floor right within their reach.

"Quick! Grab it," Väinämöinen shouted to the Concierge.

"You crazy, man? I don't do sloppy seconds." The Concierge recoiled, gazing at his chopstick, smothered in bile and saliva.

"I can do this all day," Balaam said, still hunched over and laughing through an injured cough.

"The Staff of Power!" Shiva exclaimed. "Let's see him heave that up."

Shiva snatched the walking stick from Clarence's hand and cocked it back like a javelin, preparing to thrust.

"Shiva." Clarence quickly grabbed his arm.

"What are you doing, Mister Clarence? This is our only chance."

"It's *only* a walking stick," Clarence intoned and reclaimed his staff to stand back up. "Call me corny if you want, but I'm not going to resolve this violently. I mean, c'mon Balaam, you and Shiva were the first two to step in front of Ankou to protect me, and now we're throwing chopsticks down each other's throats? Does this make any sense at all? Like it or not, we're friends. We've been to the library together, which

I know doesn't sound like the most exciting thing for a group of men to do, but it turned out to be exciting, even life threatening. And we've been on a road trip together—to a winery! And I know that's also not the most manly thing for a pack of guys or Gods to do, but they also had a brewery and we got to sit together at a bar and have a few drinks. That's called bonding, my friends, male bonding."

Balaam's hardened features hadn't softened, but at the very least his aggravated breathing had finally begun to settle as his pupils panned across the group. Though his brow appeared permanently scowled, somewhere deep within his eyes were recollections of the memories they had recently forged together. Clarence was right. He and Shiva were the first to put their lives on the line to defend Clarence, and that meant that even for the briefest of moments, they had been allies.

As Balaam tried to reconcile this, a voice broke in, interrupting his thoughts.

"This discussion about wine and ale just reminded me..." Omiokane raised a finger. "Ever since I met you, Balaam-san, you've been drinking the same wine—*your* wine. But I recall that at the winery, Odin offered you to sample their house wines. Tell me, how would you rate their wine?"

Balaam paused to think it over. "They were... acceptable."

"I believe that is the point Clarence-san is making," Omiokane nodded. "We are like the wines —"

"Oh, for Heaven's sake, do I really have to listen to this? I thought you were a God of Wisdom, old man. At least try to upgrade your two cents to a nickel."

"He's not listening," the Concierge said. "We gotta bum rush this fool. *Now!*"

He prepared to charge forward, but Clarence quickly reached out and snagged him by his hand, then did the same to Omiokane, forming a three-man chain. Right away, Omiokane understood what was happening and extended his hand to Shiva, who extended one of his to Väinämöinen.

"What in blazes are you doing?" Balaam objected.

"We're bonding," Clarence answered, "and we're going to sing you a song, Balaam."

"No, you're not."

"An uplifting song."

"Don't do it."

"About friendship." Clarence closed his eyes and raised his chin.

"Stop that."

The other Gods closed their eyes as well. With hands bonded, a Finnish God of Song, an African God of Music, a Japanese God of Wisdom and an Indian God of Destruction held hands with a godless American and swayed their bodies in unison as they hymned and hummed the iconic '70s song by the funk and R&B band War.

> ♪ *Why can't we be friends, Why can't we be friends*
> *Why can't we be friends, Why can't we be friends* ♪

"Bloody hell! Alright, alright. We can negotiate this. Just don't sing any more bloody songs. DON'T TELL ME YOU'RE CONSIDERING LISTENING TO THESE HEATHENS!"

Clarence and his companions flinched from the sudden outburst, and their five-man chain reflexively coiled into a tangled and protective knot. Though the tantrum came without warning, it shouldn't have surprised. It was only a matter of time before Balaam's personality split and exploded like an atom. He was nearly fulminating at the mouth as he heaved in and out.

"I think the wine is kicking in," Väinämöinen whispered.

Finally, Balaam recomposed himself. Switching to his alter ego, he spoke with the stammering humility of a subject addressing his superior.

"Oh, Father, it's you. I— I— I didn't see you there. You just kind of snuck up on me."

"And the rest of us!" Väinämöinen added.

"SILENCE YOU FOOLS! THIS IS A FATHER AND SON MOMENT! NOW, AS I WAS SAYING, SON, WHAT IN MY NAME ARE YOU THINKING? PLEASE

TELL ME YOU'RE NOT CONSIDERING COOPERATING WITH THESE INFIDELS... Well, dad, I— I— I... Aren't you the one who told me to love my enemy?... I NEVER SAID THAT—YOU SAID THAT! DON'T PUT WORDS IN MY MOUTH... No, heaven forbid I would do such a thing, but, technically speaking, if I said it, *you* said it, no?... THAT'S ABSOLUTE RUBBISH! WHO TOLD YOU THAT?... Well, sir... NO NEED FOR THE 'SIR,' SON, 'FATHER WHO ART IN HEAVEN' WILL DO JUST FINE, OR IF YOU WANT JUST 'FATHER' OR EVEN 'DAD'... Thank you, *Father.* Well, take for example your use of the word 'rubbish?' When have you ever used that word? If I may say so, I believe you borrowed that little bit of parlance from me, which is, of course, to say, from *Us*... WHAT ARE YOU SAYING? A FATHER CAN'T USE THE LINGO OF HIS CHILD? AM I NOT *'COOL'* ENOUGH FOR YOUR GENERATION? I'M JUST TRYING TO RELATE WITH YOU, BOY, CUT ME SOME SLACK... No, no, no... That's not what I meant, dad. Whatever, this is all trivial. The point is, you taught me to be kind and considerate to others. What kind of son would I be if I didn't obey the word of my Father... Who art in Heaven... I SENT YOU TO SAVE THE WORLD, BOY! ARE THESE HEATHENS SAVED?... Brilliant point, Father."

Balaam turned to the group. "Listen ol' chaps, I would love to accommodate you all, but to do so means that you first have to accept me as your Lord and Savior. Do you think you can do that?"

"WHAT?!?" they all exclaimed together.

"Merely a formality, I can assure you." Balaam grinned.

Still clenching to each other, they all blinked, looking crossly at the offer.

"Of course. These types of details We can attend to later. Okay, Father. I'm sure they'll agree later to... INSOLENCE! ... Oh, come on; work with me here... DON'T TALK BACK TO YOUR FATHER, BOY!... I'm not talking back to you, I'm talking *to* you. Or, at least, I'm *trying* to talk to you, but one of Us seems to be having some difficulty with listening... OH, HERE WE GO WITH THAT AGAIN. 'I NEVER LISTEN.' YOU'RE BEGINNING TO SOUND LIKE THE HUMANS... Well, sir, or dad, or Father Who Art in Heaven, or whatever it is your ego craves at the moment, as painfully circuitous as it may seem, perhaps it is high time you start *listening to your children*!... I DON'T NEED TO LISTEN TO THIS CRAP. I'M OUTTA HERE."

Balaam threw down his bullhorn and stormed out of the retirement home, being sure to kick the door that was already off one hinge. An awkward silence followed.

"You know," the Concierge broke the silence. "This is even creepier if it turns out that he's not who he thinks he is."

"It's now or never," Väinämöinen whispered.

"What are you talking about?" the Concierge asked, but the answer was right in front of him. "Oh, the bullhorn!"

"No, we can't. What if he comes back in?" Shiva said.

"Well, if we hurry we can get it before he does. So who's going?" Väinämöinen looked around for volunteers, but no one stepped forward. "Oh, for the love of ale, I'll go then."

"No, no, no. He might hear your footsteps"—the Concierge pointed to the ground—"but I can float there." He pulled free from the group and began to glide for the bullhorn, but before he could get far, he felt a hand grab him. He looked back and saw Clarence holding him by the wrist. He vetoed the move with a shake of his head.

"It'll just make him an enemy all over again. We have to trust him."

"Trust him?" Väinämöinen nearly shouted. "Which one of him?"

"Mister Clarence is right," Shiva added. "We must put our faith in our friend."

"Shhhh," Omiokane shushed them as his ears twitched. "He's coming."

A few short seconds later, Balaam reentered with an entirely different composure.

"Sorry that you had to sit through that, ol' chaps," he said. "There's a bit of a history there that needs some sorting out."

"Is He going to be okay?" Clarence asked.

"He'll be fine. He just needed some air. Okay, so where were we?"

"From the sound of it, I think you were considering—"

"Oh, yes, yes," Balaam cut him off. "You all want Us to share the retirement home. Here's the thing, mates, I have to admit that I have more or less grown fond of some of you, and I hear what you're all saying about the virtue of sharing, I really do. If it were up to only me, I'd say, 'sure, why not.' Unfortunately, it isn't only up to me, it's up to Us. And as dreadful as this may sound, this ultimately is a committee decision."

"Can you vote on it?" Clarence asked.

"Voting would be a good idea, but I'm afraid it would only be a split decision."

"Well, no... There's three of you, isn't there?" Clarence added. "Where's the other board member? Get him out here, so you three can vote on this."

"Brilliant," Balaam agreed. "Let me go see if Father will talk to me. More importantly, let's see if the old crank is willing to *listen*."

Balaam walked back out of the retirement home and disappeared again around the corner. This time it took markedly longer for him to come back. The group could hear mumblings as he petitioned himself to return to the meeting and settle the issue democratically. After a brief pause, Balaam conceded and begrudgingly re-entered the lobby.

"Splendid," he said. "I am hereby calling to order a Trinity meeting for the purpose of holding a vote on whether or not to share the retirement home with the other heathens and false gods. For the purposes of keeping minutes, I ask that the three presiding board members please confirm their attendance. When I call your name a simple 'here' or 'present' will suffice." Balaam cleared his throat. "The Father?... HERE... The Son?... That's me and, yes, I am present." Balaam smiled and looked around. "And I am informed that our third board member is with us in spirit, which means we may begin. So, with no further ado, the question, which shall be repeated, is whether or not to allow the heathen gods to take residence in the retirement home. To avoid any confusion, as I call your name, please raise your right hand to vote *yes,* or your left hand to vote *no.* We will begin with myself. Balaam, do you vote yay or nay on permitting the heathen gods to live in the retirement home?"

Balaam stopped and thought about it. He bobbed his head back and forth, equivocating, before finally raising his right hand to vote yes.

"Father, do you vote yay or n—"

Before the question could be finished, the left hand went up.

"Okay, still not listening, I see. We now have one vote for yay and the other for nay. Finally, Holy Spirit, do you vote yay or nay to permit the heathen gods to live in the retirement home?"

Balaam stood still, waiting. The group waited also, each on the edges of their feet.

"What is happening?" Omiokane whispered. "Did he raise his hand?"

"Shhhh," the Concierge hushed him. "Not yet. He's thinking about it."

Clarence, more than anyone, was gripped by the suspense. He didn't so much as blink, not even once, as he stared intently, waiting for the vote. His eyes widened when he saw a stream of sweat trailing down Balaam's brow. As difficult as it was to imagine, even Balaam didn't know which way the third and final vote would swing. Suddenly, Clarence breathed in as he saw Balaam move.

His left shoulder flinched. And then it flinched again before falling into convulsions. It was trying to vote *no*, but Balaam was doing the best he could to suppress it.

"Fight it, Balaam, fight it!" Clarence whispered. "You can do it."

But maybe he couldn't. The left arm appeared strong and nearly made it mid-way before Balaam tried to beat it to the punch by raising his right arm. This time, it was the Father who made the interception. Suddenly, the poor ogre was in some strange tug of war with himself. He vibrated violently before finally falling to his hands and knees. Sweat fell from his head as he breathed deeply. It was a brief struggle, but one that left him nearly incapacitated. With one last concerted effort, he threw back his head and applied the last of his strength to stop the inevitable.

Everyone gasped as they saw the fire in Balaam's eyes blow out as quickly as a candle. His head lowered as if he had passed out. Simultaneously, his left hand went up, with the right hand only a split second behind it. His head down and both arms raised high, Balaam looked as if he were frozen in a moment of passionate worship.

"Is that yes or no?" the Concierge asked, confused.

"I believe it is… *both?*" Shiva said. "Another split decision."

"I guess they'll have to settle it over an arm wrestle," Väinämöinen added.

"No, wait." Clarence's eyes widened. "Look."

Balaam ground his teeth and gyrated his hands. He found his second wind, and with all the strength he could muster he fought back the resistance, allowing his left arm to go limp and drop to the floor. But he wasn't finished. With dramatic flair, Balaam lifted one leg and powered himself back to both feet. His right hand, still beaming skyward, sealed its decision by clenching into a powerful fist.

"Praise Jesus," Clarence whispered.

"Praise him," the group chanted in unison.

Swept up by the moment, Omiokane shoved everyone aside and ran over to Balaam, fell to his knees and embraced him. Balaam responded by placing his right hand on Omiokane's brow. He whispered unintelligible words before removing his hand. Omiokane blinked several times before he slowly opened his eyes and looked around.

"Sweet Hops from Heaven," Väinämöinen shouted and looked around, "he can see!"

"No... I just... I have something... in my eye." Omiokane blinked and rubbed his eyes.

"Here, let me help." Balaam leaned Omiokane's head back. "It's an eyelash, my child." He blew into his eye and turned Omiokane around to face the group.

"Now he can see!" Väinämöinen shouted again.

"No. But the eyelash is out." Omiokane bowed to Balaam. "*Arigatō*."

"You are most welcome, my child." Balaam spread open his arms. He looked down at the stray bullhorn at his feet and kneeled down to retrieve it, making sure to do it with his right hand. He snapped the chain upward and spun it around, causing everyone to stand back. But the threat was over and Balaam tossed the bullhorn through the air for Clarence to catch.

"Words are power, my child. Use them wisely. But please, don't sing any songs."

Clarence smiled. They all watched as he walked in slow, exhausted steps for what used to be the lobby desk. It was now in shambles. He stepped over the still unconscious body of 007-2 and saw what he was looking for underneath a pile of rubble. With some effort, he leaned down and came back up with Ptah's tool chest. He set it down on her back and opened it. He rummaged through the tools, pushing aside the ruler, compass, T-square and hammer until he found what he needed.

He stood and held up the flute.

"Let's jam."

Chapter 14

The Gods awakened around the same time that the Sun was tip-toeing into the West. *Breksta*, the Lithuanian Goddess of Twilight was the first to open her bleary eyes. She announced her awakening with an unexpected belch that acted as an alarm for the others and was seconded by a booming voice that carried over the sleeping masses.

"Good Evening!"

One by one, they stirred and sat upright to observe the human figure supporting his frail weight on a wooden staff and speaking through the government lady's bullhorn. They looked confused.

"She's history," Clarence announced while pointing at the mouthpiece, practically reading the Gods' thoughts. "So, it's just us now—all thirty-three million of us. I've only met a handful of you so far, but my understanding is that most of you already know who I am. I'm the one who is going to rebuild your temple. Well, up until a day ago, I thought that's who I was. With the help of Veritas... Where is she?" He made a visor with his hand as he scanned the crowd. He spotted her waking up in a bikini. "There she is. With her help, I was able to design your new temple. Let's give Veritas a round of applause."

The few Gods who were fully alert put their hands together into a golf clap.

"However," Clarence continued, "I'm not going to build your temple." He looked around at the score of Gods. "You are." He paused to let that sink in. "My new friend—excuse me—my *old* friend, Vynamomen, told me that the Gods are numbers. But where do we find numbers? We find them in music. Harmony occurs naturally according to numbers. Just plain old counting numbers: one, two, three, four—voilà—there's your formula for music. Which means that music *is the art of making numbers speak*—it makes them sing. And that's what we're going to do to build your temple. Whatever your differences are, I don't give an S. Put them aside. You all just drank beer and wine together. Now we're going to make beautiful music together."

He paused again and looked around at the enormous crowd of Gods.

"But before we make beautiful music"—he cracked a strangely sinister smile—"we're going to make some NOOOOOIIIIISSSE!" Clarence shouted as loud as his fragile voice could muster before it quickly collapsed into an old man's cough. Not wanting to lose the momentum, he pointed to his four-armed friend, who sat behind a damaru drum.

"Shiva," he said still hacking a bit, "kick that beat in!"

Shiva nodded to the cue and slammed two of his hands down, one after the other, producing a slow and heavy plodding drum beat. With his other hands, he raked an electric guitar, creating an arthritic bass line that crunched and grated like grinding bones. With each pulse, Clarence bobbed his head. He looked out at the crowd and saw thirty-three million Gods bouncing their heads right along with him.

"Yeah, yeah, yeah, one-two, one-two." Clarence waved his arms like a hip-hop artist. "The name of this song is 'Maybe.' As in, maybe I need a better song title, but this was the best I could do on short notice. And it goes a little something like this:

> ♪ *My life just got a little bit crazy, a little bit hazy,*
> *Stuck between these if's, and's and maybes,*
> *Like I'm trapped in the head of an old timer,*
> *Maybe I'm dead, maybe I have Alzheimer's.*
> *I need a reminder, so call me Charlton Heston,*
> *Indigestion every time I swallow these life's lessons,*
> *Doubting every minute, second-guessing this second,*
> *Maybe I have the answers, or maybe I forgot the question* ♪

"MAYBE!"

That cued Omiokane, Balaam, Väinämöinen and the Concierge to swing open the front door and swagger from the lobby as they took their positions next to Clarence. As his chorus, they pumped their arms in the air and shouted: *"MAYBE."* The Concierge prowled the air, pointing to the audience and stoking them to join the chorus and shout: *"MAYBE."* The repetition of this would-be magic word thundered through the air, causing the ground itself to shake.

"MAYBE!"

For the second verse, Clarence handed the bullhorn to Väinämöinen, who prepped himself by stroking his beard and punctuating his rhymes with vivid hand gestures.

> ♪ *Maybe I lost the point, but the point doesn't matter,*
> *Like the Mad Hatter's riddles that were scribbled with Scrabble.*

Maybe I'm on to something, but I'm off on a tangent,
These tall tales of Tobias mean I fell off the wagon,
'Cause I'm swimming in Kvas while reality shatters,
Wandering in Wonderland like a wandering bladder,
Still seeing crazy things only seen in a dream,
The first Gandalf is back, but now it's Lord of the Bling ♪

"MAYBE!"

The front door to the retirement home swung open again and out came 007-2. Her body was making strange mechanical, epileptic movements that seemed random at first, but it quickly became apparent that she wasn't having a seizure—she was dancing! Taking it back to the '80s, she spun into a series of seamless break-dance moves, winding up her arms and strutting like a dancing robot. Even she couldn't resist the allure of music, which soon had her on her back spinning around like a human carousel. This was exactly what Clarence had hoped for. With everything still going according to plan, Väinämöinen handed the bullhorn to Balaam who finished off by throwing his arm around Omiokane as he rapped the third and final verse in an old-school rhyming style:

♪ Maybe it's the mind playing tricks on the brain.
If you can't change your mind, maybe change up the game.
Maybe I'm a figment of my own imagination,
Or maybe I'm the product of all these calculations.
Maybe you're the fool who needs proof to exist.
That's why ignorance is bliss, so go to sleep in the mist.
Pleasant dreams 'til the time that you open your eyes,
And recognize I'm the Word, my homie Omi is Wise ♪

"MAYBE!"

Balaam dropped the mic and threw both arms to the sky as thirty-three million Gods ripped the air in half with deafening chants and cheers. Shiva rattled the drums with all four hands, adding even more noise to the climatic energy. Clarence and Väinämöinen walked to the front of the crowd and like actors before the bow, they held up their hands and looked at each other with mutual admiration.

"Sell-out crowd for our first gig. Well done, ystäväni." Väinämöinen winked. "But you never told us what the point of this concert was."

The answer came with a tremor that Väinämöinen felt in his belly.

It even induced him to belch. He looked around as if he had caused the quiver but quickly realized that it wasn't him. Something else was shuddering. He turned back and saw the retirement home coming alive, dancing to the vibrations made by the voice of the Gods. Each shake compounded with the next until, finally, its walls made their last quake and every stone went crumbling to the ground.

The applause came to an abrupt stop. Everyone stared at the ballooning cloud of debris, their eyes filled with dismay—except for Shiva. His pupils flared up at this awe-inspiring masterpiece of destruction. It took several long minutes for the air to clear, but when it did, it was apparent that the retirement home for the Gods was no more. Everyone was thinking the same thing, but it took Väinämöinen to say it.

"Maybe this was a bad idea, ystäväni."

*

As all the Gods know, man works in mysterious ways. Clarence's folly turned out to be a blessing in disguise. Väinämöinen and the Concierge had their old jobs back, albeit now that the retirement home had been turned from an old ruin into rubble, the job description changed. They were now taskmasters and traffic controllers, directing the chaos of thirty-three million homeless Gods, a formidable task by any estimation.

"I want ya'll to form twelve rows on all sides. The ones on the North and East sides will sweep going southwards, and those on the West and South sides will sweep northwards. We're going to get all this reflective glass into one big pile." Väinämöinen was issuing orders to several dozen *Domovye*—domestic Slavic deities who were like miniature versions of himself: thick-bearded and woolly all over. Their wicker brooms were twice their size, so they looked like hairy children doing their chores.

"Don't bother stopping to look at yourselves in the mirror; there isn't much to look at and you know it. And watch your feet," Väinämöinen continued barking orders. "There aren't any shoes or sandals to spare for anyone. Hey you! That's a broom not a back scratcher. Oh, look at ya, you've gone and shed hair all over the place."

Actually, all of the Domovye were shedding, which is why Frigg, Gabija, Matka Gabia and Brighid—Nordic, Baltic, Slavic and Celtic Goddesses, respectively—took it upon themselves to begrudgingly sweep up behind the Domovye.

"Typical. Just typical," Brighid bemoaned with an Irish lilt. "Whose idea was it anyway to send the men to do detail?"

"It's the twenty-first century, Brighid," Matka Gabia replied. "A man's home can still be his castle as long as he cleans it up himself."

"Have you ever known a man to clean anything?" Gabija griped. "They're only good at making a mess. Open your eyes, girl; we're sweeping up the proof right now."

"It's not their fault that they shed," Frigg defended.

"No, but whose fault is it for picking them to do sweep duty in the first place? It's his." Brighid pointed at Väinämöinen. "Look at him. He sings one stupid song, and all of a sudden he thinks he's a rock star."

"And he didn't even write his own lyrics," Gabija added. "I heard the Concierge was the ghost writer."

"Reeeaaally?" they all wooed. They stopped sweeping, spiked their brooms into the ground and leaned on them as they admired the Concierge from a distance. "He's gorgeous."

Narcissus, the infamous God of Vanity, walked up to the Concierge and handed him a new pair of shades. As the Concierge put them on, Frigg, Gabija, Matka Gabia and Brighid sighed like Cinderellas with stars in their eyes. To them, he looked like a celebrity. To the other Gods, he looked like a police officer, especially as he went about the business of turning the melee and mayhem of millions of Gods into the miracle of law and order.

"Single lines, people. All the Gods of Fire over here, and the Gods of Earth will go right next to them." The Concierge paralleled his arms. "Gods of Air and Water over here, please."

"Where do I go?" One God raised his hand, looking a little confused.

The Concierge frowned at the lion-faced figure in front of him. He had no idea who he was and was a little embarrassed by this. He looked over both shoulders, ensuring no one, especially not Väinämöinen, would hear him. "Who are you again?" he asked.

"Nusku," the God answered timidly, like a lost boy.

"Oooh, right. Babylonian God of Fire."

"Yes."

"Well, there's your answer right there. Get in line with the Fire Gods."

"I know, but I was a God of the Earth, too."

"Ugh." The Concierge palmed his face. "This is why I hate syncretism. Okay, I tell you what, Nusku, we're going to do the Fire, Water, Air and Earth game. It's like Rock-Paper-Scissors."

♪ Rock, paper, scissors
Will it be rock, paper, scissors ♪

Nusku blinked with confusion at the singing outburst.

"Sorry," the Concierge said with an abashed smile. "Made me think of that song by Melanie Fiona. Anyway, Fire burns Earth, Water puts out Fire, Earth drinks Water, Air feeds Fire and… You get the idea. So let's go."

They put their fists forward, bobbed them four times as they made the Rock-Paper-Scissors chant—*"Fire, Water, Air, Earth"*—then held up strange alchemical symbols with their hands: the Concierge was Fire, and Nusku Water.

"Water puts out Fire!" Nusku said victoriously.

"Yeah, but I can't have you standing next to the Water Gods. Get in the Fire line."

"But I want to be a Water God."

"I know. Next time, I promise."

Nusku slumped over and kicked a stone as he moped away. The Concierge shook his head and sighed. This was tough work, and it wasn't anywhere near being complete. It was problem after problem, and now eight more were on their way. He turned and saw an octad of African deities donning black leather jackets approaching him in smooth, slow steps like a pride of panthers. They were lead by a woman who wore a head crown and a screen that obscured her face.

"What's up, Oya?" the Concierge asked, greeting her with an intricate handshake that ended with a clap.

"That's what I was going to ask you," she snapped in a strong voice.

"What has happened to the temple? Before, it was overcrowded. Now, it's in complete ruins. Who must we punish for this crime?"

Before the Concierge could answer, lightning flashed through the sky followed by a terrible thunder that ended with the sudden and startling appearance of Zeus, who rudely cut between Oya and the Concierge.

"Insolence!" Oya shouted, furious from the interruption. Her eyes flashed and glowed even brighter than Zeus' lightning. But Zeus, either oblivious or indifferent to his intrusion and her protest, ignored her. With his arms folded behind his back, he arrogantly surveyed the situation, as if he were an inspector. When he saw the ruin of the retirement home, he turned to face the Concierge with quiet contempt in his eyes.

"Give me *one* reason"—he held up a finger—"not to hang you from the peak of Olympus by your *balls*."

"How about I give you *eight*?" Oya stepped in front of Zeus and pointed to her pack of panthers, who stood solid with their arms locked across their chests.

Bemused, Zeus turned to size up her threat, but quickly found that he was staring into the barreled chest of his old wrestling competitor, Shango. Zeus swallowed hard before recomposing his poker face. He stepped back several paces.

"Back for a rematch, I see. Well, as you can see we no longer have a wrestling ring, so you'll just have to wait," Zeus said while walking away. "Sike!" He flung himself around and threw a fake jab at Shango, trying to psyche him out, but the burly God didn't so much as flinch.

"C'mon, big boy," Zeus taunted as he held his fists in front of his face, swinging his shoulders in and out and pivot-dancing like a boxer. "What you got? What you got?"

Shango yoked Zeus by his beard, hoisted him high and heaved him into the ground. Lightning flashed and cracked from the impact. Zeus quickly countered by throwing up his legs, scissoring Shango around the neck and somersaulting him to the ground. He clamped tight, squeezing a solid promise to never let go. Shango was unperturbed. He pushed off the ground and stood up with Zeus dangling upside down, wearing him like an Olympian necklace. Before the battle could go too far, the Concierge rushed in to break it up, which he did by rapping

Afrika Bambaataa's song "Frantic Situation."

♪ *Isn't it a wonder, We are the Gods of thunder*
We're on the same mission, Come on everybody listen ♪

"Listen," he continued, while unclamping Zeus' legs from Shango's neck, allowing him to hit the ground with a dull thud. "This is all part of the plan, okay? We're expanding the retirement home. When we're done here, everybody will have their own space. What we need now is less grief and more peace."

Disheveled, Zeus picked himself off the ground and dusted off his robes. He looked at Shango and Oya and sneered.

"Hey, Zeus, look over there. Isn't that Hera?" The Concierge pointed, hoping for a diversion. "She's lookin' mighty fine today, man. You know, if I were you—"

"That's my baby mama!" Zeus flashed his eyes.

"Word?"

"Yes, *word*," he intoned.

"That's beautiful, brotha. How's the kid?"

"Kids, *plural*," Zeus corrected. "I have sired many children, and yes, they're doing just fine. Thank you for asking."

"Anytime, my man. But you know what, there's a lot of cats out here. Maybe you should go stand next to your baby mama and make sure there's no drama. A lot of G's out there would love to be a step-daddy, you know what I'm sayin'?"

"I know what you're saying," Zeus confirmed, but after an awkward pause, his face suddenly appeared constipated. Tears welled up. His cheek trembled and his voice cracked. Finally it all came out: "But... Hera doesn't want to see me anymore."

"What? Why?"

"She caught me in bed"—Zeus flung out his arms and began bawling into the Concierge's shoulder—"with another man."

"I see." The Concierge patted him on the back, consoling him. "Okay, check this out, bro. I want you to dry those eyes and look over there. A lot of fine looking brothas, do you see them?"

Zeus sleeved his eyes and looked at Shango. Shango flinched, threw up his hands and stepped back, abashed.

"No, over there," the Concierge clarified. "Where my finger is pointing." Zeus looked yonder and saw several Nordic Gods with lean biceps and blonde hair burning in the starlight. "Happy fishin', my brotha." The Concierge gave the mighty Zeus an encouraging nudge, sending him off to find true love again. With that out of the way, he turned to Oya.

"Don't even think about trying to smooth-talk me," she warned.

"I won't have to," he replied. "When you see the new temple, it will speak for itself."

Oya's stern expression didn't relent, but she accepted this answer, turned to Shango and the others and gave an approving nod.

"I hope this architect knows what he's doing. For his sake—and yours." With those parting words, she prowled off with her pack.

The Concierge removed his shades and wiped sweat from his brow. Another problem resolved. Deciding that he deserved a reprieve, he reached under his shirt and pulled out a fresh set of chopsticks and an unfinished box of Rice Krispies. He leaned back in the air, levitating as he snapped, crackled and crunched away on his lunch break. But the bliss of this midnight snack was soon blistered by the approach of 007-2. She marched in his direction with plodding boot steps, glowering the entire way.

"Slacker," she jibed. "That's why I fired you."

"And that's why we fired you," he fired back.

"I wasn't fired. I quit."

"Yeah, well, the point is that you don't work here anymore."

"I don't have to work here to know that you're the worst excuse of a concierge I or anyone has ever seen. If it were up to me, I'd have you arrested for trespassing on private property."

"And I should have you arrested for trespassing on my lunch break.

Now run off and find yourself a new hobby, girl."

"Excuse me?"

"No, seriously. If I were you, I'd get out of here. Balaam is coming this way."

These words were like a code-red warning, setting her on high alert as she turned tail and scurried off. The Concierge helped wave her away with his chopsticks. Balaam, of course, saw the whole thing and proudly whistled while casually gaiting over and swinging the bullhorn by its chain.

"Careful with that," the Concierge shielded his face with his arm. "I've seen what you can do with that thing."

"And We've seen what you can do with those chopsticks." Balaam winked.

"Tell me, man. How did you do all that stuff you did with the bullhorn?"

This question made Balaam smile. "Well, ol' chap, We were known as the Logos in the old days, which translates to mean *the word*. However, it also means *ratio,* which brings a whole new meaning to John chapter one verse one: *'In the beginning was the* Ratio.' As a well-cultured connoisseur of music, you'll no doubt appreciate knowing that this old verse was referring to music theory—the relationship between two numbers. For example, if one were to count *one, two*, the ratio of these numbers is $1/2$, known as the Octave. If one were next to count *two, three*, their ratio is $2/3$, a Fifth. And if one continued counting *three, four*, well, that's $3/4$, a Fourth and so on. Music, it would seem, is the very cradle of counting, which made measuring, in those days, a form of music. Temples were therefore measured to be—you will forgive Our poor attempt at poetry—a silent symphony in stone. In other words, the temple *is* the Logos. Which, I suppose, means that Clarence is building *my* temple after all."

The Concierge was noticeably disquieted by these words, and he peered at Balaam from the corner of his eyes, thinking that the possessive troll was about to relapse. Balaam guessed his thoughts and gave him a teasing wink.

"Apologies, ol' chap—I meant to say *our* temple."

*

"Okay, I admit it. I have no idea how to build a D. temple." Clarence threw down his walking stick at Seshat's feet in desperation.

"Easy, easy. Don't let the others see you do that." She quickly retrieved his cane before anyone noticed. As she bent over, the strange plant flowering from the roof of her head whisked him across the nose, causing him to sneeze. They both said excuse me at the same time, making for an awkward moment that demanded an explanation of why a Goddess of Architecture's head was being used as a flower pot. But Seshat was noticeably shy about the whole thing and brushed right past it.

"Listen," she continued, sticking to the task at hand. "This is how we did it in the age of the Pharaohs: Every temple has four sides which are aligned with the cardinal directions. So we start by figuring out which way is North, South, East and West."

"How are we going to know that without a compass? It's the middle of the night. We're going to have to wait until sunrise to know which way is East."

"No, we can find North with this." She used his cane to tap the bulge in his pocket.

"The Pole Star," Clarence nodded.

"The *North* Star," she added with a wink.

Seshat took Clarence by the shoulders and pivoted him around, prompting him to look up and identify Ursa Major or, as he knew it, the Big Dipper. Standing behind him, she lifted his arm and pointed out the Big Dipper's ladle, which she used to locate the Little Dipper until his finger stopped at the North Star.

Next, she positioned herself with her back against the canopy of the Northern constellations. The seven-petal plant sprouting from her head appeared as if it were blooming from the ancient light of the stars. Clarence thought to ask her again about the flora on her head but was cut off as she placed a long rope in his hand. As he backed away, he saw that it was knotted at equal intervals.

"A measuring cord," he said, looking up at her. She nodded affirmatively and tossed Clarence his walking stick.

"Back up half the length of the cord and then use your harpoon to spear the tail of the Bear."

Clarence looked at his cane. Of course, it was a "harpoon" now. But at least this time, he understood the symbols. This was how the North Star came to be known as the Pole Star. A pole was spiked into the Earth, establishing North—a ritual Clarence re-enacted with his harpoon.

"Now swing the cord around it and pace out at a right angle." She pointed East.

He turned his back to the East, made only a single pace backwards then stopped. He leaned his head back, allowing his eyes to travel along the Ecliptic. A diffusion of white fires burned in the sky, and from the embers emerged the animal forms of the Zodiac. Just like before, their subtle forms appeared and vanished as if the imagination had blown away the ashes. His mind moved backwards, re-gathered the cinders and remade them into new constellations. He saw the starchitecture of his younger days. They were so different, the stars, when moved from the page and returned to the marquee dome of the sky. They weren't just dots anymore. They were eyes. And just as we might wonder about a stranger's brooding thoughts, it is hard not to look up at these distant eyes and wonder what is behind their ambient silence. The great neurons of the sky were quietly thinking, silently watching the young starchitect at work.

"Ahem," Seshat coughed. "Sometime before dawn would be nice."

Clarence shook the stars from his eyes and began making his slow steps Eastward, looking Westward at the Decans. Never had he embarked on anything like this. Never had he built buildings with the preternatural presence of a small mountain. Never. Until now.

He stopped when the cord reached its end. He looked down and grabbed a small piece of rubble to mark East. Then he repeated this ritual for South and West.

"Well done," Seshat said with an encouraging smile. "You just re-enacted the ritual of the Pharaohs."

"That wasn't so hard." Clarence smiled back.

"Yeah, but temples are star maps. So now we have to align key elements with important stars at their point of culmination."

287

"Man alive," Clarence groaned.

"Don't worry, I'm with you every step of the way. Do you have a building plan?"

"Yeah." Clarence grabbed his sketches and laid them out. "What about this?"

Seshat looked them over, critically contemplating with her hand couched just beneath her nose. After a long minute, she looked up at Clarence and smiled.

"She's beautiful."

"*She?*" Clarence peered at her curiously. "How did you know?"

"Well these are obviously legs." She trailed two fingers along the contours of a double colonnade. "These convex walls here are the hips with a door right in the middle... You dirty dog." She winked. "Which leads to the concaving walls, the waist, and then a pair of very, very large symmetrical towers. You're not one for subtlety, I see. And this here, the Holy of Holies, must be the head."

"The *head*quarters," Clarence intoned his correction. "That's where I want to start building. There will be a subterranean space in that area, like the subconscious."

"I love it," Seshat said with full sincerity. "Reminds me of the Temple at Karnak built by Senusret, except he used the subtext of a man's body. So cliché." She shook her head and Clarence nodded his. He appreciated this. "I do see one problem," she continued. "Where will you get the extra materials to *expand* the temple?"

Clarence kneeled down and pulled up a handful of soil. "Rammed earth," he said, gyrating the soil between his fingers. "The heavier recycled stones will make the temple's base. The earth we dig up for the subterranean headquarters will be compressed with sand and gravel to make building blocks—just like the ancients used to do."

Seshat smiled again. She was impressed.

"So what do we do now?" he asked.

"I think you know the answer to that, or at least you should." She smacked him on the back. "Now we *measure*."

*

Nearby, atop a small mound of rubble, Omiokane sat in silence alongside Shiva, listening to Clarence and Seshat. His acute hearing had picked up on them counting off measures for the feet of the temple.

"The First Dance!" Omiokane's gray eyes opened wide as he whispered excitedly.

"Excuse me?" Shiva asked. He turned and saw Omiokane watching Clarence and Seshat with his ears.

"I'm sorry, Shiva-san. I just overheard them counting. It reminded me of *saru-maï*, the monkey-dances performed very long ago by the *Sarumè*—the monkey-women of the Shinto ceremony. A strong and fierce Kami known as *Sky-Frightening-Female* performed this dance with bells fastened to her hands. She stamped upon a hollow tub— *boom, boom, boom, boom*—while playing a flageolet made of bamboo. The other Kami joined in by playing harps and wooden clappers to measure the time. This put the Sky-Frightening-Female into a deep trance so that she uttered the first words of divine power: *one, two, three, four, five, six, seven, eight, nine, ten, hundred, thousand, myriad.* The song was found to be so sweet that the eight hundred Kami who heard it all began to laugh."

"They laughed at a God?" Shiva exclaimed, not believing his ears.

"They laughed *with* a God, and for good reason. They were happy. The knowledge of number had been revealed."

"Were you there, Mister Omiokane?" Shiva asked.

"Oh, no. I am no musician. And laughter is difficult for me."

"I have noticed this. I have seen you smile, but never laugh. Why is this?"

"Because Ignorance is bliss and Knowledge is sweet, but Wisdom is very bitter."

Or, perhaps, *bitter-sweet*. The sound of Clarence and Seshat counting was deeply nostalgic for the ancient God of Wisdom, who couldn't help but smile wistfully at the beautiful melody of numbers. Like feet tip-toeing soundlessly in his mind, he listened to them dancing while recalling, too, the sound of laughter. It is an altogether different experience when the Gods laugh. If one can imagine, it is like a loud, bottomless thunder, only it doesn't strike fear in the hearts of men, but rather, it strikes their funny bone, bringing them to tears, then to rain, and finally to rainbows. Such is the laughter of the Gods.

"Mister Omiokane," Shiva snapped him from his trance. "Perhaps you should consider learning an instrument. Then you could become a God of Music."

"If I understand what Clarence-san has said, Gods are numbers and numbers are music, which means there are no Gods of Music—the Gods *are* music."

"This is very true," Shiva nodded. "I was thinking about what you said about the monkey dance. In my land, we also have a story of a monkey who was quite skilled in the art and science of song. As monkeys tend to be, he was quite vocal about his mastery and bragged about it to anyone who would listen. But he was not quite the singer or player he believed himself to be. He was performing on a *vina* while passing through the forest, and seven Goddesses suddenly appeared from out of the strings of his vina and dropped dead right in front of him. A *rishi* who lived in the forest heard the awful singing of the monkey and came running. He took the monkey's vina and began singing, this time playing all the notes correctly. The Goddesses were alive again and returned to their home inside the strings of the vina. So you are right about Mister Clarence. What he said is quite true. The Gods are music."

"Except for us."

"Ah, different strokes for different folks." Shiva shrugged.

"But you are a really good drummer."

"I am more of a visual artist than a musician. My drums are for making *this*," Shiva chuckled as he patted the demolition with his hand. "Creation for the Hindus is the opposite of what humans believe. They believe that creation began with a Big Bang. But we believe it ends with it."

Shiva struck the face of his drum creating a thunderous boom, then laughed loud enough for the both of them. As his chortle slowed to a chuckle, he saw the sweet melancholy still loitering in Omiokane's mind. With four free arms, he decided he might as well use one of them to comfort the old, wise God with a firm hand on his shoulder.

"So now that you are retired, Mister Omiokane, what will you do?"

"Retirement is not always easy, Shiva-san. For people who are accustomed to having a purpose, it can make them miserable. But I think I will begin by enjoying three glasses of Kvas. The first, I will enjoy on my own. The second, I will enjoy with Clarence-san, and the third with Ahura Mazda if he will agree to join me. He is a God of Wisdom too, you know. He also served his last client. And as a wise man once said"—Omiokane smiled—"*misery loves company*."

*

With mapping and measuring out of the way, the real grunt work awaited—digging. Needless to say, no one wants to do this kind of unskilled labor, especially not the Gods. Indeed, so much are the Gods averse to menial labor that in virtually every mythology, this task is delegated to man, hence the term *man*ual labor. In fact, in the Babylonian myths, manual labor is the reason the Gods made men in the first place. Even in the Abrahamic traditions, the task of tending to the garden is assigned to Adam, who was conned into accepting the first recorded system of sharecropping by being told it was *his* paradise. It took a serpent snitch and Adam's wife to open his eyes to the fact that he was being scammed.

Now the tables had turned, and it was a human looking for the Gods to be the grunts. The only takers were the Moai of Easter Island. Famously known as "the stone heads," the Moai were stocky and sturdy and spent most of their lives neck deep in dirt, making them perfect diggers. There was also a staggering eight hundred eighty-seven of them. Many hands make for light work, and the combined effort of hundreds of Moai meant that in a few short hours, they had dug halfway to Hades, which is to say, with a little less hyperbole, they carved out a massive multi-level underground parking lot.

A single Moai stuck his large head from the depths of the Earth, before extracting the rest of his body and raised his hand in the air. "We found something!" he shouted.

He made a plodding run past his chain gang of digging co-workers, declaring his discovery. Clarence and Seshat were nowhere to be found and everyone else was too busy to notice or care. It was Shiva and Omiokane who heard the excitement from their resting post. They climbed down from the rubble to see to the commotion.

"What have you found, Mister Moai?" Shiva asked.

"Look at this." The Moai coughed and held up a small, circular silver-like amulet. "Careful, it smells awful," the Moai warned as he handed it to Shiva.

Shiva toyed with the talisman by knuckle rolling it across all four of his hands before it dropped free and Omiokane caught it. Stoically, Omiokane raised the token to his nose and sniffed. The serious look on his face broke as his expression buckled.

"Hai. It smells terrible." he agreed. Next he ran his fingers along the surface. Like an Egyptian relief, it was embossed with the face of a man.

"Do you know what it is, Mister Omiokane?" Shiva asked.

"Hai," he answered ominously. "It is a *God*."

*

The discovery of this new God was unbeknownst to Clarence, who hid behind Światowid, away from the public gaze, while Seshat peered over the corner to see if anyone was looking. Seeing that the coast was clear, she cracked open two bottles of beer and handed one to Clarence. They clinked the neck of their bottles to inaugurate a much-deserved break, laughing both at their secret mischief, but also at the awkward silence flirting between them. They took a single step backwards to add a little more padding to their personal space, then looked at each other again and offered clumsy smiles. *This is like running into a co-worker outside of the office*, Clarence thought to himself. He had no idea what to do with his eyes, so he fixed them on his feet. Then hers. Next he glanced up and stole a peek at the roof of her head.

"I'm going to finally ask," he began, breaking their awkward silence with what promised to be an awkward question. "What the H. is growing out of your head?"

"A symbol," she answered flatly. "What's growing out of yours?"

Confused, he reached up to touch the roof of his head, where his hair had receded. The answer, of course, was *nothing*.

"Sorry about that," he frowned. "I've never had a symbol grow out of my head before."

"So you've been bald your whole life?"

"No, I ju—"

"So you've had hair at one time?" she interrupted.

"Of course."

"Then you've had a symbol sprouting from your head too. Like the story of Samson and Delilah, where she cuts his hair and he loses his strength. You never wondered what that symbolized?" He shook his head *no,* and she shook hers. *Pathetic.* "Hair symbolized sunrays coming from the light of the mind. Knowledge is power. She cuts his hair and he loses his power."

Clarence rolled his eyes. "Because hair could never just be hair. Everything is a D. symbol around here."

"Now imagine me coming to your world, rolling my eyes and saying, 'Of course! Everything is *matter* here.'" She rolled her eyes and mimicked his voice.

"No need to take it personally. I'm just saying."

"And I'm just saying *yes,* I have a plant growing out of my head. You try having vegetation grow from your skull and not be sensitive about it."

"So when you walk around as a Cheetah is that to hide the, the—" He circled his finger, not wanting to name it.

"Nah, that's just to scare off the herbivores. You have no idea how hard it is to keep them from grazing on my head. Of course, if I had any sense, I would let them. It would save my hairdresser the trouble. She does my hair with a weed whacker, if you can believe that."

"Well, I did a bit of exotic gardening on my spare time, if you can believe *that.*"

"Why would I not believe it?" she answered vapidly. "It's not like you're telling me to believe that you were an astronaut on your spare time. You were a gardener on the weekends, so what? That's supposed to impress me? If you want to impress a lady, try proving that you actually practiced architecture *full time*, because so far I'm beginning to wonder if your only experience was building with Legos. I mean, seriously, is this your first real building or what?"

"Cut me some slack. I'm trying."

"I understand. But what *you* need to understand is that planning and plotting the temple is as far as I can go with you on this. You're the one who has to move those massive stones."

"I'm not going to move them; the Gods are."

"And how do you plan on getting them to do that?"

"The way they did in the age of the Pharaohs or, at least, the way the legends say they did it."

"Which was…"

"With music," his voice cracked.

There was a grin on her face that he couldn't read, though it had all the condescending curves of a skeptic's smirk.

"Hey, *all* the legends say so. Orpheus supposedly charmed rocks with his lyre."

"His flute."

"Exactly. Ever heard of Mozart and his famous opera **The Magic Flute**? There's gotta be something to it, right?"

"Meh," she shrugged. "I'll see it when I believe it."

"You mean… You'll believe it when you see it."

"No, that's your reality. Not mine."

"Okay, fine. But weren't you there when the Pharaohs did this? Tobias, or Toby, or whatever that crazy broad's name is, saw you in a book stretching the chord with the Pharaoh."

"C'mon, you really think I was there? In person? I'm an idea, Clarence. *A symbol.*" She rolled her eyes and mocked his voice again. "Haven't you ever had an idea before?"

"Of course. I'm an architect. I have ideas all the time."

"Do you really feel as if you found all of your ideas—and not the other way around? How often were you in the shower or lying in bed when, for no reason, an idea appeared from nowhere, poking you in the head, trying to get your attention? Perhaps what you are doing right now, at this very moment, is causing someone to wake up in excitement and say, 'Aha! I have an idea!'"

"In my day, we called that a *Muse.*"

"Yeah, well, in mine, they called it the *Gods*. What I'm saying is that yeah, I was there with the Pharaoh—*in his head*. Outside of the head, you have to see it to believe it, but the mind works differently: It has to believe it to see it. The good news is that I believe in you."

She threw her arms around Clarence and guided him from the protective oversight of Światowid into the panoramic overview of the assembly of thirty-three million Gods, organized in tidy rows, awaiting orders from a commanding officer.

"So I'm ready to see it," she finished.

*

Whereas before the Gods had been a congested concert mass, they now stood in the perfect arrangement of an orchestra, with their strong and sturdy lines sprawling outward and curving into a single elegant arch. From afar they resembled the contour of a cathedral's dome, and the exotic individuality of each deity was its ornaments. This was the masterwork of Väinämöinen and the Concierge. They had arranged the Gods into architecture.

Every building has mastered meditation. It has achieved enlightened emptiness. Silence is a temple's virtue, but in the end, sound is its purpose, just like the Gods. In patient repose, every building waits for its visitor, and the Gods waited for theirs, but not just any visitor.

He entered from the rear and rippled through their lawful lines like a sound wave. The disturbance was almost undetectable. Only the slightest movements could be seen as each God looked down and shifted sideways to make way for their maestro. He travelled the long walkway until finally emerging from the front as a young boy—Harpocrates, a God of Silence, Sound and, of course, Bartending.

Today, however, with baton in hand, he was a conductor. A God of the Gods.

Stoically dignified in his face and mannerisms, he said not a single word nor wasted a movement. Every action of his was economized for form, function and efficiency. For a moment, he stood still and silent until finally the perfect symmetry was broken. He raised his arms slowly like wings preparing to fly and brought them down, but his feet never left the ground, nor did those of the Gods. It was their voices that lifted up and took to the air as they began to sing.

And what a song it was, immersive and ambient. Beautiful, but also tragically penetrating, like the pining of a bird whose pinions had been cut and who was now banished to a life weighted to the ground. The song of the Gods was a lamentation.

They mourned not over death, but over the heartache of life, which demanded that every soul have its pinions cut, spending a lifetime behind the prison bars of a body, ministering to its appetites. There were no words to their song, but their heavy tones spoke of every creature's burden: That life is brief, but the days are long, and each soul would count its days until the end. Only then would the adamantine bands be broken. Life would take its leave, abandoning the body and leaving it as prison food for those still numbering their days.

This worship of sorrow continued for nearly an hour, until the boy gave a signal for the Hippopotamus, Raret, to step to the center of the orchestra. With all the force of a plus-size opera singer, she opened her toothy mouth and cried a tantric eulogy for the soul so universally painful that all present were moved—including the stones. Each massive block in the rubble began shifting its weight, restlessly vibrating. Stirred from their slumber, the stones were, at last, awakened.

Chapter 15

"BOOMBAYALA! What's up everybodeeee! We got a full house of the Zodiac tonight, and all my real G's are large and live from the Other Side. This is yo homeboy DJ OGO puttin' these beats in orbit with an eclectic mix of old school myths and new hits so hip-hop and jazz yo big ass to the central, raise yo antenna for the signal. It's all fundamental as we keep it simple with some Icelandic downtempo and Asian instrumentals. So walk, stride, gliiiiide, ride or get a rental 'cause you don't want to miss this soul food for your mental."

Translation: LISTEN UP! The tavern is now a full house of Gods and the Concierge, now known under the spin-name DJ OGO, is their official self-appointed Disc Jockey. His music repertoire is an eclectic and ethnic mix of old school myths, hits, hip-hop, jazz, downtempo and instrumentals. Yada, yada, yada. Be there.

Of course, they were already there. The tavern was reopened and teeming with Gods. Not a single one of them knew what the Concierge, a.k.a. DJ OGO, was saying, but it didn't matter. The bass spinning from his "wheels of steel" spoke the universal language of music that everybody understands, especially the Gods. The room was energized and the name DJ OGO was now immortalized.

"This next jam is for my beautiful black and white Goddesses in the hizzle, and let's not forget all the caramel shades in the middle."

Frigg, Gabija, Matka Gabia and Brighid threw up their hands and screamed. Matylda, who was in the front row, fainted.

"That's right, ladies, I'm the lyrical lover for hire, mixing some acoustic alchemy with a little Earth, Wind and Fire. And it's about to get hectic. But don't forget that DJ OGO said it when he told you to go electro with *Magnetic.*"

As the '80s jam "Magnetic" came on, the door swung open and in walked Lucifer, prowling through the party with a seductive catwalk and showcasing her curvaceous contours. The lights went out, allowing the stout starlet to strobe the room with her Venusian glow. Many of the Goddesses tossed up their noses as she sashayed past them, but Lucifer's insatiable appetite for attention devoured their sneers as mere appetizers. This playground was strictly for the big girls, and any wafer-thin wraith who came in with a man wasn't going to leave with him. The cougar was on the hunt and did a little runway reconnaissance until she finally identified the sexiest God in the tavern.

She took a seat next to him, looking the other way, feigning disinterest and yet effervescing pheromones in his direction. But two could play that game. The godly stud gave as good as he got by showing absolutely no interest, and yet the scent of desire lingered about him. He kept his cool and flexed his VIP status by chatting it up with heavy hitters like the King of Olympus himself—Zeus. Undeterred, Lucifer cleared her throat and ordered a glass of water, which she purposely spilled, breaking the concentration between Zeus and her target lover.

"Oh, I'm so sorry." Lucifer covered her mouth, abashed. She leaned over to clean up the mess, purposely flashing a bit of cleavage.

"Oh, no, it was probably my fault. Please, let me buy you another drink," the dashing deity offered.

A stud and a gentleman, Lucifer thought as her eyes beamed. She glanced up at Zeus who silently snarled like a lion. The bisexual sybarite of Olympus made it clear with a sneer that this hunk of heaven was his and his alone. Luci hissed, accepting the challenge.

"Oh, no, no, no. It's okay," she coyly refused. "I'll pay for my own—"

"Nonsense. This is on me."

The gentleman God signaled to Shiva, who was putting all four of his hands to work as the assistant barkeep. Lucifer was winning the catfight, and she rubbed it in by flashing her fangs at Zeus, then quickly reverted to a congenial smile for her new boy toy.

"My name is Luci," she said, wisely abbreviating her name. "And yours?"

"Thor." He smiled sweetly. "And this is my boyfriend Zeus."

*

While the other Gods partied, Ahura Mazda sat next to Omiokane, enjoying a glass of Kvas and bickering about his stolen Mazda. Väinämöinen basked in the attention of two old Goddesses, one under each arm, while in each hand was a mandatory pint. He boasted and toasted, then chugged-and-hugged on his two ladies, little realizing that Matylda was right behind him doing the same with Shango.

Behind the scenes of it all was Odin, making a back-door delivery of wine and ale to the Barkeep, who, even with Shiva's help, could barely fill the glasses fast enough. Väinämöinen, being especially proud of the tavern's success, began rapping the bar with his empty pints, cueing all the others to do the same.

"Speech! Speech! Speech!" he shouted for the Barkeep.

A hush washed over the room as all waited. The Gods stepped aside, clearing a path for the Barkeep who reentered the tavern from the rear and made his way to the bar. They could hear him climbing a stack of phonebooks until finally he stepped on the bar as if it were a stage. Standing under the halogen spotlight, he flanked his body with his arms, graciously bowed, then made his exit, stage right.

The tavern erupted into a cheer.

"Wait, wait, wait," Seshat shouted over the wall of voices as she inched herself higher using her stool. "I have a speech to make. EVERYONE LISTEN UP!" The command of her voice brought the crowd to a murmuring silence.

"Buildings are no different than people—they want to be seen. They want to matter. Every building is waiting for the right person to chance along and stop, look and pay attention to the story of how they were made and all the pain they endured from the constant grinding, hammering and pounding from the hand of the builder, who wants only to see his creation be made beautiful. The hand of Life is no different. Her covenant is that if we survive Her fire, we rise as magnificent as Her mountains. So, with these words in mind, I want to make a tribute to architecture—and to the architect." Seshat proudly raised her glass, and the others followed suit.

"TO THE ARCHITECT!" they saluted in unison.

Seshat drank, then looked around the room at the ennobled, even if inebriated, faces of the Gods. But her smile faded into a frown when she realized the most important face was missing.

"Wait," she said. "Where *is* the architect?"

*

Back at the newly completed temple, Clarence sat alone with his back against the wall of an empty room. He rolled the Heart of the Pole Star from hand to hand as he brooded, then looked up at the sound of feet approaching. After a delayed silence a familiar celestial bear, bright and massive, stopped at the mouth of the door. He looked around as if lost but then fixed his eyes squarely on Clarence.

"Hi, Charles," Clarence said.

"Hello, Clarence."

"So... What do you think?" Clarence threw out his arm to showcase the new temple.

"Impressive. Clean lines, ambitious angles... I like it."

"Thank you. Man alive, this heart of yours came in handy—or is it an eye? I'm getting conflicting reports. Some called it 'the Eye of the Sky' and others the Sky's Heart."

"Meh, I'm used to it. Some people call me a dipper, some a wagon... But for the record, it's my heart. Though sometimes I use it as an eye." Charles winked.

"Right. Well, it was very useful. For my trial *and* building the temple. I guess you want it back."

"Keep it. A third eye might come in handy."

"No, thanks. Carrying around an iron ball just adds weight to my knees and legs. Besides, I understand you need it to keep a watchful eye on Big Momma. You know, so that guys like me don't make a move on her." Clarence smiled jokingly, but Charles didn't smile back. "Ahem... Sorry. The Concierge told me that you two are sort of love birds."

"I want *you* to have it, Clarence—until your task is done."

Clarence's head dropped. *That's right,* he thought. *The other task. Because building a temple wasn't difficult enough.*

"You are still bound to your duties to help Big Momma."

"So you want me to save the world?"

"I want you to help the Earth."

"What's the difference?"

"The world—your world—is raping the Earth. Humans have created a new God who is eating the Earth's offerings. Have you forgotten our contract? Now that the temple is built, you must return to your world, kidnap this new God and bring him back to the temple—"

"For an early retirement," Clarence finished his sentence for him. "Yeah, I didn't forget. But I noticed that this time you used the word *kidnap*."

"Yeah?"

"Kidnapping is a crime."

"And?"

"*And* I want to make sure that when I do this—assuming I can do it— I'm not going to be charged of another crime and then owe you another favor for getting me off the hook, and this keeps going on and on like I'm locked into some kind of deal with the mafia. I mean, there is an end to all of this, isn't there? I seem to be the only person here who actually wants to retire. Who is this God that we invented anyway?"

"His name is Mark."

"Mark?" Clarence intoned. "Are you sure? I never heard of a God named *Mark*. What does he look like? Do you have a photo or sketch or something?"

"*Hai.*"

That, of course, was not the voice of the Celestial Bear, but Clarence recognized it right away. He looked past Charles' massive body to see the figure of Omiokane in the doorway. The blind God could not see the bear, but could sense his presence and bowed.

"*Kon'nichiwa,*" he said, rising and bowing three times. "Great Bear of the Sky."

"Actually, I'm the Little Bear. Just call me Charles."

"Of course, Charles-san. I believe I have what Clarence-san is looking for. During the building of the temple, the Moai discovered this..." Omiokane held up the circular silver amulet with the embossed face of a God.

Clarence stood up and removed his glasses. As he approached Omiokane, he cleaned them with his tie before placing them back on for a clearer view. He couldn't believe what he was seeing. There had to be some mistake. If this were in fact the God that Clarence must kidnap then there was no way his name was Mark, more like...

"George Washington?" Clarence said incredulously, pointing to the face of the First American President minted on a U.S. quarter. "You can't be serious. You told me his name was Mark."

"Clarence-san," Omiokane began. "When human beings discovered numbers they arrived at the conclusion that the Universe was ordered by them. The Gods, it was believed, had ordered the world using the numbers found in music. Order was considered a sacred thing—the most sacred of all things—and wherever it was found, it was seen as divine. A colony of bees, a flock of birds, a small tribe or even a great country—all divine because of their natural order. I am not well versed in Greek philosophy, but I recall that even the philosopher Herocles referred to a country as a *'secondary divinity.'*"

"So the God I'm looking for is a country... named Mark?"

"Clarence-san, what I am saying is that this God will most likely be some principle of order."

Hmmm, Clarence silently mulled this over. *There's a statue of George Washington as Zeus. It was done by a guy named Horatio Greenough. Maybe Ol' George actually became... a God. Do I have to kidnap— No. Kidnapping a president is impossible. Well... It was done before in a movie, but still... Kidnapping a dead president... Argh!* He dismissed the insane idea and kept brainstorming. *Who is this new God?*

As these thoughts jostled around in his head, he looked again at the quarter. Four simple words embossed on the coin arrested his eyes: *In God We Trust.* But it was the words just above George Washington's head that made him blink from his brainstorm:

Liberty

"We need to call a meeting with the gang," he said, still looking at the inscription. "And we'll need a God of Money to join us."

*

302

A knock on the door sounded and Matylda came clomping out of the kitchen. She dodged and kicked aside every stray article and grumbled about never having a moment's peace. She stopped at the door and peered through Triglav to find Ahura Mazda standing next to two Gods who looked similar to him, only they donned strange conical caps. Matylda grumbled some more as she answered the door.

"Greetings," Ahura Mazda said, while making a single nod with his head. "My wise counsel was requested. With me are Mithras and Shamash, Gods of—"

"Yeah, yeah, yeah. Just come in. They're all waiting for you. And take off your shoes."

Clarence, Omiokane, Väinämöinen, Shiva, Balaam, the Concierge and Seshat were all crouched on the floor in a huddle. Everyone quickly tucked in their legs to avoid being recklessly trampled by a stampede of two pink bunnies as Matylda passed through with Ahura Mazda, Mithras and Shamash right behind her. Shamash stopped in his tracks, instantly hooked by the small medallion in Clarence's hand.

"In God We Trust," Clarence read the four words minted on the coin. He looked up at Ahura Mazda and his two companions. "So money is man's new God?"

"Correction," Shamash said, as he stepped forward and stood with a proud poise. "Money is man's *old* God. Though the idol of this God did not always take this form." He helped himself to the bullion for closer inspection. "Sometimes it took the form of cattle or even grain. It matters little what form or symbol the God assumes; what is important is the *value* entrusted to the symbol."

"This is Shamash," Ahura Mazda introduced. "Babylonian God of Banking and Justice. And this is Mithras." He motioned to the younger fellow, whose Phrygian cap sagged ever so slightly at the tip. "Mithras is a God of Contracts."

"Ah, you forgot something." Mithras stepped forward and extended his hand for someone to accept. Shiva obliged and reached out one of his four hands to shake. "I," Mithras continued, "am the inventor of the handshake."

"No," Shiva whispered in awe.

"Yes," Mithras whispered back. "With a simple handshake, honorable men sealed their words through *me*."

"Who cares?" Seshat interrupted. "What do you know about money?"

"What do I know about money?" Shamash jumped in front of the question. "My dear flower-child, I—yes, *I*—was the recorded creditor of over eighty percent of all loans issued in Old Babylon. In other words, when men needed grain or silver, they came to *my* temple."

"You mean to your *bank*," Clarence corrected.

"Ancient temples were banks, yes." Shamash returned the coin to Clarence with a flick of his thumb. "But they were also courtrooms, cathedrals, congresses and, yes, collections agencies—all rolled up into one. It wasn't just about money, my friend; it was about order—having a system to mitigate people's interests. Correction: their *conflicting* interests."

"And interest rates," Clarence snidely retorted.

"Thirty-three percent interest rate, yes," Shamash casually replied.

"Bloody hell!" Balaam blurted. "Brings new meaning to 'bank robbery,' wouldn't you say? Maybe it is high time We start flipping over some merchant tables again."

"Merchant tables?" Clarence said. "Today's banks are bigger than merchant tables or even temples. They've grown to the size of nations. What we're dealing with is a little more complicated."

"Complicated?" Matylda dug her hand into her cleavage and pulled out a book. "Incomprehensible is more like it."

She dropped the book in Clarence's lap. On the cover was a fourteenth century drawing of a merchant. In one hand the merchant held a measuring rod. In the other hand he held a scale identical to the one held by Lady Justice and in the Weighing of Words trial. But the scale of the merchant served no lofty mystical or moral functions. It weighed not the hearts of men or their words. Its only purpose was for the weighing of precious commodities.

Clarence frowned at the title.

The Science of Economics

"That's my book, woman." Väinämöinen snatched it away.

"No, it's *my* book." Seshat snatched it from him. "You stole it from *my* library."

"And now it's under *my* roof in *my* house." Matylda snatched it back and returned it to Clarence.

"But he stole it," Seshat argued.

"Of course, he stole it. You think that's the first time he's stolen things?"

"Dirty snitch," Väinämöinen grumbled and grabbed the book from Clarence.

"Wait a minute," Clarence jumped in. "Why *did* you steal this?"

"Because, ystäväni, in all my golden years of counting, I've never seen numbers like these." Väinämöinen opened to a dog-eared page and drilled his finger on an equation.

$$\frac{\partial V}{\partial t} + \frac{1}{2}\sigma^2 S^2 \frac{\partial^2 V}{\partial S^2} + rS\frac{\partial V}{\partial S} - rV = 0$$

"And while I'm a master counter, I'm not ashamed to admit that I have no clue how to count these numbers," he continued, "much less how to make music with them."

"They're not for making music," Clarence rebutted, brooding over the equation. "They're for making money."

Clarence paused to quietly page through the book until an excerpt jumped out at him. He began reading it: *"The produce of the soil maintains at all times nearly that number of inhabitants which it is capable of maintain—"*

"See there, you lost me already, ystäväni."

"Me too. And I'm a banker," Shamash added.

"Now, when the book says 'inhabitants,'" Mithras began, "is it referring to... Gods?"

"No. It's referring to people, rich and poor," Clarence answered, then continued reading: *"The rich only select from the heap what is most*

305

precious and agreeable. They consume little more than the poor, and in spite of their natural selfishness and rapacity, though they mean only their own convenience, though the sole end which they propose from the labors of all the thousands whom they employ, be the gratification of their own vain and insatiable desires, they divide with the poor the produce of all their improvements. They are led by an Invisible Hand to make nearly the same distribution of the necessaries of life, which would have been made, had the earth been divided into equal portions among all its inhabitants, and thus without intending it, without knowing it, advance the interest of the society, and afford means to the multiplication of the species."

All the Gods looked blankly, blinking three times: WTF.

"This means"—Clarence sighed—"that if you let the rich bake a bigger pie, there will be more crumbs falling from the table."

"Crumbs?" Väinämöinen looked confused. "For whom? Dogs?"

"For the poor," Clarence answered. "This quote is from a famous book on ethics called ***The Theory of Moral Sentiments***."

"This does not sound very moral to me." Omiokane shook his head.

"That was the point," Clarence replied and then turned to Shamash. "The guy who wrote this believed in a system of *self-interest*: that when two sellers compete, they'll do the right thing for the buyer not for any moral reason, but for competitive reasons. Capitalism was supposed to create a moral society without morals, or even a lawful society without laws."

"And common good without common sense." Matylda huffed, puffing on her pipe. "Smells like a crock of crapola to me."

"And to Us. And, presumably, the rest of us," Balaam agreed looking around. "Seriously. Who's the wanker that wound up this wobbling wheel?"

The wanker in question was a reputed absent-minded professor of the Enlightenment, who, by his own admission, fit the caricature description of having an unpleasantly plump nose with eyes swelling out of the sockets, a lower lip that stuck out like an open shelf, a nervous twitch and a speech impediment that coupled his curious and maybe even comical habit of talking to himself. Also, he was the Father of Modern Economics and Free Market Economic Theory.

"The author's name was Adam Smith," Clarence answered.

"A priest?" Mithras asked.

"No, but Adam is considered a prophet by the people who put their faith in mark—" Clarence stopped short of completing the sentence as his own words hit him.

"Mark?" Mithras smacked the name with a sour flavor. "Who is *Mark*? I never heard of this God."

"I'm sorry," Clarence said with blinking revelation. "I meant to say *markets*. People put their faith in markets."

This triggered a signature song outburst from the Concierge. It was, of course, only a matter of time before this was to happen.

> ♪ *I had a dream I could buy my way to heaven*
> *When I awoke, I spent that on a necklace*
> *I told God I'd be back in a second*
> *Man it's so hard not to act reckless* ♪

"Kanye West." The Concierge smirked. "'Can't Tell Me Nothing.'"

"Can't tell me *anything*," Balaam corrected. "But point well taken: Faith in markets is reckless and, We might add, complete rubbish. And while We make no expert pretenses on this dodgy doctrinal dogma, it sounds to Us that there's a proverbial devil lurking somewhere in those details."

"Not a devil, Balaam-san," Omiokane said solemnly. "A *God*."

"But how will we locate this God, Mister Clarence?" Shiva asked.

A good question. How does one find *any* God? Some would say that the seeker must look within himself, because God is in the heart. Indeed, if greed were a God then such advice is not without merit. Where else is greed found if not in the hearts of men? But others have said that God can be found in Nature, or even the stars. To find God we must look to the Heavens. But Clarence found his God by looking closer at Adam Smith's quote where three seemingly unassuming words jumped out at him: *The Invisible Hand.*

"Find him?" Clarence sighed. "I'm not even sure we'll be able to *see* him."

*

WANTED

Mark a.k.a. "The Invisible Hand"

Like every "hue and cry" of its kind, this one had a square box for a head-and-shoulders illustration dominating the center of the page; only in this case, the square box was blank. Beneath the invisible profile was a description.

**Ruthless and untamable eater of good(s)
and hoarder of wealth.
Known to have a voracious appetite.
Possibly assumes the form of neither man nor animal,
but of a beast.**

Clarence taped a large poster on a wall-length whiteboard and turned to his audience. The Gods had reconvened in the underground headquarters of the new retirement home, where Clarence conducted a military-style briefing. He used his cane as a pointer to tap the wanted poster, then locked his arms behind his back as he paced to and fro.

"The Invisible Hand," Clarence began, "was the invention of human hands for the purpose of shaping a selfless society through selfishness." Clarence picked up the economics book and read a short excerpt.

"They are led by an Invisible Hand to make nearly the same distribution of the necessaries of life, which would have been made, had the earth been divided into equal portions among all its inhabitants, and thus without intending it, without knowing it, advance the interest of the society, and afford means to the multiplication of the species."

He turned a few pages to locate another excerpt.

"He intends only his own security... only his own gain, and he is in this, as in many other cases, led by an Invisible Hand to promote an end which was no part of his intention... By pursuing his own interest he frequently promotes that of the society more effectually than when he really intends to promote it."

Clarence paused to let this sink in, as he walked over to a desk, grabbed an apple and held it up above his head. "This is Adam's apple," he continued. "Rich or poor—everybody wants a bite from this apple, but there are only so many apples to go around. In Adam's Eden, the rich own all the apples. They hire the poor to grow and pick them and then they pay them a wage to buy their own apples. To many people, this sounded good on paper and to most of them it still does.

"But the rich did more than select only the most precious resources; they selected them all. And they did not consume only a 'little more than the poor;' the smallest fraction of them hoarded far more than the entire number of the poor ever could. Needless to say, the Earth was never equally divided—she was decimated. By our consumption and waste. And the only solution anyone could think of was to save Mother Nature by owning every inch of her and putting a price on it, so that only those who could afford it could continue living off her. They called this a Natural Order and rationalized it as a 'Rational Market.' " He leaned forward to make sure he had every grain of attention. "And that's why I need *you* to help me hunt down and capture this "rational" God. Human beings used *you* to parent this demon of a deity, and I believe you are the only one who can help us stop him."

He stared intently at one person. What appeared to be a briefing of an entire army was in fact a secret meeting to conscript the service of a single assassin: *Raison*, the Goddess of Reason.

Donning dark shades and a trench jacket, the femme fatale sat alone with her legs crossed, holding a burning cigarette in one hand and her trusty blunderbuss in the other. She smoked casually while contemplating the assignment.

"A Natural Order without Nature?" Raison asked in her velvety French voice. "This sounds neither natural nor rational to *moi*. Are you certain this is truly my child, mon-chéri?"

"Very certain. That is why I want you to help me find and capture him."

"Capture?" She dropped her cigarette and stepped on it. "Not *kill*?"

"I was instructed to capture and retire this God. Besides, the Gods are ideas, and if I've learned anything at all from all my years as an architect, the only true way to kill an idea is with a committee."

"What about them?" She thumbed to the back room, where Clarence's companions stood against the wall. Väinämöinen sat with a beer. "Isn't that your committee?"

"C'mon, Raison, can I can count on you or not?"

"Pathetic," she said and chuckled. "The last time I opened my door to you, you turned around and went running right out of it. And now you're back, knocking on my door again. Pathetic."

"You tried to kill me."

"You rejected me."

"Because you pointed a gun at me!"

"And who is to say I won't point it at you again?"

Quick on the draw, she grabbed her blunderbuss and leapt to her feet. Clarence, of course, was too old and too slow to react. He gripped his cane to swat her rifle, but he was already staring deep into the eye of her barrel. She smiled cunningly and aimed carefully, this time making sure she would hit her target. Before Clarence parted his lips to plead, she pulled the trigger. He dropped his cane and fell to the ground. The blast caused his companions to freeze in shock.

Breathing hard, Clarence looked at Raison, who wasn't looking back at him but at her real intended target. He followed the direction of her stare and saw that she had shot a bull's-eye directly in the center of the wanted poster, filling the empty square with a bullet hole.

"Even if this God is my son, how do you expect me to recognize him if he is invisible?" she asked, lowering her blunderbuss.

"He may be invisible, yes. But that doesn't mean he's inaudible." Clarence used his cane to get back to his feet. "If he's a God of numbers, then that means that he makes a sound like the rest of the Gods."

"And you expect me to know this sound?"

"Every parent recognizes the sound of their own child's voice."

Raison nodded slightly to this and lit up a second cigarette.

"And where do you plan to find this child of mine?"

"In somebody's head."

"*Oui*, but whose?"

"Everyone's."

Clarence's tone revealed how daunting this prospect really was.

"You are joking, no?"

"We'll go from head to head following the word signs."

"You thick-headed imbecile!" Matylda rudely interrupted as she barged through the door. "Do you even know how the word signs work? They are there when two people are having a conversation and use those words."

"Trust me," Clarence rebutted, "right now, in a meeting room somewhere, dozens of people are talking about 'the rational market.'"

"And you think a New Age wolf-woman with crystals wrapped around her head will be invited to this meeting?"

"Actually," Clarence rebutted. "A lot of libertarians are hippies. And hillbillies."

"And you really plan on travelling from head to head of a few billion people until you find these hillbillies? I'd hate to be your travel agent."

"I'm sure there's a God of Travel somewhere in this temple who can help navigate us."

"Yeah, and by the time you find your Invisible Hand, it will have finished destroying what's left of your planet." Matylda gave a mocking clap. "Genius idea, genius!"

"Do you have a better one?"

"As a matter of fact, I do." She held out her hand, showcasing a ball of dung. "I'd say *this* is a pretty darn good idea."

"Dog dung?"

"How many times do I have to tell you? It's *God* dung. When I said that book smelled like a crock of crapola, I wasn't talking figuratively. If you want to catch a God that's completely full of shinola, then what better God to lead you right to him than the God of Dung?"

"TO THE GOD OF DUNG!" Väinämöinen raised his beer and saluted the name. Matylda looked at him and shook her head.

"How do we find the Dung Beetle?" Clarence asked.

"She'll find us. With the right bait, of course."

The right bait. It didn't take long for everyone to figure out what this meant. They all began looking around for volunteers, but no one stepped forward. Finally, Väinämöinen stood up and began loosening his belt.

"Well, I was holding on to this for centuries. Now I know why."

"Aaargh. You're as thick as he is, you idiot." Matylda swatted him across the head. "Not in here. We do this outside. And we already have the bait—*this!*"

"You're expecting the Dung Beetle to come back for the same dung?"

"No," Matylda said. She pierced the ball with her fingers, and the crap crumbled to the floor, leaving behind a penny in her hand.

"But she will come back for this."

*

They baited the penny on the sidewalk, in exactly the place where Clarence had nearly stepped in the ball of dung. They all huddled around, looking down at it as if it were a seed planted in soil, waiting for it to suddenly sprout up and grow.

"You're just going to stand there?" Matylda snapped. "There's no telling how long it will take for that beetle to come back for this thing. When she does, the last thing she'll want to see is you lot of dolts hanging around the nest, so come inside." She motioned for them to follow her back into the house. "And take off your shoes."

"How do you know that she will come back for it?" Clarence asked.

"Don't you know anything at all about Dung Beetles?" she answered belligerently. "They roll that crap cradle as a protective nest for their eggs, which they put inside. I'm hoping the smell on that penny will attract her again, and that she'll follow its scent directly back to its source."

She opened the door to her shed, and Raison was instantly appalled by the cluttered condition of her house.

"Take off your shoes!" she commanded again as she shooed them all inside.

Everyone crammed behind the one window in the narrow house, while Matylda used Triglav's magnifying eye for a better view. Like watching a proverbial pot of water refusing to boil, absolutely nothing happened, at least, not on the outside. Inside, the Gods irritably poked, prodded and pulled each other's limbs as they tried to make their crammed accommodation more comfortable. Shiva got the worst of it. Others complained about the odor of Balaam's feet. Raison cursed in French at Seshat, who hissed back, threatening a cat-fight. Inevitably, all the old wounds were re-opening. Väinämöinen and the Concierge blinked silent sparring quotes.

"!!!!!!!!!!!"

♪ !!!!!! ♪

Matters worsened after a pudgy happy go-lucky Buddha strolled by and chanced upon the penny on his way to the tavern.

"Oooh!" he exclaimed with great delight as he hunched over to claim his winnings. "A good-luck omen!"

Everyone stopped and watched in dismay as he plucked his prize off the ground, popped it in the air and caught it before stashing it away in his robe and trotting into the tavern.

"He stole our money!" Väinämöinen hollered.

"Pipe down," Matylda snapped. "We still have the one the stone heads found."

"We do? Where is it? Which one of you has it?" Väinämöinen looked around.

"You do!" Matylda snapped again and helped herself to the quarter in his pocket. As Väinämöinen grumbled at his second loss, Matylda smell-checked the coin. Sure enough, it had the scent of stool.

Clarence, Raison, Seshat, the Concierge, Balaam, Shiva, Omiokane and Väinämöinen looked out the small window and watched Matylda as she waddled out the front door and made the replacement. She turned around and saw the eight deities bunched together like sardines behind the window. It was as if they had fought over front row seats to watch paint dry. Deciding that there was no point in explaining to any of them how long this was going to take, she shook her head and walked back inside to return to her post.

All that could be done now was wait and cross their fingers that another lucky fellow wouldn't come along to take the last of their bait.

As the hours passed, a steady traffic of drunken deities came in and out of the tavern with their feet treading over the stray quarter. So far no one noticed it. But another problem was brewing.

The background of amusement and jovial chatter travelled from the tavern, through the air and located Väinämöinen's spine, where it splintered off into a series of nervous signals and triggered his limbs to vibrate. At first it was only a tremor, but as the partying increased, his entire body began to quake. The poor guy was hankering for hops. Seconds later, he cracked.

The group wailed as he dislodged himself from the wall of bodies, sending them all toppling to the ground. No sooner had they stood up to stop him, he shoved them all aside, stormed out of the house and disappeared past the tavern's front door. Matylda made no effort to stop him.

"Are you aware that your husband has a drinking problem, Madam Matylda?" Shiva asked, politely.

"What do you think?"

"Ah, let him have a sip," Seshat defended. "We've been smashed together smelling each other's breath for hours. I could use a drink myself."

"So that afterwards we can cram back into the stench of each other's beer breath?" Raison countered.

"Yes," Seshat snapped.

"I agree with Seshat," Omiokane added.

"Whatever." Raison sighed and rolled her eyes, but then widened them when a thought occurred to her. "Wait a minute. Why is a blind man cramming to look out of the window?"

"Perhaps a better question is..." Omiokane raised a single finger. "Why would a blind man cram himself between two sexy Goddesses *pretending* to look out of the window? The answer to that, I believe, is self-explanatory."

"Ugh." Seshat and Raison looked at each other and shook their heads.

"Do you have any beers?" the Concierge asked Matylda.

"If I did, that fool husband of mine would have run into the kitchen, not the bar."

"What about water?" Balaam asked.

"You plan to get drunk on water?"

"After We give it Our blessing, yes."

Matylda looked around counting all the thirsty mouths. She looked at Shiva and motioned for him to follow her.

"Come with me. I'll need an extra pair of hands. Clarence, come here and keep your eye on the ball."

She handed over the cross handles to Clarence, went into the kitchen and came back with a gallon of water, which Balaam promptly made into a gallon of wine for the group to pass around like homeless winos.

While the group intoxicated themselves, Clarence remained vigilant using Triglav's all-seeing eye to keep close watch over the coin. Powerful magnification allowed him to see every detail of the pavement and that Matylda's plan was working. The faint scent of turd and money had attracted several bugs. Dozens of brown and black critters restlessly scurried around the quarter, almost as if they were fighting over it. Suddenly, they all scattered as several pairs of feet stepped into close view and stopped at the quarter. Clarence decreased Triglav's magnification and saw a procession of twenty-four animal headed Gods carrying the emblem of the Sun and forming a protective circle around the coin. Clarence's eyes widened as he watched a tiny Dung Beetle come crawling out from between their toes.

He increased the magnification to observe the Beetle as it followed the scent and went directly for the coin. With its thin legs, it propped up the quarter.

"Oh no, you don't!" a voice shouted. "That's my money!"

The sudden voice came as a war cry and immediately after, one of the Watchers was sent tumbling across the pavement. Clarence zoomed out and watched in horror. It was Väinämöinen. And he was juggernauting a queue of Gods, knocking them down like bowling pins.

"Holy S." Clarence exclaimed as he went for the door.

He burst outside and waved his arms for Väinämöinen to stop, but the big man was on a rampage and heard nothing. He squatted like a linebacker and darted forward, bowling over anyone who was in his way. For the Dung Beetle, each step was like a giant's stomp, and the two-dozen bodies falling around her were like skyscrapers collapsing from an earthquake, threatening to topple down on her.

Matylda and the others finally came barreling out of the house, adding fourteen more feet to the Dung Beetle's nightmare. They piled up on Väinämöinen, tackling him to the ground, which, to the Beetle, seemed like an asteroid had just struck the surface. The Earth violently shook and coughed up stray limbs, funky feet and a pair of pink bunny flip flops before it finally settled. Clarence alone remained standing.

He surveyed the aftermath: thirty-three Gods scattered across the pavement and a missing Dung Beetle. Not only was this mission over, it had been a complete failure. To the victor goes the spoils of war and, as the proverbial last man standing, Clarence decided the antique quarter was his.

He took one step to claim his prize and heard a crunch.

Chapter 16

"SOB!"

His eyes instinctively clenched shut. A sinking feeling dropped through his stomach and descended all the way to his feet, where he felt a warm, wet, unmoving texture. *No!* he thought as he lifted his bare foot. Reluctantly, he opened his eyes and found the insect crushed into small bits and blood-juice. The God of Dung was dead.

He groaned and cursed as his bad luck flashed before his eyes. On day one, right here in this same GD spot, he came *this* F'n close to stepping in S. and D. near broke his F'n bones trying to dodge the GD S. and now, today—in the SAME F'n spot—he stepped on the GD, small piece of S. rolling dirty A. Dung Be—

He felt a strange sensation tickling his *other* toes. He looked down.

Holy S!

The Dung Beetle, still very much alive and wedged in the cavity of his big toe, was wiggling to get free. Carefully, he spread his toes to release her. She sniffed around and followed the distinct smell to Clarence's other foot where she found not a pile of poo, but splattered goo from some other stray bug his foot had crushed. After a cursory investigation of the fresh carcass she moved on, this time locating what she was looking for. Gripping her limbs on the coin, she propped it back on its edge and, picking up where she left off, made her rolling getaway.

Matylda stuck her head out from the crevice of someone's armpit and shouted: "The ship is setting sail. Follow her!"

"Raison, are you coming with me?" Clarence called to the heap. She was buried in there somewhere.

She answered by pulling herself from the pile, running back into Matylda's home and returning with her blunderbuss. With legs spread and one arm hanging by her side, she cradled her long rifle against her shoulder, ready with her back against the Sun. An unexpected ally stepped behind her and mimicked her heroic poise with four fists punching into his waist.

"Shiva, what are you doing?" Clarence asked.

"Mister Clarence, I am coming with you."

"No, you've done enough already."

"Mister Clarence, though Madame Raison is standing like a noble super-heroine, the fact is, she is very drunk at the moment. Our other companions are also severely impaired by their addiction." He pointed to the pile of chaos. "I am very certain that you will require a sober assistant to help you complete this mission. Besides, I saw a quote in the stolen book by a priest named Warren Buffet who said, *'derivatives are financial weapons of mass destruction.'* I do not know what these derivatives are, but if this priest is correct, I would very much like to see this masterpiece for myself."

Clarence approved by stepping into their ranks with a valorous stance. Fresh sunrays spangled over their shoulders as baying horns sounded in the distance, heralding their courage, their camaraderie and their covenant. He turned to face them and to make a climatic speech, the kind made by all war generals before leading their beleaguered soldiers into the battlefield.

"When I first wondered into this land, I saw nothing but misfits: a Japanese God of Wisdom *and* Larceny, a Finnish God who stretches tall tales to be even taller, a Messianic troll with British trimmings, a happy-go-lucky Hindu with no taste for meat but an appetite for destruction, a cross-cultural connoisseur concierge with chopsticks, a flower-child librarian with an actual flower potted on her head and a boot-stompin' blunderbussin' disbeliever deity with all the tolerance of the Taliban.

"Misfits you were, but now you are mavericks marching into the marshes of the marketplace. You will encounter terms like *obsolescence.* To be outdated. Outmoded. Out of sight and out of mind. They'll tell you that you, the Gods, belong to the past, that you are the defective products of a Dark Age. The past can be discarded; it can be ignored. It can even be covered up like an embarrassing secret. But every robust and regal tree has its roots, though they be buried from our eyes and forgotten by the mind. They can raze these trees for paper to write their history books by the volumes, but no amount of revisionist history will change the fact that page one belongs to you, the Gods. The first chapter is yours. History begins with you. They can climb whatever mountain they choose, journey across vast terrains and travel the distance of the Earth, but the first step was yours. You are the cornerstone of every building and the alpha in all architecture. What reaches the stars starts from the Earth, and therein is your purpose: *to be the beginning.* Obsolescence is the end, and that chapter is not yours; it is theirs."

Clarence raised his cane as if it were a sword. He crunched the ground with his heel and swiveled around to point the way for their voyage to begin. Had this played out as cinematically as he imagined, they would have galloped off on warhorses, a three-man infantry charging into battle. But the Dung Beetle, while capable of galloping, doesn't charge forward; *it chugs* and it does so at the dawdling rate of 7.6 millimeters per second.

Fifteen minutes later they had only travelled the distance of a single step.

"This is going to take quite long, Mister Clarence."

"No," Clarence said looking around. "She's head-hunting."

"Excusez-moi?" Raison said.

Clarence pointed to the street post, which had the word *Religare* emblazoned on the sign sheeting. This was the line he crossed, bringing him to the world of the Gods.

"Conversation is two brains exchanging information, wirelessly. Ideas are uploaded and downloaded via words. Looking for a word sign is like roaming for a signal: Once you find it, you're in someone's head. She's going in the direction of the next word sign. We don't need to follow her; we just need to use her like a compass." Clarence turned to face Raison and Shiva, then pointed. "She's headed West. Run ahead and see if you can find the next word sign. I'll stay here in case she changes course."

Shiva and Raison rushed off down the main road, stopping at every deserted side street, checking for word signs. But the entirety of the town was unmarked. Even the storefronts were missing any signage that might have indicated what they used to be before being abandoned.

"What kind of words are we looking for?" Raison shouted from a distance.

"Words that describe my world," he shouted back while cupping his hands into a bullhorn. "Words like *derivatives, return on investment, vertical markets* or even *planned obsolescence.*"

"What about... *Psilocybe semilanceata?*"

Psilo-what? Clarence frowned at the syllables. He checked on the Dung Beetle's ETA and saw that she was still working on her second lap. He grabbed one of Matylda's bunny flip-flops left over from the fracas to use as a landmark, then hobbled off towards Raison's discovery.

The long Latin words *Psilocybe semilanceata* were printed on a picket and planted in a mushroom field—a *magic* mushroom field—the kind where the mushroom cap is not flat and wide but shaped like a liberty bell or, as Clarence suddenly recalled, like the conical Phrygian caps worn by Shamash and Mithras.

This must be it, he thought. He looked back at where the Dung Beetle was heading. Fittingly, *'shrooms*, as they are psychedelically codenamed, thrive on dung.

Raison ran back for the Dung Beetle, but stopped and cringed at the thought of what had to be done. *This has to be done. This has to be done. This has to be done. One. Two. THREE.* She scooped up the arthropod and screamed as she felt its limbs crawling around in her palm. At lightning speed, she hand-delivered the blood-curdling bug to the mushroom patch and flung it away from her body. Clarence and Shiva stood by and watched as she went into an erratic dance of slapping her skin, trying to rid herself of the scaly after-touch. Finally, she calmed herself and looked abashed at her companions.

"I don't like bugs," she admitted.

This was understandable. Insects are as ugly as they are strong. The Dung Beetle, which boasts the ability to move well over a thousand times its own body weight, is the world's strongest. It's also very ugly. But strength doesn't necessarily mean stamina, and Clarence watched with some anxiety as the Dung Beetle recovered from being cannoned from Raison's hand. After some stupor, the stout bug found her footing and her coin and marched into the mushroom forest with single-minded tenacity. Like a mirage, she disappeared.

"Psilocybe semilanceata."

The words had swallowed her whole. Clarence, Raison and Shiva looked at each other, confirming that they were ready to begin this cross-cognitive road trip. They nodded, took their first step and tripped.

They dove headlong into a subaqueous hallucinogenic dream. The mind splashed and mushroomed. Clarence, Raison and Shiva kicked and flailed while sinking into a kaleidoscope of surfaces and solids shape-shifting all around them. Even the ground refused to stay grounded.

The world was experimenting with itself, exploring new psychoactive possibilities of space and time, and it had three new *psychonauts* as its intrepid explorers: two Gods and one human.

Everybody knows what happens when humans trip out on mushrooms—*everything happens*. Including visions of being God. But when Gods trip out on mushrooms they become überGods, which is as difficult to imagine as a hypercube expanding three dimensions into four. Raison, now amplified as überRaison, discovered the unifying theory that merged the electromagnetic, weak and strong forces with quantum gravity. Shiva marveled at how his four arms had squared to sixteen. Clarence, however, had no such expansion. Time rolled him back into a monkey, one now high on mushrooms. The psychotic monkey was kicking, screaming and cursing unintelligibly, and not without reason. He was being attacked by a colony of fractals armed with forks and wallpaper walk-a-thon stitches glued to his britches and visions of a cure for conjunctivitis and what not. No, none of that made any sense, and to make matters worse, the fractal colony had a banana and wouldn't give it to the poor monkey.

Thankfully, this was all washed away in a shower of synesthesia. Chameleon colors began singing a strange song in his head.

I am the smell of blue. Me too, y tu?

What the hell does that mean?

Am I the sound of green?

The touch of Spring?

So many questions

So many things

Don't ask, but

Do tell me

About

"Eburnean"

Just like that, the hues, hymns and hallucinations were whitewashed away. Clarence, Raison, Shiva and the Dung Beetle had reached the bottom of this oceanic subconscious. At such depths, they should have been swallowed by darkness, but the vast space around them became a soft, empty eburnean—an ivory-like color, akin to a blank canvas.

That word had taken them inside the imagination of a painter, where the background filled itself with sprawling pigments condensing into a wet sunset. A waterfall of watercolors splintered into tiny tributaries, cascading and coursing across the canvas. They were witnessing an artist's geology, where landscapes accrete and dreamscapes ablate. Shiva recognized this as creation and his eyes ballooned with burning visions of destruction. Now was his chance to show off his artistic muscle. But Clarence stopped him and pointed at the Dung Beetle. She was marching across the artist's signature.

"Thomas Girtin"

This name transported them to an amber-colored cliff overlooking Bolton Abbey. They were in the heart of Yorkshire Dales, surrounded by a countryside roaming free in every direction. Of course, the question now was *which direction*. They checked the Dung Beetle's course and saw her treading for a teal river running through a pair of rugged hilltops hidden in a fog. Shiva pointed to a word sign at the peak of the cliffs.

They ran over and began rock climbing, presumably inside the head of some bloke with vivid visions of hiking up Crag Hill and crimping up Great Coum. That was the path Clarence and his crew took as they bore their naked fingers and swollen feet into solid rock. Shiva, having the hands to spare, cupped and carried the Dung Beetle. Fatigued and funky from sweat, they reached the summit, where they were rewarded with a God's eye view of the naked Earth, flat-bellied and breasted with hills. Respectfully, Shiva covered his eyes.

"I think the point is that we are supposed to look, Shiva," Clarence said.

"Oh no, not until She puts on a robe."

"No, I mean that's what the sign is telling us. Look." Clarence pulled down Shiva's arms and directed him to the next word sign.

"God's Window"

God's Window is the name for Blyde River Canyon in Mpumalanga, South Africa, which is where the word sign transported them. Here, they stood at the edge of the end of the world, overlooking a boundless blanket of clouds that bridged Heaven and Earth. This time Shiva could look. The Earth was covered in white silk.

Clarence recognized this soft scenery from a '80s movie and concluded they were inside the head of someone watching a re-run of **The Gods Must Be Crazy.** He even noticed a Coke bottle nested in a rocky cavity. Deciding he would re-enact the famous scene where Xi tossed the God's imprudent gift over the edge, Clarence dislodged the bottle from its nest but stopped when he noticed that the word "Coca-Cola" was printed in a foreign language.

He looked up and around to discover that they were now at a bottling plant in Mongolia.

The beetle started leading them on a scenic pilgrimage along a wide and nameless dirt road, across golden-green steppes and through barren plateaus so vast as to make even the Gods appear small and mortal. Clarence, most of all, was swallowed by the open immensity but also by the sick sinking feeling that they were helplessly and hopelessly lost.

Overtaken by fatigue and despair, he plopped to his knees and blankly studied the horizon, so heavenly and yet still so aloof. That was always the damning thing about Mother Nature: Like all beautiful women, she attracts attention but rarely gives it. *Casual Gods*, as Jerry Harrison called them. Clarence thought about his conversation with the Concierge when they first met. *Broken Hearts, Broken Worlds and Broken Gods.* How right he was. Clarence nodded, rubbed sweat from his brow and blinked away the cloudy tears in his eyes. He looked back out at the horizon and blinked again. A figure trekked along the horizon's edge, rippling in the heat waves.

"Who is that?" Raison asked.

"A God," Clarence answered. He leapt up and stumbled after the shimmering silhouette. Shiva and Raison couldn't stop him even if they tried. Instead, they just peered dubiously at each other. Even at this distance, they could see that this was no God.

Clarence tripped several times on his way to the mirage, but his final collapse sent him head first to the of feet a Bactrian camel—a plump, two-humped stallion with a broad drooping neck wrapped in a thick mane. Clarence looked up at the rider. The rider looked down at him. It *was* a God.

"Alec Issigonis," Clarence said while coughing up dust.

"*Sir* Alec Issigonis," the God corrected.

Sir Alec Issigonis was a Greek automobile designer imported into the UK around 1923. He studied engineering and became famous for designing the Mini automobile for the British Motor Corporation. He became a Royal Society Fellow in 1967, was awarded knighthood in 1969 and, throughout his professional career, was known by the nickname "the Greek God." Befitting of his royal godhood, Sir Issigonis projected an intensely noble character. Clarence probed deeply into his exacting eyes and saw a sharp, sagacious stare signature of the intelligentsia.

"Rise, fellow designer," he bid Clarence.

"How did you know?" Clarence asked in a raspy voice, while standing and wiping dirt from his eyes. "How did you know I'm a designer?"

"It is in your eyes," he said.

"The light?" Clarence asked.

"No, the defeat. Every designer has it. Even me."

Clarence blinked and reappraised his "exacting eyes." They were still sharply sagacious, but he understood now this had been from his suffering.

"What kind of design do you do?" the Greek God asked.

"Architecture," Clarence answered and looked around. "How did you get here?"

"Some chap or chairman somewhere just quoted me—that favorite line that everyone enjoys tossing around. I'm not even sure the quote is truly mine, to be quite honest."

"A camel is a horse designed by committee," Clarence repeated the famous quote.

"Yes," Issigonis nodded. "And now here I am, riding a strange camel in Mongolia. Not sure how Mongolia fits into all of this."

"Maybe your name came up at a committee meeting at the bottling plant we came from. It's not too far from here. No, what am I talking about? It's actually very far from here. We've been walking so long that by the time I get back into my own body, I'll probably be dead."

"Nonsense. Two minutes in the body is two decades in the mind. Haven't you ever had an adventure dream you were certain lasted the whole night, only to wake up to find you dozed off on your smoke break? Which reminds me..." He pulled out a pack of cigarettes from his breast pocket—Camels, of course—and lit up. He glanced over Clarence's head as Raison and Shiva arrived, carrying the Dung Beetle.

"Mister Clarence, who is this?" Shiva asked.

"Sir Alec Issigonis," Issigonis answered for himself. "Born in Smyrna, died in England and known in my own time as *The Greek God.*"

Once again, Shiva and Raison peered dubiously. They were not convinced.

"Automobile designer," Clarence hastened to add. "Amazing work. Really."

"And now tell me what brings the three of you into this head?"

"We're head-hunting," Shiva answered, "for a God."

Issigonis' eyes shot open as he instinctively grabbed a pistol from his camel pouch and pointed it at Clarence. Raison reacted even faster and had her blunderbuss aimed at Alec. A stand-off. Raison's aim was focused and her limbs locked. She wouldn't miss. And neither would Alec, whose nerves were as sturdy as steel even as he looked down the barrel of the blunderbuss. But then his eye twitched at the sight of the Dung Beetle crawling up his shirt and disappearing into his breast pocket. He lowered his gun and dug his fingers in search of her, only to discover that the Beetle had vanished.

"What kind of wizardry is this?" Alec asked.

"We're searching for Mark, the God of the Marketplace, a.k.a. the Invisible Hand." Clarence pointed to Alec's pocket. "That Dung Beetle is leading us to him."

"And so you passed through the mind of a committee chairman along the way." Alec smiled and put his gun away. "I would say you are on the right path, alright. Though I don't envy you. Committees are dangerous entities. Even the esteemed 'Greek God' was no match for them. Smoke?"

He pulled out his cigarette pack, jerked it upwards to get a stick to stand out and offered it. Clarence noticed the packaging: a short-skirted dame donning a bob cut and basking in a self-aristocratic aura of cigarette smoke. She had her head tilted back as if she could hear the Jazz.

In those days, they called these women "flappers." They were the Riot Girls of the Roaring Twenties. Raison latched on to the image instantly. She reached for the cigarette and, in a flash, was gone. Clarence looked closer at the package and saw why.

"Packaged in New York, NY, 1920"

Shiva reached for the same stick and slipped into the Roaring Twenties, with Clarence tumbling right behind him. Flat and face-down on a frantic dance floor, they watched as several dozen feet bobbed and bopped, swinging to Jazz and nearly slamming down on the Dung Beetle. A dancer's heel sideswiped the beetle's quarter and kicked it away, sending it rolling across the dance floor and delivering it to another man's foot. He reached down to claim it, but a blood-curdling scream stopped him. Every man and woman scattered like roaches, not from the Dung Beetle, but from the terrifying sight of a blue man with four arms standing in the center of the dance floor.

Shiva snatched up the Dung Beetle, Clarence grabbed the quarter and Raison reclaimed her rifle. The three ran out the front door, crashing into a newsboy. A stack of papers broke apart into the air and came down like confetti. A shower of lithographic text rained down on them, but all Clarence could see was the headline. In blocky bold san-serif letters it read:

"Black Tuesday"

Society had danced and drank itself into a *"Great Depression"* and now everyone, including Clarence and his crew, were running for their lives as the sky was falling with the bodies of broken brokers. They ran right into a *"New Deal"* and a *"Keynesian"* economy that put thousands of carpenters and masons, pipe fitters and plumbers, welders and window glazers, and, of course, artists and architects to work on public buildings that were designed to capture the spirit of populism. The stuffy, vanilla aesthetics of the classical era were pushed aside for red brick walls, rectilinear forms and murals of men at work. Tall vertical edifices reached as high as the dreams for the future and stood proud, even through a *"World War,"* before it all came crumbling and crashing into an ocean of oil shock, followed by an *"Economic Malaise."*

They were getting close.

Despite the erratic beginning of their voyage, the latter half of their journey had at least a domino's logic about it, although the latest domino to drop came as a strange detour. Leaving behind a stagnant economy, they suddenly walked into a **"recession"** so severe as to, literally, be *ruins*, which is to say, they had somehow roamed into...

"Rome?" Clarence looked around perplexed at the capitol buildings decomposing under the heavy hand of time. The ancient past had the aura of a post-apocalyptic future. All of the signature elements of classical architecture—the arch, the dome and the regal white columns capped with floral capitals—were recognizable, but in a state of broken decay, wrecked and war-torn. The remains were all withered away by the weather. He checked the Dung Beetle's course, wondering how and why she brought them here.

"These appear to be ancient temples, Mister Clarence," Shiva said. "If the Dung Beetle has led us here, then perhaps the last God is already dead. We are too late."

"But she was in such a hurry to get here," Raison quipped sarcastically as she motioned to the slow Dung Beetle, who was still trudging forward.

"This doesn't make sense." Clarence shook his head. "Charles said that this was a new God. But if this God came from ancient Rome—"

"Ancient for you, Mister Clarence," Shiva rebutted. "But when you come from a civilization as old as mine, Roman Gods are but children."

"But Charles told me that this God was alive and destructive."

"He must have meant *self-destructive*," Raison said. "And apparently *dead*, and we're all the better for it. The only good god is a dead one." She mounted her blunderbuss on her shoulder and kept moving.

"Where are you going, Madam Raison?" Shiva asked.

"Home."

"But you do not know the way."

"*Je suis une femme intelligente.* I will figure it out."

"Raison"—Clarence began following her—"you need the Dung Beetle to guide you back, and she's still following the scent —"

"Of a dead God who forgot to clean his *cul* before he keeled," she cut him off. "If you want to follow her to see that, be my guest. *Au Revoir.*"

Walking away, she waved an indifferent goodbye while Clarence watched her without saying a word. He had half the mind to abandon the mission and follow her. One look in Shiva's eyes and he could see that he, too, agreed. Only the Dung Beetle was determined to see this through to the end. Clarence looked down at the sound of her tiny legs crunching the dirt. He lifted his foot as if to put the poor thing out of her misery and brought it down alongside her. *Fifteen minutes*, he thought to himself. *It would take her fifteen minutes to travel this far.*

"I'm staying." Clarence sighed. "She's on this stupid journey because of me. It's not right to—"

He stopped mid-sentence, noticing that Raison had spotted something. She threw up a hand and pointed at a familiar figure in the distance: a stone needle—Światowid!

It would have been a sight for sore eyes, had it not been for the fact that the tall standing structure had been decapitated. Clarence walked off in that direction, past Raison, until he came upon the broken remains of the once tall, vertical pillar. This wasn't Światowid. It was a wrecked obelisk standing at only half its original height. The top half had crumbled to the base as a rubble of scattered bricks.

"There's something wrong with this obelisk," he said.

"You think?" Raison quipped, laughing as she kicked one of the bricks.

"No, what I mean is, this shouldn't be made of individual bricks. The Egyptians quarried their obelisks from a single slab of granite. The Romans imported their obelisks from Egypt. This should be one big polished piece of granite—not bricks."

"But I thought we were in Rome, Mister Clarence."

"So did I." Clarence stepped into the rubble and pronged the bricks with his cane. "There is one obelisk that I know of that was made of bricks, thirty-six thousand of them. But it's not in Rome." Clarence looked around at where they were. Finally, he recognized these ruins. "This is the Washington Monument."

The Dung Beetle's course confirmed where they were and where she was going, though at this stage, he didn't need her compass. Her destination—the White House—was right in front of him.

The former architectural icon had lost its regal white sheen for a rotted and ruinous grey—soot left over from pollution. The high ceilings and wide-open walls gave the long ago abandoned White House the appearance of a haunted house. There were no Gods squatting in these halls, only ghosts loitering around fallen paintings of past presidents. Shiva carefully stepped through the scattered shards from shattered chandeliers and tip-toed around toppled Turkish-style furniture, looking on in rapt awe.

"Admiring your work?" Clarence asked.

"Oh no, Mister Clarence. This is work wrought by some other hand."

"The Invisible Hand."

"Then I am very eager to meet this God and congratulate him on his masterpiece."

For Shiva, the battered mansion was a museum, which he strolled through with two arms bow-tied behind his back, one hand perched on his hip and the last cradled around his chin as if surveying the walls of the MOMA. He finally stopped at the most interesting exhibition of them all: a plaque icon of a man, nailed to a door.

"Your God is in here, Mister Clarence." Shiva tapped the plaque.

"That's a restroom sign, Shi—" Clarence paused and looked down. The Dung Beetle slid her quarter underneath the door and then scratched at the base, like an estranged house cat wanting inside.

All at once, Clarence, Raison and Shiva placed their ears to the door and could hear someone stirring and letting out pellet-sized farts. Clarence looked at Shiva, Shiva looked at Raison and Raison looked away, turning up her nose as if to say, *There's no way I'm going in there.*

"Oh, to H. with this," Clarence grumbled. He gave a polite knock to announce that he was welcoming himself inside.

The door squeaked open and Clarence nearly crapped his pants when he discovered former President Ronald Reagan squatting on the proverbial porcelain throne, struggling to liberate his bowels and the marketplace. Mortified, Reagan grabbed his copy of **Capitalism and Freedom** by Milton Friedman and used it to shield his lower half.

"Who are you?" Reagan asked in his usual airy voice.

Clarence was a stuttering mess as he struggled for an answer. He blurted the first thing that came to mind: "The help."

Reagan sized him up, noted Clarence's color and accepted this answer. "Help with what?"

Before Clarence could answer, Reagan noticed the Dung Beetle trying to crawl into the seat of his pants. He leaped up and looked at Clarence for an explanation.

"Help with that." Clarence sighed and grabbed nearly a half-roll of toilet sheets. He moseyed back to the door, glowered at Shiva and Raison and closed it.

Shiva and Raison pressed their ears against the surface and heard a scuffle. Seconds later, the president yelped. Stray items were heard being thrown and tossed about, followed by a punching thud. Finally, the skirmish settled and the toilet flushed. Water from the sink turned on and they could hear hands being washed excessively. Shiva and Raison stepped away from the door as it re-opened and Clarence emerged with a wad of toilet paper and a lump of presidential dung in his hand. The Dung Beetle pawed at his feet as if begging for table scraps.

"Tell no one about this," Clarence implored his friends.

"I will take this with me to *your* grave, Mister Clarence," Shiva promised. Raison blurted an ego-injuring laugh but still gave a consensual nod.

Satisfied, though far from happy, Clarence inserted the quarter inside the lump of crap and placed it on the floor. The Dung Beetle promptly rolled it away, but she only went as far as the neighboring door with its own plaque bolted to the surface.

"Logistics"

They opened the door and found themselves back in the outdoors, standing in the middle of a quiet, isolated highway stretching well beyond the horizon. Long ago this must have been a turnpike. Clarence could see the sunken impression of where a tollbooth had been removed. Now it was, quite literally, a freeway—an open road for roaming traffic, though at the moment it was vacant. A few chucked cigarette butts and faint tire treads on the asphalt were the only evidence that it was still being used at all.

The lonesome ambiance of an empty highway has a meditative quality, but the serenity of this secluded road was short lived. The ground began trembling, and Clarence turned his head to the familiar sound of metal thunder. Shiva did too. He recognized that ominous death knell. His eyes dilated from the fresh memory of the beast he had failed to conquer. He gritted the beast's name through knotted teeth:

"A Dragon."

Chapter 17

At 65 mph, several massive wheels passed over a pothole causing the semi trailer to bump and clamor. The small bounce made a cup of coffee spill over and into the lap of the driver, who ignored it as he reached out with his tattooed arm for the volume on his dashboard and cranked up his heavy metal music.

With the windows rolled tight, every sharp note that sliced through his speakers filled the small space and the driver's vicarious imagination with images of being on stage in front of thousands of fans. With one arm, he air-played his imaginary guitar with such energy that the strings sizzled with electric fire. His imaginary stage was smothered in a dense fog, courtesy of the electricity in his fingers and the exhaust from his cigarette. He closed his eyes to play out the last minute and pounded the dashboard like a drum as the acid-song fizzled out to its end. He re-opened his eyes to thank his fans, but they had all vanished. Except for one. She was standing in the middle of the highway pointing a blunderbuss directly at him.

"What the—"

He slammed the brakes. The truck came to a grinding halt only a foot away from Raison, who hadn't so much as flinched. He blinked in disbelief at the sight of a woman wrapped in vintage French fashion holding a weapon from the eighteenth century. He went for the door latch, but was intercepted by the jarring sight of a blue four-armed man standing in the window. The driver froze up, speechless.

"Mister Clarence has informed me that what you are experiencing is a car-jacking. For your own safety, please step away from this Dragon. She is very dangerous," Shiva said in the most non-intimidating Indian accent he could muster.

The driver stammered silently until he was finally able to stutter out a jittery *"What?"*

"He said to get out of the F'ing truck!" Clarence commanded from the opposite window in the most gangster voice he could muster, but it was all belied by his elderly face and form. This was even more disturbing for the driver, who reached again for his latch, but Shiva beat him to the punch and yanked the door open. The driver went hurling from the seat and smacked the ground with a single thud. Strangely enough, the Dung Beetle began walking towards him.

"I can't believe it!" Shiva exclaimed with excitement. "We have found the God! The beetle has chosen him. We can go home now!"

"No, he's not the God," Clarence said, pointing to the man's moist buttocks. "He just crapped in his pants. The beetle is distracted."

"So which way do we go now?" Shiva asked.

"In the same direction the driver was going," Raison answered while stepping into the driver's seat, but Shiva blocked her. "I am sorry, Madam Raison, but it is I, and only I, who must do this."

She glowered at him, thinking this to be some kind of stupid chauvinism, but Shiva, guessing her thoughts, shook his head. "The time has come for Lord Shiva to redeem himself against the she-dragon."

The Dragon opened its mighty jaws, releasing a scream of metal music. The door, decaled with flames, closed and locked shut. The engine roared and the Dragon swooped off with Clarence and Raison sharing the passenger seat. They crashed their heads with chaotic rocks and rolls as the ambidextrous Shiva horned the sky with one hand, air-guitared with another and steered the road serpent with the others.

At 100mph, the God of Destruction was the new ruler of the road. But with every king comes a contender for the crown. Trouble arrived. An ominously armored black military vehicle snapped at the Dragon's tail.

"Mister Clarence," Shiva turned off the music. "I believe these other Dragons are trying to get our attention."

Other Dragons? Clarence thought, and Shiva pointed out the window to a flank formation of two Hummers and a jeep accelerating ahead as if to escort them. The Dragon was caged in, with no hope for escape. Raison spotted something ahead.

"Another word sign!" She pointed out the window.

Shiva pulled the reins by pressing the brakes, this time keeping control of the Dragon as it pulled its neck to the side and veered. The metal beast restlessly resisted its harness, but eventually conceded to the command and came to a rolling stop directly behind the sign.

"Inventory"

Clarence gazed out the window at an industrial landscape. Scores of breathing obelisks exhaled cloud-white gases, giving this grungy colony of temple-factories the serene illusion of life. At this distance, they looked like windpipes to a small city—one that apparently needed military protection.

The armored trucks came alive. The doors opened and armed soldiers emerged from their bowels, brandishing black metal assault rifles that made Raison's blunderbuss look like a toothpick.

"Who are these people, Mister Clarence?"

Clarence didn't answer right away. He looked at the small militia, wondering how to explain this to Shiva. Finally, he answered in a graven voice: "They are Ankou."

"Ankou? And what is it that they want? The Dragon?"

"Yes"—Clarence swallowed—"and us."

Raison grabbed the keys from the ignition and her blunderbuss. "Guess they'll have to settle for me."

She stepped brazenly from the passenger door with both hands raised in the air and holding her rifle. Unfazed by the number of weapons aimed at her, she scanned around taking inventory of any possible escape routes while plotting her next move. She did a quick headcount and identified six targets. But she was getting ahead of herself. First things first. Introductions.

"My name is Raison, and I understand that you six are personifications of Ankou. It is a pleasure to finally meet the mighty Ankou. I have heard a great deal about you. But tell me, mighty Ankou, was it wise to send six soldiers to claim one Goddess? Would it not have been wiser to send more?"

At the speed of thought, Raison spun through the air with her leg outstretched and brought it down like a sword into the skull of one soldier. The blow rocked through his cranium, dislodging all consciousness from his head and the rifle from his hand. Before he could drop his weapon, Raison had already laid claim to it. If only she knew how to use it. Despite her unparalleled speed, the delay in her counterattack would cost her. The remaining five soldiers opened fire. She dropped the gun, crouched low, dodging the bullets, and spun out again into a sweeping roundhouse that swept her next target off his

334

feet and into a half-somersault that ended with him falling flat on his face, unconscious.

But she underestimated their numbers. Even at her lightning speed, she was unable to get the drop on the remaining soldiers. Four of them stood side by side with their guns aimed and ready. But they never fired. Instead they collapsed to the ground, revealing that Shiva had been standing behind them. He held up his four hands, flexing them as spearheads.

"The problem with guns is they protect everything," Shiva quipped, "except the body's pressure points."

"*Oui*," Raison agreed with a sigh and a nod of gratitude. She looked down at the six soldiers spread out at her feet. "But what were *they* protecting?"

The answer to her question must have been hiding inside the trailer. They walked to the truck's rear and pulled on the handle of a sliding door, which mechanically rolled upward and back. Inside was nothing more eventful than a freight of smart phones.

Shiva helped himself to one, turned it on and tried his hands at playing with it, but his twenty fingers got in the way. Raison impatiently snatched it from him. Within a short span, they were already taking selfies. She even made the duck face.

"Mister Clarence, you must come and see this— Mister Clarence?"

They looked around and found Clarence standing at the end of the road. As they rushed to join him, Raison dropped the truck keys on the chest of one of the soldiers.

"Here's your truck back," she said and kept moving.

Clarence was watching the Dung Beetle's path. She was only a few centimeters away from the next word sign. But where the road abruptly ended, a conveyor belt began. It was a moving highway with a mechanical stream that grabbed hold of the Dung Beetle and her quarter and pulled both into its current.

"Well, at least, she'll be moving faster now," Raison said as she grabbed her companions by the hands and stepped onto the conveyor belt.

The conveyor, with its inexorable forward movement, was an apt symbol of industry: restlessly moving and relentlessly staying the course to fulfill its single-minded purpose of product transport.

"Mister Clarence, look at this." Shiva handed the stolen smart phone to Clarence. "We found this in the belly of the Dragon. Where do you think this moving road is taking us?"

Before Clarence could answer, he noticed a moving shadow sway over his feet, prompting him to look overhead. Directly above were multiple monolithic overpasses of even more conveyor belts. Each one overlapped the other, and all were transporting a steady line of products. Finally, Clarence looked back at Shiva.

"It's taking us to the market."

The only problem was that each conveyor was going in its own direction, and there was nothing to say that their moving road was leading them in the right direction. In fact, when they checked the Dung Beetle, they found the poor girl pushing the coin in a circle. She had become a spinning compass.

"I was afraid of this," Clarence sighed.

"What's wrong with her?" Raison asked. "Where is this God we are looking for? Is he even here?"

"Not just here." Clarence walked dangerously close to the conveyor's edge and looked down at a convoluted crisscross of currents. "This God is *everywhere*."

He walked back to the center of the conveyor and lay flat, staring into the screen of Shiva's new phone. He tapped it, prompting it to glow with playful rainbow colored icons. One of them was a mini-Buddha, smiling with a gumdrop face and wearing a modern medical white coat. Underneath was the app name:

"MEDitation."

The mini-medical Buddha smiled at Clarence, but he declined to smile back. He was hypnotized. Time ticked and tocked in his ear. All the while, the Buddha continued smiling, inducing him into a meditation and eventually lulling him to sleep.

*

The phone buzzed with a mystic ring tone.

Clarence opened his eyes, looked around and wondered why he was in his sofa chair and not on a conveyor belt. Then he remembered: *MEDitation.*

His phone was still chiming, but at least not belligerently. The music was soft and New Agey. It helped his mind descend with a gentle landing. He grabbed his phone and touched the audio icon to stop the meditation session. His phone spoke with a synthetic Buddhist voice.

"How was your guided MEDitation?"

"Good," he mumbled, "but I didn't experience emptiness."

"What did you experience?"

"An adventure."

"Would you like to record your experience in your journal?"

"Sure."

Instantly, the phone made a ding and the screen displayed a flat sound wave, which undulated at the sound of Clarence's voice.

"Today, I did a half-hour morning meditation where I tried clearing my mind, but I had this question sitting in the back of my head the whole time, and I just couldn't get myself to ignore it. Is it time to quit my job and retire? That was the question. Anyway, I did a visualization exercise, where I rediscovered some old passions: music and painting. I was even relearning how to build. I think what I'm craving is not so much to retire, but to be creative again. Clients make it really difficult to be creative, but they're the only ones with the money. How do I create without a client?" Clarence paused to think about this and then added his last thoughts. "When God created the world, I think he was working for a client. That would explain why the world is so screwed up."

Clarence tapped a button and a Buddhist voice returned: *"When would you like to schedule your next MEDitation?"*

"Lunchtime."

MEDitation closed by showing his heart and breathing rate, then dimming out. With his guided meditation complete, Clarence let out a great big groan as he propped his hands on the arms of the chair, anchored his legs and lifted himself to his feet. With slow, elderly steps he tottered off to the shower.

*

Clarence lived in a moderate apartment reflecting the life of a moderately successful man with a moderate income. He no longer dressed as the celebrity architect he once aspired to be, but as the average architect he had always been.

Every morning, he went through moderate motions that involved getting dressed and getting *away* from his apartment building, which was hopelessly noisy, particularly from the neighbors next door who were constantly running around trying to regain control of their reckless child. The apartment building was built by some average hack settling on cheap materials that only succeeded in permitting the boy's irritating voice to travel through walls and hit every nerve in Clarence's body. Once dressed, Clarence escaped from his home as quickly as possible. Each time, he promised himself that some day he would go over there, knock on the door and choke the parents. If no one was looking, he was going to punch the child, as a bonus.

Outside, in the public, was no refuge either. This was a big city, congested by the lingering walks of pedestrian traffic. Hurried people aggressively pushed through the crush of bodies, with little care or concern for who or what was in front of them. This almost always resulted in a series of small collisions.

Because Clarence moved slower than the herd, he always felt as if he were on the verge of being trampled. He would try to step off to the side, but that usually meant a game of chicken with someone so immersed in their phone that they didn't even know the game was being played. Every so often, he just allowed the collision to happen. Only for a split second did the other person realize that they had almost knocked over an elderly man. They would glance up, make a feint apologetic murmur and revert their attention back down to their phone to repeat the stunt with someone else. So much self-obsession. So little self-awareness. This bothered no one. Only Clarence. Occasionally he stopped to ask himself, *Who are all these reckless people?* The answer: *They are called society, not to be confused with civilization.*

*

He missed the first trolley and watched it rumble down the road without him.

He waited with a small crowd for the next one. He was surrounded by mutual strangers who had all agreed to an unspoken truce to neither look nor speak to each other, to engage with machines only and to follow a strict Darwinian code: When the trolley arrives, it is a first-come, first-served rule of law. Being old and slow, Clarence was just barely capable of getting his share of the scraps, which meant that, quite literally, he was always the last man standing. Everyone else had a seat, and there would be no offers of charity. With each stop, more bodies loaded, and now he wasn't the last man standing anymore; he had more company then he knew what to do with.

If everyone had suddenly disrobed, the trolley would instantly become a Roman orgy. This gave Clarence an idea. If he stripped down naked right here, people would back away in absolute horror, giving him the room he craved. If he walked down the street naked, the mere sight of his saggy skin would mean no more collisions.

This made him laugh, and a few people broke the truce by looking at him.

*

He walked into work and was greeted by his fellow moderately successful colleagues. As depressing as it was to be in such company on a Monday morning, there was at least a kind of ambivalent camaraderie to be found among them. They were like a team of players habitually breaking even on the season's record. Such players resign themselves to how unremarkable they really are. There was no in-fighting here, no quiet competitions. They exchanged vapid greetings, they worked and went home, then came back to work again.

The firm was like the employees: moderately successful. It was a loft where everyone worked in cubicles. Certain office trimmings found on people's desks provided evidence that the firm had tried to be hip in some heyday that never happened. The hipness had long ago gone stale, but for some reason the evidence was all still sitting there, on every desk and shelf, with faded colors. Maybe people kept these little dated tokens because it fit right in with everyone else. Every now and then, the office experienced a slight renovation. It would be cleaned up, jazzed up and made ready for a visiting client. This day was such a day.

Clarence walked to his desk and looked down at a bunch of mounted boards with renderings of yet another unremarkable building. That was the part that really hurt. It's one thing to start a race with both engines blazing and then burn out before the end, but there are few things more pathetic than the sight of someone who starts the race with no enthusiasm to finish. There is no sympathy for such a spectacle, no mantras about *at least you tried*. No, the only fitting mantra is to ask, *Why did you even bother?* With this mantra floating in his head, Clarence grabbed his boards and went for the conference room.

The door was closed.

He looked through the window and saw a bunch of talking heads huddled around the conference room table. It was a full house with his younger colleagues sitting on one side of the table and primly professional property developers on the other. Much like watching the missed trolley rumble up the road without him, he looked on as the morning meeting went on despite his absence.

He looked down at the obsolete renderings in his hands and set them back down on his desk. He stepped closer to the conference-room window, not so close to be noticed, but enough to see what was going on.

In the center of the conference-room table was an all-white scale model of yet another sky tower. The model was only paper and wood now, but someday it would be glass and steel and swaggering curves—all complimenting the property developer's braggart lifestyles. That was usually the subject of all small talk at the start of the meeting: the client's pastime, which would include anything from extreme sports to extreme sunbathing with the deep-fried suntans to prove it. But the client never boasted about this. Extremely wealthy people never do. They don't have to, and not because of the suits and watches and luxury cars that do the talking for them. They don't have to brag about their wealth because everyone can already see it in their eyes, their poise and their stride. It's like an aura. It's a vibe that everyone feels, especially the hired hands that shake and smile and start the small talk with *"you had a good weekend, I hope."* To which the client will answer, *"I did, got to spend some time out at—"* Anywhere. Pick a place. The Moon. They can afford it. The hired hands nod admirably, feigning fascination. Or maybe they're not feigning at all. People who aspire for success love to hear about it. It's a reminder that it's real. Someone in the room will follow up with the time they spent with their kids, and this is good because it keeps one foot grounded in what really matters:

family, allegedly. With soul and values duly calibrated, the small talk shifts to big talk, to what *really* matters: plot ratios, absorption and capitalization rates.

In order to add value to their image, designers learn to talk like their clients. For instance, the term "value added" is not one Clarence ever used until he began working closely with his firm's clients, which consisted primarily of property developers. They use the expression *value added* a lot. This means perceptual value as opposed to true innovation. True innovation means added cost and they don't want that. "Value added" refers to features that look like innovations but actually aren't. Designers are really good at adding value without adding cost to the client, who will, of course, use the "added value" to raise his capitalization rate—all terms Clarence came to loathe.

He could hear these words being slung around even from where he stood. This wasn't the first time he found himself on the outside *listening* in. In fact, it was becoming a trend. The first few times, he felt snubbed. Lately he felt spared.

It wasn't like he was being punished. When the door re-opened, they'd greet him and ask how he was and professionally smile away the answer no matter what it was. They'd ask, "*Hey guy, how was your weekend?*" It didn't really matter how he answered. He might say, "*Awful, I lost control of my bowels again.*" They'd smile as if he had just cracked a joke. "*Oh boy! Gotta get a handle on 'em next time.*" After that comes the affable pat on his arm. Then they walk away.

And that's how you know when your career is over: When they like you more than they respect you.

Clarence's *MEDitation* app chimed. Lunchtime. The place cleared out, leaving only Clarence who brought his low-sodium lunch with him. He sat alone at his work desk. It might have looked as if he was a dejected child unwelcome at the playground, but the truth was this was his favorite part of the day. It gave him time to think and to make a decision.

The next day, Clarence submitted his resignation. He retired from architecture without a swan song.

Chapter 18

"Why do you want this job?"

For all of their inanity, answering job-interview questions requires a special skill not unique to humans. Computers are better suited to the task; they are programmed for placating, for consistently saying the right thing with remarkable indifference to disingenuousness. Some humans are able to pull it off, but Clarence wasn't one of them. He suspected the woman in front of him wasn't either.

He sized up the poor woman across from him—a motherly looking manager who appeared both professional and tired, or just professionally tired. She was completely out of place in her own office, which looked and felt more like a waiting room lobby. The fact that a man Clarence's age submitted an application for employment sparked a lively curiosity in her otherwise weary eyes. *Why would a recently retired architect want to work at a restaurant—as a waiter?*

"I don't," he answered laconically. "It's not that I *want* this job; it's that I *need* this job."

She looked at him, speechlessly blinking. But her eyes were saying everything: "!!!" The wrong answer that is, in fact, the right answer has a way of doing that.

"Okay," she smiled, playing along. "Why do you *need* this job?"

"For money," he answered flatly. "C'mon, you know this already. Just like every person applying for this position—I'm not even sure 'position' is the right word, by the way. This is more like a *condition* than a position. I'm broke, that's my *condition*. That's why I'm here. I'm too old to be a mediocre architect anymore, so I need a new gig. Something where I can make just enough money to fix my fixed income."

"So you want to wait tables?"

"I *need* to wait tables," he corrected. "I *need* the tips."

"And you plan on waiting tables walking around with a cane?"

"What does that have to do with anything?"

"This is a position—"

"Condition," Clarence corrected again.

"This is a *condition* that requires the use of both hands."

"See that? You're hung up on what I can't do and completely missing what I *can* do. Don't focus on my disabilities; focus on my missed abilities."

"Fair enough," she chuckled and rephrased using air quotes. "So what are your *'missed'* abilities?"

"For one, I have three legs." Clarence paused, looked at her and grinned, but she was unresponsive. "*And* I have a sense of humor."

Finally, she cracked and laughed. She shook her head in disbelief at this crazy old man sitting in front of her. She liked him. There was no way she was going to hire him, but she liked him.

"Are you sure you were a mediocre architect?" she asked, still chuckling.

"I'm very sure," he said, as if it were the only thing he was sure about. "Too bad humor and honesty didn't earn as many points at my old firm as they do with you. Not that I'm complaining. Most places would have retired me a long time ago."

"Why didn't they?"

"Because I was really good at designing mediocre buildings, and as my manager used to say, *'That's what the market wanted from a firm our size.'* The market doesn't want art; nobody wants art. They don't even want art-chitecture; they want walls to cram in customers and employees and a roof so that they can't escape from the top. The market has no interest in things like art and culture. They want filing cabinets enlarged to the size of tall buildings. That's what the market wanted, and that's the mantra of this age: WTMW—What The Market Wants. Doesn't matter what you do—if it's selling crack to children or, or, or... filming your own daughter for a viral twerk video—all you have to say is WTMW and people nod their heads and say, *'yeah, you're right.'* WMTW—it's like What Would Jesus Do from the '90s. We might as well be walking around with WTMW bracelets and T-shirts."

"There you go." She gaveled her desk gently with a fist. "Launch a line of WTMW shirts. You said it yourself. It's what the market wants."

Now it was her turn to be funny and Clarence, being the good sport that he was, shared an agreeable laugh with her.

"Do you know what the market wants in a restaurant like this?" she continued, leaning back in her chair to level with Clarence. "They want the daughter from the twerk video serving their food. And if she doesn't do it the way they want it, they want a woman who looks like her mom to come over and fix it."

She paused to let Clarence see just how much she looked like that professional mom, which meant, just as Clarence surmised, she was professionally tired.

"Maybe what your market wants is a grandfather," Clarence added. "You know, to give the mom a little back up with the kids."

She gave Clarence a little smile, and for a moment it seemed she might even reconsider.

"Okay," she leaned forward. "I know this is a stupid question, and I'm only asking because I can't wait to hear *your* answer. Where do you see yourself in ten years? And don't tell me that it's waiting on tables in a wheelchair."

"No, no, no, I'm not going to tell you that. What I will tell you is that the road behind me is a lot longer than the road ahead of me. I'm not even sure I have ten years of road left. As far as what happens after the road ends, I can't tell you."

It wasn't the gag she was hoping for, but she appreciated his witty sincerity and leaned back in her chair again to level with him.

"You know I can't give you this job, right? And even if I could, I don't think I would. When I ask people why they want this job, they give me the usual answer that they're a people's person and they love being around people and helping people. But the truth is waiting on tables isn't something anybody enjoys. I'm probably too young to give you any advice, but you should consider spending the last part of your road walking, not waiting. Especially not on tables."

Clarence was wrong. This wasn't a smart woman; this was a *wise* woman. He nodded knowingly at her words and conceded: "No, it's good advice. The problem is that I can't afford my apartment anymore. Every year the rent goes up, but my income stays flat. If I'm lucky, I'll die before I go broke, but I don't want to wait around for that either."

"I know you're going to hit me over the head with your cane for asking this, but can you take what money you have and *put it in the market?* Invest it. Who knows, maybe your money will make money."

"Or maybe my money will become someone else's money, and then I'm back here robbing this place and making a fast getaway on three legs."

"Yeah, I know." She laughed. "It's tough out there. This morning on my way here I made a stop for bagels and coffee. Do you know who served my bagel and coffee to me?"

"Who?"

"My mom." She let that sink in before continuing. "The woman spent her whole life working so that she could retire to a life of serving bagels and coffee. She'll tell you that she's doing it to keep busy, but—"

"Ah." Clarence waved that away. "There are other ways to stay busy besides serving people coffee. What the H... Grandchildren can keep you busy."

"I'm sorry... What did you say?"

"I said grandchildren can keep you busy."

"No, before that."

"Oh, that. Yeah, I don't swear, at least not all of the letters. No need for me to be a cursing cliché just because people can't do a crossword puzzle in their head. S."

"You are something else." She shook her head looking at him. She wanted to hire him just for entertainment purposes. "Your grandchildren must have a lot of fun with you."

"I'm sure they would if I had them."

"No kids?" she asked and he shook his head. "Wife?"

"Nope."

She speechlessly blinked three times: "???"

"What can I say?" he shrugged. "I guess I just wasn't what the market wanted."

Suddenly she found herself shifting restlessly in her chair, although it was what she felt going on inside her that had her so discomfited. She looked at Clarence with no idea what to do, and it was only from a hard study of the look on his face that she realized he was thinking the same thing. She took a deep breath before responding.

"I feel really uncomfortable saying this, but... If cost of living is the real problem here, maybe you should consider ditching your apartment and..." She stopped and swallowed before spitting it out. "And moving into a retirement home?"

He knew those words were coming, and he knew she meant well. Just the same it was tough to hear it. She didn't expect a witty response and that was for the better because he was at a loss for words. All he could offer as his rebuttal was an audible exhale.

*

The Golden Age Retirement Home brochure arrived in the mail only two days after he requested it. It was a conspicuously anti-climatic little instrument, consisting only of a single piece of paper twice folded, creating three panels of photos and sales text. However, the usual photos of a happy staff and even happier old people were replaced with a magnificent photo of an estate so grand that it seemed more befitting of Olympian immortals than mortal old-timers waiting to die. He wasn't sure how he felt about the home itself, though. On one hand, there was something profoundly confident about its simplicity: Instead of a rigid box, one got the impression they were looking at a Platonic cube—pure, idealized geometry—crystallized as stone. But it was also covered in reflective glass, which he had seen too much of in financial-district architecture.

He turned a fold of the brochure and saw the face of the concierge, who didn't look at all like your typical front man. He looked like a Maasai man shoved into a suit. Printed above him was a map to the home and an open invitation for anyone to visit. Clarence closed the brochure and secured it in his pocket. His mind was made up. He was going to go there and do some reconnaissance.

Immediately after he left his apartment, he could hear the boy next door driving his mother crazy. *Maybe now is the time to knock on the door and strangle whoever answers it*, he thought to himself. He surprised himself by actually getting as far as the door with his hand ready to knock. The door was actually vibrating from the commotion inside.

Instead of knocking, Clarence placed his ear against the door.

"MINE! MINE! MINE!"

These words practically shoved his head back, and Clarence stared at the door as if the wood itself had just screamed into his ear. In-between the terrible toddler's chants were the unmistakable sounds of broken property. Meanwhile, Clarence could hear the parents huffing and panting, not from chasing after the rabid child, but from chasing after a coveted coital orgasm. That was all he needed to hear to know that the advice of the woman who interviewed him was spot-on. He didn't want to spend the rest of his years listening to this kid tearing up the apartment while his completely useless parents were waging war in bed.

He stepped away from the door without knocking or strangling anyone, but the commotion began to pick up. The mother screamed for the child to give something back. This turned into a long heavy-footed pursuit that went from one end of the apartment to the other and ended with the door exploding open and the mother tumbling out, wearing only a brazier and panties. She wasted no time in shoving her back against the door to trap her child inside. Immediately the door banged from the inside as the child pounded for escape. Clarence could hear him shout, *"Mine! Mine! Mine!"* What the child wanted was answered the moment he saw the mother protecting, with both hands, several hundred-dollar bills in social security money. She looked desperate to keep it from the child, and the look in her eyes was an obvious plea for assistance. Her eyelids sporadically twitched from a pending breakdown. She reached out her hand. Clarence reached out his in solidarity and began to approach her, but she shook her head.

"No, I need your cane," she said in a Russian accent.

"My cane? For what?"

"To give it to him."

"You want to give him *my cane*?"

"As a distraction, please," she pleaded. "He wants everything he sees. It's just the way he is. Please help me."

"I'm not giving you my cane to give to that brat!"

"Then what am I supposed to give him?"

"Maybe a slap upside his head for starters."

"No, we don't hit people in this home."

"Sounds like he's hittin' the H. out of you. I heard that boy kicking your a—"

She cut him off by lunging towards him for his cane, which was a mistake. The boy shot through the door, pounced on his mother and slapped her hard enough to dislodge the money from her hands. It scattered in the air, which put a smile on the brat's face. To him it was colorful confetti, which he celebrated with a giggle as he held out his hands to catch it.

"MINE! MINE! MINE!"

The shrill of his voice was unbearable, and Clarence decided he was finally going to put a stop to this. He took up his walking stick as if it were a katana. Just as he made his move, a single gunshot roared through the air. He heard a bullet whistle past his ear and saw the boy tumble to the ground, struck down by the bullet.

Clarence looked on in disbelief. *Did that really just happen?*

The boy didn't move. Nor did the mother, who was frozen from shock. After a long delay, she blinked and her pupils dilated with rage. Her head swiveled towards Clarence with her eyes laser-beaming in his direction.

"No! It wasn't... I didn't... It wasn't me."

He tried backing away, but he bumped his spine into the barrel of a rifle. He turned around and his mouth dropped at the sight of Raison who started reloading her blunderbuss for another shot at the boy.

"It's him," she said, looking squarely at the body of the kid.

The boy twitched. He wasn't dead. As the boy pushed himself up from the ground, Clarence was struck by the realization that he was doing it with only one hand. The other hand was missing.

"The Invisible Hand," Clarence whispered, then blinked absently. "But how? Where are we?"

"The conveyor belt dumped us into *your* head, Mister Clarence," Shiva answered, stepping beside him. "We are in the memories of your life and your world."

Clarence turned again and saw the toddler standing strong next to his mother, unfazed by the bullet that had sought to slay him. His eyes were no longer on the money that lay scattered across the floor, but on the blunderbuss in Raison's hand.

"MINE! MINE! MINE!" With this battle cry, he charged after the gun, holding out his Invisible Hand. Raison wielded the rifle like a baseball bat and swung a Grand Slam that sent the boy soaring. He struck the wall behind him and slid to the ground.

Enraged, the mother leapt into the air and came down with an iron fist that spiked the floor. It ruptured under Raison's feet and cracked opened into a small chasm. Clarence and Shiva went tumbling sideways, while Raison went plummeting inside the fissure.

The mother straightened her stance as her son joined her at her side. She looked at Clarence with eyes of fire and stuck out her hand. "The cane," she said in a demonic Russian voice, "give it to me."

"Mister Clarence," Shiva pleaded. "If you surrender the staff of power, we are all finished."

"Mark, silence the four-armed freak!" the mother commanded.

Mark fired into the air, but Shiva was ready and caught him like a flaming football. Still, the force was too much and they both went skidding across the floor, leaving a fiery trail before crashing into the wall. Shiva wrestled the boy down and pinned his arms. The boy retaliated by sinking his teeth into Shiva's hand. The God of Destruction yelped.

"We must leave at once, Mister Clarence. I am no match for him!"

But getting away wouldn't be so easy. The boy's mom stood opposite of Clarence with her arms flexed near her waist, as if ready for a gunfight. She walked forward, curling and clenching her fists. As she drew closer, her sullen visage became clearer. Clarence recognized her. He knew her Russian accent. He knew her—a woman who escaped the clutches of the Iron Fist for the embrace of the Invisible Hand.

"Ayn Rand," he whispered.

She confirmed with a sinister scowl. With little interest in introductions, she raised two clenched fists above her head and brought them down like a hammer. Clarence instinctively gripped both ends of his walking stick and held it out to block the blow. Her hands came down with such thunderous force that Clarence's knees buckled and gave out. He fell downward. His cane was intact, but he was not. Ayn grabbed him by his collar and threw him across the room like a ragdoll, then let out a mocking cackle.

Clarence smacked the ground, and his cane slid just beyond his reach. Dazed, he gazed up at Ayn and shook the dizziness from his head.

"I... read... your... book..." he strained to speak. *"Atlas Shrugged."*

She smiled approvingly. "Did you enjoy it?"

"Meh," Clarence shrugged. "I liked *The Fountain Head* better."

"And yet you learned nothing from it, you miserable excuse of an architect!"

She leaped into the air again and came down with her foot on Clarence's hand, intercepting his feeble attempt to regain his cane. He let out an agonizing cry as she reached down and claimed his staff of power. It was now hers and hers alone. The room flashed and flickered with electricity as she howled in victory. But it was to be short lived. An annoying voice cut in: "MINE! MINE! MINE!"

Mark darted through the air and tackled Ayn to the ground, causing her to lose her grip of the cane. It slithered across the floor and stopped at the edge of the chasm where it teetered, threatening to fall.

"You fool!" Ayn shouted. "I was going to give it you!"

They both stretched out their hands to grab it, but a third hand, reaching up from the rupture, beat them to it. Mark and Ayn shielded their eyes as the blunderbuss opened fire, creating a mist of gun smoke. They fanned the fog away and reopened their eyes to find Raison standing strong, cradling the blunderbuss in one hand and wielding the staff of power in the other. Mark glowered at her before retaliating with his ultimate weapon—his annoying voice.

"MINE! MINE! MINE! MINE! MINE! MINE! MINE! MINE! MINE!"

"For God's sake, just let the boy have it!" Ayn shouted, covering her ears.

"Madam Raison"—Shiva pleaded with all four hands—"*nooooooooo!*"

It was too late. She conceded the staff to Mark, who raised it above his head like He-Man but did nothing more eventful than take the stick and start swatting the floor and the wall with it.

"What is wrong with all of you?" Raison shouted. "You're fighting over a superstition! It's not a staff of power; it's a walking stick! It doesn't have any power! Oww!!!" she yelped and fell to the ground, clutching her shin after Mark whacked her with it. Ayn stole the opportunity to grab the blunderbuss, which she held by its neck like wild game killed from the hunt.

"You claim to have read my book, but apparently you missed the words," Ayn said. "'*So long as men live together on earth and need means to deal with one another—their only substitute, if they abandon money, is the muzzle of a gun.*' Destroy money and you destroy democracy. Money is a symbol of freedom and for free men's right to choice. Destroy that symbol and what will you replace it with? Tyranny? Oh, let me guess... religion."

The room went silent, save the sound of Mark's incessant whacking of the wall with Clarence's cane, which appeared to float all on its own in the grip of the Invisible Hand. Mark was oblivious to her words and their meaning. The others were speechless. Ayn figured her point was made and looked down at the scattered money.

"Look at this... Money everywhere," she muttered, while gathering her social security income or, as she would call it, restitution for money stolen by the government as taxes.

"Wait!"

A voice shouted out from Ayn's apartment, and a naked man, wrapped in a white towel, came bolting out, disheveled and dripping wet from a post-coital shower. He had an Anglo beak-like nose and Rococo white hair that curled into an S on both sides. Clarence blinked from bewilderment at the man who appeared as if he had walked right out of the eighteenth century. It didn't take long for him to realize who he was.

"Adam Smith," he whispered in awe.

"This is wrong. This is all wrong!" Adam shouted. "When I wrote about free trade I was referring to family farms and small neighborhood shops. Not behemoth industrial corporations the size of governments.

The whole idea is to keep the market from concentrating into one—"

"Shut up." Ayn commanded and blasted him.

Every face dropped, including Mark who turned and looked at his fallen father. Adam's hand trembled as he reached out for his son.

"That's... *my*... baby!" Adam grunted with his last breath before his hand fell to the floor.

"Not anymore," Ayn quipped.

Mark's face buckled as if on the verge of crying, but he didn't. He simply turned around and resumed smacking the wall with his toy stick.

Ayn laughed as she went back to shoveling her social security money into her arms. But the last unclaimed dollar lay next to Clarence's feet. She leaned forward to grab it, but reflexively yoked back her hand and released a blood-curdling scream.

"What is that? Get it away from me! Kill it! Adam, get over here and kill it!"

But Adam was dead. Clarence, on the other hand, was unruffled by his old travel companion, the Dung Beetle, trotting across the face of ol' Benjamin Franklin. He bent forward and pulled the one hundred dollar bill from underneath the beetle. Taking a cue from the Concierge, Clarence began to sing "Paper Gods" by Duran Duran.

♪ *Bow to the paper Gods in a world that is paper thin,*
Fools in town are ruling now
Bleeding from paper cuts ♪

"Shut up! Give it to me!" she hissed, but Clarence responded by gripping the bill at both ends and ripping it in half. Ayn's eyes widened from shock. "How could you?"

Another bill fell from her hand and drifted into Clarence's lap. Foolishly, she dropped the stash of money and dove for it, but it was too late; Clarence had already severed the bill. Enraged, she grabbed Clarence by his lapel and balled her iron fist, ready to crush his skull against the wall, but she was distracted by the sound of crackling coming from behind. She turned and saw a single C-note burning in a small fire. The flame had come from Shiva's hand, which he slowly extended over her pile of money as if ready to light a bon fire. Mark stopped banging the wall to look. In a searing flash, a fire engulfed the money.

352

"A masterpiece," Shiva whispered, complimenting his own creation.

"Noooo!" Ayn shouted. She dove to stop it, but it was too late. The entire pool of money was incinerated.

Heartbroken, Ayn threw herself into the ashes, sobbing. Mark, hearing his mother cry, heedlessly dropped the toy stick and dove head first into an insatiable appetite to own everything—even the ashes.

The cane lay abandoned. Clarence reclaimed it and stood up, looking down at Ayn. She looked up at him.

"Why do you hate freedom?" she asked.

"Why do *I* hate freedom?" Clarence was taken aback, paralyzed not by the question but by her sincerity in asking. "I can't believe you just asked me that dumb ass question. Woman, when freedom is brokered by money instead of personhood then the only free man is a rich man. And I gotta tell you," he continued, "as someone who lived through the Civil Rights era—a fight for *true* freedom—my real answer to your question is fuck you and fuck off."

He flicked the Dung Beetle's quarter into Ayn's hand and ran off. Or, at least, he tried to. He was too slow, and Mark was already moving to tackle him. Acting fast, Shiva snatched Clarence with one arm, revved up his other arms into a propeller motion and rocketed off. Raison aimed her blunderbuss and blasted Mark backwards. But the boy quickly recovered and was hot on their tail.

Ayn, meanwhile, stayed in the ashes, sobbing.

*

The side of the apartment complex exploded into a debris of bricks after Shiva and Raison barreled through it. At first, it seemed as if their momentum would carry them through the air, but they were soon falling several floors before they struck the concrete. Once again, the cane shook free from Clarence's hands. It rolled and settled into the middle of the street.

Mark smacked the ground and came to a tumbling stop at the curb. Undeterred, he was back on his feet and, as every unmonitored two-year-old is wont to do, darted off into the busy street for the stray cane. A cab zipped through and struck him, sending him soaring back into the air. The door opened, revealing the cab driver to be none other than Shiva. Wasting no time, he ran around to the rear off the car, grabbed the stick, handed it to Clarence and helped him into the back seat with Raison. He then leapt into the driver seat, ready to zip off.

"Wait!" Clarence said, looking through the back window at a man flagging the cab. "Someone wants to come with us. Who is he?"

"He is the proper owner of this yellow Dragon. Please ignore him, Mister Clarence." Shiva looked into the rearview mirror and started the meter. "Where to?"

Clarence answered by digging into his pocket, fishing out the folded retirement home brochure, which he shoved in Shiva's face and pointed to the map. "Home!"

That was music to Shiva's ears. He turned forward, ready to slam the pedal but abruptly let out a terrified scream when he saw Mark with his face pressed against the windshield, staring at him. Shiva screamed again as the boy leaned back and slammed his head into the windshield, cracking it, all the while crying "MINE! MINE! MINE!"

Shiva threw the cab into reverse, and Mark went toppling backwards. Shiva shifted into drive, then burned forward. The cab screeched and skipped skyward as if hitting a speed bump. The muffler was knocked loose and moaned as loud as a fighter plane as the stray piping snagged the boy by his diaper and dragged him haplessly across the asphalt while he continued shouting "MINE! MINE! MINE!"

"What the hell was that?" Clarence shouted.

"The boy," Shiva shouted back. "We just ran him over."

"No, I mean… What's that loud sound?"

"The boy is now stuck underneath the Dragon. I believe our Dragon is arguing with him. Shall we stop and put the boy inside with us?" Shiva asked.

"Are you crazy?" Raison shouted.

"It doesn't seem right to leave him there. He is only a kid."

"No. He's a God," Clarence said and sunk into his seat. "He'll be fine. Just drive."

The roar of the muffler came to a puttering stop as Shiva's Dragon, worn down from the mileage, called it quits. Her last breath ended with fumes silently seething from underneath the hood. The long drive home had exhausted even the boy who had somehow managed to fall asleep in the dying Dragon's arms.

After miles of dragging the recalcitrant toddler by the arms of a roaring muffler, the silence that followed somehow seemed strange and untrustworthy. Only after Clarence directed his weary eyes out the passenger window and saw the familiar sight of the town tavern did it sink in that the long journey was finally over.

Clarence, Raison and Shiva climbed out, wiped the weariness from their faces and stretched their legs. They leaned against the cab to settle down their nerves when a door from the small shack across the street opened and out came Matylda as their only welcoming committee. Her presence immediately made Clarence realize that he had forgotten something.

"Aw, crap," he said, palming his face.

"What?" Raison asked.

"The Dung Beetle. I left her back there." He rapped his head with his knuckles.

"Does this mean we must go back to get her?" Shiva asked.

"No," Matylda said while bending down and smoking her pipe. She examined a long trail of dung and pennies that followed the path of the car, like skid marks. "Something tells me she'll find her way back just fine. Hmmm... I better get my share, before she rolls all of this up into a nest."

With little or no reservation, she grabbed a sample of the dung with her hands and placed it in a small pouch.

"What are you going to do with that?" Clarence asked with a disgusted expression.

Matylda answered by lifting her foot and planting it in a mound of soft shit. She let her foot marinade, even grinding it in for good measure.

"For good luck," Matylda answered.

"Say what?" Clarence blinked.

"I'm a Polish Goddess. Stepping in shit is considered good luck in Poland."

This is true. Poles never clean up their dog shit, especially in the winter. So when the snow melts there's a goldmine of good luck waiting to be stepped in by people like Matylda. Clarence, Shiva and Raison watched as she strutted away in her bunny flip-flops, leaving behind a trail of soiled footprints.

"This is why I have no tolerance for Gods," Raison said. She straddled her blunderbuss across her shoulder and started walking back to the retirement home.

"So what now, Mister Clarence?"

"Now, we get this boy from under the cab and check him into his new home."

With great effort, Clarence used his cane to kneel down, and, with Shiva's help, he tried dislodging the boy without awakening him. This was a surgical procedure that required the steadiest of hands. Each attempt caused the boy to stir, and they found themselves fumbling with every false start. Finally, fed up with the whole affair, Clarence just grabbed the boy by the leg and dragged him free. The boy woke right up, immediately saw Clarence's cane and reached out for it.

"MINE!"

"NO!" Clarence pulled the cane away. "This is *mine!* Not yours, MINE."

The boy was taken aback. He stared into Clarence's face, trying to understand. This was the first time that he had been refused so sternly and the first time that he had heard the voice of discipline. His first reaction was to cry, but this quickly turned into anger. Old habits are hard to break, especially for a two-year-old, and the boy reacted the same way he did with his mother: He pulled back and slapped Clarence across the face.

"That does it."

Clarence threw down his staff of power, unfastened his belt buckle and unsheathed the true source of all parental power. The boy saw what was coming. His eyes buckled as he began to cry.

"Oh no, you don't, you little bastard. Don't you start that crying now. You earned this ass whoopin'!"

WHAP

"Boy, don't you ever—"

WHAP

"Ever—"

WHAP

"Put your hands on an adult again! Not yo momma! Not yo daddy— God rest his soul—and you damn sure better not put your hands on me again. Do you hear me, boy?!?"

WHAP

"That's right, welcome to the old school, where you don't just get a slap on the hand. You get a slap on the ass!"

The prohibition of profanity had long ago been broken. With all arms folded, Shiva looked on as Clarence introduced the boy to obedience.

Shiva had always wondered about Clarence's curious name and his mysterious identity, but now, seeing this, he figured out who Clarence truly was.

A God.

At least, that was Shiva's first guess. He wasn't sure. What did seem certain was that after this ass whoopin', Mark would never clamor for the staff of power again.

Chapter 19

A year later, young Mark was holding two bronze bowls in both hands—one filled with grains and the other with water. He made slow, steady steps as he tried not to tip and spill the offerings. Of course, as his small legs tried to keep balance while pacing up a hill, the water splashed a bit and soaked the sleeve of his shirt.

"That's okay," Clarence said softly and placed a paternal hand on the boy's shoulder. "Here we come to the entrance. It's a little small... Now bend down."

Mark was small enough that he didn't have to, but he still crouched a bit as he passed through the door and entered Big Momma's temple.

"And now set the offerings down here."

The bowls were set before the idol of the Earth, and the boy followed Clarence's lead in closing his eyes and bowing his head in silent prayer. The boy didn't have much to say other than what Clarence had taught him. When he opened his eyes, he saw Clarence with his head still tipped in reverence and his lips silently moving. When he finished, he looked at Mark, rubbed his back and smiled.

"When we are children, our parents give to us, but because we are children, we are not able to give back much but our love," Clarence explained. "When we become adults, our parents become old, and it is our turn to provide. That is why we do what we do here. This ritual is to keep alive the idea that we must give back love and offerings to our parent, the Earth."

"Is the Earth a God?" Mark asked.

"The Earth is your *home*; therefore, it is a temple. So don't shit where you eat, okay?" He paused to see if Mark understood. The boy looked back, attentively. "Okay, we can go," Clarence said, satisfied.

They made a final bow and left the intimate darkness through the small doorway. They emerged back into the spring day, turned and appraised Big Momma's temple, which had been resized and redesigned to the shape of an elegant cube, reminiscent of the old retirement home. But Clarence had not been the builder.

"You know that he is too young to know the real meaning of what you are saying, don't you?"

Clarence turned to the familiar African voice and saw Ptah coming forth from the grove with his arms positioned proudly behind his back.

"It's okay. As he matures, he'll understand."

"We hope." Ptah raised an eyebrow. "Young people do not take well to tradition."

"Then hopefully they'll make new rituals and celebrations that keep the ideas of the old traditions alive."

"Yes. Hopefully."

"That's what you did here, right?" Clarence said, sizing up Big Momma's new temple. "I have to tell you, it's really impressive. A+."

Ptah agreed with the compliment by smiling and sizing up his own masterwork. Clarence could see his self-satisfaction and was happy for him.

"So I guess you were right," Clarence continued. "You are still an architect. I'm sorry... Architect. Capital A."

"It's okay," Ptah laughed. "But this place does not need two Architects. This was my last work."

"Your swan song?"

"Yes. My swan song."

"So what now?"

"Now?" Ptah pursed his lips as if mulling it over. "I suppose I am no longer Ptah, God of Architects." He unfolded his hands from behind his back, revealing that they were empty. "Now I am Ptah, God of Science and Technology."

Four arms swiftly sprouted from behind Ptah's back. Clarence flinched and stepped backwards. These were not the wooden arms from before, but arms made of elaborate electronics and stainless steel. After regaining his composure, Clarence relaxed and nodded at the prosthetic upgrades.

"Where I'm from, we call that a cyborg."

"Then go back to your world and tell them that Ptah is coming."

"Will do," Clarence nodded and turned to leave, but stopped as a thought occurred to him. "Wait a second. I almost forgot something."

Clarence crouched low as he went back inside the temple and kneeled again in front of Big Momma's idol. He reached into his pocket for the Heart of the Pole Star. He placed it at her altar, between the offering bowls. He bowed his head again and, with no words, left the temple.

*

Ahura Mazda sat behind his new writing desk in his new bachelor apartment. Sitting on the floor, with legs crossed, was his visitor—Omiokane. The two turned their heads as someone stepped in the doorway.

"Mark is here! Let me see him!" Omiokane said, reaching out his arms for the boy.

"See him?" Ahura Mazda huffed, pushing from his desk. "Old man, have you forgotten you are blind?"

"Not all sight comes from the eyes," Omiokane quipped as he used the back of his hand to survey the contours of the boy's profile. "Hai," he said approvingly, "you are growing up quickly. Soon, you will be ready for your own room, and before you know it, you'll be moving out and going back into the world again."

"Not until I teach him a thing or two," Ahura Mazda added.

"Not until we *all* teach him a thing or two!" Raison said, stepping into the doorway. She leaned against the wall with her arms folded.

"She's right, Mazda-san. It takes a village to raise a child."

"Thirty-three million Gods is a bit more than a village," Mazda rebutted.

"I thought you didn't care for the Gods, Raison." Clarence smiled and winked.

"I don't. But these guys are okay. Plus, old people are kind of cute."

"Well, I have to get going," Clarence said. "So who's doing the babysitting today?"

"You ask as if it matters. Our rooms are right next to each other!" Mazda complained. "Anyway, let the boy stay with me today. He can help me work on my new book."

"What book is that?"

"A book on copyright law. And I'm reserving a free copy for the Mazda Corporation."

"And where are you going, Clarence-san?" Omiokane asked. "Are you heading back to your world?"

"No, I'm just on my way to the tavern."

"For a drink?"

"No," Clarence answered. "For a job."

*

The Barkeep sat silently behind the desk without saying a word. Had it not been for the phone books stacked on the seat of the chair, he would have vanished behind the desk and Clarence would have been left staring at a painting on a wall. Not that he wasn't staring at the painting anyway. Read from East to West, it showed a circle, a triangle and a square—a strangely simplistic composition made even stranger by its title: *"The Universe."*

Clarence pulled his eyes from the Universe and fixed them on the Barkeep, who was still looking at him, as if waiting for Clarence to start the interview.

"Employees drink for free," Clarence began. "That's what you told me. At first, I thought that you wanted me to wait tables or bartend for you, but let's face it: An old man getting around on three legs isn't going to cut it. When Vynamonen was your only customer, maybe, but this place is packed now. You now have what every tavern dreams of—thirty-three million thirsty customers. The tavern is too small. Which brings me to my proposition. You're a God of few words, right? Well how about I pitch this idea to you in only one word: *barchitecture*." He paused to let this sink in. Then drilled his finger into the boy's desk. "You need a barchitect."

Clarence leaned back confidently and locked his fingers across his belly, waiting for the boy to say something. But, of course, he didn't, so Clarence took the lead again.

"So now this is me asking, I mean, *me* really asking *you*: Do I have the job?"

"Yes."

"Excellent." Clarence clapped his hands once. "Now, I understand that you may not have the budget for this. But that's where the free beer comes in. Keep the tab open for me and my builders, and you'll have yourself a new and bigger tavern. Deal?"

"Yes."

"Perfect." Clarence stood up and saluted the boy with his cane. "We'll get started right away—with the drinking, I mean. We'll start working on the expansion of the tavern next week. Pleasure doing business with you. That painting looks great on your wall, by the way."

Clarence whistled as he walked out of the office, but in a few moments he turned back and stuck his head through the door. "Oh... Uh... Are you going to be long? My crew needs another round."

The boy leapt down from his stack of phone books to answer the call for more ale. The second he stepped past his office door, the walls of the tavern rattled as hundreds of Gods, crammed shoulder to shoulder, raised their empty mugs with a cheer. The Concierge—or DJ OGO as he preferred—was back on the turntables. He raised his hand to Clarence and saluted him. Clarence waved back with his cane, then pushed his way through the crowd until he found Väinämöinen, Balaam and Seshat breaking bread and snacking on chili chips at a tavern table. Clarence grabbed a seat and joined them.

"So how did it go, ystäväni?"

"I got the job!" Clarence smiled broadly to Väinämöinen.

"Ahem!" Balaam purposely cleared his throat. "Perhaps the question he means to ask is did *We* get the job?"

"We sure did."

"Brilliant!" Balaam raised his glass of wine, tipped it back and downed it all in one hasty gulp. "In celebration of our new architectural firm We will, for this night only, set aside Our proverbial wine and switch to beer."

"Now we're talking!" Väinämöinen roared. He fingered to the Barkeep for four beers and motioned with his lips that he wanted all four to be Kvas. The Barkeep gave the signal and Shiva made the delivery.

"To the Architect." Seshat raised her glass and toasted.

"To the Architect!" they all repeated, clinked their glasses and imbibed.

"Speaking of Architects," Seshat continued. "What will be the name of our firm?"

"What about Clarence & Co?" Clarence proposed.

All at once, they rejected this with a clamor, resulting in a dispute over alternate names and whose moniker should go first.

"Hold on, wait a second. Wait just a second," Shiva interjected. "I believe the firm should have Mister Clarence's name."

"No offence, ol' chap, but you're just a bit too destructive to be a builder. You don't get to vote on this one," Balaam said.

"And no offence to you, ystäväni," Väinämöinen added. "But the name *Clarence* has no order to it. And architecture is about order."

"Oh no, Mister Väinämöinen," Shiva rebutted. "I don't believe that Clarence is the true name of Mister Clarence. I believe that his true name is *Kalki*."

"WHAT?" they all exclaimed in unison.

"Please allow me to explain: Kalki is the last incarnation of Lord Vishnu. He is the Destroyer of Filth and Ignorance. He is the next avatar, who will appear to mankind to restore peace and order. After seeing how

Mister Clarence disciplined Mark, I now believe that *he* will reincarnate as Kalki." Shiva turned to Clarence and placed a hand on his shoulder. "Mister Clarence, you have been on a very long journey and have learned many great things. It is my belief that when you return to your world, you will be a great teacher. Your mission will be tough, but your tough love will be tougher."

"So he's going back into the bloody world as a *crime fighter*?" Balaam asked.

"Hold on just a minute." Väinämöinen slammed his beer down. "How are we going to have an architectural firm if he's back in his own world to fight crime?"

"He's right," Seshat agreed. "Exactly when is Kalki going back to his world?"

"At the end of the Kali Yuga age," Shiva answered.

"So what? Tomorrow?" Väinämöinen asked.

"Oh, no, no. We have plenty of time, Mister Väinämöinen. More than enough time to rebuild the tavern. And so, my friends, I, Lord Shiva— God of Destruction—especially when I do not get my way—hereby propose that your architectural firm be named Kalki & Co."

The group looked at each other, shrugged their shoulders in agreement and ratified the decision with a unanimous chug of the beers.

"Okay, so now that that's settled, on to the name of the tavern," Väinämöinen said.

"Actually, I already have the name," Clarence said. He stood up with his beer and made a motion with his head. "Follow me."

*

A sign, hand painted in broad black brush strokes, hung above the door. It was an exotic fusion of Asian calligraphy with the hard curves of Celtic lettering. The sign read:

House of the Gods

"It would have been nice if you had run this by us first," Seshat said.

"That would make us Kalki and *Committee*," Clarence answered. "Trust me, if you want anything to get done before the end of the Kali Yuga age, then we're better off not making decisions as a committee."

"We love it!" Balaam looked at Clarence.

"Has a feeling of a home away from home," Väinämöinen nodded approvingly. "Good work, ystäväni."

Clarence accepted the compliment with a nod and stole a final look at the horizon, where the new retirement home peaceably rested. He imagined that Światowid, reaching skyward, could see him and was saluting him from a distance.

"Okay everybody"—Väinämöinen turned to the group—"don't over-think this. Back inside, all of ya. It's high time for me to make an offering at the porcelain altar."

He shooed them back through the door and into the joyous sound of singing Gods, blissfully slurring an ancient anthem about the God of Dung, whom the ancient Egyptians knew as Khepera, a name that means "to become," as in what will become of the human mind as it evolves in the future. After all, the God of Dung is still out there.

Somewhere, in the sprawling network of the human mind, she is slowly rolling her big ball of crap from head to head. People fill their heads with a lot of shit, and the ideas of religion, government, economics and even science all demand their fair share of fertilizer.

End

About the Author

A.A. Jordan is one part writer and one part graphic designer. He writes novels with an anime tone, which only means that his creative process begins with visualizing anime-style characters (the kind without the whiny voices). He was born in Buffalo, NY, and lives abroad.

Other books by A.A. Jordan:
The Gene Hackers

www.ingramcontent.com/pod-product-compliance
Lightning Source LLC
Chambersburg PA
CBHW060350260626
47160CB00006B/2264